Advanced Praise for

# DOORMAN WANTED

"This gem of a novel is equal parts wit and heart. Set in a Manhattan luxury condominium and its environs, *Doorman Wanted* is written with flair and elegance and has a cast of believable characters whose actions surprise, infuriate and ultimately, inspire us."

—**Lorna Landvik,** author of *Last Circle of Love*

"In *Doorman Wanted*, Miller shuttles between privilege and reality by giving Henry, reluctant heir of a luxury condo building, the guise of a doorman. 'Franklin' is more at ease picking up litter and characters off the noisy streets than Henry ever could be in the hushed corridors of wealth, where his conscience stumbles. An entertaining debut."

—**Sarah Stonich,** author of *Vacationland*

"A fun, beautifully written story with plenty to think about. I'd recommend *Doorman Wanted* to any book group."

—**Robert Alexander,** author of *The Kitchen Boy*

"With the deft touch of a master storyteller, Glenn R. Miller brings us into the life of a New York City apartment building and peoples it with individuals whom we want to know. In the process, Miller examines what it means to find oneself, to learn who we are and where we belong, despite the press and pressures of forces we cannot control. With a style that flows like a soft breeze and characters as distinctive as the city in which they live, *Doorman Wanted* is a delightful, meaningful, and important book that belongs on the top shelf of any library."

—**Greg Fields**, author of *Through the Waters and the Wild*

"Can you ever have too much money? Thirty-something Henry is about to find out. When he inherits his father's massive estate the irresistible force of his progressive ideals slams headfirst into the immovable object of a dubious inheritance. What's a reluctant plutocrat to do? Assume an alias and work as a doorman, of course! True, the rich are different from you and me, but thanks to his touching sincerity, insightful wit, and liberal angst, one-percenter Henry—aka Franklin the doorman—is my new best friend."

—**Brian Malloy,** author of *The Year of Ice* and *After Francesco*

"Fans of P. G. Wodehouse will delight in Miller's witty wordplay as they cheer on his doorman hero's page-turner odyssey through both the ground floor and upper echelons of a tony New York apartment building."

—**D. M. S. Fick,** author of *Lewis Sinclair and the Gentlemen Cowboys*

"A comedy of manners for an era of cavernous income disparity, *Doorman Wanted* contains satire serrated enough to cut an overdone steak, but it's also light on its feet and undauntedly optimistic. Its droll narrator, Henry Franken, is a scion with a heart and vault of gold, and Glenn R. Miller—clever about identities unwanted and mistaken—will have you rooting for him all the way."

—**Dylan Hicks,** author of *Amateurs*

"Succession by way of P. G. Wodehouse? A comedy of manners with a dash of Wilde? Miller has written an entirely modern novel with roots in an earlier era, one in which wit, charm, and lightness were supreme virtues. *Doorman Wanted* welcomes a reader into the private world of L'Hermitage, where you'll want to linger and even take up residence."

—**Colin Hamilton,** author of *The Thirteenth Month*

"Bravo! I loved this book. Franklin Hanratty (aka Henry Franken) is at turns sharp, witty, sensitive and profound. But he begins this novel confused. He quickly applies his myriad talents to becoming the finest doorman in New York, and to navigating more misconceptions than a Jane Austen novel. Thankfully, Franklin is also a wonderful human being—and so are many of the characters that help him find his way. I raced through the last fifty pages, excited to see Franklin's final metamorphosis into Henry, a man who finally comes to terms with his wealth and figures out how to use it for good. I don't know what Glenn R. Miller is planning to write for an encore, but I'll be waiting in line to read it."

—**Cary Griffith,** author of *Wolf Kill*


"With eloquent prose and an uplifting tone, Miller paints characters who come to feel like old friends and illustrates the power in shedding the identities that have been assigned to us, as a means to uncovering the one to which we truly belong."

—**Rachel Stone,** Author of *The Blue Iris*

*Doorman Wanted*

by Glenn R. Miller



ISBN 979-8-88824-231-5



Published by

3705 Shore Drive
Virginia Beach, VA 23455
800-435-4811
www.koehlerbooks.com

# DOORMAN WANTED

A Novel

## GLENN R. MILLER

VIRGINIA BEACH
CAPE CHARLES

# PROLOGUE

## Four Months Ago

I turned the corner off Park Avenue and started looking for my newly acquired home. *There it is*, I thought, *that one there.*

On the tree-lined stretch of stately condos and apartment buildings, the structure that had technically been in my possession since 7:37 p.m. two weeks ago Tuesday—the determined hour and minute my father suffered his heart attack—announced itself like Dad invariably did when entering into any setting: loudly, with exuberance, and flashing money. I hadn't seen the building before, much less entered its premises, but I recognized Dad's unique style from a half block away.

The building burps marble, if not taste. White marble blocks, set at incongruous angles, cover the building's twelve-story facade; black distressed marble spans the distance from the gold-plated front doors to the curb; delicate, pink marble flower boxes hang beneath the second-floor windows and outside the building's retail space; and finally, a marble statue of a bull protrudes from the building's front niche. While fervidly embracing his marble phase during the renovation of the building last year, Dad had informed me in one of our rare cross-country phone conversations that he had removed a headless Greek statue from the recess and replaced it with this commissioned bull. "Bulls signify wealth, Henry. Did you ever know that? Who knew that? But they do!" Adorning the building's facade with marble blocks did not suffice in announcing my father's arrival on the Upper East Side. He needed to ride in on a white bull.

Dad's long-standing financial attorney and closest friend, Judith

Guncheon, had reached me early that Wednesday morning, just as I was sitting down with my team at St. Benedict's Shelter in Los Angeles. Had there been openings at a San Diego agency—or Barrow, Alaska, for that matter—when I was applying for such jobs, I would have gone after them, thereby putting a few more miles and hills between me and New York City.

Sadly, nothing was available.

Judith informed me that Dad had died the night before from a massive coronary. One of his construction foremen had discovered his body behind a desk that morning within a small onsite trailer—an ignominious departure for the king of displaced and gentrified real estate development in the Triborough region. It should be noted that that is not an official title, simply an honorific bestowed upon Dad by me, in one of my sniffier and more heated exchanges with him. It was yet another in a list of disparaging comments I aimed his way, immediately regretting, yet incapable of uttering anything that approached even a mumbled apology.

"It's time to come home, Henry," she proclaimed. Serving in the dual roles of both family lawyer and personal godmother, Judith was accustomed to issuing such opinions in my direction. Regarding moving back to New York, for the past ten years, ever since I'd landed on the West Coast following my college graduation, she had been sharing this perspective with me during our sporadic phone calls. I assumed she did so on behalf of Dad, whose hope was to groom me for the eventual takeover of the business.

"And when I say, 'come home,'" she continued, "I mean move here. You'll be one of New York City's wealthiest thirty-four-year-olds—"

"Thirty-three."

"Better yet. That moves you up a couple of slots. Very, very eligible. Oh, and you now own that building your dad insisted on buying last year up near the park. You get the top floor. Nice views. Come pick up your keys."

At this, I started to dry-retch.

"All right, it sounds like our conversation is wrapping up," she said. "As is your time in California. Oh, and Henry?"

"Yeah?" I said, wiping my mouth.

"I'm sorry for your loss. And mine. I know you and your dad had your issues, but I loved him like a brother. I wish you had known him like I did. See you soon."

◆　◆　◆

I stood outside the building—*my* building—L'Hermitage by name, attempting to delay my entrance and forestall my future. I had come from Judith's office after signing documents, meeting with on-staff financial managers, ignoring said financial managers' brilliantly colorful PowerPoint presentations, and sitting down in a darkened "soft" conference room with two people named Kim and Terry. Or was it Tim and Carrie? Unclear. The two introduced themselves as financial therapists, explaining to me that there is a very real connection between money and mental health. They informed me that, as part of Judith's team, Judith had asked that they sit down with me and that we would have as many of these meetings as I would like.

"Great," I said. "In that case, I think we're done."

They gamely pushed on, letting me know that in the weeks ahead we would go over not just the value of money, but the value of *me*, the value of myself within society, the value of my time, my energy, my gifts, and my unique skill sets. They stressed that the three of us were, indeed, in a safe space, a judgment-free zone.

"Hmm, not entirely," I said.

"Henry," one of the Kim-Terry team said.

"Yes?" I responded.

"Henry," the other said, unwilling to be topped by his teammate. "What is it you want? How can we help you?"

"I haven't a clue. I don't know what I want."

"Well," one of them said, "I think this has been a constructive first session. Are you available again next Tuesday?"

◆   ◆   ◆

And so, after ten or so minutes of standing in front of my newly acquired building, stalling, reading a sign posted near the building's front door that stated *Doorman Wanted*, observing people walk in and out of the building, watching others walk up and down the street, going back to more closely inspect the help-wanted sign—this time with a particular interest in the listed qualifications—giving the look-see to my fingernails, assigning various nicknames to pigeons strolling by—Throttle-Neck, Pretty Boy, Whompa Bompa, Cannonball, Leslie (coloring reminded me of a previous work associate's bouffant), Future Shock, Future Shuttlecock, Ratface, Rat-a-Tat-Tat, RattyRat, etc.—I worked up my nerve and entered.

The interior space, unlike the flashy exterior, was tastefully appointed. There was an office immediately to my left with a sign reading *Charlotte Marbury, Manager*. Deeper into the interior was a large, open . . . what shall we call it? A living room? A parlor? Certainly not a common area, for there was nothing common about this space at all. One immediately wanted to enter—warm tan wood paneling enclosed the room, with black walnut framing the doors and windows. There was a large unlit, but seemingly working, fireplace at the opposite end of the room, framed in floor-to-ceiling brick and millwork.

Alcoves contained shelves of hard-bound books; two Italian leather sectionals occupied the middle of the room, separated by a low leather-wrapped block serving as both coffee table and supporting foundation for a scattering of art books dedicated to German expressionism, Scandinavian landscapes, Asian prints, International Pop, and a robust volume entitled *Anti-Art*. Modern lounge chairs were arranged in couplets throughout the rest of the space, each pairing separated by sculpted wooden side tables.

Opposite the parlor and across the central hall were elevators. Two men were in midconversation, waiting for an arriving car.

"My doctor said one glass of red wine each day actually has beneficial health effects, that there are antioxidants—"

"Whaddya talking about, '*one* glass each day'?"

"That's what my doctor told me. A glass a day. I have mine every evening before I go to bed."

"Well, if one is good for you, glasses two through six must be even better."

"Nah, it's just one a night. But I have a work-around. The glass I use is sixty-four ounces. I'll get you one so you can be in compliance, too. We can be on the same healthy diet together—"

The doors closed and the remainder of the dietary-insights discussion was lost to me. On the right of the elevators was a hallway, presumably to a mailroom. And finally, to the right of that hallway, and near the front door I'd just entered was a large, wooden reception counter. Behind it was a woman, about my age, with a large spray of black hair.

"Can I help you?"

"Well, yeah, maybe. I'm here for the . . . uh . . . for the . . . well, uh—"

"For the pickup? For the drop-off? For directions? Use your words. You're here for the . . .?"

"I'mhereforthebuilding," I blurted out, a tad less elegantly than one might normally when assuming ownership of an Upper East Side residential building.

"Aren't we the eager beaver," she asked. "The employment agency said they'd be sending you over later this afternoon. And, by the way, you don't get the whole building, just the door. You're the doorman, not the *building*man. Here, fill this out; we need it for our records."

She held out a clipboard to me with a sheet of paper attached. I've thought back numerous times to that moment. I could have—*should* have—immediately said, "I'm afraid there's been a misunderstanding. You see, I *do* get the whole building." But I didn't. I didn't say anything. In the flicker of that moment, I felt she was handing me a life ring, a preserver. No, that's not quite right. More like a means of flight, a means of escape, if only momentary. No, no, that's not quite right, either. She was handing me an opportunity to hide.

"Thanks," I said. I started to fill out the form by writing my full name—Henry Franken—but realized this probably wouldn't do. I scratched it out and took another run at it, writing, "Frank Henry." Stupid! Too obvious. I crowded in "-lin" after "Frank," forming "Franklin," turned the "e" in "Henry" to an "a," scratched out the "y" in "Henry," and added "ratty," my pigeon nicknaming game seemingly still rattling around in my head.

"I promise, the form gets easier once you get past the name part," the receptionist said. "In case I can't read all that talon-scratching, what's your name? Temp didn't tell me."

"Who?"

"Tempositions? Your agency? Remember them? They're the ones who sent you over here. They're also the ones taking a fifteen percent cut of your pay for the next year."

"Oh, right, of course. Sorry, I misheard you. My name is Franklin Hanratty," I said.

"I'm Charlotte," she said. "A bunch of guys report to you, you report to me, and I report to the new owner, so there you go. You're pretty close to the top of our elaborate hierarchy. You have a few days to work out your jitters. I need you in here Monday morning at eight."

I finished filling out the sheet, a little more comfortable and seasoned with the fictitious information I was laying out. I exited L'Hermitage in a slight daze, mystified by what I had just impulsively done. Within his business dealings, Dad had always, shall we say, skirted the law. Is this how he got his start, by falsifying documents? It all felt too easy. Could I undo what I had just done, without seeming entirely crazed? Hardly, at least not in that moment. So how was I now going to assume Dad's unit within the building—the penthouse? That had been my initial mission, assigned by Judith just a few hours earlier. At the very least, I needed to come clean to Judith. Right after I called Tempositions to cancel L'Hermitage's need for a doorman.

# CHAPTER 1

Thursday, 7:53 am

As I root around in the building's boxwoods, crawling, pulling out newspapers, flyers, and stray gum wrappers that collected over the weekend, I catch sight of a man walking toward me, occasionally pausing to bend over and inspect some scrap or other on the sidewalk. I've seen him before. He's overlayered for the late-spring weather, wearing a ski jacket, a knee-length paint-flecked smock underneath, and a Giants baseball cap. He normally stays on the other side of the street, walking slowly with a shuffling limp, looking over at me, sometimes waving, sometimes just smiling and nodding, but always standing out. People like him can't help but stand out in this neighborhood. Not me; I'm just the doorman.

"Hey, young man, what are you doing down there?" he says once he reaches me. "What are you doing crawling around like a little boy, huh? They couldn't pay me enough to root around in other people's trash like they got you doing."

I stand up, realizing that, perhaps, he has a point and that I'm taking my tasks a bit too far.

"Holy cow, I never seen you this close up. You're no little man! You're just one more city skyscraper," he says, referencing my six-three frame. "And by the way, Skyscraper, you got a nice-looking penthouse, if you know what I mean." At this, he lets out an open-mouthed, gap-toothed laugh.

I've noticed this guy two or three times each week. In the months I've been working at L'Hermitage, there are certain people of the street—neighbors, workers, dog walkers, walking commuters, homeless people—I've come to recognize and expect. This guy, I presume, falls under my "homeless" categorization.

"And speaking of tall drinks of water, which we *were,*" he continues, "where'd you find yourself one of those?"

He's pointing at my cup of coffee, set upon the low marble balustrade under the building's front awning. It's a tin cup that was sent to me in appreciation of a financial gift I once tendered my childhood camp—a device successful in jogging pleasant memories of a time long past, wholly unsuccessful in containing hot liquids in a manner that would be regarded as comfortable to the holder.

I look at it for a moment before turning back to him, saying, "Would you like a cup?"

"What?" he asks with mock surprise. "You've got coffee in there? I thought you just kept rich people in there. This building spits out coffee, too? Hell, had I known that I would have been here"—looking at his watchless wrist—"an hour ago." Again, the loud—too loud—open-mouthed laugh. "Yeah, man. Shit, I'd love one of those cups of coffee. But I don't want to put you out or anything. That is to say, I don't want to take you away from your rooting around in the bush."

"We'll be okay," I say. "Wait here."

With the exception of Mr. Harrison, 10A, working his morning crossword puzzle in his usual place near the living room hearth, the lobby is empty. I walk to the coffee and tea service set up across from my front counter and pour a cup. I add generous amounts of sugar and cream and go back outside.

"Aw, that's very cool of you, Skyscraper, very cool. God bless you. God bless. This coffee's a whole lot better than the swill I get at Sacred Heart. I guess you could say, I've been in a rut."

"Yeah," I say. "Aren't we all?"

By looks, it was a rough weekend for him, given what appears to be a fresh cut on his forehead. He's a short guy with deep green eyes and a nose with an inclination to hang out on the right side of his face. From one angle, he might be a rough-worn forty-year-old; from another, a down-on-his-luck sixty-year-old. Unlike other street people, he tends to travel light. On the occasions I've noticed him, he's not had a shopping cart or large plastic bags stuffed with aluminum cans with him, as others I've seen do.

He takes a long, loud slurp from the cup before saying, "Ooh, that do fill a void, Scraper, that do-oo fill a void that was rattling around down there. Say, ain't it a beautiful day to be walking the streets of New York City? A gorgeous day. Buds are popping, pigeons are mating, things are maturing. Life is good, Scraper, eh?" Despite his volume, there doesn't appear to be a trace of mental illness in his words or actions, just high spirits. But there's something behind the facade. There often is.

"Since we're out here sharing a cup of coffee and what have you, we might as well know each other's names, wouldn't you say?" he asks with a large grin. "My name's Terry, but you being in what I'd call the service industry and all, feel free to call me *Mister* Terry, if that makes you feel more comfortable. Now, what's your name? I know what your *fake* name is but what's your real name?"

I look at him a moment to gauge his intent with this question.

"My fake name?"

"Yeah, yeah," he says. "Scraper. Your nickname, I meant. But what's your real name?"

I point to the nameplate on my uniform. "Franklin," I say. "Franklin Hanratty."

"Franklin Hanratty. Well, that's what I'd call a damn fine blueblood name. Even better if you stuck a 'von' somewhere in there. Scraper to me, though, huh, since we're friends who share coffee in the morning with each other and all." He takes a large, loud sip before announcing, "Well, gotta keep moving, Scrape. Thanks, again for this. God bless."

"Busy day today?" I ask him. As soon as it comes out, I realize my question sounds more biting than I intended.

"Damn straight," he says. "I'm making my way over to the Met in time for the doors to open. A new show opening there, you know."

"The Met, huh? Well, enjoy yourself." Yeah. The Met. My question deserved his answer.

"I will! Trust me, I will. We all need our sources of inspiration, right? Our spiritual connections?" he says, tapping his chest before heading up the sidewalk. "Hey, thank you for this!" he shouts over his shoulder, holding up his coffee.

"Mister Terry, wait a minute," I say. "I have a question for you." If he is, in fact, heading to the Met, I assume he's doing so to sit in the cafeteria and nurse another cup of coffee for as long as the guards allow. I occasionally see folks like Terry in the Met's large cafeteria, sleeping in the deep corners or behind the broad pillars. The guards tend to escort them out, as if they have finely calibrated sensor devices attuned to such presences in their midst.

"That's expensive, isn't it, going to the Met? Their cafeteria can be pretty pricey." I offer him a twenty-dollar bill. "Here, today the Manets are on me. Get yourself a sandwich. With lots of mayonnaise." Whether he eats at the Met or not, Terry deserves a nice meal.

"Oh, that's good. I like that. Manets. Mayonnaise. Hah! That's good, Scraper. You could be a stand-up with that kind of—what do they call it?—with that kind of wordplay. Shoot, you don't have to do that, though," he says, taking the bill and putting it into his coat pocket. "But, that's awfully sweet of you," he says as he heads in the opposite direction of the museum.

"By the way, Scrape," he shouts back, turning around and walking backward from me, "I'm a Friedrich guy, not Manet. Romantic, that Friedrich. 'Two Dudes Checking Out the Moon,' Gallery 807. You ought to check it out, once you're done picking up trash, that is." He turns back around and hurries away.

Friedrich. I'll be damned.

"Oh, wait," he shouts back at me. "Friedrichs ain't as good on sandwiches as Manets, though! I'll give you that." He booms out another loud laugh and heads toward the corner.

# CHAPTER 2

Thursday, 9:32 am

As she enters the building each morning, a whiff of tension is cast upon my otherwise pleasant lobby. There is scary Charlotte and friendly Charlotte, depending upon the day and depending upon the person she's chatting up. Mr. Stewart gets friendly Charlotte. Mrs. Hill gets a hybrid Charlotte, occasionally friendly but most often impatient and condescending. Mr. Harrison, gentlemanly Mr. Harrison, gets a version of Charlotte that I would categorize as coquettish Charlotte.

I rarely get friendly Charlotte or, I should say, I rarely do anymore. Jacob, our night doorman, gets get-the-hell-out-of-my-way-before-I-bust-your-balls Charlotte in those rare moments when their shifts overlap. Mister Terry . . . oh my God, poor Mister Terry would get she-devil-out-of-the-blackest-hole-in-hell Charlotte if the two of them were to ever bump into each other in the lobby. Charlotte is a complex figure, some might say.

But that is, perhaps, understandable. After all, we have a complicated relationship, she and I. She doesn't have a full appreciation of its complexity, its richness, its nuances, its true depth, but someday I suspect she will. Someday, she must. For now, however, she sees her relationship with me, Doorman Franklin, as being straightforward. She is my boss. I report to her. She gives orders; I follow said orders as I see fit.

But then there's the issue of the orders she must take from her unseen and irritatingly perplexing boss, L'Hermitage's recently arrived building owner, Henry Franken, living, presumably, within the building's 9,500-square-foot penthouse. And that's where the complexity enters into her life. She has never met her boss, which is frustrating to someone like Charlotte. She seeks approval, affirmation, stroking. She must, in this case, get it from a distance, through an intercessor, my lawyer Judith Guncheon. Charlotte does, on occasion, express begrudging astonishment and surprise by the direction she receives from her boss. Trenchant, incisive, almost omniscient instruction stemming from a person who has, to her knowledge, rarely stepped foot inside the building's public spaces. It is said that Mr. Franken travels a great deal and is seldom home, which lends an inordinate amount of intrigue and fascination among the denizens, who speak often of Franken sightings. "I caught a glimpse of him from behind yesterday," they'll say, while idling away in the lobby. "Or, at least I think it was him. Short, balding. Very dapper, *very* wealthy—oh, yes, that much was obvious."

"What are you talking about, bald?" the other will say. "He's just a kid, that guy. Got the place when his old man croaked. Where've you been? I saw him the other day, heading out of here wearing a cap and those work boots—what are they called, Red Wings? Fat, short kid, and I can tell you, he had plenty of hair. Didn't so much as utter a grunt when he passed me. That's what massive bucks can buy you—lousy manners."

Charlotte stops at my desk as she enters, gesturing with her metal canister of tea, wafting fragrances of hibiscus or chamomile or some such meadow-laden concoction within my space. "This place is crazy," she says, taking off her sunglasses and jangling. Charlotte has a constant jangling noise about her. I'm not sure where it comes from—earrings, bracelets, necklace, hem accouterments, tea kettles. Mysterious female jangling.

"Good morning, Charlotte," I say.

"Yeah, yeah, good morning. I can't believe how ridiculously managed this place is."

"Aren't you the manager?" I ask.

"Oh, nice, that's very funny, Franklin. You know what I mean."

Charlotte's annoyance with the building owner's distant managerial style flairs up on various occasions, most often when an edict comes down from above via the intermediary, Ms. Guncheon. That's when Charlotte feels her most impotent, as in this morning's case.

"I'm nothing but an order taker; that's all I am," she says. "I might as well be working at Starbucks. So last night, I receive a call from Gitchygoomee or whatever the fuck her name is,"—Guncheon, I'll assume she means—"and she says that Franken wants that I get more involved in the day-to-day matters of our retail space renovation. Can you believe that bullshit? How crazy is that?"

"Yes, well, I suppose it would feel a little overwhelming to suddenly have to—"

"It's not over*whelming*, Franklin. Who said anything about over*whelming*? Do I look like I'm over*whelmed* to you? I've managed lots of projects far bigger than that in my life. Believe me—*lots*. Do I look like someone who gets overwhelmed?"

"No, not at all. But if it would be of help, Charlotte, I'd be happy to lend a hand in managing the oversight of the renovation work going on in—"

"Franklin, you're the doorman. I . . . am the manager. Of course, I will manage the Fitzger's renovation. I am well-studied in Six Sigma management techniques—"

"You know, I think that if we can bring our sigma count up to even four or five, we'll be in fine—"

"Franklin! Use your head!"

"Good morning, you two." Mr. Harrison enters the front reception area from the living room, heading for the coffee urn, crossword puzzle in hand.

"Oh, ho, ho," Charlotte coos. "Good morning, Mr. Harrison. How are you?" That smile of hers. When used, it can be disarming.

"Fine, fine. Puzzle in hand; all is right with God's children." He turns from the coffee cart with his cup refilled, lifts it in our direction, and returns to his seat in the living room.

"Yeah, fine, good for him," Charlotte mutters to me under her breath. "All's right with God's children. Anyway, so do you believe that crap? Not only do I hafta manage the residential part of the building, but I now need to oversee the retail space renovation. What, so I know retail or something? My ass! What am I? Both Lord *and* fucking Taylor? Gimme a break. If that's the crap I've got to get into, I'd rather just be a simple doorman."

I allow this somewhat inelegant statement of Charlotte's to linger upon the air for a moment, to meld with the tincture of hibiscus. I'm nothing if not patient with Charlotte.

"Oh," she says. "Sorry. That might have—I didn't mean that in a, in a condescending way, or anything. Or, at least in a 'I've got to take this to HR' level of condescension. I just meant that . . . Anyway, what a joke. You know what? I bet Franken's a drug dealer or something . . ."

"Hmm, doubtful," I say. "Bit of a longsh—"

"Never showing his face down here. Living up there in his penthouse and never interacting with anyone from the building. Trust me, I know these things. There's something underhanded going on," she says, wagging a jangling finger at me. Ah, it's the bracelets.

"Maybe just shy?" I suggest. "Reclusive? I'm sure he means no ill intent with his antisocial behavior. He actually strikes me as a very decent fellow."

"How can someone issue orders like that, having absolutely no clue what I do on a day-to-day bas—Wait a minute."

And now it's her opportunity to insert a pause within the rhythm of our morning conversation.

"What do you mean he strikes you as a decent fellow? How would *you* know?"

"Well, I just . . . you know, from what I've heard."

"You've met him, haven't you?" she asks, leaning toward me.

In the short time I've been in this position, the issue of Charlotte's noninteraction with Mr. Franken has played as an established leitmotif, sometimes tinkling quietly and softly in the background, other times bassooning loudly in the foreground, as it is this morning. Her lack of access to this all-important presence diminishes her standing and threatens her distinction within our encapsulated world.

"Goddammit. You've met him, haven't you?" My personal space is further encroached upon.

"Well, I, no, uh, no, not really—"

"'Well I,' blah, blah, blah, 'no, not really' blah, blah. Fine. You got a little bromance going with the man; I'll let *you* deliver this to the penthouse. He's not there anyway. I signed for it while coming in this morning. Something, I might add, that *you* should have taken care of. I don't know why I keep covering for you."

She tosses the envelope onto my desk and, having completed her unloading for the morning, and, no doubt, upset by this revelation of mine, spins on her heels and heads to her office, but not before offering to refill Mr. Harrison's coffee cup.

There is much for me to process following our five-minute interaction. To begin with, Charlotte's reaction to the retail space request, quite honestly, surprises me. I would have thought she would have enjoyed the additional responsibility. The jeweler, Fitzger, who had occupied the space for decades, retired a month ago. Architects, contractors, and subcontractors have been crawling over each other for the past two weeks, trying to bring the space up to date so as to be marketable for a future long-term renter. What Charlotte failed to share with me is that Judith also offered her an attractive raise for further oversight of this activity.

"Oh, by the way, guess what?" she asks, scurrying back to my desk, dark mood having lifted. "Guess who drove to work today in her brand-new red convertible Miata?"

"Ah, good for you. You picked it up, did you?" I ask, genuinely excited for her. Charlotte has been talking about the purchase of a new car for as long as I've worked here. I've noticed an inordinate amount of her time each day has been devoted to researching cars on the internet, speaking with dealers in New Jersey and Long Island, and seeking the advice of residents within the building. "Congratulations. I thought you were picking it up next weekend."

"No, I couldn't wait any longer. My uncle drove me to the dealer in Summit to pick it up last night. I must say, I am quite sizz-zzling driving it around the city." She emits a hissing sort of whistle as she touches her forefinger to her butt.

"And you drove it into work today? Wow, pretty brave of you," I say. "I imagine it was difficult finding a parking space in this neighborhood."

"I have my ways, you know, Franklin," she says, starting back for her office. "It was surprisingly easy. Well, I guess if you get in early enough, it's not such a problem. You ought to keep that in mind, by the way. Yep."

Nine-thirty—early enough? Her boss, who she has learned is a lenient man, allows for this fudging of arrival time only because she stays late on some days.

If Charlotte were to ever invite or accept advice from me, the doorman, I would recommend to her that she not push her boss' leniency too far. There are limits to everything.

<h1 style="text-align:center">CHAPTER 3</h1>

Thursday, 9:53 am

"The hordes have departed, Mr. Hanratty," Mr. Harrison says to me from across the lobby. "The rats are racing, eh?"

I look up from my Jeeves story, included within a Wodehouse anthology I was surprised to discover in Dad's meager book collection in the penthouse office. The other dozen or so books focused primarily on New York real estate, negotiation techniques, and the scintillating art of making deals. I can only assume that the Wodehouse volume managed its way into Dad's mingle-mangle for no other reason than he mistook it for a compendium on, well, wooden houses.

"Truth be told and between you and me," I reply to Mr. Harrison, "I thought they'd never leave."

This is a line of banter Mr. Harrison and I have picked up recently, branching out from and expanding upon our daily crossword-puzzle-related conversation. I've come to realize that friendships develop at their own pace; some gallop together in a matter of moments, others tiptoe together quietly and slowly over the course of weeks or months.

Within the lobby, L'Hermitage's branded concoction of morning smells continue to linger, the ones that are delivered via the opening and closing elevator doors—bacon, coffee, burnt toast, hints of aftershave or light perfumes—or those that join us through the front door—exhaust fumes, humidity, and the sweat from a recent run or workout.

Tall and elegant, Mr. Harrison has a bearing that speaks of balletic control and authority. Our form of address is formal. To him, I am Mr. Hanratty; to me, he is Mr. Harrison. Since his wife's death three months ago, he has become a regular morning fixture within our lobby, bringing a mug and the *Times*'s puzzle down from his apartment with him. He has told me that, since becoming a widower, it's the morning hours that prove the most difficult, the hours in which he prefers to avoid the apartment. The apartment, and the breakfast table that remains set for two.

"Toss me a clue, sir," I say. "What's got you stumped this morning?"

"Oh, lots," he says. "I'm still working on yesterday's puzzle. But since I mentioned rats a few moments ago, let me throw this animal-related clue to you. Let's stay true to theme. You know a lot about animals, right?"

Mr. Harrison considers me to be an expert in animal-related topics because, in one of our early interactions, I referenced Ms. Sillerman's—she of 3B—small arm-laden lumpen mass as a Pomeranian, shortly after the two had passed through our lobby. That I labeled it a "Pomeranian" rather than simply a "dog" apparently bestowed veterinarian-like wisdom upon me in Mr. Harrison's mind. Fact is, I refer to every small dog as a Pomeranian, and, occasionally, but not intentionally, small cats, gerbils, and ferrets, as well.

"What was the name—four letters, second letter 'L'—of the lioness in *Born Free*?" Mr. Harrison asks. "Good lord, it's not enough that the *Times* expects we know the characters' names in *The Lion King* and something called *Frozen*, now we need to know animals' names from a movie I haven't seen in fifty years. That'll probably stump you. Way before your time."

"Elsa," I say.

"Elsa," he repeats. "Well, there you go. That seems to fit. That was a nice movie, as I recall. About a lion cub that reached its full potential once it was freed. Good stuff."

My memory of that movie is more of the romping about the cat did in the long grass of Africa, along with what seemed to me to be misguided wrestling matches taking place between the owners and the rapidly growing cat. Even as a seven-year-old, watching the old videotape while curled up on Dad's lap, I had the good sense to suspect that lion-wrestling was an inadvisable activity at any point in the animal's development, unless your name is either Siegfried or Roy, and, as fate would have it, maybe not even then.

In our morning visits, Mr. Harrison has told me about his relief of being freed from his law firm, retired for close to a year. First in dribs and drabs, and finally a torrent, he informed me of his dislike of the profession, a conviction which I readily grasp. Although he excelled at his practice, working within one of the city's most prestigious firms, there was rarely a day in which he wouldn't rather have been elsewhere.

"What is the value of money if it doesn't allow you to truly do what you want to do?" he asked me one day a few weeks ago, rhetorically. "I do hope I won't look back on this all and feel my life was wasted. There are several partners of mine who have been dragged out of their offices once they hit the mandatory retirement age of seventy-five. Dear god, on and on they went, slowly becoming just another potted palm around the place, albeit with a well-knotted four-in-hand. Not me. I had been counting down the days for a decade, knowing the exact date, day, and minute that I would walk out of there for the final time. At thirty-eight years of service, Mr. Hanratty, I was eligible for full pension, full profit sharing, full dividends, the whole kit-and-caboodle. Loved the people dearly, just found the work deathly dull."

"Why did you do it? Why did you get into law?" I asked.

"Hah," he snorted. "Yes. Isn't that the question? The answer's easy, though. I had to please my father, who had also been a lawyer. One of the city's best. I had little choice in my career. To have done anything else would have severely tested our relationship, which was always strained, at best."

I'm certainly aware of how often and easily the bonds between father and son can become frayed, how philosophies and outlooks between generations can vary and clash. It is the well-recorded material of legend and mythology. Although Dad had been my singular source of comfort during my childhood, a role forced upon him with the premature death of my mother when I was six, our relationship during my teenage years became fraught with angst, theatricality, and simmering anger. My adolescent animus was aimed directly at my sole parent and only relative.

"What would you rather have done?" I asked Mr. Harrison.

"I was an artist, or so that's how I always regarded myself," he said. "I was talented as a young man." He explained to me how he had drawn from the moment he could hold a pencil. Although his mother had been supportive, to the point of enrolling him in art classes throughout his childhood, his father had seen it merely as a hobby at best, but certainly not a future vocation. It's fine to doodle on the side, his father would tell him, but it will not be a line of professional work, certainly not one that will be further explored following high school.

"And, so, here I am," Mr. Harrison told me. "I can now begin the second part of my life. I have fulfilled my obligations to both father and firm, God bless their souls. Now I get to do what I want to do."

He approaches the coffee table for a topping off of his cup before heading upstairs.

"What's on your docket today, sir? The usual full schedule?" I ask.

"Well, since you asked," he says, approaching me and tossing the half-finished crossword onto my counter, "I'll tell you. Related to what we've discussed—I signed up for art classes taught at a little place down the street called the Metropolitan Museum of Art. I felt it was time to pick up where I left off as a teen. We draw from pieces within the galleries, various paintings, etchings, sculptures. I'm rusty, so I'm going to need to shake off the cobwebs, eh? Quite eager to get started."

"Sounds wonderful. Good luck to you," I say. Remembering my earlier conversation this morning with the homeless man, Terry, I add, "By the way, I've heard there's a painting in Gallery 807 that should be checked out. What was the artist's name? Something Frederick—?"

"Of course," he says. "Caspar David *Friedrich*. Wonderful German artist—nineteenth-century Romantic movement. Very important acquisition for the museum a few years back. I've seen it several times. A peaceful, contemplative piece. You're not familiar with it?"

"No," I say, shaking my head. It's at moments like this that I regret not having paid closer attention in Ms. Baldwin's art history class during my sophomore year in college, an elective course that those who trod before me swore was far easier than Mr. Keidendahl's ball-busting astronomy course. As it played out, my proficiency around transits of Venus and parallaxes is on par with my seemingly unaccounted-for command of Friedrich.

"You've got to get out from behind this desk more often," he says, and then, dramatically, "Cast thyself free of this anchored building! Being of the Romantic period, Friedrich was one of those artists who often worked the moon into his paintings. The Romantics loved the moon—its mystery, its two-sided nature."

"So, Mr. Harrison, one moment, please," I say, half smiling. "There really *is* a painting about two guys looking at a moon in Gallery 807?"

He looks at me, blankly, a look not too dissimilar, I suspect, from those I regularly greeted Ms. Baldwin with during her early-morning lectures.

"Yes, *Two Men Contemplating the Moon*. Go see it; it's wonderful. But I'm off now, Mr. Hanratty. I'm fifty years late for my art class."

He heads up in the elevator, and my lobby is empty once again.

# CHAPTER 4

Thursday, 10:26 am

Mornings and evenings are the busiest times at my job—my rush hours. All sorts of people—busy, busy people—coming and going. Going mostly, in the morning hours; the coming happens later in the day, of course, when they return to their roosts, no longer as driven or preoccupied as they had been when the day began. The spring is gone from their step, the joie de vivre a little less joie-ful.

In the hours between 8:00 and 10:00 a.m. I assume several roles for my newly shaven and freshly eye-lined subjects: concierge, taxi hailer, Uber alerter, traffic cop, weather reporter, confidante, therapist, appeaser, listener, empathizer, and mediator. While the evening hours have their own distinct energy, they are different from the intensity of the morning's.

"Franklin," a voice booms as the elevator door opens.

I wake from my reverie. "Good morning, Mr. Stewart."

"Yeah, yeah, g'morning," he replies with a dismissive wave of his hand. "An assistant from my gallery is going to swing by this afternoon, bringing a painting over. His name's Eric. Can you make sure he gets into the apartment all right?"

"Of course, sir."

"Point him toward the large empty wall opposite the entryway, okay? I've kept the track light on for where he's supposed to hang it. It's the only light on in the place, so he shouldn't have any questions about where it goes, okay?"

And, as he heads out the door, an additional tidbit of instruction, sealing our one-way agreement. "Just make sure he gets in, would you?

It's important."

As quickly as it arrives, the morning gale passes, and the lobby is once again quiet, still. For a brief intermission, I have the space to myself. As often happens, Charlotte comes out of hiding at just that moment, making sure I have understood everything that was asked of me and that I have my tasks and responsibilities for the day under control and properly prioritized.

"Yes," I say. "It's all good, Charlotte. Thank you for checking."

"Good, then," she says, giving me a look intended to express depths of subtext and underlying meaning, "because that's what you're paid to do." She spins on her heels, comfortable in her mind that all is, indeed, under control.

"Charlotte," I start, "I'm wondering if, during those busy periods . . . I'm wondering if you could possibly lend me a hand out here. It does get somewhat crazy at times with people's requests and questions and so forth." Truth be told, I occasionally venture down this path merely for my own momentary amusement more so than to affect a desired outcome.

"No, Franklin, that's not the way we have this set up. Do the best you can. Mr. Franken does not want me out here working the front desk. My time is better spent in my office, dealing with other matters. Important matters. Juggle! That's the job of a head doorman. Once I start getting pulled into the morning's minutiae, people will be popping into my office all day long, asking *me* all the sorts of questions that they should be asking *you*. Like, 'Is it supposed to rain today?' or 'Where's my *Times*?' That kind of crap. I don't want them seeing me like that. I am the *manager*. The job of handling requests is the *doorman's*. It's your job, clear?"

"Of, course. I just thought . . ." but I let it drop as Charlotte heads back to her office. I'm tempted to suggest that her Miata chatroom moments could wait, or Candy Crush be put on pause, but I bite my tongue. Charlotte's firing of me would create a world of complications for everyone involved.

"Aren't bosses the worst?" someone quietly asks me.

I look up and it's Wendy DeLong of 8D. I thought the lobby was empty, and clearly Charlotte had too. Her language is far less earthy, shall I say, when residents are in the vicinity. But Wendy emerges from the shadows of the living room, near the coffee urn.

I haven't a perfect sense of this resident. Wendy comes and goes, rarely lingering within the lobby or living room areas. Although my snap judgments of people tend to be spot on—a long-standing point of pride—there is something about Wendy that I can't quite put my finger on. I've known her *type* for years. Attended a fine East Coast school, most likely a Wellesley or a Mount Holyoke. In the years since graduation, she has, no doubt, stayed in touch with several members of her class, getting together with them for the monthly book club or annual college meeting at, let's say, the New York Wellesley Club. Brought up in wealth, submerged in old, quiet money. Annual childhood winter trips alternating between ski resorts in odd-numbered years and Caribbean beaches in even. Owns an expensive, three-bedroom Upper East Side apartment— the aforementioned 8D—despite working in a lower-level, modest-paying marketing position in Midtown. Oh, yes, Wendy has trust fund written all over her; this I know. Perhaps even a small, discreet, ironic tattoo on her derriere, something clever like, *I Deserve Your Trust.* If Wendy's youthful age within the confines of this Upper East Side building hadn't caught my sophisticated eye, then certainly her beauty outside of it would have.

"Believe me, I know all about difficult bosses," Wendy says, nodding her head in the general direction of Charlotte's office. "But asking for purely selfish reasons, and because I need my caterers to get in easily this afternoon, you *do* have this all under control, right?"

"Well, if not," I say, "I'll do my best to fool you. *One,* I mean—to fool one."

"Perception is everything; isn't that what they say?"

"Well, that's how I've squeaked by."

All right, as vapid or inane as it may be—and I certainly don't rule out both being the case in this instance—this is the longest conversation I've had with Wendy and, for that reason alone, I feel it merits sharing. And, for what it's worth, it's the closest we've ever even been to one another.

"I just wanted to make sure that, of all the balls you've got in the air, my own doesn't fall through the cracks tonight and get busted. Am I mixing my metaphors?"

"I believe the ball-busting has been adequately covered this morning. But the others are still up in the air."

"Yes, well, you do have it down that I have a caterer coming in this afternoon for an event I'm hosting, right?"

"Artisan, at 5:00 is what I have. Is that still correct?" I ask, referring to the daily written log, an anachronism that, for some reason, Charlotte feels is necessary for lending a critical element of . . . authenticity? Retro simplicity? to our lobby. "They're bringing the canapés, bowls of mista salad, and the plates of mixed metaphors, yes?"

"Ah, wit," she says, smiling. "Almost makes me wish I had more things to check on down here every now and again at the front desk. Yes, that's it."

"Tip top go, then," I say, somewhat inscrutably, for little reason other than I had just read a similar line delivered by a lackey in my Wodehouse novel. In that setting, it was delivered and received to good effect.

"Tip top go? Hmm, tall, dark, *and* antiquated, just like my bedroom bureau. I like that in a doorman," she says, and allows her smile to hang in the air for what I *perceive* as one more second than is perhaps necessary. And I allow myself to enjoy it for one more second than L'Hermitage's bylaws dictating employee-resident relations might deem proper.

"Good," she says again. "Well, all righty, then." She turns and starts to move off, her slender, elegant frame gliding quietly toward the vestibule. Though above average height, my guess is that Wendy was never one of those tall teenage girls who stooped in an effort to appear shorter than boys of her age. Her quiet nature alone might make it easy to overlook her. What doesn't make it easy to overlook is what's been distracting me since the first time I noticed her gracing my lobby several weeks ago: her confidence, refined nature, and grace. Her humor, deep brown eyes, and shoulder-length hair suddenly provide me with a painful and untouchable diversion.

"Ms. DeLong—" I stammer.

"That's Wendy, to you."

"*Wendy*, is there anything else I can help you with in preparation for your party?"

Had we sufficiently covered this issue? Were we done? Was I repeating myself? Perhaps I should have offered up a brief weather report instead, an encapsulation, a synopsis of the climatological situation at hand. With other building denizens, weather-report repartee can go on for countless—sometimes unending—moments. The same might hold true with Wendy.

She turns before heading out the doors, regarding me with her ambiguous smile. "No, I don't think so. I think we're all . . . hmm, let's see, how might one put it? Oh, yes. I think we're all absolutely, tip-top go." And the moment has passed.

"Yes, of course. Very good then," I say. I adjust my seat, straightening my back, sitting taller, and return to the paperwork in front of me. And for a moment, just a moment of daydreaming, I pretend that this wealthy young woman might consider being interested in a doorman.

The world is full of complications, after all.

# CHAPTER 5

Thursday, 2:23 pm

So, more or less, those are my peeps, as Jacob, the night doorman will, on occasion, remind me. As in, "Frankie-boy, you need a shitload more peeps in your life. You are one lonely-assed son-of-a-bitch if ever I saw one. You put the hermit in the L'Hermitage. Hey! You know what I heard once? That being lonely is equal to smoking fifteen cigarettes a day. How do they figure that equals-to shit out? No wonder I flunked math. Anyway, Cousin-Jakie is telling you to go get your lonely-ass laid. Here's an equals-to that I understand: getting laid equals to one nice night in heaven. Bam-a-lam! Or noonday, too, if that's the way you like to roll."

But he doesn't use the term correctly. I'm not lonely. *Alone* maybe. Solitary. Incommunicado at times. But not lonely. Jacob invariably makes this proclamation on Monday afternoons during our shift change, after asking me how I've spent my weekend. He shares with me his Tinder moments, his weekend conquests, his one-nighters, his day-longers. Jacob is nothing if not pure id. There's a part of me that envies him. Assured, good-looking, never doubting or, at least never *self*-doubting; what, in my father's generation, may have been referred to as a ladies' man. He has a nonquestioning lightness in his approach to life that has never been an intrinsic part of my own fiber.

◆　◆　◆

At 2:30, Charlotte disembarks from the elevator coming from parts unknown.

"Franklin," she shouts. "Don't forget that there are three dinner parties in the building tonight—the Coopers, the Cohens, and . . ." She trails off as she enters her office.

The rest of her sentence is garbled or conceivably nonexistent. I'm not sure if she assumed that I would be bustling after her with a notepad or if I could hear her inside the recesses of her office, but no matter. The family she most likely mentioned is the McAdoos of 11A, or possibly the Stewarts of 10B, unless she somehow became aware of the fact that Wendy had late last week organized a work-related cocktail party for this evening. But I doubt it.

I get out from behind my desk and walk to her office door. Our relationship has degraded in the time that Charlotte and I have worked together. I have multiple theories around this issue, but none that are appropriately fleshed out or well-formed enough to merit sharing at this juncture.

There is no vagueness, however, in Jacob's relationship with Charlotte. "Hey, man, how's Queen Charlotta-ass tonight?" Jacob invariably asks—or some variation thereof—when appearing each afternoon for his shift. In these intermittent exchanges, I will give him updates on what has transpired during the day, what he can expect for the night ahead, and what needs to be prepared for the following day.

"Yeah, yeah, yeah, man, just give me the straight dope. The only thing I need to be prepared for is she-bitch's departure through my lobby in the next fifteen minutes. So, tell me, Frankfurter, how . . . is . . . Char-broiled tonight?" Although Jacob may, in almost all cases, have his way with whatever woman he so desires, Charlotte has proven immune to his charm. His idea of hell is working the day shift alongside her, as he had to do for a short time as fill-in prior to my arrival. "They should have given me fucking hazard pay for those weeks, Franklin! Haz. Ard. Pay. Worst fucking time of this young boy's life. They giving you hazard pay, Franky? Cuz if not, they should, you know. Shit, I'm still suffering PTS . . . LG . . . BQ, or whatever that alphabet soup is called, from when I was working your shift. As for you, take it up with the man, up in the penthouse. You got yourself a rock-solid case for hazard pay. Rock solid, bro. I'll back you up!"

As day doorman, I am, technically the boss of Jacob, the evening doorman Monday through Friday. We also have an assortment of weekend day doormen, most of whom I rarely interact with, and two elderly gentlemen who split the long weekend night shifts: Morgan, originally from Wales, and Lester, originally from England. Jacob, having little interest in differentiating between the two, simply refers to them as "More" or "Less." Other building members, perhaps equally uncharitably, refer to the two gents as "L'Hermitage's United Kingdom." In Charlotte's organizational chart, a document that provides no end of amusement to the full staff, all doormen report to me.

And I, of course, report to Charlotte. I stand inside her office doorframe waiting to be recognized in order to make sure she is fully informed of the roster of parties occurring this evening. It's a heavy load for a weekday evening, the three catered dinner parties and two bartended cocktail parties. Two of the dinner parties are scheduled for 7:00 p.m. guest arrivals, one for 7:30 arrival. The two cocktail parties are scheduled to begin at 6:00 and go until 8:00. In situations such as this, we ask the hosts to stagger their guests' arrivals, so they don't all arrive in our lobby at the same time. If not staggered appropriately, we risk sending guests to the wrong destination. This has led, on occasions in the past, to embarrassing situations. More than one guest has contributed to a prochoice cause when they thought they were attending a fundraiser for a Republican state party candidate simply because they got off on the wrong floor with a group of boisterous attendees.

"I've scheduled On Thyme catering to arrive at the loading dock at three thirty and be out of there no later than four fifteen," I tell Charlotte, who I can't help but notice is regarding me with—shall we call it a sneer? The upper lip is curled in a fashion that conveys disdain, an expression, I might add, that in toddlerhood may have been considered either amusing or, perhaps, mistaken for a cleft pallet by infrequent visitors. I push on: "Their people are handling both the Cohens's and the Coopers's parties. Huckleby and Rosemary will arrive at four o'clock for the McAdoos's setup. Artisan will be setting up for Ms. DeLong's cocktail party by five, and Murdocks is coming at five fifteen. It's a full evening."

"Franklin, when did you find out about Wendy DeLong?" she squalls. "Did she just arrange it this morning, before I came in?"

There are numerous aspects of my job that I enjoy—charming and winning over residents within the building, earning the applause of tenants by going beyond their expectations, managing and juggling complicated schedules, discretely reading humorous British novels from the previous century during work hours. But these interrogations imposed by Charlotte try my patience.

"These are the types of things you should be telling me when I come into the building, rather than asking me about my car. Do you know how stupid I look when a resident mentions something to me that they assume I know about? I'm the one with the title of 'manager.' I need to MAN-age."

I recognize that Charlotte is frustrated by her situation. She reports to an unseen entity and receives mildly tendered counsel and professional tips in the guise of questions or muted suggestions from a direct report. We're stuck, in our own separate ways, she and I. It could be stated that the solution to both situations rests in my hands, and my lawyer Judith would be quick to point out that resolution to me, were I to bring up the matter in our weekly get-togethers. But, for my immediate future—and, by immediate future, I mean the next fifteen minutes—it's far more important that I review the arrival log, shuttle the recently delivered packages to the mail room, straighten the art books within the parlor, and finish the final paragraphs of my Wodehouse chapter.

# CHAPTER 6



Chaos descends upon the lobby a little after three in the afternoon. Charlotte comes out of her office after slamming down the phone. She surveys the lobby to make sure it's just the two of us; Jeeves is, for the moment, sequestered.

"Frickin A!" she yells. Charlotte has an eager willingness to share mild annoyances, original thoughts, or abstruse observations at random moments throughout the day. I am often forced into the role of captive audience member.

"Something wrong, Charlotte?" I ask, calmly. I don my parent-of-a-child-in-the-throes-of-a-tantrum voice, one I have learned, through experimentation, to employ to greater or lesser effect with Charlotte.

"What do these people think I'm here to do all day? Do they truly think I'm their gofer? Their whipping girl?"

"What do you need, Charlotte?" I ask. "How can I be of help?" My relationship with Charlotte is such that I am able to recognize her eruptions as not so much a seeking of sympathy as a long and loud preamble to the ultimate issuance of a directive or fiat.

"Ah, gawd, how do these people get through their days? I mean, they're successful, accomplished people, right? So why does their shit continue to slide down on me, huh?"

Despite a mental image that throws me slightly off stride, I push forward. I see she hasn't vented fully enough to enter the solution phase of what's irking her, so I stand by quietly, filling out the evening's paperwork for Jacob, grunting at appropriate gaps and pauses as she emits a few more puffs and burps of irritation. Eventually, with no further prompts of empathy from me, the balloon deflates, so to speak, and she looks at me, frustrated.

"I'll be happy to take care of it, if you need me to, Charlotte. Very happy, really."

If, and only if, it serves to hasten her exit from the immediate vicinity.

"Brendan Stewart just called. He wants someone to run over to his gallery to pick up some painting that they need to have hung up in their apartment."

"I understood from Mr. Stewart that they were having the art piece delivered. He indicated that to me this morning."

"I don't know—something got screwed up with the delivery. The delivery boy is stuck somewhere out on Long Island. It really doesn't matter. All I know is he's seeing his stupid problem as now being mine. Such bullshit!"

At this point, Mr. Harrison gets off the elevator and heads to the mailroom, just to the right of my desk. With his reappearance in the reception area, Charlotte has the wherewithal to lower her voice and tone. Beyond the volume adjustment, a bit of verbal tidying up occurs, as well.

"Well, in any event," Charlotte continues, "Brendan Stewart asked me to pick it up. Could you do it? If you could get it back here, he said he'd get a professional hanger over here to get it hung. Jesus, it's like there's a specialty for everything now. Professional hanger—pfft. Anyway, it needs to be in place before his guests arrive."

"I'd be happy to have it couriered over here," I offer, picking up the phone. "The problem with my going, you see, is that this evening's caterers are about to arrive. It would be best for me to be here for the next two hours to check them in, get them in and out of the dock as quickly as possible, and make sure they head to the right apartments. They'll be coming soon."

"The dock?"

"Yes, for unloading. But regarding Mr. Stewart's issue, I'll make sure a courier picks up the painting immediately." I start to dial. Leaving my station is out of the question. After all, I do have my patrons to tend to.

Mr. Harrison exits the mailroom, pausing by our desk as if wanting to join our conversation—deathly dull though it might be—all the while sorting through the mail he has picked up.

"Hello, Mr. Harrison, how are you?" Charlotte asks. She immediately turns back to me, not waiting for Mr. Harrison to respond.

"Sir," I say, "how was your session at the museum? Your art class?" I feel that a bit more acknowledgment of Mr. Harrison's presence is required beyond Charlotte's perfunctory greeting.

"Oh, it was quite—" he begins.

"Franklin, you're not fully understanding the issue," Charlotte says to me in a loud stage whisper. She's unyielding, incessant. "Mr. Stewart insisted that one of *us* pick up the painting. He specifically said he didn't want *any* courier. If his own deliveryman couldn't bring it, he asked that someone from L'Hermitage pick it up. I'm sure he intended that I send *you* over."

"But the caterers—" I begin. "I'm afraid that if I leave right at this particular—"

"Afraid?" blurted Charlotte. "Of what? Like, the caterers are going to run through the halls lobbing bacon-wrapped water chestnuts at each other? Bwah, c'mon, Franklin, I think I can handle the—"

"I didn't mean *afraid* afraid. It's just that the delivery schedule is laid out in a very orderly manner, and I know exactly where folks should be and where they should go and . . ." my voice trails off, in a perhaps not totally-convincing manner.

"Mr. Hanratty," says Mr. Harrison. "Do yourself a favor. The caterers will be fine under Ms. Marbury's firm direction. Nothing to be afraid of. Get out from behind this desk and enjoy the streets of New York. And in terms of something to be afraid of—I suspect there's a greater possibility of dangerous situations with our fine art dealer than there is with catering machinations or schedules. Go ahead, young man. Have yourself an adventure."

Well, I'm not sure my enjoyment or adventure-seeking is entirely germane at this moment in time. I feel somewhat trapped, like a kitten in a corner as the two of them paw at me, rolling me back and forth. "Well . . . if you all feel it would be for the best," I say, with an intended lack of conviction. "Huckleby and On Thyme will be here soon," I say. "They'll need to be properly directed—"

"Franklin," Charlotte says, smiling and winking toward Mr. Harrison in a conspiratorial manner that I find to be immensely annoying, "*Please.* How *do* you think we ever got along here at L'Hermitage before you arrived? Yes, yes, I'll take care of the caterers and send them in the right directions. Now go. Go, go, go. Oh, but just remember—you're not supposed to be away from your desk in the middle of the day. We'll keep this breach between us. Make sure you hurry, now."

It's at moments like this that a voice clambers around in my head—a voice not too dissimilar from my own but far more reminiscent of my father's or Judith's—that says, "What the hell are you doing with your life? You've been given a gift and you're spending your time schlepping paintings for fat cats." The specific wording may vary with the occasion, but the gist remains the same.

I walk outside with Mr. Harrison. "I'd be happy to walk over to Mr. Stewart's gallery with you if you thought that would be helpful," he says.

"No, thank you," I say. "It's right here in the neighborhood. I'll be able to find it easily enough."

"Alright, then, best wishes," he says. "And Franklin, make sure you remember the agreement Brendan made with Charlotte. She was asked to have one painting brought back, not a whole slew . . . Just don't let him take advantage of you, you know—" his sentence trails off as he heads up the street.

A straightforward errand has, seemingly, set everyone unnervingly on edge. Charlotte passing up the opportunity to further endear herself with one of the building's older, more established male residents is odd in and of itself, although I'll admit, this particular delegation of responsibilities might be related more to her unfortunate selection of three-inch heels this morning than an unwillingness or discomfort in visiting Mr. Stewart's gallery. And then the strangeness just now with Mr. Harrison, normally the building's most discreet and genteel resident. All buildings, like any small community, have their tensions and intrigues. It's just that I had never seen them displayed between Mr. Stewart and Mr. Harrison.

In terms of the catering issue, I'd like to say I'm leaving L'Hermitage with total confidence that all would go well in the next thirty minutes, but Charlotte has repeatedly disabused me of that notion in the past whenever she's been placed in charge. She's smart; she's accomplished; and she carries herself quite well in certain moments. But as a handler of *chaotic* moments, she isn't worth a damn.

# CHAPTER 7

Thursday, 3:21 pm

T his might prove an opportune moment to share some incidental notes about my past, now that I am away from those who reside and work within the cosseted environs of L'Hermitage. I hesitate to share too much, however. I recognize how self-loathing can all too easily spill out into the general atmosphere and contaminate others' opinions.

My childhood was a normal one. Well, of course, it was *not*; why else would I be bobbing adrift—Dad's voice, again—for the past several years? While experiencing it—my childhood, that is—I assumed it *was* normal, with the notable exception of my mother's death when I was an impressionable six years old. The travel, the *means* of travel, the schooling, the weekends, the weeknights, the friends, the acquaintances—it all seemed deathly dull and prosaic to me. It wasn't until I achieved a broader worldview, largely during my teenage years, and saw what others had—or *didn't* have—that the resentment and the utter disdain for my father's work began to settle in. It was around that time that my lack of direction—again, Dad's depiction, not mine—or my seeking of a broader and more enriched understanding of the world around me—my more favorable characterization of this era—settled into my inner fiber.

But why ruin a perfectly good walk? Plenty of time to seek solutions to the dilemmas within one's life. What else should one do while lying awake at 2:37 every morning? And so, with a certain amount of trepidation I head for the Stewart & Company Gallery on East 82nd Street.

Mr. Stewart's gallery is a distinct building on a tony street, one I've noticed on previous late-night neighborhood strolls. The gallery is a four-story building, designed in an Italianate style, with exterior pillars scattered about, rounded arches between them, and small ornamental balconies. The most eye-catching and noteworthy feature of the property, however, is a full-sized, iron sculpture of a man standing out front dressed in a business suit, his hands tucked in his pockets and gazing in a wistful manner toward the park. While neighborhood pigeons may be appreciative of the statue's presence in the middle of the sidewalk, pedestrians aren't. If this statue is intended to represent Mr. Stewart, then he might have done his neighbors a favor by having his iron likeness stand off to one side. I don't know Mr. Stewart well, but it seems the artist has caught his general mien. Iron-willed. Strong-jawed. Inarguably in the way.

The gallery is highly secured; the only way to enter is by being buzzed in. It's not the type of gallery that one visits on a window-shopping or sightseeing whim, wondering what might be hidden behind curious doors just off Madison Avenue. I go into a small vestibule, ring the buzzer, and look expectantly into a camera—or is it a fire sprinkler?—five inches from my face.

"Sxk-ay-I-elp-oo?-ksx?" a voice squonks at me through the small appliance.

Assuming the intent of this noise was to ask if I could be helped, I take a leap of faith and say, "Good afternoon. I'm here to pick up a picture for Mr. Stewart. I've come over from L'Hermitage."

Another unintelligible utterance from the box but this time, with a more excited, perhaps even anticipatory, inflection, followed by an absurdly loud buzzing emanating from a device even closer than the camera/sprinkler.

I open the door and enter. The smell of closed spaces hits me, something between musty European museum, grade school textbook, and Mrs. Cooper's weekday perfume—not altogether unpleasant. As my eyes work to adjust to the darkness within, I hear the clattering heels of either a receptionist or resident tap dancer approaching me rapidly.

A man with short, spiked hair comes into focus. "Are you from L'Hermitage?" he asks.

"Yes, I am," I say, pointing to the branded name pin on my breast.

"Before I give you the litho, could I please see some identification?"

"ID?" I ask. "I would have thought that my outfit and name tag might have proven sufficient. I'm not sure I brought my wallet—" As I self-administer a pat down, knowing that this pantomime will produce no means of identification, I fill the silent void by lobbing a bon mot his way, "This happen often? Folks popping in using the ruse of picking up a painting for the owner of this place?"

"Mark, it's okay." Mr. Stewart approaches us, having materialized from the vicinity of a stairway behind the reception desk. "Thanks for coming over, Franklin. We were expecting Charlotte; that's the only reason Mark was asking for an ID. Thanks, Mark, I got it."

Dismissed, Mark spins and taps back to his reception desk, looking put out by not being able to follow through on this important matter.

"Come here, Franklin. The painting's up here," Mr. Stewart says. He leads me up the staircase past two galleries of work. His office is on the third floor.

"You've never been here before, have you?" he asks.

"No, I haven't. It looks like quite a beautiful collection."

"Yeah, we got some good-looking stuff here. I've done alright for myself." He pauses and looks at me for a moment, studying me. "You like what you see here, Franklin? You know, I was a kid just like you, working a series of dead-end jobs—like you—one after the other, going nowhere. I looked around me, saw all the stinking rich people and you know what I said? I said, Fuck this. Who needs these bullshit jobs I was in, you know? I'm as smart as them. So, I saw a guy, just like me right now, owned a dozen galleries, king of the world. He said to me, 'Bren, if you ever wanna be someone, you gotta make a character of yourself.' That's what he said to me. Make a character of yourself. I said, hell, I can do that; been working on that for years, you know? The guy didn't know shit about art, but, god, could he grease the rich folks. Smooth as silk. So, I said, yep, that's for me. I can learn enough about art to do the same thing. So, I got a loan. Easy as pie, by the way, leverage is the key in life—and opened up a gallery. This isn't my first; it's the third location. And ka-boom! Landed in the uppity-upper class. Everybody looks at me now and thinks I'm some Upper East Side tycoon. Me! Let me ask you a question. Who's the greatest American who ever lived?"

"Lincoln?"

"Okay, next greatest."

"Washington?"

"My point is, PT Barnum belongs somewhere high up on that list of yours. You can't believe how easy it is to fool people by selling them shit, you know? You could do it too, Franklin."

"Quite an impressive journey, sir."

"Well, like I said, you could do it too, kid. Just strap on a pair of balls and away you go. Zoom zoom, to the moon, know what I mean?"

At this point, we have landed slightly shy of the moon, at the building's second floor. Our assent continues.

"Yeah, people said to me—Christ, *family* said to me—'Bren, you're too rough around the edges; you ain't got no class. You can't be no art dealer.' Hah! Know what I said to them? 'Too rough around the edges? Fuck you,' that's what I said to them, straight up. Look who's laughing now, huh? I got more fucking edges—rough, smooth, in between—than they'll ever have. Yeah, Franky, you can do it too. You got far smoother edges than I got, you know? You're halfway there, pally-boy. Just need the money part. Leverage, Franky, leverage."

"I don't know a great deal about art, sir."

"Phht. I told you, like *that* matters. Neither do the buyers. You think I knew art? Art Carney—that's the only art I knew, okay? He was a customer of mine years ago, by the way, bought a couple of pieces from me. Anyway, you just gotta know people and how to sell to them and put on a little act? And you, *you*, got showmanship about you; I can see that much. You just gotta get out of those doorman duds.

"Here's one more tip for you, Frank, if you find yourself getting into this game. Make sure your artists paint on small canvases. Sell more that way. They all want to paint on these big fucking canvases, make a big fucking statement to the world. Who's got the wall space? I say to them *small*. I want small canvases. Sell a ton more—it's a volume game. By the way, you know what the deal is with all Upper East Side buildings? The floor plans are all the same. The only difference is the art on the wall improves as you get higher up. Okay, art class is over."

We're near the top of the third staircase and Mr. Stewart, winded, pauses for a moment.

"Speaking of higher up—whoo man! I should take the damn elevator more often. Either that or move my office down to the first floor, huh? Yeah, so anyway," he says, continuing up the stairs, "we normally hold the receptions within the gallery space, but tonight we gotta do it at our home. It's not so much that we're trying to sell the art as we're trying to sell the artist, you know? But we gotta have something that represents the artist on hand. We're introducing Willem de Smet, the Belgian guy, to a patron."

"Aha, excellent," I say. And then, to further solidify in Mr. Stewart's mind my interest in the matter, I toss out, "What's his medium?"

"Soot."

"I'm sorry, it sounded almost like you said 'suet.' Say that again, please."

"Soot." Damned if he didn't utter the same concise syllable again.

"As in the animal fat, sir? The bird feed?" I ask, trying to hide any level of surprise and, perhaps, display an interpretable lack of artistic sophistication.

"Nah," Mr. Stewart chuckles. "Not suet. *Soot* is de Smet's medium. Only the Japanese guy, Kanaberi whats-his-fuck paints in suet and Goldenson's got him. Lucky bastard. Willem would never cross over into that medium. He collects soot from the chimneys and furnaces in Wallonia, and then creates industrial landscapes. It's kinda fascinating, really, if you're inta that stuff. Anyway, we have a rich British guy in town tonight who's interested in Willem doing an entire series for his country estate."

We have arrived at the outer area of Mr. Stewart's office. On the walls are several of de Smet's framed pieces, all relatively small, depicting . . . well, as billed, sooty landscapes. Each one has a variation of a hilly countryside in the foreground with chimney stacks belching clouds of whirling black smoke in the background. All quite blackish and grayish and, most certainly, sooty-ish.

"He makes quite a—what do you call it—ecological statement, wouldn't you say?" Mr. Stewart asks.

"Yes, that he certainly does," I say. "And, quite frankly, beyond the artistic expression, I'd have to say it's a nice reuse of soot."

"Just right for these times, I think. Yeah, well, let's hope he makes the fucking *economic* statement tonight, right? God knows and between you and me, Franky, I could use it about now. Here's the one I want you to take back," he says, going into his office and returning with a large, brown-wrapped package. He hands it to me, and we begin descending the stairway.

"Must have removed an appreciable amount of Wallonian soot with this particular study, sir," I offer, struggling a bit as I follow Mr. Stewart down the steep flight of stairs.

"Yeah, sorry about that, kid," he says. "That's why I had originally lined up my firm's delivery service. Anyway, once you get back to my place, just set it inside the door. My hanger guy Ben should be arriving soon to put it up on the wall. Jeezus, the things you gotta do now to stand out from the crowd."

"Well, sir, it sounds like a worthwhile plan. Right inside your door, then?"

"Yeah, yeah, just inside the door. The caterers should be arriving right about—" he says, looking at his watch. "Goddamn, look at the time. They're probably there right now. Is Charlotte letting them in?"

"Yes, sir. I'll see you back at L'Hermitage then, unless there's something else I can do for you?"

"Just deliver the package safe and sound. Oh, and Franklin, please," he says, handing me a twenty-dollar bill as he holds the front door open for me, "for your above-and-beyond efforts. You're a good doorman, you know that? Best our building's ever had—I can tell you that, pal."

Although uncomfortable accepting such tips, I have learned that they are not to be turned down. To do the no-I-couldn't-possibly-are-you-sure? do-si-do is considered bad form within this particular stratum. A gracious thank you is all that is expected.

"You're far too generous, sir," I say, taking the bill and stepping outside with the package.

"Yeah, well, you know what? Scratch my back; I scratch yours, right? Isn't that the way this world works?" he says and shuts the door. As I turn, heading back to 5th Avenue, I narrowly avoid colliding with the metallic version of Mr. Stewart, sidestepping him gracefully. At the corner, a saxophone player is working over the strains of "Someone to Watch Over Me." Before crossing the street, I drop a tip—the twenty-dollar bill—into his sax case. He sees what is dropped and acknowledges me with an exultant, brassy blast on the "lost in the woods" bar, normally a languorous note. Given that the twenty's only company within the case is a handful of quarters and a few stray singles, the misinterpreted rendering is understandable. The player quickly moves to his final note, reaches down, pockets the twenty, and shouts out a, "Thank you, sir!" before launching into what is either "All the Things You Are" or "More Than You Know;" I'm not sure which.

# CHAPTER 8

Thursday, 3:52 pm

When I turn the corner onto my street, it's immediately evident to my professionally trained eye that things are not as they should be. A measurable portion of New York City's motorized street transportation has come to a stop at or near the front of L'Hermitage. Cars honking, people shouting from their vehicles—a radically different scene from the relaxed atmosphere I had left just twenty minutes earlier. Certain folks—those in what I would refer to as highest dudgeon—are standing alongside their vehicles with car doors open, one foot in, one foot out, fists in the air, yelling detailed suggestions and, presumably, unsought counsel toward the head of the column. Some are hollering to the driver behind them, some to the driver in front, others to mere passersby. Those who aren't shouting are actively adding their horn to the discord. One seems to be tossing words in my direction, but I can't quite make them out. The majority, however, seem focused on one person in particular.

Charlotte.

"Goddamn it, lady, get that damn truck out of the way."

"For the love of fuck, lady, you can't block the whole goddamn street!"

Charlotte is having none of this impertinence. "Oh, you shut the hell up back there! We're trying to solve it." Charlotte's unrefined and churlish communication, while not appreciated within the hallways of L'Hermitage, serves her modestly well in this setting and under these conditions. As Dad used to say, there are times when it's appropriate to muck yourself up and crawl down into the gutter.

I approach the event's epicenter, attempting to appraise the situation before throwing myself unto the breach. I can't help but be struck by how much Charlotte resembles a small, leashed dog who strains lustily against her chain and collar at all perceived threats to her territory, yaps for one moment in one direction, turns, and begins yapping at the next approaching distraction before returning once again to the initial threat. On and on the energy is spent. And, like that small yapping dog, Charlotte solves nothing. She is standing between the white catering van labeled *Huckleby and Rosemary*, which has arrived early, and the red van labeled *On Thyme*, which has arrived, well, not on time. Stretching back behind both vans is a line of angry cab and sedan drivers. Charlotte is, in essence and in keeping with the spirit of catering-related matters, in the midst of her own version of a flambé. The liqueur has been poured and ignited.

"Charlotte!" I offer up, crossing the street to alert her to my return.

"Oh, thank god you're back," she says, but quickly catches herself. "Where the hell have you been? You've screwed up the catering, Franklin."

Not yet convinced that this debacle should rest upon my shoulders I, nonetheless, push on. From what I can best make out, there are four issues to be solved: First, relieve Charlotte of her streetside responsibilities. Second, get the catering trays off the delivery trucks as expediently as possible and, by the way, why were they not directed to offload back in our dock area? Third, clear up the traffic jam. And fourth, ensure that Mr. Stewart's Wallonian painting makes it safely inside the building; this was, after all, the point of my outing.

"So sorry, Charlotte. Let me see if I can't solve it. Why don't you head back inside? I'll take it from here."

"Yeah, get your ass back in there," shouts the cabbie behind the Huckleby van.

"Let Doorman solve it."

"Oh, *you* shut the hell up," Charlotte shrieks and then, turning back to me, "If it's a matter of *solving* it, I could *solve* it. What I want, though, is for you, *Franklin*, to *take care* of it. I'm delegating here, see? This is me delegating. Give me Brendan's painting. *I'll* take care of that. You tend to your mess out here. Jesus, this thing is heavy." With that, she turns and heads toward the safe and quiet confines of L'Hermitage's lobby.

I approach the driver of the Huckleby van and ask him why he's delivering to the front door when caterers are always instructed to bring their goods to the dock elevators in the rear.

"Because *she* told me to bring it in the front door. I went to the alley, but your dock was blocked. When I came to the front desk to check in, she told me to bring the van around front and unload there. She's the boss, right? I don't care where I offload; I'm just the delivery guy. I'm happy to double-park if I need to. If I get a ticket, it's just charged to the job, that's all," he adds with a shrug. "And you know what? One order's already been screwed up today with some lady over on 62nd Street saying I brought her lobsters for a rooftop clambake a week early. What am I gonna do with twenty-four lobsters, huh? So like I say, one order's already been screwed up. That's my quota for the month."

By this point, the driver with the On Thyme van has approached us. Within the Upper East Side, there is a firm and distinct pecking order among caterers. There is the lower substratum, which handles the one-offs—inexpensive, serviceable food for the younger crowd, the crowd that might require a caterer every year or two. Then, there is the midstratum within the pyramid, comprised of those caterers who have a regular set of customers for whom they service two to three events each year. And finally, there is the top tier set of caterers, who are passed around among a very small, select clientele list for every needed event. And so, for some of the more upper-crust East Siders, they, in effect, are exposed to just a handful of caterers—those top-rung suppliers of small, bite-sized morsels, who go from one party to the next, serving the same visitors and party goers, only in a different setting. Huckleby and Rosemary holds the coveted status of one of these top-level caterers. In Huckleby's mind, On Thyme is little more than a start-up wannabe ("Truffled mashed potatoes? Pumpkin pizza? Quail eggs with poached bacon? What a fun niche—being the first to present retro food from the late teens.") Even its overly reaching name—*On Thyme*—indicates how desperately it wants to be a part of the elite club, to be accepted in the inner reaches of the social sphere, to serve the crème brûlées to the crème de la crème. But not today, and not with this afternoon's crisis. Today, at this moment, at this location, Huckleby will hold supreme. And there is nothing the On Thyme deliverer can possibly do to help unplug this jam. Although she stands on the periphery of the action, she lobs in a weak attempt at supremacy, or, at least, equality.

"Sorry, but if I don't get these trays upstairs to the Coopers and the Cohens, both of their dinner parties are going to be shot," she says.

"Oh, is that right?" says Huckleby. "They're going to be wrecked, are they? What are you taking upstairs?"

"I've got chicken that needs to be sautéed for the Coopers and salmon that needs to be poached for—"

"Oh, yeah. Chicken and salmon. That's great. 'Dja find a special on unused airline food on your way over here? You got a pan of macaroni and cheese in there, too? Well, guess what. If I don't get the filet mignon that's been soaking in portabello sauce for four days up there in the next five minutes, it's gonna taste like the bottom of an ashtray. That's the problem *I'm* facing, friend. Or my shrimp and tzatziki over to the other side of town in forty-five minutes, there's gonna be hell to be paid. Got it? So, your little chicken and salmon McNuggets can wait till I'm done unloading. For all intents and purposes, you can consider those front doors to be the loading dock and I'm parked in it."

With her one feeble attempt at supremacy, the On Thyme deliverer pulls back to a more neutral position, at least in relationship to Huckleby. She turns her energy on me, in the hopes both she and Huckleby can be a unified front.

"And so, what are you going to do, Doorman?" she says. "I can't get back to your loading dock. I'm blocked in and in about thirty seconds, I'm going to have to leave the trays out here on your front step, too."

An option that wouldn't bode particularly well for me. Nor for my residents. As I look back and forth between my two yammering caterers, as the cabbies and drivers on the street raise their shouts and increase the frequency of their car honking, two faces come into focus: Charlotte, who is peeking out of the window blinds in her office, and Wendy, who is standing at the front doors of L'Hermitage. Despite the fact that she is wearing oversized sunglasses that cover much of her face, I detect a whiff of nervousness about her expression, as if she is wondering how this specific circus is going to affect the event taking place in her apartment later this evening.

And then it strikes me, an idea of such sheer brilliance, such utter magnificence, something which brings such a level of circular closure to my day that I couldn't help but grin and say out loud, "Of course." I say to Huckleby and On Thyme, "Wait here, I'll be right back."

"Yeah," says Huckleby. "'Wait right here,' he says. Where the fug he thinks I'm going?" I run—far more nimbly than I, or anyone else for that matter, had a right to expect—toward the construction entrance of Fitzger's, our building's retail space. With Fitzger's renovation work having ended for the day, a number of hard-hatted crew members have congregated outside the entry point before heading their separate ways.

"Jimmy! Is Jimmy around?" I shout, looking for the head contractor. One of the throng turns to me.

"Doorman, what's up?" Jimmy approaches me while the others look on.

"I have a favor to ask of you guys," I explain to him the reason for the backup on the street and say that I would like him and his men to help remedy the situation. I wrestle with just how much detail I should share with them in order to properly develop a case around our brothers-in-arms moment. Is it necessary to impress upon them the number of social events taking place in the building this evening? Charlotte's insistence that I abandon my post and pick up a soot painting from the Stewart Gallery? My budding and flirtatious friendship with Wendy, nervously observing the goings-on just down the street? I land on the side of brevity; after all, I've become extremely good at leaving out key details of my day-to-day existence.

"Yeah, I was wondering what's up with the roadblock back there," Jimmy says. "I gotta tell you though, man, I'm not exactly sure lugging trays of food up several stories and waving on traffic is going to hit the spot with my crew right now. They're spent. They ain't on my clock any longer—they're on their own time. The only order I could give them at this moment that they might follow is to head over to Folliard's and have a cold one. And even that one would be questionable."

Oh. I was hoping and aiming for some sort of musketeers moment, all for one and one for all and whatnot. But, seemingly, such may not immediately be the case. Jimmy's particular brand of esprit de corps doesn't seem to extend much beyond four in the afternoon. A bit of wheedling, cajoling, and whining would probably not play to my benefit with this particular crowd.

"Well," I put forward, "what say the first round at Folliard's is on me, then?" What was it my father used to say? If you can buy your way out of a problem, then you don't have a problem. Sheer and unmitigated brilliance, if not entitlement, that one.

He wavers. I see my initial poke has tapped the target nicely. Perhaps one more thrust and we'll be at the promised land.

"And . . . and the second round, as well," I say, continuing to toss chips into the ante. "And . . ." Marvelous! "what if everyone gets a sackful of lobsters? Fresh, live, succulent lobsters for everyone. Lobsters and two rounds of drinks. Deal?"

By now, the construction crew members have gathered around us as we negotiate. When Jimmy turns to them, he is met with supportive and, increasingly, enthusiastic nods of assent and agreement ("Hell, yeah!"). He jumps into the spirit of the moment by assigning four of the crewmembers to catering duty, telling them to offload the trays from Huckleby and On Thyme so as to at least free those impediments from the street. The other two are assigned to traffic control, heading down to the intersection, slowly easing cars back a few inches here and there to open up a flow. Once the catering trucks are unloaded, Jimmy directs both vans to temporarily park in the side alley across the street from L'Hermitage, thereby clearing the street. In less than ten minutes, the street is flowing again like sweet sap on a crisp March day, or some such poetic analogy.

"Hey, Huckleby," I call out, approaching the catering van still in the alley. "I just took care of your lobster problem for you. Let me buy fourteen of them off of you."

"Fourteen? Well, guess what, Doorman? Today's your lucky day. Fourteen'll get you twenty-four. You give me a couple of Bennies for the lobsters and they're all yours. Such a deal. Who can refuse?"

I pull three one-hundred-dollar bills out of my pocket and hand two of them to Huckleby. I hand the other hundred-dollar bill to Jimmy, who is approaching me with the rest of his crew.

"All right folks, thanks much to all of you. Jobs well done, all around."

"Yeah, thanks," says Huckleby. "Next time, Doorman, let us go 'round the back, where we normally unload. Can you do that, Doorman?"

"Yes, about that loading dock issue," I say. "I'm not sure why Charlotte would have turned you away from the dock."

"Oh, I know why," says Huckleby. "I was back there. The reason I couldn't unload is because someone's sports car is parked back there."

"Sports car?" I ask.

"Yeah, blocking the entire dock area," he says. "Your lady friend said she didn't know whose it was, and she didn't want us working anywhere near it. That's why she had us unload through the front door. She's pertectin' one of her friends, I guess."

"It wasn't a red sports car by any chance, was it?" I'm nothing if not detail-oriented.

"Yeah, yeah, red," he says. "Like a little cherry."

Ah. A brand new red Miata. I thank the caterers and Jimmy and his crew and head back across the street to L'Hermitage. As I approach the building, Wendy, who had been watching the goings-on, gives me a smile and turns toward the building.

"Swoon—my hero," she says.

"Allow me," I say, grabbing the large brass doorknob. "It is, after all, within the job description." And, out of the corner of my eye, I notice the blinds within Charlotte's office ease slowly, though perceptibly, back into place.

For just a fleeting moment it occurs to me that, were one to be generous in their assessment and evaluation of my actions over the past half hour, they might toss about terms such as *heroic* or *intrepid* to capture the manner by which I dashed into the breach. Were they of a more literary bent, the admirer of the cleverly-crafted solution might even insert the expression *Jeevesian*, not caring one whit if the person with whom they were speaking understood the reference or not. Were I to overhear the gushing, adulatory praise, not mere modesty alone would force me to interrupt and say, "No, no, ma'am. You're too kind. But if you insist, the solution is Jeevesian only in the sense of a predicament Jeeves might encounter early on, toward the beginning of a Wodehouse book, say on page fifty or thereabouts. Certainly not the closing climactic scene. That level of dynamism is held off until later."

# CHAPTER 9

Thursday, 4:13 pm

Jacob enters the lobby. Though he's thirteen minutes late for his scheduled in time, he's actually ten minutes early for his normal entrance time.

"Coast clear, Frankie?" he asks.

"Yes, Jacob. All quiet." Although I have attributed Jacob's tardiness to his untroubled approach to the world in general, there are times I can't help but wonder if it's because he's going out of his way to avoid interacting with Charlotte. We all understand our limits.

"Good. Just the way I like it. I'm sure she's gone home to get all gussied up for your date tonight. Where you taking her, man? Or maybe the two of you are staying in tonight for some quiet action, huh? Or maybe nothing at all. Maybe you've been going at it all day down in the boiler room. Checking the pipes, right? Don't worry, your secret's safe with me," he says, giving me a hard jab to the ribs as he comes behind my desk. This is Jacob's latest course of humor.

"Yes, yes," I respond. "Very good, Jacob. All right, you've got a busy night ahead of you. Several guests heading to multiple parties."

As I say this, five people enter our lobby, two couples and a single. I direct one couple to the Coopers on three, one couple to the Cohens on five, and the single to Wendy DeLong's on eight.

"Geez, Mandy, this is a fancy place," says a short man, heading with his wife to the Coopers. "They got *two* doormen. These guys are doing all right."

"'Dja hear that, Frankie?" Jacob asks me. "We're a *two-doorman* place. That's how fancy we are. Hey, boss, since I'm working at an uppity-scale place, can I have a raise?" Another loud laugh followed by more rib jabs. "At your next building board meeting, make sure you tell Franken that his main man Jacob needs a raise. Tell him we're going to lose ole Jacob's ass if we don't kick up his pay, bring it more in line with all the other two-doorman joints. You tell him that, okay?"

"Yes, very good. Duly noted. I'll add it to the top of our agenda."

"And put it in bold, could you, so nobody overlooks it?"

"Yes, certainly, in bold. Spare no ink."

"Oh, and do you think Italians would help?"

"How could Italians help with—"

"You know. The slanty letter shit. It's kind of eye-catching."

"Italics. Okay, um, Jacob, could we focus on the matter at hand? Do you have the lineup all straight? Here are the start times of the parties. People associated with the events are starting to arrive, coming for the Coopers, the Cohens. The McAdoos's people will start coming in an hour or so. Folks will be trickling in for Wendy's starting at—"

"Say what, now? Did you just say people are going to be tickling Wendy?"

"Trickling, Jacob—"

"Because if there's some tickling of Wendy going on tonight, I may just have to head up that way myself, check in on the festivities—"

"*Trickling. Trickling* into Wendy's much of the early part of the evening. And the Stewarts's guests will be coming in about half an hour."

I walk out from behind the desk, preparing to leave.

"You DO have a date with Charlotte tonight, don't you, you cheeky ass? Otherwise, what's your rush?" he asks while tossing the guest log under the desk.

"Jacob—"

"Okay, then. You schtupping Mrs. Hill up in 8B? That who you hurrying off for? Get her out from behind that walker of hers and I'm going to bet you she's a spitfire, that one." Last week's running joke was that it was Mrs. Hill, at eighty-seven, who was my conjugal liaison.

"Good night, Jacob."

"Doorman by day. Gigolo by night. You are *one* major man of mystery. Haw!"

# CHAPTER 10



Transitions can be the most difficult part of our lives, of our existence. We come into this world, screaming, terrified by the light, the sounds, the pokings, the proddings, and the pain of a backside slap. We exit, afraid, spent, used up, physically depleted, with nothing more to give but hoping to hold off for as long as possible our foreordained appointment with the back half of the eternity that awaits us. Every takeoff and landing between these milestones—the first day of a new school year, the arrival at a party, the entrance on stage, the beginning of a speech—induce various levels of sweat, anxiety, and nervously chewed bottom lips. Planes rarely drop out of the sky after having reached their cruising altitudes of 35,000 feet. It's the bit of getting to that point that can be white-knuckled terrifying. That's when crashes happen.

I'll be the first to admit that, within my own life, I haven't yet attained that elusive cruising altitude. I like to regard myself as being in a slow ascent. And so, within my world of daily transitions, it is with a certain amount of trepidation that I arrive and depart L'Hermitage each day.

After I give Jacob his update, fill out my timecard, and retrieve the envelope that Charlotte had asked that I deliver to Mr. Franken's residence, I head out to the street. On most nights, if anyone were inclined to give it a moment's thought, they might imagine me heading off to grab the 6 downtown, transferring to the R, and heading to some dingy apartment deep in Queens. That's what I imagined, anyway, when I had to list a street address on the forms that Charlotte put in front of me during my first week on the job. Where would a doorman of my type and age live in New York City? Turns out it's 90 Steinway Street, Apartment 409, Queens. It's a lovely studio apartment, a tad bit underfurnished, allowing for more than enough room to receive the occasional mailing that needs to come from L'Hermitage. My official mail, however—that from lawyers, accountants, financial management team members, old college chums, and the gobs of magazines that I'm a sucker for—simply comes directly to L'Hermitage, addressed to Henry Franken.

In actuality, when I leave the building each evening, I turn toward the park, round the corner, and take the next left into the alley. One of the selling points of L'Hermitage's penthouse on the twelfth floor is its private entrance off the back alleyway. There is a vestibule that gives access to a small elevator, slightly larger than a phone booth. Although there are windows from our building that overlook the alleyway, they tend to be rooms that are not often frequented by residents—third or fourth bedrooms, utility rooms, or service areas. Nonetheless, I try to make my presence in the back alley plausible, typically carrying reception-area refuse for the building's dumpsters or, as in the case of this evening, something for delivery to the penthouse. Before entering the vestibule, I glance up at the nearest windows—out of a developed habit—to make sure no one is looking. I go up.

The elevator opens onto what architects and real estate agents refer to as the Grand Foyer, a round room with a black-and-white checkered marble floor, a large round table with an oversized eucalyptus—or do they call it a gum tree?—arrangement upon it, and an umbrella stand. Across from this private entrance is the elevator that goes down to the main lobby, the one by which most visitors, were I to have them, would enter. From the foyer, the unit's main hallway stretches past the sunken living room, the powder room, the library, the kitchen, the dining room, bedrooms four and five, and the media center, once marketed as the "safe room." The unit continues to be tended to, with a cleaning staff and, apparently, a florist, arriving at regular intervals. With the curtains pulled, the rooms are dark and cool, cavelike. I toss the envelope intended for Mr. Franken on the tabletop, and then remove my doorman's suit coat and hang it in the closet. I'm home.

My departure each morning reverses this nighttime ritual. If I am to be caught or spotted, I have my story created. As the doorman, I, of course, am privy to all shared parts of the building. I come and go as requested, delivering items, and picking others up. If confronted within the alleyway, I will simply say that Mr. Franken requested that a package, just delivered to the lobby, be brought up directly via the private elevator. To say anything further on the subject of deliveries or packages would, of course, be regarded as indiscreet and unprofessional.

Yes, transitions. Once I'm in my hideaway, all is well. Having set up this secretive existence, however, I'm not sure exactly how to extricate myself from it; I haven't determined what *that* particular transition will look like. I hope to make it smooth, effortless, but I realize the potential for it to be messy, especially the longer I continue the charade. I enjoy my work as a doorman; I enjoy my living conditions; I enjoy the fact that the only expectations anyone has of me is that I get a painting hung within their unit or that I schedule the caterers' arrival times appropriately. But I recognize that I'm like the bald man who feels he must wear a toupee to attract the woman of his desires. Once accomplished, how does the conversation occur by which the hairpiece is addressed? *Oh, by the way, you know what? This virile mop on my head that attracted you to me? Funny thing—turns out you can take it with you when we're apart. Just a little memento of the sincerity of our relationship.*

Nah. That's the part that has me most worried. But I continue on, following the marble-bricked road that goes deeper into my own personal forest. For years, therapists have assumed that my rejection of my family's wealth is due to a deep-seated antipathy toward my father, that money represents him and his way of life, and that by rejecting his wealth, I am, more pointedly, rejecting him and all that he represents.

Or, they say, it's an indication of my unwillingness to grow up, to assume the responsibilities of an adult, that I'm mired in that teenage period of expansive opportunities with minimal responsibilities. I point out to them that I've been independent and on my own since college, having worked and lived off of a full-time job during that time. Wouldn't my refusal to accept Dad's financial support—or help from him of any sort—indicate an exuberant embrace of adulthood and all the lovely things that come with it?

So, the mystery continues and my inability to act ossifies. It'll be solved. But not tonight.

# CHAPTER 11

Friday, 8:07 am

"Hey, hey, Scraper! Yo!" Terry greets me from a two-building distance. I'm pulling pieces of paper, bottle caps, and other discarded items from the front shrubs. The street still has the bluish hues of early morning, but the sky is brightening from crack-of-dawn pink to early-morning yellow.

"Scraper! Quit messing with them little trees—let them live, man. You're going to stunt their growth, reaching in there and tickling their undersides. Don't you have some awning poles you gotta be polishing, or something?"

Terry has a friend with him today who finds amusement in Terry's comment. "This guy a pole polisher?" he asks. "Nothing better than polishing your pole." The two of them burst out laughing.

"Shit, man," Terry says to his friend, chuckling, "Don't go talking about pole polishing around here. We ain't in the park no more. We're up in the fancy area. Up here they call it stanchion shining." Another explosion of loud laughter from the two.

It would appear that, indeed, no good deed goes unpunished. My dispensing a cup of coffee to Terry yesterday earned me this morning's comedy routine. I turn back to continue pulling gum wrappers and cigarettes from the potted shrubs.

"Hey, hey, man, we're just messing with you. Don't go getting all hepped up and serious on us. Scraper, this is my friend, Tomata. He doesn't like coffee as much as I do, but he tolerates it pretty well, especially this time of day. You know, in case you were wondering about such things."

"Hello, Tomata," I say, thinking it mildly odd that a grown man be named after a vegetable (or is it a fruit? I'm yet to avowedly master that object's proper classification). "Are you a chef?"

"Yeah, right," Terry says, spitting out a laugh. "My man Tomata's a chef, over at 21 Club. Nah, his name's Tom, but we call him Tomata. Has something to do with the color of his schnoz. He's lucky we don't call him fucking Rudolf. I mean, that sucker could light up the night. And often does."

"Fuck off," Tomata says. "It's a family trait. We carry our emotions close to the surface."

"Yeah, whatever," Terry says.

"Coffee?" I ask.

"Coffee! Well, now that *you* brought it up, Scrape, that's a great idea. Wasn't I just saying, Tomata, that my friend Scraper comes up with the finest ideas? The finest ideas of any of the doormen in this district. In fact, he's the only doorman that actually talks to us. Oh, wait a minute, that's not entirely true."

"Yeah, you're not being fair to some of the others," says Tomata. "Lots of them talk to us."

"Yeah, yeah, that's right. Lots of them talk to us. There's that one guy who always says, 'Get the hell out of here,' when he sees us. That guy talks to us."

"There's him, yeah, the nice one," Tomata says. "And don't forget the one who says, 'Get the *fuck* out of here' every time he sees us. He talks to us, too. He's a talker."

"Spss, spss," Terry sputters, bringing his fingers up to his lips, "I told you, we aren't in the park, man. Bring it down, bring your *goddamn* voice down. But, yeah. There's him, too. He's pretty consistent with his talking to us. He-he, hyeah."

"Oh, yeah. Shh, shh." Tomata says, immediately following Terry's orders and lowering his voice. "Anyway, that guy, that doorman, he whispers it all quiet-like so no one but just us can hear him. He's a scary dude when he does that whispery shit, huh? But, anyway, I guess that's talking to us, isn't it?"

"Hell, yeah. And there's the guy over on 83rd who says, 'Get your shiny asses out of my sight.' Why, he gives us a little bit of conversation, too. Passes the time of day with us, real nice. So, yeah, Scrape, I guess you got some brethren who acknowledge us."

"That's right. Give them their fair shakes, Terry."

"Yeah, but I'm not shitting you, Scrape, you're the only dude who says, 'You want a cup of coffee?' Man, I'm starting to think you went to the wrong doorman school. Either that, or you weren't taking good notes in class like your other friends around here." At this, the two of them let out more squelched laughter, with Tomata thumping Terry on the shoulder for further emphasis.

"Let's keep this our secret, shall we, men?" I say, opening one of the doors. "Wait here. I'll be out in a moment with some coffee for you both."

"Okay, but make it quick, Scraper. We got appointments to keep, you know. Some business up the street. We're busy men. Places to go, people to see, things to do, you know." The two of them laugh again before Terry blurts out, "Oh, and Scraper, if my cup of coffee were to bump into some of that cream and sugar on its way out here, I wouldn't mind that, you know. I wouldn't turn my nose up at it."

"Yeah, I wouldn't mind some of that stuff slopping over into mine, either, please," says Tomata. "A little Kahlúa'd perk it up nice, too. Then you'd have something, then you'd have a true morning concoction."

"Shut up with that noise, man. You always push it too fucking far," I hear Terry say just before the door latches.

In the lobby, I fill up two large cups of coffee, both with generous helpings of cream and sugar, and bring them out to the two of them.

"God bless you, man," says Tomata. "You know, Terry, there are some damn fine people in this world."

"Told you. Thanks much for this, Scrape," he says, holding up his cup of coffee before turning and heading off.

"Mister Terry, wait a minute. I want to ask you something," I say.

"Mister who now?" Tomata asks.

"I wanted to ask you something. Your visit to the Met, how was it?" I ask, halfway wondering whether I'll receive even a glimmer of recognition of what it is I'm referring to. "Did you go?"

"Oh, yeah, yeah, it was awesome, man. I took this bum with me," he says, gesturing to Tomata. "We had some research to do, the two of us. We needed a . . . what would you call it? A guiding light."

"And remind me. Who was that artist you mentioned to me? The one you recommended I go and check out? Tell me who it was again." I'm testing him. Let's see how far I can push this. Was it a fluke? Did he just pull out a name to toss my way, throw me off base? Ensure another cup of coffee on another day?

"Shit, I don't know. Who are you talking about? They got lots of artists in that place. Some are even good."

Yes. That's what I thought. "I suggested you go see Manet, remember? But you had said you preferred someone else. Who was it, again?"

"Hell, man, I don't remember. Sometimes my memory's not so good. Today it's a little slow. It'll kick in later, I think, after I down this cup of coffee. I'll have to get back to you on that."

"His memory ain't worth shit. Drank too much turpitude in his day," Tomata says in what theatrical circles would refer to as a stage whisper.

"Turpentine, dumbass, and I did no such thing. May have *sniffed* too much of that crap, but sure as hell didn't drink it. That stuff'll kill you. Unless, of course, you water it down." At this, they both laugh, Tomata slapping Terry on the back in a show of effusive appreciation.

"Stop it, godammit! You're spilling my coffee," Terry says.

"Oh," I say, attempting to quell the squall. "Sorry. I thought you might remember. You had suggested I go see some artist in a certain gallery in the Met. I have an off day coming up. Thought I'd go over there." I turn to go back to my work.

"Well, I don't happen to remember what I said. There's lots of art pieces over there, you know. But I can sure as hell give you some tips if you're going. One dude I like really well is Caspar David Friedrich—"

"That's it!" I say, turning back around to him quickly. "That's who you told me to go see. Caspar David Friedrich. Tell me about him. What's his story?"

"Well, his story's done been writ. He lived a couple of hundred years ago, but, yeah, that don't surprise me that I would have mentioned him," he says. "Friedrich's a favorite of mine. I recommend him to lots of people. I just didn't remember there for a second. The Met doesn't have many of his works, though. You gotta go across the lake if you want to see his pieces. Tomata and I are a little short of funds for that these days, but the library has books full of his prints. That's where I do most of my research. Either the library or the museum."

"Your research," I say. "What are you referring to, research? What kind of research do you do?"

Terry looks at Tomata, smirks, and looks back at me. "Ah, man, that's cold. Just because Tomata and I are in a little bit of a rough stretch right now, that doesn't mean we can't do research, that we can't appreciate the world around us. The beauty of art. We're artists, man," he says with a broad grin.

"I wasn't doubting you," I say. "Just curious."

"Yeah, well, Tommy and I met at RISD, used to have a studio before the big bust. Not here, though, not in Manhattan. Somewhere else. These days we specialize in, what's it called? What's that French term? Oh, yeah—*pine-air* art, you might say. Always painting in the great outdoors. Central Park, that's our studio now—when we have materials. It's got plenty of natural light, doesn't it, Tom? Can't complain about the light. C'mon, we gotta get going. We'll see you later, Scrape."

The two of them start to head off. "Mister Terry," I say. "Would you go with me, someday, to the Met and show me some of Friedrich's work? Explain to me what it is you like about him?" Although I, as with most people, like to regard myself as a spontaneous creature, one who grabs life's moments by the collar and shakes them in a fun and free-spirited manner, nothing could be further from the truth. There's not an extemporaneous bone in my body. That I issued the invitation at all reflects, perhaps, poorly on the third cup of coffee I downed just moments ago.

"Hah!" Terry shouts out. "Old Terry's going to be a museum guide. How do you like that, Tommy?"

"You? A museum guide at the Met?" Tomata asks. "Jesus, I used to think highly of that joint."

"Well, that just might be the only way I can make my mark in *that* museum," he says, ignoring Tomata. "Yeah, man, happy to. You'll trip when you see this guy's stuff. I'm warning you though, they only have one painting of his. But it's a good one. If you had to have just one Friedrich, that's a pretty damn good one to have. I'll meet you there tomorrow on the front steps when it opens, at ten. I might bring this chump here with me—the two of us'll introduce you to Herr Friedrich. He's going to blow your mind, Scrape. Blow your mind!"

◆　◆　◆

Judith has said repeatedly during our Saturday morning tête-à-têtes that I need a cause of some sort, something that might shake me out of my months-long malaise and move me beyond what she refers to as my *Hamlet phase.*

"At the very least, sugar plum, go out and do something different each day. Start with that, just start with a single step. Because you're stuck in a rut," she said. "You're depressed. You're de*pressing.* If you can't do it on your own, I'd be happy to find you a doctor for your situation and they'll be happy to hook you up with some meds. We'll get you all taken care of. But you've got to get out of your rut."

"I've been making a point of trying to visit a different Pret a Manger at lunchtime, does that count for anything?" I asked. "I've been branching out to Lexington most recently, sometimes as far south as 68th."

"Let's get you aiming higher, could we?" she said.

For tomorrow's meeting, I have something to share with her and it will blow her mind. Blow her mind.

# CHAPTER 12

Friday, 3:34 pm

Toward the end of the afternoon, Mr. Stewart erupts out of the elevator, pauses momentarily to give me what my father would commonly refer to as *the hairy eyeball*, and storms into the mailroom. He comes out a moment later with a stack of letters, peers at me over his half-rimmed reading glasses—no diminishment of the aforementioned hairy eyeball, it might be worth stating—and says, "Hello," far more coolly than one would have expected, given the recent bonding experience at his gallery the two of us had.

"Crap, crap, shit, more crap," he says, sorting through the mail.

"All went well, sir, with your showing?" I offer, attempting to sway the subject area away from that of crap.

Mr. Stewart views me over his glasses. Were I a talking simian, I suspect I may have received the same sort of withering glance.

"Yeah," he says. Back to the mail sorting activity.

"All right. Very good, then."

One needn't smack me on the nose with a rolled-up newspaper twice to make me understand that one is seeking privacy, public space or not. I avoid the seductive call of personal reading—a book tucked discreetly under my desk's overhang—and turn to my paperwork, laying out Jacob's responsibilities for the evening, as well as Morgan and Lester's for the weekend.

"No, that isn't exactly true, Franklin." Ah, back in his confidences. "It was shit, actually."

"Shit, sir? Not soot?"

"No, Franklin. Not shit. That's Anton Henning, if you're talking about shit as a medium, which I was not. If you're talking shit as a subject matter—which I also was not—you're probably talking about Piero Manzoni"—the man does have a firm grasp on varying media, I'll grant him that—"I'm talking neither. I'm talking about shit as in presentation. I'm talking about Willem de Smet and soot and the fact that he does absolutely nothing to help me sell one of his paintings."

"The artist didn't connect with the collector?"

"Oh, he connected, all right, Franklin. A real charmer, he was. Talked all night about the medium, where he paints, the gradations and tones of the soot he uses, how many paintings he's painted, everything."

"And that presents a problem? Sounds like he was pouring it on."

"Damn right, it's a problem. I might as well have invited a goddamned art historian from The New School for the evening. At least that way we could've snuck in a nap. I realize now that de Smet hasn't a clue how to sell himself. It was a huge mistake bringing him and Stansfield together. Couldn't turn him off."

The picture was starting to come into focus. "Ah. Overindulged in the medium of alcohol, did he? Got swept up in the excitement of a pending sale?"

"No! No such thing. A perfect gentleman all evening. I wish he *had* drunk too much. I wish he *had* become a blithering idiot and passed out on the couch, maybe even after grabbing Mrs. Stansfield's ass. Act like a . . . like an artist. A *tortured* artist . . . a *troubled* tortured artist. Act like Pollock, for Chrissakes. Now *there* was a guy who knew how to act like an artist. Do something inappropriate. Brood. Give the collector a goddamned story to take home with him *along* with the painting. He did nothing of the sort. He hasn't the faintest idea of how to look and act like an artist. Goddamn him, what a mistake." And back to his mail.

"Sorry to hear that," I say, hoping to calm Mr. Stewart's comportment as others pass through the lobby.

"He sounded like a docent, explaining all the painterly qualities of his work," he says, back in the fray. "Jesus, who gives a shit? Do I have to give him sales lessons, in addition to flying him over here? One beer! That's all he had. Just one beer—and it was a light beer, to boot. I wanted to slosh my Bombay Sapphire all over him, douse him in it. At least then he might *smell* like an artist. Oh, the perfect gentleman, all clean-shaven and shampooed. Jesus, the Stansfields couldn't get out of there fast enough. They weren't here to just buy a painting. They were here for an experience, a story to be able to tell, along with the displayed painting, to entertain their dinner guests. Stansfield was yawning and looking at his watch by ten-thirty. 'Jet lag,' he said. Jet lag, my ass. De *Smet* lag is what it was."

Mr. Stewart was working up into quite a lather, given the hour. "I'm sorry it didn't go fully to your satisfaction," I offer in an effort to console him. When all seemed to have settled down, another thought leaps into his mind. "And here's the other thing," he says, crumpling a recently distributed delivery menu and staring intently across the desk at me.

"More problems?" I ask.

"There's no, whatdoyoucallit, *irony* in the guy. He's deadpan. I thought his representation of Wallonian factories and landscapes was meant to be ironic or something, you know? But it turns out he wants his scenes to actually look like, like . . . sooty things. I assumed they were thick in metaphors and shit. Why it was purely . . . purely . . ."

"Rockwellian, sir?"

"Ah, Jesus, Franklin, why don't you just bury the shiv a little deeper into my heart? It wasn't *that* bad, but pretty damn close. Just give him a paint-by-numbers set next time."

"Sorry, Mr. Stewart. My apologies for, perhaps, going too far with the analogy."

"God, I guess, Franklin. You'll have to give me a little bit of credit for being good at what I do. The day I start dabbling in artists who appeal to . . . um . . ."

"Emotions?"

"Yeah, yeah, who appeal to emotions, or who actually represent the . . . the . . ."

"World around us, sir?"

"Yeah, the world around us. The day I start representing *those* types of artists is when it's time for me to hang it up."

"I suspect those types of artists appeal too much to the masses to be considered popular?"

"Yes, appealing to the masses. Horrendous. And de Smet truly rocked my foundation. I can only hope Stansfield doesn't breathe a word of this debacle to his friends back in London. If he does, I could be finished in that market."

The art world is a complicated one. I'm glad it rests in the talented and capable hands of Mr. Stewart.

# CHAPTER 13

Friday, 3:52 pm

With my paperwork and notes for the weekend completed, I head to my position at the curb, the place where doormen are most visible and, given my title, most expected. The traffic within L'Hermitage's lobby is at full throttle, with residents milling about, greeting one another, and welcoming visitors. Charlotte is among them, entertaining Mr. McAdoo, 11A, and Mr. Longworth, 7E, with stories of her newly formed adventures in a red convertible. Although Mr. McAdoo—a sports car aficionado himself—might, in fact, be interested in the topic being discussed, Mr. Longworth appears to be more interested in Charlotte's Friday night attire and its flattering accompaniment of décolletage. L'Hermitage, in the spirit of large, progressive companies, is receptive to a casual Friday dress attire that, thus far, only one employee—that being Charlotte—is in a position to take advantage of, given that doormen must adhere to a strict uniform policy whenever on duty.

The street has its evening hum about it. Cabs shooting by toward Madison Avenue. Clusters of people walking by, those heading home from work carrying briefcases and backpacks, others bound for best seats within bars and restaurants. A cab and a black limo, in quick succession, pull up in front of the building. I open the door to the first one and Ms. Pelletier, 5D, steps out, briefcase in hand; from the limo, Mr. Wallin, 2B, steps out. They greet one another and nod to me as I rush to open the front door.

I return to the curb, look west and see Wendy walking toward our building. She doesn't see me yet, looking down at the sidewalk, appearing exhausted, carrying a large work satchel, a shopping bag, and folded newspapers.

It should be noted that I like to regard myself—whether anyone else does or not is entirely beside the point—as one who can deliver a clever riposte at the drop of a hat, something so crafty, so witty, that the recipient is immediately disarmed, if that, indeed, is the desired outcome. And, in fact, on this particular Friday evening and at this particular moment, the spirit moves me in such a manner that sharing one of my witticisms, one of my quips as I will occasionally refer to them, is exactly what I want to do. It is only coincidental that Wendy happens to be a convenient and nearby mark at this very moment. "Ms. DeLong. You appear to be deep in thought." Hmm, yes, a bit flat, that particular effort. Give me a moment; still warming up.

"Oh, hi, Franklin. Sorry. I *was* deep in thought. Lots going on."

"Well, it's Friday," I point out. "And there's a beautiful weekend forecast. I hope you get a chance to enjoy it." Whenever I descend into the ever-present arms of weather-related raillery, you may read that as a sign that the mental gears are still not meshing properly.

I open the door for her, and she passes through. She spins before I shut the door and says, "Franklin, by the way, thanks for your help last night. I mean with the catering details. You, like, solved that problem on the street perfectly."

"You mean the traffic jam?" I ask. "That was pretty minor. All in a day's work."

So, so humble. Heroically so.

"Well, it was good problem-solving," she points out. "I mean, who would have thought to go pull in a bunch of construction workers to help deliver trays of food. That was, I don't know, kind of brilliant."

"Let's just say that a little leverage goes a long way, shall we?"

"I've heard that. Yeah, well, anyway, thanks again. Have a good weekend. By the way, I've often wondered—what *do* doormen do on weekends? Your job has to be exhausting, having to be friendly to everybody every single moment. God, I couldn't do it. So, Franklin.

How do you relax?"

This is far chummier of a conversation with Wendy DeLong of 8D than I've yet had. Although always friendly, she had, for the most part, created a set of interactions that went little beyond the fleeting morning and evening greetings, always delivered with a smile but with the understanding that the conversation was not bound to go much beyond that. In doorman-resident relations, it is understood that the resident is the one to dictate the terms of engagement. My sorting out of matters yesterday evening—of which she had a curbside seat—must have presented myself to her in a different light altogether.

"In the usual way," I say. "Theater, trendy restaurants, Tribeca art openings, Lincoln Center, and unending fundraisers. And you? How do marketing executives relax over the weekend?"

"Well, if it's me you're referring to, it sounds like you and I may be on the same circuit," she says, "because that's exactly what *I'm* doing. I hope to see you out there."

"Yes, well, Ms. DeLong, be so kind as to save me a seat at all of them, if you would."

"And you the same, Franklin, should you arrive ahead of me. And remember what I said. Call me Wendy."

She heads to the mailroom along with two other residents who have entered. She returns to the lobby, looking through the mail she has just retrieved, but instead of going to the elevators, she returns to my front desk.

"So, what *are* you doing this weekend?" she asks, without looking up from her bills and flyers. "Any fun plans?"

This is unexpected. A different note has been inserted into our discussion, into the cut and thrust. The salient charm has overpowered the target.

"Well, as a matter of fact," I say, "I was thinking of going to the Met tomorrow morning."

"Oh!" she says, looking up from her items, "I've been wanting to do that for a couple of weeks. Are you going to the Dutch painting show?"

"No. Yes, I mean. Maybe."

"Hmm, decisive," she says. "Well, *maybe* I'll see you there. I just decided that I'm going tomorrow morning."

"It's a big place," I say. "We might not cross paths."

"Good point. It's probably best to go together if we want to cross paths there."

At this, I smile. I'm being gently led down a path, uncertain of the destination but willing to sniff about.

"Would you like to join me?" I ask.

"I'm sorry," she says. "I'm probably insinuating myself into your plans. Sorry about that. But, yes."

"No need to apologize," I say. "We'd love to have you join us." The issue of personal relationships between doormen and residents is always one of balance. There are perceived boundaries, but they are fluid, moveable—depending upon the person, the request, the time of day, and the time of year. For the most part, our residents are appropriate in their interactions with us, striking a balance between the formal and the informal. There are those who brush by me each day as if I were a lobby fern; others who regard me as a trusted confidante. But those are the extremes.

"Great. Who's 'we'd' and what time should I meet you?"

"Nine forty-five, here in the lobby? We'll make it to the museum right around their opening."

"Why don't I just meet you at the Met? Wouldn't that be more convenient for you?"

"Well, sure. But wouldn't the lobby be most convenient for both—" Oh, right then. She lives here. I live somewhere else, as far as she knows. Public transportation and whatnot. "Good point," I say. "I'll meet you on the front steps of the Met, ten o'clock? Right at opening?"

"Fine then. And again, who's 'we'd'?"

I look at her for a moment, wondering if I heard her correctly. "Whose weed? I guess I wasn't planning on bringing—"

"No, no. *We'd*, as in 'we would.' You said, 'We'd love to have you join us.' Who's 'we'd'?"

"Oh, right," I say. "There are a couple of acquaintances—artist acquaintances, of a sort, really—who might be accompanying us. There's a specific painting and artist that they wanted to show me, and then, presumably, show me around some other galleries, as well. Is that all right? Their names are Terry and Tomata—uh, yeah. Tom."

I become aware of the potential clash of worlds within our gallery visit tomorrow morning, a loaded concoction that might not make for a perfect outing. I'm not yet sure which invitation was a mistake—the one issued earlier to Terry and Tomata or the one I just accepted from Wendy DeLong.

"The more the merrier," she says. "Terry and Tomata … intriguing. Could be two men, two women, a man and a woman, a human and a vegetable. We just don't know at this point—but I want to keep the mystery alive until tomorrow morning, so don't you dare spoil the surprise for me. But what we *do* know is that, whatever form they take, you're bringing two art experts to the Met with you. Our very own docents. You are quite resourceful, aren't you, Franklin?"

"Well, just to temper all expectations, 'art experts' might be a slight overstatement. I'm not totally aware of the type of art they are involved in. I might need to warn you—they're quite, well, *earthy* might be the best way to describe them, these two. We'll see how it goes."

"Earthy? Aha, yet another clue. Still not totally ruling out that Tomata is a straightforward vegetable. I'll see you then. At the Met. Tomorrow at ten. I look forward to it, Franklin." At this, she turns and heads to the elevators, entering a waiting car. I watch after her as she departs. She turns to me quickly before entering, and then the doors shut. I can't help but think that—

"You dirty dog," I hear someone say quietly from the living room. I look and see Jacob sitting in one of the stuffed chairs, right leg dangling from the armrest, peering at me over a magazine he's holding. At this particular moment, he and I are the only ones in the lobby area.

"Jacob, what are you—"

"You dirty, DIRTY dog!" he says, leaping up and tossing the magazine aside. "Is this what goes on during the day? No wonder you like this shift! I was just kidding you yesterday about tickling and schtupping the ladies of the Hermitage but look at you! Whoa, boy, plant a little seed in ole Franky's soil, and stand back, people. Watch that stalk grow!"

"Jacob, what are you—? No, this isn't what goes on during the day. But what are you doing here so early? You normally don't show up until—"

"It's a quarter after, isn't it?" he says, approaching me. "And isn't that the time I'm supposed to be here? Punctual as always, dog. Besides, I accidentally caught an earlier train. Haven't a ka-lew how that catastrophe happened, probably won't ever happen again, so don't go getting excited on me. But, I'm sure glad I did! Otherwise, I'da missed the whole damn floor show . . . coo, coo, kachoo."

"Jacob, stop it," I say. "We're simply—"

"Dirty dog!"

"Jacob, knock it off. It's not appropriate. We're just going to the art museum, and I would appreciate your not saying anything to Charlotte about this. I realize that this outing might be a bit irregular and—"

"Nah, that's a pretty safe bet there," he says. "To *tell* Charlotta-ass means I'd have to engage in a conversa-she-on with same Charlotta-ass, least the way I understand how that all works. And while I may have been blessed with the gift of gab and a couple of big nads, they ain't armor-coated, Franky. Any-ways, I know al-ll about your little art scene. Take her to those nice, big paintings with half-naked people lying around in togas and shit. Get her all hepped up. We used to go there on field trips back in grade school. 'Oh, look, Ms. DeLong, look at the nice painty qualities Ren-what's-his-shit was able to attain right around the heaving bosom area there, you see it? Look close, go ahead, get on up to it. And, my, didn't Michel-asshole do a nice job with the firm buttocks on that young lad, yonder?' Believe me, I know *all* about that shit. That's a masterstroke, Franklin. It's always you quiet ones, you know? Here I thought you had nothing going on, but you're out there escorting the young hotties to art museums. Awesome, man. I might have to rip a page or two out of your skinny-ass book." At this, he lets out a loud laugh.

"Okay, Jacob, let's kick up the professional demeanor a tick or two, could we? Are you ready to take over the shift, or is your floor show not quite finished?"

"Give me a minute to recover," he says, bending over, hands to knees, shaking his head as if he's just run a sprint race. "I'll come up with some more shit. I'm tapped out for the moment, but it just takes me a second or two to power back up."

"Very good, then. But if you don't mind, I would now like to begin my weekend."

"Oh, oh, look out now," he says, "I just bet you would. I think you done started your weekend about ten minutes ago, by my watch, baby. Counting down the hours until tomorrow morning, are you?"

"Goodnight, Jacob. Have a pleasant evening."

"Yeah, dog, you, too."

# CHAPTER 14

Saturday, 8:12 am

I wake up and stumble around the miles of square footage available to me within the penthouse. Weekend mornings, unlike Monday through Friday, are disorienting to me. If I were a different type of penthouse dweller, I might wander down to the lobby, pick up a cup of coffee, chat for a moment with doorman Lester, Jacob's weekend replacement, step outside for a test of the temp and a feel of the wind, sit in the reception area for a moment to see if any other interesting denizens appear, and then head back upstairs to the roost.

But I don't. On mornings such as this, I'm a hermit, a prisoner. My lie, which began so simply, has become all-consuming. I am the cartoon character who stupidly, yet comically, paints himself into a corner. To take the primary elevator down to the lobby would be daring and bold, but it would also elicit reactions that I, quite simply, have neither the energy nor the inclination to deal with at this point in time.

I make the coffee, preparing for my weekly in-home visit with Judith Guncheon, our family—well, at this point, *my*—lawyer. Beyond deferring to her on all legal and financial matters, I have forced a role upon Judith that she is not comfortable in, that of go-between, middle-person, and condo-building overseer, not to mention managerial interface with Charlotte. Each week I assure her that I will come clean, that I will assume my rightful role within the universe of L'Hermitage— as well as the broader world in general—and that I will do it in the not-too-distant future. But, for the time being, the doorman outfit remains comfortable and, so, I continue to wear it.

I have known Judith since I was a child. She was one of my father's closest friends—the two of them having attended college together—and was named as my godparent upon my birth. This was a perfunctory title allowing for little more than a tenuous connection between the two of us as I was growing up; the true relationship was between my father and Judith. If I was ever in Judith's presence, it was more so because she and Dad were spending time together, not because she was calling upon me or bestowing birthday gifts or coming to offer godmotherly advice. Given Judith's sexual orientation and demeanor, I suspect my mother never experienced a moment in which she felt threatened by the closeness of Dad and Judith's relationship. That closeness was founded upon a decades-long respect for each other's business acumen, a shared love of the political scrum, an unexpected appreciation of musical theater, and a mutual hatred of the Boston Red Sox. But during our meeting in those tornadic days following the funeral, Judith and her staff laid out facts before me that my father had never done or, perhaps more correctly, I had never allowed or encouraged him to do. I'd had no idea of the size of Dad's wealth. I knew we were well-heeled, or, as Dad would often say dismissively, *comfortable*, ("I guess we're supposed to downplay this stuff, Henry") but he had never divulged to me the extent or measurement of our resources, all of which stemmed from the construction and building management company he had started as a young man. Dad recognized my aversion to the source of his wealth. Informing me of the metrics would have only contributed to my teen hormone-induced brooding and enmity.

But what brought true focus to my animosity regarding his wealth and professional occupation—or shaped my personality pathology, as one of my therapists was fond of saying—was an incident in college, an event that was so instantly mortifying that the shock and humiliation has reverberated within me for years.

During my sophomore year at Northwestern, I fell in with a group of public policy and journalism students who spent their weekends either loudly protesting against or quietly distributing flyers on the longstanding inequities associated with Chicago zoning policies. These policies, we assuredly claimed, were enriching developers while displacing their poverty-level renters. It slowly dawned on me that this topic and activity dangerously approached my own family's background. In our relaxed and less dogmatic moments, whenever the subject of parental professions arose, I would invariably duck the matter, either by attempting to change the subject or simply excuse myself and leave the room. I was becoming comfortable with the concept of hiding behind a cloak, as it were.

My point of entrée to this circle was a fetching junior from Hinsdale who lived down the hall from me that year. I met Joan, along with her all-consuming earnestness and mile-long legs, during move-in day to Willard Hall's coveted garret rooms. Because she was so convincingly passionate about the ills of Chicago development and the detriment of gentrification, so, too, was I. Not only was I realizing the connection between this claque's improvised, pentameter-tortured slogans and the Franken family wealth, but I was also feeling a profound relationship between the bimonthly protests and the nightly benefits garnered within the gentle confines of Joan's dorm room.

And then it changed. A group of us were sitting in Joan's room, reveling in our latest adversarial adventures while passing around quickly draining bottles of Jägermeister, when our self-proclaimed leader, Matthew—a senior poli-sci major who I suspected to be equally attracted to Joan—inelegantly brought up Dad's business. It was as if he had been lying in ambush for weeks.

"It's funny, Henry, that you feel so strongly about these issues," Matthew said.

"These are important ithews . . . ishoos," I said in my Jäger-infused state, not yet comprehending the baited trap I was entering. "Pass the pizza, could you?"

"Hmm, yeah, important issues. By the way, remind me what it

is your dad does." The enjoyable and effervescent buzz within the room was abruptly pricked. Everyone was looking at me, including Joan. Were it not so painfully obvious and trite, one could have made the argument that I was entering a rezoning process myself. With Matthew's pointed question, there was no changing the subject or excusing myself to visit the bathroom.

"He's a developer," I said.

"A developer?" he asked. "Such an imprecise term; I'm not quite sure what that means. Tell us what it means."

"Come on, Matthew," Joan said.

"No, tell us. What's a developer do, Henry? What is it exactly he develops?"

"He builds buildings, Matthew," I said. "It's kind of straightforward."

"Yeah, pretty straightforward. Except when it's not. You could say he's a landlord, too, right? A corporate landlord?"

"Well, his company is, yeah. I s'pose you could say that."

"Hmm-hm. The company that he started and owns, right? I'm amazed this topic hasn't come up before, given how much we've talked about *development.* I did some reading on Daddy's company. Your dad—sorry, your dad's *company*—buys buildings, forces out tenants, jacks up rents, and then resells the buildings for a really nice profit. When he can't force out the tenants, he—sorry, *it*, the company— makes life a living hell for the remaining tenants through ongoing construction—noise, dust, all sorts of shit—until they're so desperate they leave. Your dad—oh, shoot, I mean *Franken Companies*—isn't a developer. He's a fucking manufacturer. Of homelessness. Enjoy your skiing in the Alps this winter, you fucking phony."

Both the evening, immediately, and the relationship with Joan, within a week, was over, the latter due less so to her than to my personal discomfort and embarrassment around her. I began conducting my own research into Franken Companies, information that any fourteen- year-old could have easily unsurfaced within minutes were he to have a modicum of curiosity. I knew what Dad did; I even understood that there was a whiff of impropriety around his activities—he was often involved in class-action or community lawsuits, all of which were invariably shrugged off. My research confirmed that Dad's millions were built on dishonesty and unethical procedures. Months later when I confronted him on the issue, the best defense he was able to muster was, "Henry, everybody in the city does it. I play by the rules that are in place—if I didn't, I wouldn't have my license, okay? It's all in the game. Besides, do you think I'm doing this for myself? Hell, no. I stopped working for myself a long time ago. I'm working for you. No, wait, you've been covered for years. I'm working for your kids."

At nineteen, I wasn't equipped to push back on this line of reasoning—it was too emotionally confusing to me. How could I be angry with Dad if his reason for working was entirely for my own well-being—for my *kids'* well-being? Isn't that what good fathers are supposed to do? It was during those idealistic college years that I began to consciously deny, not just hide, our family's money and its source—our dirty little secret. I was incapable of distancing myself from my father but not so his money.

So, immediately after Dad's death, when Judith and her team informed me within their Midtown offices that I was now worth hundreds of millions of dollars more than I had been the previous week; my reactions had bounced between being excited, repulsed, overwhelmed, scared, thrilled, and disgusted.

"I can see you're going to need some time to let this all soak in," Judith told me in that meeting as she sat at the oversized mahogany desk in her wood-paneled office, stirring sugar into her coffee mug. "Realize that when the partners buy your family out—buy *you* out—you'll be getting another chunk of change. Can I assume that your father hadn't had the financial chat with you that I had been begging him to have?"

"No," I told her. "Whenever I came to visit him from college, we'd spend time doing this or that, but never going over the finances. I know he saw it as a loaded topic, one we—*I*—could not rationally discuss. With each visit home during those college years, I guess you could say I was becoming more and more judgmental of his life and his things. He probably thought there was plenty of time at a later date to get into the finances—after I had matured."

Judith sighed. "Well," she said after a moment's pause, "you're about to grow up. Fast. You'll need our financial guidance immediately. Your father, as you know, has retained our group for years. Following our discussion, I would like you to get to know the full team, especially two of our financial therapists, Jim and Mary."

For the next thirty minutes or so, Judith offered a mixture of sympathy, guidance, and reflection upon how much Dad had talked about me, as well as advice on the life adjustment that had just been forced upon me. At a certain point, her assistant, Thomas, entered the room and offered me a cup of coffee. Leaning on her desk with her arms folded, Judith smiled slightly as she watched Thomas exit the room. "He's very good under certain circumstances," she said, "but he ain't worth a shit when it comes to the needs of people during times of full-on stress." At this, she leaned down to her right, opened a lower desk drawer, and pulled out a bottle of Blanton's. "Pour your coffee into the plant stand behind you—wouldn't be the first time. Make room for a real drink."

During the course of our conversation, there were ample, *You'll want tos* and *You'll need to considers* tossed at me from her side of the desk. My side of the desk tossed back head nods, weak *Okays*, and unintentionally encouraging *Good ideas*. Judith and her caffeine-pushing assistant, Thomas, weren't fully appreciating the fact that my life had changed inexorably not only because my personal net worth had increased dramatically, but also because my ability to ever see my father again had decreased precipitously.

"And Henry, regarding the building I'm about to send you to. It's not just the penthouse you own. You own the whole damn thing. Your dad, god love him, excelled at taking advantage of desperate rich people. He caught wind that the L'Hermitage's debt was beyond the means of the residents, so he swooped in and made them an offer they couldn't refuse. He would assume all debt and wipe the slate clean, as long as he owned and controlled all public spaces. The owners could own their individual units, but he, in essence, owned the entire building. So, when you go to the building this afternoon, don't be surprised if you get a stink eye or two from your new neighbors. They appreciated the bailout but may not fully dig Baby Warbucks walking amongst them."

◆　◆　◆

The coffee is done brewing at 8:30 and, on cue and quite theatrically, the penthouse elevator doors open. Judith has a key to my unit—the only person besides me who does—and, for these scheduled meetings, she lets herself in. Presumably, she acknowledges Lester below as she marches through the lobby. I imagine some sort of grunt emanating from her, but certainly no chitchat and nothing that would allow for questions to be posed by Lester, were he the type to exhibit any traits that border on curiosity.

"Good morning," I say.

"G'morning, Henry. This place is a goddamn cave. You live in the goddamn penthouse, and you keep all your curtains shut—why not just live in the basement? Where's my coffee? And don't forget the cream. And don't even think about pulling another soymilk gag—and, I stress, *gag*—like you pulled on me the other day."

As Hurricane Judith makes shore, my oversized unit immediately feels crowded. It's not so much that Judith is tall—she's not—or broad of beam—she is; it's more that she carries herself as a very large presence. It has to do with her demeanor, her ever-present dress suit, the manner in which she stands, the way in which she walks, and the well-regulated volume by which she speaks.

We take our customary seats at the kitchen bar. Rarely is there an agenda created in advance of these gatherings. The meetings had been her idea when I moved back from California, I'm sure, for no other reason than to try and talk sense into me, to convince me that I've gotten off trajectory. To assume the role of head doorman—a lofty title that, for whatever reason, she belittles—while living in the penthouse unit is, to use her characterization, fucking featherbrained. On her more charitable days, rare though they may be, she refers to it as ill-considered. Like too many of my associations these days, there is a complexity between Judith and me. She is, as noted, my godmother, a role fraught with literary expectations, fairy or not; yet as my financial and legal adviser, there are transactional expectations. She is, after all, paid to follow my instructions and orders.

Complex, indeed.

I apprise her on incidents that have taken place within the building over the past week, more gossipy in nature than anything else. She updates me on financial and legal matters, pulling paperwork from her attaché case, papers that need to be signed, documents concerning the retail space's renovations, bank statements, city and county assessments, upkeep payments, issues that, largely, induce an overpowering urge to curl up in the corner and take a nap.

"For pure entertainment value," I offer, "I will match my traffic jam and red Miata stories any day against your lien assessments and bank statements."

"Lovely," she says. "Become a novelist and tell fascinating stories about some cheeky bimbo who parks her sports car convertible illegally in her apartment building's loading dock. That will be absorbing, Henry. You can play the role of the starving artist up in his garret penthouse. But in the meantime, and before we reach that juncture, sign these papers. The rest of us will keep the world moving smoothly. And, by the way, remember when we first set up this charade, you said you were going to make a firm decision within a few months? Well, guess what? Happy anniversary. You're rapidly coming up on six months. It's getting time to revisit the issue. Shall we go over your options once again?"

"There's nothing more I would enjoy doing right at this moment than reviewing my life's options, but I'm afraid we're almost out of time. I'm about to meet some folks at the Met. At ten." I look at my watch, take the last few sips of my coffee and head for the kitchen sink.

"You have plenty of time, unless you're heading there via Fort Lee. Get yourself a second cup of coffee, sit down, and relax. I have a story to tell you."

Unusual, this. I don't think of Judith as a storyteller. Carnival barker, yes. Opinionated, sure. Overbearing, most certainly. But a spinner of yarns she's not. So, mildly intrigued, I refill both of our cups and sit back down.

"My older brother Nate was popular in high school. Nate the Great everyone called him. They called him that because he was not only the smartest kid among us, but he was also the best athlete and the most charming. He was great at baseball. Back in those days, in Williamsburg, that's what everyone played. These were in the days before every child ran around on a soccer field, and soccer moms? That wasn't a term then. Anyway, every free minute, the boys'd get together after school—and it was always only the boys who played, but we girls—*young ladies*—would hang around the fields, too. If I had any level of popularity among the girls, it was due to Nate being my brother.

"If enough kids showed up—as they typically did—the boys would play five-on-five or six-on-six, whatever it was, however many we had. They'd play for hours. Nate was the best of them all. He was the one who pitched the hardest, hit the farthest, ran the fastest. Typically played middle infield, either second or short, and nothing got by him. And that was on the hardtops of the empty lots that they'd play on. Those lots were *fast*. You hit a grounder on hardtop, and it skips by you before you know it. But they didn't get by Nate. He was a starter for our school team at Loughlin. He'd always tell me, 'Jude, once I get onto those grass fields, it's like the ball's moving in slow motion.' He was so good. Hit .450, .500, something like that, each of his varsity seasons. I think his senior year, he was close to .550 or something crazy like that. He was a straight-A student. Just a brilliant kid. Charming. Good looking. Everyone wanted to be with him. Everyone wanted to *be* him.

"But he had one fatal flaw . . . maybe two," she stops to take a drink of coffee. "You don't happen to have any pastries to soak up this mud with, do you? Maybe a roll or an old bun? I have trouble drinking coffee on an empty stomach, Henry. It's worth your while to take good care of your adviser."

I go to the counter and open a bag of pastries I picked up earlier in the week. I put some croissants and rolls on a plate as Judith continues her tale.

"So, aren't you kinda curious what his fatal flaw was?" she asks, taking a bite of a croissant.

"Yes, of course. You've left me absolutely on the edge of a cliff. Do you need to be prompted? Go on."

"Yeah, yeah, I will, but give me a minute. Don't rush me," she says, taking another bite of croissant. "You need to appreciate the art of the pause. Oh, wait a minute. Maybe you've nailed that. Anyway, back to brother Nate.

"As a kid, of course, I should say that I didn't see this particular character trait of his as a flaw; it was just who Nate was. But now, with the fat part of sixty years under my belt, I recognize it. It's pride. Hubris. *Stubbornness.* They're all related. So, here's what happened. Nate got a full ride to our father's alma mater, Fordham. He received a baseball scholarship. Our dad was a tough old bird. He and Nate had their stress, butted heads. Always something bubbling beneath the surface with those two. Subtle, too. They'd be in the middle of a conversation, talking about something or other, and all would seem fine but then, all of a sudden, bam! They'd be screaming at each other out of nowhere about who knows what. I hadn't a clue what would ignite it. I'd replay the tape in my mind, but it was all too faint, too subtle for me. There was something there, though, between those two.

"Anyway, all that notwithstanding, when Nate got that full ride, Dad was bursting at the seams. Crowed about it for weeks, telling everyone in the neighborhood that his boy was going to Fordham on a scholarship. Nate this, Nate that. I'd never heard Dad go on like that about him. Even through the years of straight As. Even through the baseball seasons that Nate had had. But this . . . this was something; his Natey was going to *his* Fordham on a full boat. And Nate let him go on and on. He was Dad's Exhibit A. Dad would haul him out to show him off to friends or relatives when they came over.

"And then, one day, Nate stabbed him in the heart. Told him that he wasn't going to go, that he had never wanted to go to Fordham, couldn't care less about the school and their scholarship, had no interest in going to a stupid Catholic university, much less the one that Dad had gone to. 'That was *your* dream,' he told Dad. 'Not mine.' Instead, he was going to try and make it in the pros, head south the following spring and try to catch on with one of the minor league affiliations. That damn near killed Dad; he thought Nate had lost his marbles. Nate couldn't have done anything more hurtful to him. It was almost like everything Nate had done in his young life had been done purposely to lead up to this very moment. Like he had been waiting for one special moment to spring the trap, to renounce everything that was of any importance to Dad." Judith sits back in her chair, takes a sip of coffee followed by another bite of the croissant. "And then he finally got it."

"Hmmph," I say. "Sad story. So did he make it in the pros?"

"Of course not," she said. "This isn't a fairytale. Nate bumped around in the minors for years—single A was the highest level he made—when he was twenty-four or twenty-five. Over the hill for that league. He was in the Yankees minor league system for a while and I was able to follow him in the *Times'* box scores, but, even at that level, he was clearly learning that minor league pitching was a whole different animal from his high school league. He never batted higher than the low .200s."

"So, given your path, you were the one who lived out your father's dream."

"Yeah, I suppose you could say that. That episode in our family's life left a big impression on me. Lotta drama between the male units back then in the Guncheon household."

"Well, if you're concerned that I'm puttering with the idea of running off to the minor leagues, you needn't worry."

"No, Henry," she says, shaking her head, and smiling. "I wasn't concerned about that. I've seen you toss a ball. Naw, I just thought it was an interesting story, that's all. Just passing the time of day on a Saturday morning."

I look at her and offer a small grin. "Sure you were. By the way, is this going on my tab? Because if it is, you're greatly eating into the profitability of L'Hermitage—the *vast* profitability, I might add."

"Ahh, listen to you. Such a businessman. Talking about profitability and stuff. Throw in a few *ROIs*, *loan-to-value ratios*, and *indexed ARMs* and we'll promote you from head doorman."

"Yes. Well, anyway, was there anything more to your story? A moral in case I'm missing any fine points?"

"I don't know what made me think of it. Maybe it's just about the choices we make in life, and the paths those choices take us down. Sometimes we get a little off track, Henry. That's what happened to Nate. Who knows? But I can tell you this: he's still searching for himself. He was successful in destroying Dad's dream, but he failed at living his own."

I pick up the dishes from the table and bring them to the sink. "Judith, I'm sorry. I really need to go meet some folks. But I do appreciate your story, and I do appreciate these discussions. If I'm off any track, I'll get back on it. I just need some time to adjust, okay?"

"Yeah, well, welcome to the Upper East Sider club, made up of a bunch of people constantly talking about all the money they can't talk about. So, what do you need, Henry? What do you need to move forward?"

"I need to become comfortable with who I am, okay? I'm thirty-three years old, I'm a multi-millionaire—"

"Multi-, multi-, multi—" Judith interjects.

"Got it. I'm a multiple-multi-millionaire, all of which has been gained through miserable and unethical practices. How do I reconcile that? I need to get my mind around that and if I need to hold off that reality for a few more weeks or months, so be it."

"Here's an update: add another week to your recovery period if you need to. The portfolio is currently twenty-five million dollars more than our last update. It's been a good couple of weeks," she says, shrugging.

"Okay," I sigh. "Twenty-five million dollars *more*. And I'm thirty-three years old."

"Yeah, well, it could be worse. Lucky for you, your assets haven't climbed over a billion dollars yet. Those are the really fucked-up kids. There's some sort of tipping point that happens with that number. Here's the weird thing about America: you're living in a world of milk and honey and boo-hooing because you want more vinegar. Well, at least you folks keep the therapy set in the pink."

Judith gets up from the table and carries her cup to the sink, recognizing that we are revisiting old ground. Judith is not patient with repetition.

"I know you've been pushed into a position you weren't ready to assume, but that's the hand you've been dealt. Most people would kill for it. I also know that you've got more in you than opening doors for rich people for the rest of your life. I get it—you want to do more with your life than sit on a beach. So, what does that mean?"

"I know. I know. And I appreciate your help on this, Judith. I do. I'll figure it out."

"Fine and dandy," she said while moving toward the elevator. "Anyway, what are your plans?"

"Oh, god, Judith, I don't know. I don't know! Please, I'll figure it out, but I need more time. I'm certainly not ready to do so this morning. Please, just give me more time. I'm figuring it out. But it's going to take time, all right?"

She looks at me with a cocked eyebrow. "Hey, Lady Macbeth, settle down. I meant this morning. What are your plans for this morning?"

"Oh, right. Sorry. Going to the art museum with some friends. Well, a friend and two acquaintances. Well, three acquaintances, really. They're all just acquaintances, I guess. I don't know them really. In fact, I—"

"Will you require nametags for this outing? I can't tell if you're meeting with three or ten people, but if this is some form of online or app dating, Henry, you're going to want to be careful."

"No, really, I'm meeting some folks there. One's from the building here."

She gives me a sideways glance as she pushes the elevator button. "Hmm. Well isn't that interesting. Girl or boy?"

"Girl . . . woman. But it doesn't mean anything. She kind of asked me, just spur of the moment."

"How old is she?"

"I don't know. Twenty-eight, twenty-nine, somewhere in there. It's Wendy DeLong in 8D."

She chuckles. "It doesn't mean anything if someone who's sixty asks you spur of the moment because she happens to be heading in the same direction as you are. If she's your age, trust me, snookums, it means something. My guess is next week you'll have a story to tell me."

# CHAPTER 15



And finally, I'm free. I burst from the rear entrance of L'Hermitage and jog down the alley to the street. Our building's rear security cameras faithfully capture my movements but because Charlotte has indicated, if not declared, an indisposition toward anything within L'Hermitage that smacks of technical or mechanical know-how, the management and oversight of the recording system resides under my purview.

Although it seemed like a terrific idea at the time, I regret the cohort I've arranged this morning, an agglomeration of souls that, when combined, may either repel each other or combust. With the exception of the past couple of days, my conversations with Wendy—if that is, indeed, how we can even classify them—have been little more than pleasantries. This morning, I suspect, she might express a certain level of curiosity about my background or where I live. A few stories above you, love, in the biggest damned apartment on the block. A thinking person's game plan might be to keep today's discussion focused on safer topics, to corral the dialogue neatly within a neutral territory, a demilitarized zone, if you will—coffee brands, favorite books, preferred jazz recordings. But even those topics are rife with class strata data, clues, and understandings. I'll do what I can to adhere to subject matter that dives deeply into the calming waters of weather-related concerns and recent streaming series.

And then, of course, there's the additional issue of Terry and Tomata joining us. I might just as well have snagged Jimmy the lobster-sated foreman and the Huckleby caterer while issuing invitations to this utterly arbitrary and haphazard gathering.

I cross 5th Avenue and look over the wall at the line of strollers heading to the zoo. They jam together at the park's entrance, each parent aiming to entertain their toddlers for the next hour or so. Buses and cabs zip by me on 5th, with an unaltered level of urgency from that observed on weekdays. Fifth Avenue is still cast in the morning shadows created by the buildings lining the east side of the road, with shards of slanted light emanating from each of the cross streets, providing punctuated hash marks as I head for my goal of the museum.

I enter the park, choosing greenery over city sidewalks. To the south, in the East Green section of the park, clusters of nannies and toddlers are arranged in the shade. The tired-looking women lie under trees while the children toddle about, the braver of the lot exploring nearby groupings. Large-wheeled carriages, many of them sporting cup holders, blanket racks, dangling mobiles, and duffel bags, are tethered together under the sycamores and beeches like barges in the East River.

I aim for the pond, where three or four boys are engaged in ramming their remote-controlled sailboats into each other. My own past metamorphosis notwithstanding, we must recognize and acknowledge the all-too-well-documented fact that boys are a deranged and berserk species unto themselves. The very fact that they, at some point, theoretically, evolve into responsible, productive members of society . . . okay, let's move on, shall we? Back to the monsters before me—good lord, one of them has now thrown his sailing ship remote into the water itself, presumably trying to hinder the progress of his brother's speedier clipper. The cannonball, as it were, missed by several scale miles. The cuff on the ears administered by his nanny was well-warranted, resultant caterwauling or not.

At the water's northern end, young girls are clambering about the base of the Alice in Wonderland statues, two young boys once again displaying their annoying brand of disorderliness by sitting atop Alice's head in a most inappropriate and ignominious manner and, from their vantage point, lobbing pinecones at the girls, much to their feigned disgust.

"Stop it!" they shriek, goading on and challenging the demons all that much more. Two older men, somewhat stooped, stand nearby, one leaning on the other, smiling and enjoying the action.

I head back toward 5th Avenue. As I enter the street's pedestrian stream of traffic, I pass the gauntlet of artists selling their watercolor prints, Haring knock-offs, photo tints, leather goods, vintage signs, and colorized New York City landmark posters.

I look to the Met's steps and, after a moment or two, spot Wendy. She's standing near the top step, leaning against one of the green metal railings, looking in my direction but not yet seeing me. I get a slight quiver of nervousness in my stomach—a ridiculous response for a man my age to experience. This isn't a date, no matter what Judith or Jacob may have thought or intimated. It's an outing, a jaunt, an escapade, perhaps. Nothing more than two people who happen to know one another—not terribly well, mind you—and have a shared interest, apparently, in art. Not entirely sure about that, never having uttered a syllable on the subject to one another, but nonetheless, here we are. She with me, and I with her. Not a lobby desk to protect me, nor a lobby elevator to take her away after our routine greetings.

"Hullo!" I shout to her, waving.

No reaction. That she's wearing sunglasses and tilting her head upwards toward the sun makes it moderately difficult to ascertain whether she sees me or if she's simply meditating.

"Hullo, hullo!" I try, a tad more animatedly, purposefully leaving out a rousing "Huzzah!" Other than annoying the older couple walking ahead of me, who turn to administer a nervous look at the yammering one-worded parrot behind them, my greeting fails to bring about anything resembling a response from its intended target.

Perhaps interjecting a name into the effort might prove useful at this juncture. I give it a stab. "Hello, Wendy!"

This seems to have successfully awakened her from her reverie. But just as she tilts her head down in my direction, raises her hand and hints at a smile, I hear a commotion off to my right. Commotions are common in New York City. The entire city is a commotion. But this particular ruckus, at this moment in time, seems to have something to do with me.

"Hey, Scraper! Scrape-MAN! Ha-HA!" Ah, yes, very good. A member of our morning's merry band, Terry.

"Door-door-DOOR-MAN! Yo!" Ah, there we go. And his loyal friend, Tomata.

"Looking good in your civvies, man! Damn good! You are wuh-hun tall drinka water, you are."

This exchange has further unhinged the older couple in front of me. The man grabs his wife's elbow and ushers her to nearby safety. I'm sure that, in moments such as this, they're both wishing they were back in the safe environs of Tewksbury or Peapack or some such place. No loud, shouting men out on those sidewalks.

"Good morning, Mister Terry and Tomata," I say. I glance somewhat nervously at Wendy, who remains standing on the Met's front steps, but the hinted-at smile has gone away, as has the waving hand. No doubt, something to do with worlds colliding and all that.

"Tour begins in five minutes, man. You ready?" Terry asks.

"Oh, yes, indeed I am," I say, infusing an additional air of brightness and conviviality to the outing. "And, by the way, someone will be joining us. That woman standing over there, looking in this direction—"

"You mean the one wearing a . . . what do you call that, a housedress?" Tomata enquires.

"No," I say, "Not her. The one in white a couple steps behind her."

"Oh, yeah, there we go now," Tomata says. "That one in white. Howdy, missy!"

"That's Wendy," I say. "She'll be coming with us this morning."

"Ooh, nice, Scrape," Terry says quiet and low. "Another drink of water. You tall folks all find each other, don't you? You all seem to kinda pair up when teams are being drawn. But hell, I didn't know we could bring dates on this outing. Did you hear anything about dates, Tommy?"

"Nobody tells me shit, Terry, you know that. Too late to go get the Sooz, you suppose?"

"Suzie don't give a rat's ass about old dead man art. Forget her, I told you."

At this point, Wendy has come up and joined us.

"Franklin, I didn't recognize you at first," she says with a large smile. "I've never seen you out of your uniform. This works." The "this" she's referring to is a pair of jeans, a black T-shirt, and an old pair of loafers.

"Oh, yeah, Scrape's got it working," I hear Terry mutter to Tomata behind me. I catch out of the corner of my eye some elbow nudging taking place between the two of them.

"You be given a build like a skyscraper, you can make it work any which way," he says for the benefit of all to hear. "Tommy and me, we're built more like double bungalows . . . more like Arts-and-Crap style architecture. I'm arts, he's crap." Both of them emit loud chuckles with this jibe. It occurs to me that our exploration into the world of high art was getting off on a questionable foot.

I attempt to reassert myself by tossing introductions about. "Wendy, may I introduce you to two gentlemen from the neighborhood?"

"From the neighborhood," Terry says, laughing. "I like that. Never thought of it that way. You have a pretty way with words. Yeah, we're a couple of Upper East Siders."

"Yeah, we live right over yonder," Tomata says, broadly gesturing to the backside of the museum where the park lays. "In this place's backyard. Six rooms, pond view. You all gotta come up sometime."

"Mister Terry and Tomata have offered to be our tour guides this morning," I say, trying to push the action along, glossing over their banter. "Our assigned docents. They have a special affinity toward one of the museum's pieces that they would like to show us. Eh, me. Us." Awkward. Rough takeoff.

"You got it straightened out yet, Scrape?" Terry asks. "Listen, don't worry about it. We do individual and group tours. This morning, the two of you get a twofer. One tour for both of you, same price as for one. You, me, we, us, don't make no difference." And then, turning to and addressing Wendy, he says, "Morning, ma'am."

"Good morning, gentlemen," Wendy says. "I've been looking forward to this event."

Really? I think. Splendid. "Well," I utter, "shall we, then?"

The four of us walk up the stairs, ascending the twenty-five steps to view some of humanity's greatest accomplishments, all contained within one building.

Once inside, Terry starts fumbling in his many pockets. "Dammit, man. I think I forgot an ID card. I gotta pay thirty dollars. I don't have that this morning."

"Dammit double," Tomata says. "My membership pass hasn't come in the mail yet. They've been promising to mail it for weeks."

"Oh, yeah, yeah, that's right," Terry says. "Well, I do have ways of slipping in, but it's not normally with groups of this size."

"Oh, please," Wendy says, "let me get this. It's on me. I insist."

I had not thought through this part of the morning adequately. The entrance fee, steep as it might be without licenses or IDs, certainly presents an impediment to Terry and Tomata and should, by all rights, do the same for any city doorman. I know that Wendy, on the other hand, should easily be able to pick up the cost. But given the fact that it was I who assembled this excursion, a modicum of effort should be offered from my side.

"Please, Wendy," I say, "let me get my own. And theirs, too."

"Of course not, Franklin," she says. "I'd be happy to pick this up. It's nothing. I'm happy to do so."

Well, it's not nothing. Even I know that. It's over fifty bucks for forty-five minutes—maybe an hour—of visual entertainment. I don't care how wealthy she may be or the depth of her trust fund. There is a level of commitment being made here, if not to the institution, then, at least, to the young relationship we're establishing off the grounds of L'Hermitage.

"Oh, but please—" I say.

"No, really—" she counters.

"But—"

"I really should—"

"Is this here going to be much longer between you all?" Terry asks. "Because if it is, we might all soon be able to get a senior discount. Which is not to say that we're not finding this fascinating, isn't that right, Tommy?"

"Fascinating. Spellbinding, you could almost say. Almost."

"Yeah, great stuff."

At this, Wendy puts her credit card down on the counter. The admissions agent goes over the New York residency pricing policy.

"Yeah, that topic's been well covered," she says, glancing at me. "Let's just go with full adult admission."

With the dispensation of the pass buttons and layout maps, we head to Gallery 807. There are a number of distractions to slow down our progress. Terry and Tomata, especially, get drawn into the various rooms, each insisting on showing the other—and us, as well—some detail within this painting or that. Wendy and I follow along; I, somewhat amused by their antics; she—I'm not so sure. Although she smiles, it's not clear whether it is with amusement or mild, stifled irritation. At one point, while they are carrying on in their own inimitable, loud manner, she quietly asks me, "So, who *are* these guys, Franklin? How do they know so much about art?"

"I think they're artists. They seem to study the subject quite closely. Terry mentioned something about RISD the other day."

"So, they're artists? How do you know them?"

"We have coffee together," I answer.

A bit more context might prove useful. "Terry wanders by L'Hermitage a couple times a week, early in the morning. He has referenced a shelter that I assume he stays at, but I also know that he spends a lot of time in the park. Earlier this week we got to talking about art. He mentioned that there was a favorite piece of his hanging here. I'm hoping that, at some point this morning, we'll actually see it, current progress notwithstanding. I asked him, somewhat on a whim, to show it to me and, well, here we all are."

"And the other one? How do you know the other one, Tomata?"

"I don't. He showed up yesterday with Terry. They're a package deal."

"Hey, Scrape, have we lost your attention already?" Terry shouts from down the hall. "C'mon, man, shake a leg. The gallery closes in ten hours or so."

"You bring a date to the Met, and you're just bound to be distracted," I hear Tomata say. "Just going to happen, that's all I know. That's been my experience."

As we leave the seventeenth- and eighteenth-century European art galleries, Terry and Tomata continue their animated conversation, perhaps, as is often the case, too loudly for the comfort of those around them. I say "too loudly" because, as we're about to enter a dark hallway dedicated to photographic arts, a guard puts his hand up to stop them. "Excuse me," the burly man says, "may I see your pass buttons?" He's speaking specifically to Terry and Tomata, not realizing that they are with Wendy and me.

"What do you want?" Terry asks, fumbling in his crowded pockets as if looking for something.

"Your passes. The buttons you would have been given when you entered."

"Oh, yeah, yeah," he says. "Yeah, I know what you mean. One of those little green buttons. I got it here somewhere. I got one of those. Uh, Tomata, did I give a little green button to you?"

Tomata produces his, but not Terry's. "No, I don't got yours. But I got mine; there you go, sir."

"You folks can pass through," he says to Wendy and me.

"But, they're with us," I say. "We all have those passes. We got them together. He probably just dropped his."

"Nah, I got it here somewhere. I paid to get in here," Terry says, continuing to fumble in his vast array of pockets. "Well, she paid, anyway. But we paid to get in here. I'll pull it out. Just give me a minute."

"You don't need to keep looking for it," I say to Terry.

I turn back to the guard and say, "Do you stop everybody like this? I'm curious as to why we were being waved through. My pass was in my pocket. You didn't see it on me."

"Nah, Scrape, let it go," Terry says. "I got my pass here. Let me show it to him."

"You can all go through," the guard says, clearly wishing to be done with us. "We do spot checks at various times, nothing more than that. Enjoy your visit."

"Nothing more than that, my ass," Tomata mutters. "And to think, I combed my hair special this morning for this outing, what little I have left. They can spot us a mile away."

"Nah, they sniff us out," says Terry. "I'm used to that shit. So are you, Tomata. Get over it and 'enjoy the visit.'"

I lead our party deeper into the photographic exhibit. After a few steps, Terry erupts in a gung-ho manner with a bit of rah-rah thrown in.

"Hah! I found it. Here's your damn little button! Take a lookee here, guard man!" Terry waves his arm, holding the button out for our guard friend to see. The guard, still near the entryway, gives a slight smile and does a mock salute in acknowledgment of what Terry has just produced. Terry turns and says, "I knew I had their damn little button somewhere on me. Who can keep track of these stupid little things?"

"You better, brother," Tomata says. "You needs the button to get through the door."

"Oh, it doesn't matter," Wendy says. "Forget him. Let's go see our painting."

"Does that happen often," I ask Terry, "that type of checking?"

"Ffft," Tomata spits. "Please. Were you just beamed down yesterday, Scrape? It happens hourly. There's few places that we're accepted for the way we look and dress. Shelters. Churches—some, not all. Libraries, if we're not sleeping. And a few other places for a few minutes, but we always get nailed at some point. Moved on. We don't need to be panhandling to annoy most folks. Just the way the world works."

"Yeah, yeah," Terry says. "Let's get off the pity potty and move on, okay? Drop it, Tomata."

"Well, I'm just saying, since he asked. Fight in a fucking war in oil land and this is our thanks . . . it sucks, that's all I'm saying. It sucks," Tomata says, having the last word on the subject.

"So, you guys are artists, Franklin tells me," Wendy says, effectively changing the subject.

"Yeah, yeah," Terry says enthusiastically. "Landscapes and stuff. We've had shows around here, here in New York. Tomata and I have."

"Have you really?" Wendy asks. "What gallery?"

Tomata lets out a loud laugh at this question. "Yeah, Terry, what's the name of that gallery again? The gallery you've been having all your shows at. What's its name? Fifth Avenue or something? Or was it Bryant Park Gallery? Or is it Sidewalk Gallery? Which one?"

"Shut up, man," he says. "Honey, we haven't been in any galleries in a while. I guess we fit more into the street artist category. We live on the streets, we paint on the streets, and we show our stuff on the streets. Got any gallery connections for us? We've been working that angle for years, ever since we got up here from Florida. But if you have any connections, or can make any introductions, we'd love to hear about it."

"Well, there's Brendan Stewart in our building," Wendy says. "But I'm not sure he—no, I guess I don't. I just assumed when you said you had shows—"

"Someday, honey. Someday. Let's forget about all that for now and just enjoy my boy, Caspar."

We arrive at a small, tucked-away gallery, number 807. Terry places us in the center of the room—empty, except for our outfit—and looks at us with his huge grin.

"Are you ready?" he says, with a nod of his head and an upraised eyebrow. "Behold." And he slowly spins his body, with his arm extended, and points to a rather smallish-framed painting across the room.

"It's not as large as I would have expected," I say.

"Size doesn't matter when it comes to beauty like this," Terry says.

"Man, I'm saying that to Suze all the time, but she don't buy that shit," Tomata says, laughing a cigarette-laden rumble.

"Shush. Keep that noise out of this here gallery. Go on, you're in deep beauty here. You're in my temple. Go check out your Pollocks and your de Crappings if you wanna get into that nonsense."

"Come on, I was just kidding. Continue."

"Anyway," Terry says, turning back to Wendy and me with a large grin, "here is Herr Friedrich's masterpiece. It's one of a few that he painted with these two cats looking at the moon. They didn't have Xeroxes back then, but ole Friedrich could make copies, and each one got better. This is the last one and I think it's the best of them all. Speaks to perseverance."

I walked up to the painting for a better look. Unlike the impressionistic paintings, which I tend to appreciate more from a distance, this one merits a closer viewing, partially due to its size, but also due to the fine detail Friedrich included within the small canvas. Two men with their backs to the viewer look out from a wooded hillside at a sliver of a moon and—I'm assuming—the evening star. One man is leaning congenially upon the other and the two are, given the title, *Contemplating the Moon*.

"It's a beautiful piece," I say.

"I love it," Wendy adds. "What is it about it that captures you?"

"Just look at it," he says. "The first time I saw this painting a few years ago, I was blown away. I've been doing a lot of studying of Friedrich and his painting pals ever since. That's how I wanna paint, man. Romantic. Loving nature. I just wanna walk into that painting, where everything is cool. Sometimes, when I'm not pissed at Tomata, I see me and him in it, together, enjoying nature."

"Aw, is that us, man? I didn't know that, you old softie." Again, Tomata slaps Terry on the back, but not quite as rough as usual. More tenderly, one could even say, if backslaps could be categorized as such.

"Yeah, whatever. Anyway, I like these two guys looking out at the night sky. I think of them trying to figure out the world. Trying to figure out their place in it, that kind of stuff. Deep thoughts. We have them now and again, don't we, Tomata? We get kind of philosophical out there on our summer nights, in the middle of the night, when the city's nice and quiet like, huh?"

"Yeah, especially when we run out of hooch and there's nothing else to do," Tomata says.

"Ah, man, why don't you just head out for a while?" Terry says. "Seriously, go sit in that gallery over there. Go on now. You're not helping my tour one bit. Fact, you're detracting from it, you and your noise."

Tomata heads out, mumbling about folks not being able to take a joke and taking themselves too seriously, glancing over his shoulder as he's doing so, and sits on a leather bench in the next gallery.

"That's better," Terry says. "Now, where was I? What was I talking about again?"

"You were telling us about the two men trying to find their place in their universe," says Wendy.

"Yeah, yeah. So, I just find it kind of peaceful. I'll come here when I'm down or something, and it makes me feel better right away. Here these two guys were, amazed at the moon, feeling so small and insignificant and I realize I'm not alone in this world, that I'm not the only one feeling what I feel. That people have been trying to figure out their place in the universe forever. You know, sometimes, when I'm sitting in the park, or walking along the streets, I see folks rushing here, rushing there, all dressed up in their suits, talking on their cell phones, carrying their stuffed cases and whatnot, and I can't help but think, they got it all figured out. They know exactly what they need to be doing, where they need to be going, who they need to be meeting with. And that's when I start to feel just a little down, when I focus on that stuff. It's like watching the carousel at the zoo . . . kids going round and round and I'm just sitting on the side, not knowing how to get back on the damn ride. But when I look at this painting, I realize nobody got it all figured out, that we're all just a bunch of bluster and show. Hell, even ants on the sidewalk can look busy. I mean, all they're doing is moving little grains of sand here and there; they don't even need to think about it. Activity doesn't mean accomplishment, right? Anyway, Friedrich, with this painting, with this composition, with the way he put all these elements together almost two hundred years ago, makes me think every time I look at it. I know he's thought of as a painter, but I think of him more like a philosopher. He wasn't just slopping paint onto a canvas, you know? He was thinking. Looking at the moon and *thinking* things. Yep. That's the way I want to paint. I want to make people think, too."

"Well," I say, "I find that to be a worthy goal," which is about the best response I can muster at this particular moment. Wendy rises to a different level, however.

"Yes, I see what you mean," she says. "The two figures are small, diminutive, against their surroundings. What the artist is saying is that nature is—and will always be—a far stronger and more powerful force than man. Also, the fact that their backs are toward us immediately draws us in as viewers. Their positioning forces us to look at what they're looking at: the moon. We are also forced to contemplate the moon, nature."

By this point, Tomata has crept back in and rejoined the tour. "Hey, hey, Terry, she's better than you," he says softly. "I want her to lead this tour from now on. And I bet she don't get all rude on me and give me a timeout in the next gallery, either."

"Oh, I don't mean to take over the tour," she says. "I took a lot of art history in college. I just remember learning that the Romantics used their portrayal of nature as a way to explore their own personalities."

"See man," Tomata says, "you didn't know none of that shit. Hah! The best you could do is, like, 'It makes me feel all good inside.' You didn't even know why you liked the painting. But now you do!"

"Shut up, man. Go look at your damn drip paintings."

"Were you an art history major?" I ask her.

"Yeah. I wanted to get into museum administration or maybe gallery work. But the job with BergMan came up and, well, I headed down a different path. I guess we can't always live our passions."

"Hey, Wendy," Tomata says, "Did you go on break? What else is Terry supposed to know about this painting?"

Wendy continues, pointing out that the tree stump in the foreground represented death, a life shortened before its due time.

"The clear sky, however, represents the promise of eternal life," Wendy says.

"Eternal life!" Tomata says with a broad grin. "I don't need no promise of this life going on eternally. It's wearing me out. You see that, Terry? See that eternal life painted in there?"

"Huh," Terry says, ignoring Tomata's comment. "I guess I didn't know he was saying all that. I just liked the painting because it kind of calmed my brain down. Well, anyway, I think I might be done with the touring for today."

"Oh, shoot," Wendy says. "Please. I'm sorry. I didn't mean to take over. I'm just spitting out what my professors said, throwing out buzzwords. Once you learn the terms—*painterly brushstrokes, evocative, diminished perspective*—you can ace all the tests. It becomes a game after a while. In fact, you barely need to look at the paintings anymore. You'd do far better to listen to Terry. He's actually speaking from the heart. I envy that quality."

"Thank you, ma'am," Terry says. "Nice of you to put it that way. I think I'm done tour guiding today, though, anyway. If you all don't mind, I think I might just kind of look at some of the other paintings around here on my own. See if I can't brush up a bit on my painting knowledge. Painterly brushstrokes and perspectives and stuff." He smiles and then says, "Come on, Tommy. Let's go look at the Turners for a while."

"See you all," Tomata says with a slight wave and a grin. "Don't worry about Terry. He gets a little tongue-tied in the presence of beauty, if you know what I mean." And with a wink, he turns to follow Terry.

"I hope I didn't upset them," Wendy says.

"No, I'm sure you didn't," I say. "I think, perhaps, the two of you were just approaching the painting from different angles."

"I tend to do that too often, you know, blurt out something. It's a fault of mine, really. Nervous energy. Do you want to get something to eat? Can I buy you a cup of coffee?"

As we leave Gallery 807, I can see Terry and Tomata walking down the extended hallways of statues, Terry pointing out certain pieces, Tomata pointing in the opposite direction. Terry appears to have recovered his spirit, his animation, once again.

# CHAPTER 16

Saturday, 11:17 am

Before sitting down with Wendy for a cup of coffee, there's something I want to take care of.

"Can I meet you in a moment?" I ask. "I'll see you in the café, the one that overlooks the park."

I leave Wendy behind, presumably with the impression that I'm heading to a washroom. Instead, I head back to the main entrance. Over on the left is a prominent desk with a large sign hanging above it proclaiming, 'Membership.' I approach the woman under the sign and ask how much an individual membership is. "We have several levels. Is it for you or would it be a gift?"

"A gift. Gifts. A couple of friends of mine," I say.

She lays out a brochure in front of me, explaining that memberships range from just over a hundred dollars to $25,000 per year, the higher level, no doubt, allowing opportunities to become close friends with the museum's president and directors.

"I think the introductory level will be sufficient," I say.

"Name?"

Oh. This part hadn't quite played through adequately in my mind yet. "Uh, Terry," I say. "Just Terry."

"Last name?"

"Can we just go with Terry?"

"We'll make it work. Address?"

These confounding questions. The grilling one must go through to buy a friend a simple present. Ceaseless!

"Is 'Manhattan' sufficient? 'Central Park'?" I ask, knowing

perfectly well it won't be, but it may successfully buy me time.

"South, East, or West?"

"Hmm?"

"Central Park South, East, or West?"

"How about Central Park Interior? No, wait. Central Park *Central*. Can we go with that?"

"No, not really," she says, biting her lower lip, "because that's not an address. Without specific addresses, your friends won't benefit from our mailings, discounts, announcements, and so forth. Would you like to call back with an address?"

"No. Let's use this one," I say, giving the address of L' Hermitage. "Unit number 12A. How does that address sound?"

"Ah, perfect," she says, visibly pleased with the sudden gush of information. "That will make sending our renewal notice to Terry much easier. Phone number?"

"He's unlisted—"

"Email?"

"No. And before we go there, I should probably say that he's also unwebbed."

"Text? Social media accounts?"

"I'm sorry," I say. "I'm no doubt frustrating you with my lack of information about Terry, but he's really more of an acquaintance. I just want him to be able to enter and roam about the museum whenever he wants over the next year without it being a hassle. All renewal information should be sent to my attention. Can we do it that way?"

I give her the rest of my contact information, which, it might be noted, is no straightforward matter in and of itself given multiple names and addresses, but we finally come to the end of our negotiation session. The world desperately wants us all to be well-rooted and grounded.

"Did you say you wanted to get two memberships today?"

"Yes, two. We did have fun with that first one, didn't we? Why end it?"

"Name, please?"

"Tomata."

And so it goes. Having worked out the rough edges with Terry's membership, Tomata's enlistment is an absolute breeze by comparison. Within five minutes, I am again on my way to the café to reunite with Wendy.

She sits by the window overlooking the park, one cup of coffee in her hands, one cup on the table in front of her. She is leaning forward, hunched, observing the goings-on in the section of the park she can see from her post. Looming over the table she has selected is a suggestive statue of a woman's body, headless and armless; a very attractive, seductive form—missing body parts notwithstanding. A simple plaque on the plinth says,

*Semele.*

"Coffee for me?" I ask.

"Yes. It may not be as good as the coffee you brew at L'Hermitage, but it's the best I could scrounge up."

"I'm sure it's fine. Thank you, both for the coffee and treating me to the museum today. By the way, I hope you didn't mind our tour guides."

"Mind *them?* The question is more, did they mind *me*? This was supposed to be their tour. We would have all been better served had I simply shut up and listened. I'm afraid I stifled the conversation."

I ask her about her work. She is an account manager with a boutique-marketing firm on the Upper West Side. The firm specializes in nonprofit organizations, especially museums and small galleries, as well as the occasional corporate work.

"We have one client who I'm working with right now who is about to launch a new high-end protein bar—"

"High end? That's an end that exists within the protein bar universe?" I ask, seeking clarification.

"Oh, yes, of course. They use only organic, nonprocessed ingredients. It's called the On the Gaux Bar, spelled G-A-U-X, but pronounced 'go.' Kind of like faux, but gaux. It's one of those spellings that marketers love—it's supposed to grab your attention."

"Well, it's certainly grabbed mine, right by the very throat. But unless your target audience is made up of creative wordsmiths with a rock-solid foundation in romance languages, aren't you afraid they'll be pronounced, 'On the Gacks?' Which, by the way, has an unfortunate connotation in street slang."

"Oh, no, we know that won't happen, or, at least, that's what we've communicated to the client. The people it's aimed at—those making at least a hundred and fifty thousand dollars and up a year—will get our play on words; we're confident of that. And they'll probably feel clever in doing so."

"Hmm, I see—the endorphins kick in upon purchase. And that demographic is lacking a quality protein bar, are they?"

"Oh, my god, they're starved for it, Franklin, you must know that," she says with a hint of sarcasm. "We're making the world a better place. Are you truly unable to tell, when I rush by you each day, the important work I am heading off to do? Our market research indicates that filthy rich people are distressingly underserved in that area. We're going after the Type A, well-paid demographic that eats their lunches or breakfasts on the go—"

"You mean, on the gacks."

"Stop it, this is my work. Monday morning, I'm coming down early to heckle you. On the *gaux*. But these bars won't taste chemical-ly, like those—ew—lower-end snack bars do. These are delicious, with fresh ingredients. We tell the client it's going to be a big seller. Huge!"

"Is it?" I ask.

"Franklin, it's a protein bar. Anyway, we have a focus group to help us determine that answer coming up on Monday. We'll have them rate the product on packaging, the eight-dollar-a-bar price point—"

"Sorry. It sounded for a moment like you just said eight dollars. *How* much do they cost?"

"Yeah, I know. A little bit high, huh?"

"Well, we are still talking protein bars here, right? I didn't, like, black out momentarily while you segued into the topic of gold bars or anything, did I?"

"Yes. I mean, no, I didn't move on. Our earlier research indicated that that price point wouldn't be a problem for our target demographic. Do you know that when Perrier first came out in America in the seventies, everyone said that no one would pay two dollars for water in a bottle? Yeah, well, we know how that all turned out."

We sit quietly for a few moments, letting the people walking outside the café windows entertain us. My mind momentarily races as I search for pertinent and trenchant protein bar follow-up questions, but I appear tapped out on the topic. I am hoping to avoid a subject that I suspect might be rapidly approaching. Me.

"Tell me about yourself, Franklin," she says. "How does one become a doorman?"

"Connections in high places," I say.

"Yeah," she says, "isn't that pretty much the way the world works?"

I give her aspects of my background, not lying, but not providing any details that might merit further questioning on her part. There is an art in being able to give just enough information that it slakes one's curiosity but doesn't elicit follow-up questions. I mention that I grew up in New Jersey (true), headed west after high school (true, but I quickly gloss over the school's name), worked as a waiter (occasionally true—between school years), worked for years in the nonprofit sector (true), before veering off, quite unexpectedly, into my current position as a doorman in New York City (leaving out the nastiness of the reason behind the move). A nice story, no lies, but not a whole lot of truth either. The art of the downplay.

"Well, you strike me as someone who has broken the mold of New York City doormen," she says, once I have completed my litany.

"I suspect you mean that in a positive way," I say, "but I'm not sure what it means."

"I do mean it in a positive way. You're not like other doormen I've encountered. I can't put my finger on it. It's the way you carry yourself. It's different, certainly, from the current collection at L'Hermitage. Jacob—ha! He's quite the performer. Morgan and Lester on the weekends—harmless overseers of sleepytown. They're all very good, but they're all characters. You strike us as the one who is unlike the others."

"Us?"

"I don't mean to act as the building representative here, but you have to know that we talk about you guys from time to time. 'Did you hear what Jacob said the other night? He's *so* funny, such a troublemaker' and 'No, but do you know that I saw Lester on Saturday morning with one of his eyes open? I actually thought he was awake.' You know, that kind of stuff. Harmless."

"And me? What do they say?"

"Oh, well. Now *you* get off pretty easy. 'Did you see Franklin's new uniform, Myrtle? That boy looks just like that nice young actor in that one play we saw at the Public. You know, that tall, good-looking actor that just makes my little heart go all aflutter. Why I just become a little schoolgirl all over again.'" That's it. That's all they say. Just good stuff."

"Aha. By the way, who are they talking about? Which actor?"

"Who knows? But I'm going to rule out Nathan Lane or John Malkovich."

"Well, in any event, I'm hoping we're all behaving professionally and appropriately at all times."

"Oh, you're very professional," she says. "In fact, you're so professional that some might even say it's okay for you to let it go a little on the weekends. Anyway, my only point was that *you* are the one who seems a little different to us. Oh now look what I've done. I've gone and embarrassed you."

And, sure enough, the tinge of rosiness that had begun creeping across my face at the beginning of this conversation flares into a full-on fire, an annoying carryover from childhood that I, seemingly, have been unable to shake now that I have categorically landed in what can only be called adulthood. At the time in which whiskers first start appearing on their chins, boys tend to lose the intensity of blushing. But not me. My ability to blush has only deepened with age, flushing my cheeks and setting my ear tips afire.

"I'm sorry, Franklin," she says, putting her hand on mine. "I didn't mean to embarrass you with my compliment—"

This action certainly doesn't help diminish the flushing or extinguish the burning ears. "No, no. You didn't," I say. "It's just a little warm in here."

She suggests that we leave, and so we do. Wendy moves with a light air, smiling gently to those she passes within the museum's hallways. There is an elegance to her frame that is not always present with other tall people. Her lightness is reflected in her erect manner, the type of person you imagine who actually did, as a shy, awkward child, practice walking with a heavy book balanced atop her head during those long, lonely summer afternoons.

◆　◆　◆

By the time we get outside, the day has warmed up, but the morning's chill remains, even in the direct sunlight. Taxis are honking, people are shouting, heels are clicking on the pavement. We walk back toward L'Hermitage along 5th Avenue, past the sidewalk hawkers with their framed photos and watercolor stands, briefcased jewelry sellers, used-book stalls, and steaming hot dog carts. The wind blows, making the vendors nervous for their displays and shifting the shadows about us. Beyond the vendors, the sidewalks are crowded with pedestrians. There are children running, dressed as if it's mid-August; older men strolling, wrapped for early March; teenagers shouting and laughing, making sure as many people as possible know they're in the area; an older woman, disordered, but famous for her roles on Broadway and in film, walking her dog; a thirtysomething mother holding a five-year-old boy's hand; a father, looking exhausted, pushing a loaded-down stroller five paces behind his wife and toddler; a man in a business suit and sunglasses running toward a bus he has just missed; a woman shouting Spanish into a cell phone; two men, each wearing loudly-striped shirts, leaning against the park wall eating hotdogs; two women talking excitedly to one another, neither listening; and a young couple, both tall, walking south on 5th, filling each other in on their recent pasts, both wondering about their immediate futures.

"Busy this weekend?" Wendy asks.

"No, not particularly," I say. "This outing is my weekend's highlight. This is it. I've peaked. All downhill from here. You?"

"Nonstop action for me," she says. "Heading into the office this afternoon, followed by a couple of hours of work at home this evening, with several more hours of the same tomorrow. I'll squeeze sleep in somewhere and I'm sure, at various points, I'll have to interact with Mrs. Hill on the phone, complaining about how noisy I'm being by simply existing in my apartment, pondering the future of protein bars. It's an exciting life."

"Ah, Mrs. Hill," I say. "Lovely woman."

"Hey, you're paid to say that. Not me. Batty as all get out, as far as I can tell. But I've been wrong on such matters before. I'm horrible at making snap judgments."

"Well, she does have a certain mien or aura about her, I'll grant you that."

"There you go, that's it!" she says.

"Sorry?"

"That's it—that's what I'm talking about," she says, turning directly to me in the middle of the sidewalk. "That's what I meant before—and don't go blushing again—but that's what I meant when I said you're not like other doormen. There's a certain *aura* about *you.* Using words like 'mien' or 'aura,' and just the way you *say* it. You're definitely a different breed of doorman, no doubt about it. That's what I was saying."

"Hmm, perhaps. It would be quite contrarian of me to gainsay that, I suspect."

"Hah! See?" she says, grabbing my shirt front.

"I did that on purpose. We within the doorman brotherhood would refer to that as a joke," I say.

"Oh, yeah—good one." She turns and we resume walking down 5th.

"Well, anyway, you do seem different, not just from doormen, but from many men, in general. And I mean that in a very good way."

"You have just assured doors being opened that much quicker when you enter and depart L'Hermitage."

"That's what I'm after," she says. "Doors opening more quickly."

◆　◆　◆

When we near our street, we begin engaging in the uncomfortable banter of a long goodbye. Mindless chatter, both of us looking for the perfect send-off to properly cap the morning.

"I assume you're heading home now, but I don't even know where you live," she says.

"Ah, yes. That would put you at a disadvantage then, wouldn't it? I have a place in Queens, in a small, simple apartment. It's all I need."

"Do you have a doorman?"

"Ha! Me? Doormen buildings are expensive."

"Well, don't fret it. They're really not all they're cracked up to be. Just a lot of overhead," she says, smiling. She turns, ready to cross the street. "Thanks for letting me tag along with you this morning. I'll see you Monday."

And she's off. Floating across the street and back to L'Hermitage. I wait an appropriate amount of time, several minutes by my calculation, and then I cross the street. I meander through the colliding crowds and enter the quiet of my alley. After several steps I arrive at the rear of L'Hermitage. I look carefully at the windows above me, hoping to ensure that no one from within the building is—at that moment—taking in the view of the passageway. I enter my private vestibule and insert the key in the elevator lock. The doors quietly shush open, and I enter, push the button labeled *PH*, and ascend.

# CHAPTER 17

Having tossed and turned much of the night before, I give up on sleep and get up early, intending to get dressed and relieve Morgan before his scheduled out time, something that, when done, is typically regarded with indifference by our laconic Morgan.

The weekend was a lost one. I wasn't being disingenuous to Wendy when I told her that our art excursion was going to be the weekend's highlight for me. It was. When the competing events are moving from one couch to the next all Sunday afternoon; watching old movies on Netflix; trying, yet again, to make sense of Dad's legal and financial papers and, being wholly unsuccessful in doing so, seeking hoped-for refuge between the spines of Wodehouse; and having coffee with Judith Guncheon to kick off the two-day fun fest, then a stroll through the art museum with new friends is a strong contender for leadoff in the weekend's highlight reel.

I thought of Wendy throughout the remainder of the weekend, trying to unravel the significance of our evolving relationship. What did she see in me—I mean, what was it that prompted her to join me on Saturday morning's expedition, to touch my hand during our discussion, to grab my shirtfront? She could easily have bypassed the outing altogether. It would have been effortless to have simply said that she was working all weekend, no hurt feelings. Maybe next time.

Part of her wanting to join us could have been the thrill of "slumming it," to provide her life with a certain level of controlled—and controllable—danger. I'm aware that I've been described by people as good-looking, but that only goes so far with women of her position, women who are highly educated and wealthy. I've known of instances in which women of that status enjoy giving the gift of their presence to those less fortunate. It allows them to position themselves as being socio-economically blind, as a way to rebel against Mummy and Daddy's bestowed class system. They fight it for only so long, however; maybe through their twenties, but rarely to the altar.

So given that, were she to discover that rather than living in a studio in Queens, I actually occupied the penthouse suite of L'Hermitage, would I be as alluring or exciting to her, if that is, indeed, what I am? Would I supply the thrill that she is after, or would I be put into a category that, undoubtedly, men she has already encountered in her life occupy? Rather than representing the sexy working-man trope, a type of which wealthy young soul-saving women might daydream, would I become just one of many others she has known throughout her life?

Well, that's the issue, isn't it? Or is it? I'm assuming there's a romantic aspect to our outing because, quite frankly, in the back of my mind I'm hoping that there might be, that the possibility might exist. The thought has flitted through my own daydreams—how could it not? But what if her acceptance of my invitation was little more than the fact that she was interested in going to the Met, no matter who her company was. What if she simply wanted an outing before jumping into the work that she knew lay ahead of her over the weekend? What if?

Dressed in my doorman suit, I take the private elevator down to the back alley and walk onto the street. At this hour, when the city seems intent on extending the weekend and hesitant to engage in a new workweek, the customary river of taxicabs is only a trickle. Out of the corner of my eye, up ahead and across the street, I detect movement. A shadow, a shape, something . . . moves near one of the trees about fifty yards beyond me. I look more closely but, like a dim star in the sky, when one looks directly at it, the image disappears. The early morning light can be tricky; images move, shapes shift, and cats seen seated on front stoops twenty yards away morph into potted plants upon closer inspection.

But this, this is no potted plant. Too big to be a cat, for that matter. Raccoon, maybe? Again, there's movement. I walk toward it, cautiously, not sure what I have before me but drawn to it nonetheless, with a sense of curiosity and fascination. Whatever it is scoots and shimmies farther away from me, toward a low shrub in the small garden of a townhome toward Park. It's a hunched-over creature. Once I'm about thirty yards away, it again skitters off, this time crossing the street, fully aware of my approach and trying to build distance between us. It bolts ahead ten yards, stops, looks back at me, and continues on to its next hiding spot.

I realize it's not a raccoon but a wild dog of some sort. It has an odd movement for a dog, seeming to bounce lightly upon its paws, with a distinctive head movement, peaking back furtively over its hunched shoulder at me.

"Good god," I think. "What is that thing?"

I continue to approach it, but in a slower fashion than before, its shape continually shifting in the shadows, one moment a hunched-over man, the other a skittish dog, although of a size that I would not mistake for Ms. Sillerman's Pomeranian. It maintains the measured distance between us, refusing to allow me to get any closer to it than it's comfortable with. The creature reaches the corner and appears to enter a stairwell. I approach cautiously, making sure that it has plenty of room to bolt—should it decide to do so—without incorporating me within its flight path.

About ten feet away from the stairwell—an entrance to a small, antiquarian book shop that people from throughout the city feel compelled to support—I pause, thinking that, perhaps, I've sufficiently investigated my fellow traveler this morning. "Ho!" I call out, intending to flush my quarry from its hiding spot. "Hey, hey!" Again, nothing. I pick up a pebble and lob it into the stairwell. It pinballs and rattles around but does nothing toward dislodging the visitor.

I move slowly toward the hole, aiming to look down into it

without getting any closer than need be. The hair on the back of my neck is bristling, some genetic artifact that told my ancestors that it might be best to run like hell but, for whatever reason, today, on this particular morning, I opt to ignore. I get to the railing and slowly, very slowly, look over the edge of it. There, tucked into the black corner, poised as if to lunge at my face and tear it off is . . . a large plastic bag stuffed with newly delivered phonebooks. They're probably not capable of ripping my face off at this moment, nor, for that matter, of having flitted about the street for the last five minutes. I lean further over the railing, looking in the other corners. With the exception of two coffee cups, a sheet of newspaper, a minor squall of eddying leaves, and the aforementioned phone books, the stairwell is empty. I spin around, looking for the creature but I see nothing. Had the darkness played a trick on my eyes? Had the animal gone around the corner instead of jumping into the stairwell, as I initially thought?

I head back to L'Hermitage, wondering what it was I had seen. At that moment, I hear a couple of high-pitched, tittering yips at midblock and see the creature sprinting west. Somehow, it had gotten around me and escaped.

It takes the neck hairs a moment or two to relax and return to their at-ease positions and, once accomplished, I proceed home.

# CHAPTER 18

Monday, 7:40 am

When I enter L'Hermitage, I notice a rearrangement of items and furniture has occurred. Papers are scattered about the doorman's desk, the bench under the large mirror has been moved into the living room area, potted plants have been pushed together, and Morgan is nowhere to be seen.

I begin putting things back into place when Morgan, from the living room, calls out, "Oh, all right, Franklin. Sorry . . . must have dozed off."

"There you are. Is everything okay? What's been going on here?"

"Yeah, yeah, sorry about that. Had quite the night around here," he says, grunting, while getting up from the leather sofa. "The ambulance folks pushed things around when they were rolling their gurney in and out. Messy folks, them ambulance people. 'Swhy I try not to call them whenever I can avoid it."

Morgan is short and wiry and has a whiff of Dobby the house elf while displaying none of the scamp's plucky energy. In fact, Morgan has rarely displayed energy of any sort—nervous or otherwise—in the time that I've known him. My interactions with Morgan tend to come in five-minute increments, the amount of time our shifts overlap at the beginning of the workweek. When I arrive, Morgan gives me those updates he deems worthwhile and then heads out. But this morning is different.

"Ambulance people?" I ask. "As in paramedics? EMTs—that sort of thing?"

"Yeah, yeah, ambulance people. Mrs. Hill," he says, as if this gives the full breadth of the story.

I wait a tick to see if he will take the opportunity to voluntarily fill in the informational gaps that currently exist within his proffered narrative. None forthcoming. Stoic one, this Morgan. Professorial types might seize the opportunity to use the word *taciturn*.

"Was there an accident? Is she all right?" I ask, attempting to advance the storyline.

"Yeah. She's fine. Have a good day. See you next week," he says, as he grabs his cap from the counter and heads to the front doors.

"I, I'm sorry, Morgan, but I'm going to have to detain you just a, a bit more before you dash into your Monday morning schedule. What happened?"

"Well, she got dizzy, that's all," he says in a tone that would suggest irritation toward my inability to ferret out the full account from the rich clues he has thus far provided me. "She called down to the front desk here and asked for help. She had fallen—"

"Fallen!" I said.

"Hmm, yeah. She had fallen. But she got back up again after a while. Leastways, got up enough to get to the phone and give me a call. Anyway, I called 9-1-1. That's when the damned ambulance people came—"

"That would follow. Go on."

"They wheeled a gurney up to her apartment. I let them in. She was sitting in a chair in her living room by that point, the poor dab. Seemed fine to me, though. Anything else?"

"Is she up there now, Morgan, or did they take her to a hospital?"

"No. She's up there. I think she's fine. Just had a little spell or something. They were gone after about forty-five minutes. Anyway, is our conversation going to go on much longer, Franklin? Because if it does, I might start tipping into overtime."

"No, of course not, Morgan," I say. "Take off. I'll see you next Monday morning unless, of course, you're planning on attending this week's staff meeting."

He looks at me askance. The man hasn't an ironic bone in his body.

My stab at humor has reached a comfortable level just above his head.

"Nope. Can't make it this week," he says, turning his back on me and heading once again toward the doors. "Didn't know there was one, but I probably can't make it anyway. All right, then."

"Should I reschedule to make it convenient for your calendar?" I ask, as the door shuts quietly, in its own expensively muffled manner, behind him.

◆　◆　◆

It's early yet for our building, just a little after eight o'clock. Although it begins to stir with elevator doors opening and shutting with a heightening frequency, people quietly, sleepily coming and going—some off to work, some returning from the morning dog walk—I do feel a compulsion to go upstairs and check on Mrs. Hill.

I ride the elevator up to the eighth floor and get off. Mrs. Hill's is one of six other residences on the floor. I walk down the red-carpeted hallway to 8B and knock.

"Mrs. Hill?" I call out. "Mrs. Hill, are you there?"

Each of the units has a small talk box mounted to the left of their doors. When the building was originally constructed in the '30s, this technology was one of the key selling points. The system allowed unit owners to communicate not only with the front vestibule area, but within the units themselves. Members of a household could speak with one another from room to room, as well as with anyone standing outside their front door. Many of the intercom systems stopped working years ago, with owners not bothering to have them fixed. Mrs. Hill's, however, still works, and she employs it—with greater or lesser success—regularly, including this morning.

"—'s there?" she says.

"It's, uh, it's—" I begin, but stop, realizing that she has continued to depress the talk button from her end, preventing her from hearing me.

"You need to . . . you need to let go of the talk button," I say quietly, uselessly, and to myself. I knock again.

"Who's there?"

"It's Franklin. Come to see if you're—"

"Who?"

"Franklin, ma'am. Come to see if you're—"

"Is that you, Franklin?" she says meekly.

"Yes, Mrs. Hill. I've come to make sure that everything's all right with—"

"—in, Franklin. Just come in."

Mrs. Hill has seemingly confused her current living conditions in the Upper East Side with a home in, oh, say, a small, rural village in the Upper Peninsula of Michigan where one could, presumably, truly open a door and simply *come in* when an inhabitant calls out those inviting words. But, given that Mrs. Hill has a dead-bolt lock and, undoubtedly, a chain lock, my easy entry is not guaranteed, as much as she may like it to be.

"Are you in yet, Franklin?" she asks.

"Uh, no, ma'am," I say. And, as an audio cue, I reach to loudly jiggle the doorknob, to let her hear that I remain quite locked out. When I turn the handle, however, the door opens without further hindrance.

"Oh," I say.

The opening door reveals a dark, crowded, messy apartment. Stacks and piles of every sort—old newspapers, magazines, bills, letters, unopened mail, manila folders, notebooks, assorted sheets of paper, invitations, and solicitations—are scattered throughout the apartment. There is, however, a pathway, just wide enough for a walker to get through, leading to various areas of the apartment. Shades are drawn, making the setting dark and, to use her word, dreary. It wouldn't be a surprise if, somewhere in the bricolage, there lies a dusty, cobwebbed, uneaten wedding cake. But I defer that search for another time.

"Franklin?" Mrs. Hill calls from a distant bedroom. "Franklin, is that you?"

"Yes, Mrs. Hill," I call out. "I just wanted to check in and see that you are all right. I heard from Morgan that paramedics were called in last night."

I walk, or, shall I say, stumble, given the obstacle course before me, to her bedroom door. She is lying, propped up, in her bed, looking gaunt and weak.

"Oh, are people downstairs talking about it?" she asks.

"Well, technically, yes," I say. "Morgan and I were just talking about it, ma'am. If that counts."

"Oh," she says. And then, brightly, "Anyone else?"

"That's all that I know of at the present time, ma'am," I say. "But it's early yet. I have no doubt the building will be abuzz soon with discussions around your emergency. You know how people can be."

"Oh, good," she says. "You can tell them I'm all right. But not *too* all right," she adds, quickly correcting herself. "I'll be convalescing throughout the day, in case people wonder where I am."

"But, you're all right now, ma'am?"

"Well enough."

"Good, ma'am. I'm glad to hear that. Will you need assistance contacting family members, Mrs. Hill? I'm sure they would appreciate knowing—if they don't already—of your mishap last night."

She looks down at her bedspread, fiddling with the lace end strings. "No, Franklin. That won't be necessary. I'll call them later."

"Very good then, ma'am. Can I do anything for you prior to returning to my position downstairs? A glass of water? Anything of that sort?"

"Yes, actually. Please get me the glass of orange juice in my refrigerator. I couldn't quite finish it last night."

"Happy to. One moment."

I wend my way through the piles into the kitchen. This room is no refuge from the ubiquitous and overwhelming mess. Piles of *New York Times* are scattered on every counter and, perhaps most alarming, upon the stovetop. I notice that Mrs. Hill has underlined many of the words within the articles and scribbled notes within the margins, such as *Call Amb. Howe, seek clarification*, or *Write Simpson Demand <u>explanation</u>!* or, just simply, and, perhaps, more to the point, *Wrong!!*

In addition to the piles of newspapers in the kitchen is an interesting assortment of other household items, none of which are normally found within a cooking space: a hammer; a desk lamp; garish Lladro statues of young, bonneted girls; paperclip holders; an overflowing Rolodex container; four vases of dead flowers—two of which have been missing from the lobby for weeks; a midsized snow globe of the Rose Planetarium; *Playbills* from assorted years-old Broadway shows; and a table-top radio located next to a topless, empty cookie jar. Her visits to the lobby are beginning to come into clearer focus. She needs to escape the chaos and confusion of her cluttered existence, if even for just a few brief moments.

I open the refrigerator door and reach for one of the six half-finished glasses of orange juice, each carefully covered in plastic wrap and secured with a rubber band. They are scattered amidst a plate of grapes, a block of unwrapped orange cheese, soda crackers, and numerous containers of jellies. I pick the juice glass that looks the— what? Newest? Freshest? Fullest? Does it matter?

"Here you are, Mrs. Hill," I say, once I have returned to her room.

"You really are so kind, Franklin. Above and beyond. Next time I see your boss—see Mr. Franken—I'm going to make sure I tell him how wonderful you are. I've told him that before, you know."

"Is that right, ma'am? You've told Mr. Franken about me?"

"Oh, yes, of course. I've told him what a wonderful job you do here. I speak very highly of you to your boss, you know."

"I greatly appreciate that, ma'am. I've heard tell Mr. Franken's quite reclusive."

"Oh, he's reclusive. But he and I have been talking recently. I'll make sure to put in another good word for you. All good service should be appropriately recognized, I feel."

"Very good, ma'am. I really must head back down now. Charlotte might be upset to find me away from my desk."

"Oh, don't worry about her," she says. "I've told Henry Franken *all* about her and her rude manners. I'll see to it that you have that position, Franklin. *You* are the one who should be running this place, not her—that's my feeling. I'll take care of it for you with Henry. You may be too young to realize it, but I have quite a bit of clout, you know."

"Very good, ma'am," I say. "Rest well."

"You really are too kind, Franklin."

"And you, as well, ma'am. And you, as well."

# CHAPTER 19

Monday, 8:44 am

"**Y**ou've seen the coyote," Mr. Harrison informs me, after we've covered the topic of Mrs. Hill's episode before moving on to lighter conversational fare. I am standing behind the front counter, having straightened the reception area and my desktop from the goings-on of the night before. Mr. Harrison is sitting in his usual morning chair in the lobby's living room area. "How fortunate for you. There have been articles about it, you know, the coyote."

"Coyote, sir?" I ask. "As in the animal that roams the plains and Western states? Howls at full moons and that sort of thing?"

"Indeed. That exact creature. Right here in our very midst, on the island of Manhattan. Quite magical, I think. And you saw it. The *Times* has had a couple of articles recently about people spotting it—or them—on nearby streets, or joggers coming upon one of them in the park. How it got here is beyond me. Maybe he was a lead scout, sent to see if we humans are still occupying this island. Nature is itching to reclaim the planet, once we're done destroying it.

"Anyway," he continues, "I'm keeping you from your work. Go about it. I'll tend to my crossword puzzle—it's Monday, you know. Easiest day of the week. Barely worth filling in the spaces—I'll be here but a minute."

"By the way, sir," I say, "how was your art class last week? Were the charcoals behaving for you?"

"Ah, yes, that," he says. "A bit frustrating. Rustier than I had thought. The charcoals were, indeed, *not* behaving, to put it in your terms. Our class took a stab at a statue of Hermes holding a baby.

My version ended up being nothing more than a mishmash, I have to say. Others had better luck with the exercise."

"Perhaps they simply had a better angle on it, sir. You may have been at a disadvantage where you were sitting. That happens at times in art classes, I'm sure."

"Hmm, no. Nice of you to say so, though, Mr. Hanratty. I was sitting dead-on to the statue. Don't worry though. I'll get 'em next time," he says. "By the way, what is that? Is someone knocking? Do you hear that?"

Just as he asks, I, too, become aware of a soft tapping somewhere nearby. I hear my name—or, I should say, Terry's name for me, Scraper—being urgently shouted as if from under a thick blanket.

"Scraper!" Tap, tap, tap. "Scraper!" Again, the repeated tapping. "Hey, over here, man, over here by the door. Scraper!"

I look to see Terry tapping at one of the small, paned windows that borders the front doors on the other side of the vestibule. A rather useless adornment, really, those small windows. Until this very moment, no one has ever really put them to use, certainly not as a medium for knocking, anyway.

"Scraper! I need you, man. I got something."

I look over to Mr. Harrison, still seated in his chair within the living room. He is looking at me from over his half-framed reading glasses.

"Do we have a visitor, Mr. Hanratty?" he asks.

"I'll tend to it, sir," I say.

I walk over to the front doors and pass through the vestibule. As I push open the door, Terry backs up awkwardly, almost tripping over the front stoop planter. He is holding a large canvas.

"Man, aren't you supposed to be the doorman here?" he asks with a big smile. "Why do I gotta be knocking on your door for ten minutes before I get any doorman to come to the *door*, huh?"

"Well, I'm not used to people, uh, knocking on the front door," I say.

"Well, you ain't got no doorbell. Least, not one I could find," he says, looking around the doorframe. "Anyway, I brought something I want you to have. Here." He hands me the canvas he's been holding. It's a depiction of the Friedrich painting, with two men contemplating a moon. Although the colors are somewhat off, making the piece a tad muddy, and the perspective is flat and childlike, the overall effect is, I would have to say, quite charming. Primitive, in its own way.

"I was a little short of green, which is a problem with an outdoor nature scene, you know, so I had to go with my umbers and siennas. Stuck a lot of black in there too, to make the background dark," he says, standing back. "If I had the right colors, it'd probably look a little more like Friedrich's. But you get the idea. It's still a little wet in some places, so watch yourself."

"It's wonderful, Terry. Really very wonderful. Where do you get your paints and canvases?" I ask.

"Well, that's no canvas. It's an old board I found somewhere. The boards—the canvases—aren't the problem; those are easy to find. The paints are a little trickier. I sometimes sell my pieces to folks. I save up and buy."

"Paints are expensive, aren't they?" I ask.

"Oh, yeah. They're real pricey, some more than others. The prettiest colors are the ones that are the most expensive, of course. But those are the ones that make the paintings breathe. So, I try to just stick with some of the cheaper ones, do my best mixing with them. That's why a lot of my paintings are lacking in the color department, certainly don't have many blue skies. Also, I search for smaller boards to paint on. I got lucky on this one, though, Scrape. It's bigger than most. Thought you might like it."

"So, where do you get the paints?" I ask.

"Couple of stores up around the corner, over on Lexington, that I go to. Sometimes, if I catch the right guys as they're opening up, they give me some of the older paints, or tubes that were accidentally punctured or crinkled and won't sell so well. I maybe get something every fourth or fifth visit."

"Is that why I see you walking by here most often on certain days of the week? Is it tied in with those stores' schedules?"

"Yeah, yeah," he says. "The guy I like at Empire only works on Wednesdays. The guy at Baron's works on weekends and Mondays. Can't go over there on weekends, though. Too busy, too many customers. But if I catch these two cats as they're going in first thing on those days, they sometimes give me some supplies. They're both veterans, like me. They get my deal. That kind of thing."

"Well, Mister Terry, the painting is beautiful. Truly beautiful. You're a terrific artist."

"Thanks, man. That means more to me than a cup of coffee. Maybe you have a wall or something in your place that it can go up on. Tell your friends it's from one of New York City's finest street painters. Might be worth something someday," he says as he starts to wander off.

"Hold on," I say. "I have something for you."

I reach into my pocket to grab the member passes to the Met that I had bought for him and Tomata.

"Here," I say. "I got these for you after you left us at the museum. Now you can go in whenever you want for the next year. Just show them this and you'll get a pass button. I got one for Tomata, as well."

I hand him the two passes and he looks down, staring at them, turning them over. I've not seen Terry at a loss for words before but if I were to have, it would probably look a lot like this very moment. He opens his mouth a couple of times, as if to say something, but then stops. Finally, he looks up at me, not quite in my eyes, more in the shoulder-ish region and lets out, "Wow, nobody done anything like this for me in a long time, given me a gift without my asking for it. Especially a gift like this. I guess I'm a little rusty at handing back thanks."

"Don't worry about it. You just gave me a gift, too."

"I guess you could say it's all kind of Christmasy this morning, isn't it?"

"Yeah, guess you could say that. You're very good at what you do, Mister Terry. Just keep finding inspiration within those galleries. Within your Gallery 807."

"I will," he says, quietly. "No doubt about that. Yeah, no doubt about that, man. Well, anyway . . . I best be off, Scrape. Now when I'm asked for my pass, I can show them my goddamn button. Awfully nice of you," he says, waving his tickets to me in a mock salute. "Awfully nice."

"Thanks, again for the painting," I say. "I look forward to hanging it up."

He walks off, with a slight limp and somewhat slowly, without saying anything. I'm not sure what to make of his muted response.

"Mister Terry," I call out. "Wait a minute, let me ask you another question." A thought has occurred to me. "Those paints, you said they're expensive, right?"

"Yep. That they are."

"Here, come here for a moment. Let me do this. Let me give you some money that goes straight to buying you some colors that you might need. Not just leftovers or remnants. Here," I say, handing him a hundred-dollar bill.

"Oh, no, no, Scraper. C'mon, man. You work hard for your money too. Don't be doing that. I couldn't take a hundred from you."

"Why not?"

"Nah, man. That's too much. That's way too much."

"But the paints are expensive, aren't they?"

"Yeah, but that's . . . that's . . . just too much. C'mon, man. Don't be doing that. That's just messing with me now. Nah. No way." He rubs his large hand over his face vigorously, as if trying to erase the last moment or two.

"Please, take it. I thought, maybe, you could buy yourself some adequate paints and materials."

"Nah," he says walking off. "Too much, man. It's just too much. Keep your money. I ain't that far down. I ain't to the point where a doorman be giving me hundred dollar bills, maybe a cup of coffee every now and again, but not a hundred dollars, K? No way, man. That's just crazy. Ain't no way you can be affording that. And I ain't that far down."

"Hold on a second. Forget about the paints, then, but I have another question for you. Where do you sleep at night?"

"Aw, come on man, all I wanted to do was bring you a painting this morning, not get a goddamn grilling, K?"

"I'm just curious. Where do you go at night? I know you spend a lot of time in the park, but where do you sleep each night?"

"Fine. When it's cold, I try to get into Mainchance. But during warmer months, like we're in right now, me and my buds are just fine with sleeping in the park. It's not so, what do you call it, claustrophobic? Besides, there's better air to breathe in that park at night instead of a crowded room. If it makes you and yours feel better, we can call it urban camping. I gotta go now."

He spins and begins walking back in the direction of the park. I've, perhaps, crossed a line with Terry that I hadn't seen and he's not comfortable with.

# CHAPTER 20

Monday, 9:06 am

As I reenter the building, Charlotte is standing near my desk, hands on hips, with a less than friendly—some might uncharitably refer to it as dour—expression upon her face. Rough weekend, perhaps.

"Good morning," I offer up. For a Monday, Charlotte is in early, perhaps focused on acquiring more adequate parking this morning than she did last week.

"Come into my office, Franklin," she says before spinning away.

I lean Terry's painting against the front desk and follow Charlotte. Mr. Harrison gives me a humored, arched-eyebrow look over his newspaper before returning to his crossword.

"Quite a bit more action down here than one's normal Monday morning," he says, just loud enough for me to hear before I enter Charlotte's lair.

"Good morning, Charlotte," I say again, hoping to get our conversation off on the appropriate note. "Have a good weekend?"

"Shut the door, Franklin," she says.

"Yes." I realize this may be about Mrs. Hill's episode, but I'm not clear on why Charlotte is aiming for such a dramatic lead-in.

"As the manager of L'Hermitage, I must ask you this question: are you a drug dealer?"

A spit-take would be an appropriate response had I a mug and a liquid within it that would allow for such a maneuver. Shy of that, I let out a cough, recross my legs, interject a short nervous titter and, I believe, cross my eyes as I attempt to muster a befitting comeback to this beginning-of-a-new-workweek ice breaker.

"I'm sorry?" It's the best I can rally at present, but were I to have another go at it, a redo of sorts, I'm confident I would have come up with a stronger or, may I say, a less weak rejoinder.

"A drug dealer." There, again. No misinterpretation of what she initially said. Conceivably, she could have asked if I was a dog healer, a rug hauler, a smug kneeler, and any number of other well-known occupations or proclivities. But, no. The ears were operating accordingly. "It's a simple yes-or-no question, Franklin. Are. You. A. Drug. Dealer?"

"Well, then, a simple question warrants a simple answer. No."

"Drug *buyer*? Don't get semantical on me."

"I wouldn't think of, um, getting semantical on you. Uh, I'm sorry, Charlotte, but this is a most unusual conversation. I'm not clear on what is—" And then, of course, it dawns on me. She had witnessed the exchange out on the front stoop. Bills being pulled out of pockets, waved about, items exchanged between living souls, that sort of thing. Extended social intercourse between doorman and someone who outwardly resembles and, in fact, *is*, a homeless person. The height of a dubious and suspicious transaction in Charlotte's mind.

"I saw everything, Franklin—you handing money to that guy out there. What is *he*, then? Is *he* a drug dealer? A gigolo? You bringing gigolos around to L'Hermitage, Franklin?"

"Oh, good heavens—"

"I don't need to know your private affairs, until they spill over into your workplace. I'm an open-minded gal and all that, but L'Hermitage is your workplace. I don't know what was going on and I don't need to know what was going on, but I want it to stop."

"Please let me explain, Charlotte. Terry is someone I—"

"You know his name?"

"Well, yes. He comes by every now and again and I simply help him out."

"You help him *out*?"

"Well, not really help him out, but . . . yes. Okay, help him out.

He's harmless enough. He stops by once or twice a week—"

"Stops by?" she asks. "Once or twice *a week*? Here at L'Hermitage? Where do you think you're working, a soup kitchen?"

"Well . . . I say, 'stops by' in that he pauses as he's walking up the street and engages me in conversation if I happen to be standing out there. I don't mean to imply that he's sitting in the lobby's living room with his feet propped up on the table, warming his hands by the fire"—as contorted a position as that might be.

"Don't be sarcastic with me, Franklin. You do know that L'Hermitage has a strict rule against any employees giving money to bums on the street? You are aware of that, right? Because we went over that when we hired you. It's not a complicated rule. It's a pretty simple rule, really. Simple, and it makes a lot of sense, don't you think? You gotta think of L'Hermitage as a castle. The sidewalk is our moat. And the door you're opening is the drawbridge. You're lowering the drawbridge to an element we don't want entering the castle, okay?"

"Castle. Moat. Dragons. Yes, got it. I'm sorry. And I didn't mean to sound sarcastic. And I didn't mean to go against any rules that may have been established—"

"You're aware that employees going against established rules is grounds for dismissal? You're aware of that, right?"

I pause at this, not enjoying the turn our conversation has taken if, indeed, a turn it had taken.

"Charlotte, please. I . . . he's simply someone I give a cup of coffee to every now and again. It strikes me as harmless."

"Our rules aren't open for interpretation, Franklin. Here, look." At this, she tosses a pamphlet, labeled *Bylaws, Volume VII, L'Hermitage,* over to my side of the desk. "It *clearly* states that employees— *especially* our doormen—aren't to give handouts to homeless people. Or something like that. It's in there somewhere. Just look for it, and when you find it, show it to me. Anyway, it's like giving table scraps to a dog. You do it once and they'll sit at your feet, begging for the rest of their lives, looking for another scrap. We don't want that element around here—they're unstable. Do you get it?"

I cross my arms, looking at her. I let out a heavy sigh.

"Charlotte—" I begin but stop.

"What? You want an argument?" she says. "There's nothing to argue about, Franklin. Your job is not to tend to the home*less*. Your job is to tend to the home*more*. The home*ful*. The *homed*. Whatever. To *our* people. Your job is to arrange deliveries. To neatly pile up the Amazon packages. To call for cabs or let folks know when their Uber ride has arrived. Deal with the pizza delivery guy. The dry cleaners guy. To make sure that catering companies are scheduled at appropriate times—we can talk more about that later, by the way. Your job is to . . . is to . . . open doors and . . . and that kind of stuff. Doorman stuff. If you want to tend to the homeless, go down and work in Little Sisters of the Poor soup kitchen. Now thank me for not firing you on the spot. You happened to catch me in a good mood this morning. I don't want to see you chatting up the homeless again, you got it?"

I pause. "Yes. Will that be all, then?"

"No. Now that we have that nastiness out of the way, there is something more I would like to say to you."

She leaves a dramatic pause, inviting me for further prompting. "Yes?" I say.

"It is part of the manager's role—as I understand it—that, on occasion, compliments should probably be doled out. So, with that in mind, I'd like to recognize your assistance Thursday afternoon. I admit that, on the surface of things, it might have *looked* like I contributed—although we both know that's not true because you had wandered from your post—*contributed* to a portion of the confusion. It seems like you handled the catering situation exactly as I would have done had I not been here, no, I mean, had *you* not been here . . . or . . . whatever. Anyway, I'm glad to see you didn't need too much direct supervision from me."

It sounds—although I'm not wholly confident of myself on this matter—like I have just been thanked, so I throw a "You're welcome" into the conversation and stand up.

"I just have to remind you, Franklin," she says, having the final word, "you guys are replaceable. You, yourself, do a great job around here. I know the residents like you. But I'm not kidding about this stuff. I feel sorry for those people, too. But it's not our position to help them out. That's not what we do here. This would be out of my hands if you act in such a way that you encourage their coming around."

Well, I had to admit as I returned to my desk, she did have a point. Charlotte's style and manner of speaking may not be quite up to Letitia Baldrige's rigid standards, but one would have a difficult time refuting her key point. That is, that the residents of the building may not be overly enamored with Terry & Co. mulling about the front doors.

There is a reason, after all, that they're living in a moated castle on the Upper East Side.

# CHAPTER 21

Monday, 9:24 am

I stand behind the counter for the next hour taking care of the top-of-the-week duties, but primarily licking wounds. I hadn't given a great deal of thought to my interactions with Terry, at least not to the point of reviewing how others might interpret symposia with a person in his current state. We might lump street people into a broad category—threatening, unpredictable, unstable—but Terry doesn't fit neatly into that grab bag; he was simply friendly. To make a true connection with someone on the streets of New York can be unusual. I was on his route, and he was on mine. My inviting him to lead a tour within the Metropolitan Museum of Art may be interpreted as curious behavior on my part, but almost every single aspect of my present condition could be viewed in that manner. What's one trip to a museum? A wealthy man who pretends not to be, a penthouse dweller who hides within his walls, a beneficiary who ignores or renounces the gift he has been given, a prisoner who holds his own key—you tell me who the unstable one is, who needs to be watched or avoided. Pathologies are in the eye of the beholder.

Monday morning rush hour at L'Hermitage has commenced. Simon, the deliveryman from Lexington Cleaners, parks out front and runs in with twenty or so garments on hangers, plus one box of folded shirts. I hold the door for him as he heads toward the drop-off area within the mailroom. Ms. Sillerman from 3B comes off the elevator, heading for the front door, which I continue to hold open for her.

"Morning, Franklin," she says.

"Ms. Sillerman," I respond, nodding my head. "Gorgeous day out there today. Remember your sunglasses."

"Got them. Thank you!" she shouts, heading in the direction of the park.

I go back behind my desk as another load of residents gets off the elevator. "Finally, something worthy of our halls, Franklin," Mr. McAdoo, he of 11A, says in a rather obscure fashion, before pushing the front door open.

"Sir?" I say, but too late. He is gone.

"Really, Franklin, you must tend to that," Mrs. Cooper, 3C, says, entering from the street, dabbing at droplets of sweat with a large white towel wrapped about her porcine neck, having just finished her morning run in the park. "Mustn't leave these things lying about. Hold that please!" She lurches to the elevator, where Mrs. McAdoo has just entered from the mailroom.

Mrs. Rubin and Mr. Prasad, she of 6D and he of 4C, get off the other elevator and head outside, but not before Mr. Prasad quips, "Hung it a little low, didn't you, Franklin?"

Oh, much frivolity and jocularity going on this morning, at least more so than normal, but I haven't a clue what they're referring to as they rush about their morning routines.

"Mr. Hanratty," calls out Mr. Harrison from his living room seat, "you look perplexed."

"Well, the residents of the building are acting a bit, uh, Delphic, shall we say, this morning, that's all," I say. "Either that or I'm a bit foggy—we can never rule out that possibility."

"'Delphic.' Very good, Mr. Hanratty. There's a Friday word for you. But I would suspect that the running commentary put out by the residents of this building has something to do with your painting," he says. "Your painting that's leaning against the front of your desk."

"Ah, yes, of course," I say. "Terry's painting." I come out quickly from behind to gather it up to get it out of the way of traffic, but also— perhaps more importantly—to get it out of eyesight of Charlotte. Enough questions for one morning. "I had forgotten that I set it there."

Mr. Harrison approaches the desk. "May I have a peek at it, Mr. Hanratty?" he asks. "Is this from your friend?"

"Uh . . . acquaintance would perhaps be more accurate," I say.

"Well, friend, foe, or acquaintance, it's quite spectacular in a rather simple, almost monochromatic way," he says.

"You think so, sir?"

"Hmm, yes. He's either trained or has developed a very distinctive style through much practice. I recognize the piece. It's a takeoff of the Friedrich piece we were talking about the other day, eh?" he says looking at me over his half-rims. "Out of scale to that, of course, but an interesting interpretation, nonetheless. For instance, the shapes of the two men looking at the moon—they're more impressionistic, more organic, almost as much a part of the landscape as the trees that surround them. It's a strong statement he's making. Quite remarkable, really, I would say."

"What's remarkable?" a voice behind us asks. "What's that you have there?"

Mr. Stewart approaches us from the elevator bank.

"Brendan," Mr. Harrison quietly greets him.

"Good morning, sir," I say.

"Is that a Pandolfo? Where did you get a Pandolfo?" he asks, ignoring our acknowledgments. "Who'd you buy that from, Ted?"

"It's not a Pandolfo, Brendan. I'm quite surprised you would confuse it for one. It's a . . . a . . ." He stops himself, looking at me.

"A . . . Terry," I say.

"Yes, it's a Terry," says Mr. Harrison. "And it's not mine, either. It's our friend's here, Mr. Hanratty's."

Mr. Stewart appears confused by this revelation and turns to me. "Oh, it's yours, Franklin? Where'd you get it?"

"It turns out our Mr. Hanratty is a budding talent scout. He's discovered one of New York's greatest new talents. And who knew? The artist was here on the streets of New York the entire time. Somehow you missed him, Brendan."

"What are you talking about? *Who's* the artist? Who is 'Terry?'" he demands, while pulling a pair of reading glasses out of his shirt pocket.

"I'm not sure of his last name, sir. He's just an artist I met. Comes by the building every now and again. Seems to have a certain flair, I'd say."

"Yeah, maybe. Where'd he go to school?" he asks while carefully studying all aspects of the painting from a mere six inches away.

"Careful, sir, it's still a bit wet. His schooling? Well, I've heard mention of RISD, but I guess you'd say he was schooled in New York."

"Huh, yeah. New York University. I thought as much. It's evident. It's got all the tell-tale signs running throughout it." At this, a loud snort is issued from the direction of Mr. Harrison.

"Pretty good program, NYU," Mr. Stewart continues, oblivious to Mr. Harrison's editorial emissions. "Must've studied under Donnelly. She has a kinda post-modern approach to her landscapes, which Terry uses. Yep."

I look quickly at Mr. Harrison, who is smirking. I feel an end should be put to this conversation before Mr. Stewart embarrasses himself further. Mr. Harrison retreats back into the living room.

"I think he's, perhaps, a bit more self-taught," I say. "Although I'm not entirely sure of his full background, I'm guessing he may not have studied at NYU, sir."

"Hmm. Self-taught? I see," says Mr. Stewart. He continues to peer closely at the painting, although I sense his interest is waning. Serious art dealers are probably not terribly interested in self-taught artists. And then something occurs to me.

"If you're interested in seeing more of Terry's pieces, sir," I say, "my guess is I could easily arrange it for you."

"Who's representing him now?" he asks, licking his lips.

"Well, uh," I say, "I would have to guess that he's not currently being represented by any agencies or galleries. He's probably *between* galleries, as they say."

"There's your chance, Brendan," Mr. Harrison shouts from the living room. "Although, be careful. It may require you to stick your neck out. You wouldn't want to harm your reputation by taking too risky a chance."

Mr. Stewart looks over in Mr. Harrison's direction and then quickly back at the painting. "No, pro'ly not," he says mutedly.

"No, of course not," Mr. Harrison echoes. "Only with your clients do you care to take chances, right, Bren? Certainly never with the reputation of an emerging artist."

There it is again. Clearly, there is something going on between these two men, but I'm not aware of what it is. I decide to jump into the fray, to rescue the moment, if not too late. A bit of diversion always goes a long way in instances such as this, I find.

"So, uh, would you care to meet this artist—this 'emerging' artist—as Mr. Harrison put it?" I ask.

"Possibly."

"Careful, neck sticking out!" shouts Mr. Harrison. Quite uncharacteristic of him.

"Yes, possibly," Mr. Stewart continues, looking at me directly and trying his best to block out the vituperations emanating from the living room. "Where does he live? Is he in Chelsea? The Village?"

"Oh, yes, the Village. The 'capital-V' village. Proper art comes from nowhere else in this world. Only the Village, eh? Possibly Chelsea? Dumbo?" This is seemingly Mr. Harrison's final salvo, as he has gathered up his reading materials and crossword puzzle and headed for the elevators.

"God forbid that anyone from outside of the Village has the slightest clue how to apply paint to canvas, eh?" One more burp before the elevator doors close.

"Most unusual of Mr. Harrison," I say, somewhat apologetically. There are times in which I feel a sense of responsibility for what transpires within my lobby, as if I am the puppet master and those who pass within my hallways are under my control. This is one of those moments.

"Nah, pretty typical, actually," says Mr. Stewart, still examining the painting.

"I've become used to Ted's brand of passive-aggressive behavior. I file him under the 'Unhappy Client' category, nothing more, nothing less. Quite honestly, I find him to be a pain in the ass. He's got his story; I've got mine. It's easier to deal with him by just ignoring him. Anyway, where does your artist friend live, if not in the Village? Williamsburg?"

"He lives in the park," I say.

"On the park?" he says. "Really? Whereabouts? Is he in our neighborhood, or is he over on the West Side?"

"Well, actually, sir," I say, "somewhere in between. He doesn't live *on* the park; he lives *in* it."

A few ticks pass while I witness the Stewart brain striving valiantly for comprehension of this lump of information. "I don't get it," he says at last. "What do you mean he lives *in* the park? There aren't any places to live in the park. I'm confused."

"Yes, well, I can understand that," I say. "I believe Terry—the artist—is not only between galleries, but he's currently between homes, as well. He is actually residing in the park, if his recent statements are to be believed."

"Oh, good lord," he says, screwing up his face in an expression of deep pain. "You mean he's homeless? A *homeless* artist?"

"But, sir, might that not be quite interesting? I mean, wouldn't that provide a compelling angle for the work you represent? I don't know a great deal about marketing or public relations perspectives, but might it not be worth investigating? This particular piece is, after all, something he did quite quickly, with little resource. No studio, barely had the right equipment, scraped by with what little paints he had. But you must admit, there's a certain style about the piece. Perhaps not perfectly executed, but certainly interesting. Nicely composed. A nice use of the colors at his disposal. And, not too dissimilar from de Smet, Terry also uses natural media—a few bits of stray grass and tree seeds have affixed themselves within the drying paint, but that's perhaps to be expected, given his *plein aire* method of painting, no?"

"Franklin, I need to head into the gallery," he says, pulling off his reading glasses and stuffing them into his shirt pocket. "I like my artists to have a rich backstory, but that one's a bit too rich. There's no angle in a homeless artist other than the fact that he has no home, and he can get his hands on some paint every now and again. Anyway, the piece is quite crudely rendered. I thought so when I first saw it. My gut was right. I'll see you later." And with a flourish, he heads out the door and into the bright, warming sunlight.

# CHAPTER 22



One would normally chalk up the morning's drama as sufficient for one day, perhaps even for one week, but, as it turns out, there's more to be had.

"Shit," Wendy says upon her dispatch from the elevator. It's been a morning of uncharacteristic entrance and exit lines.

"Good morning, Wendy. Is everything okay?"

"No. It's a nightmare," she says. "I just got a call from the office. Today was the day we were supposed to have our focus group for the protein bars, the ones I was telling you about."

"The Gaux Bars," I say.

"*On* The Gaux Bars. Yes. Those. The 'On' part is kind of important. Anyway, I had arranged for the Appalachian Mountain Hiking Club of North Jersey to come in today for our session at twelve thirty."

"There are people in our midst who refer to themselves as the Appalachian Mountain Hiking Club of North Jersey?" I ask. I refuse to allow this nugget to slide by without a smidgen of investigation and, perhaps even, reflection.

"Yes. But let me finish. The AMHCNJ—"

"The A-M—yes, of course, go on."

"—were exactly our target audience. Middle-aged, active, spend a lot of time outdoors, healthy lifestyle, upper income bracket. We've been building up to this day for weeks. And now they can't make it in. They were supposed to be here in a few hours, for a lunchtime meeting. The client is going to flip."

"And why is it they're unable to make it? Too far a walk?"

"No! They got stuck in some storm in Colorado. Their flight couldn't take off."

"Colorado? Sounds like they were a bit off course."

"Franklin, you're not helping here. Turns out they travel all over North America hiking and climbing mountains—"

"The 'Appalachian' part of their name would seem to be a misnomer. Perhaps a carryover from a simpler and less adventurous chapter within their fabled history."

At this, Wendy sighs and looks out the front door. Perhaps I'm not hitting the right notes this morning. Encounters with coyotes have been known to throw a man off his game.

"Yeah, anyway, I thought they just did weekend hikes around New Jersey. It didn't even occur to me to check weekend weather forecasts in the Rockies when I invited them in. I have to figure this out." At this, Wendy turns to the coffee service and begins pouring herself a cup of coffee.

"Couldn't you postpone the session?" I offer up. It is a suggestion not terribly dissimilar from the rich vein of "Might a coat help, perhaps?" when someone has uttered the declaration of feeling cold.

"There's no chance. Our client has flown in senior management from their Milwaukee headquarters specifically for this focus group. They're just in for the day, they fly back later this afternoon. This is a really big deal for this company. God, I thought that getting the Appalachian Mountain Club was such a brilliant idea. They were guaranteeing ten people would be here—a perfect number for a focus group. Everyone loved it, including my boss who doesn't seem to like anything I suggest. They were dead center in our demographic."

"Who knew there'd be a chance that they were *too* active? Is there anything I can do to help you?"

"Very sweet of you, Franklin, but I'm not looking for you to solve this issue. This is just me venting, not asking for help. Besides," she says, turning toward the elevator, "you're good, but you're not that good."

"Well, should I happen to see a cluster of Tyrolers strolling by outside, and *if* they happen to have a free lunch hour on their hands, and *if* they indicate an inclination for focus group activities, where would you suggest I direct them?"

"Lot of ifs swirling around in that statement," she says, lingering at the elevator doors. "As resourceful as you are, I'm doubtful of your acquaintance with ten Tyrolers."

"Fine," I say, "I may not know Tyrolers—is it Tyrolians?—but you and I both know a reliable cohort of folks who spend a lot of time in the great outdoors. That is a key criterion for this exercise, yes?"

She looks at me for a moment, trying to get her arms around the direction of the conversation. She slowly comes back to my desk.

"Wait, what are you saying?"

"Yeah, kinda brilliant, isn't it? Outdoorsy, active. It might work with their lunch break."

"Are you suggesting . . . ? Franklin, who are we talking about?"

"Jimmy and crew," I say. "You know, the construction guys, who jump into catering emergencies at the drop of a hat and . . . hundreds of dollars' worth of encouragement. They'd be perfect for you. Certainly jumped into the fray in an admirable way last week, didn't they? Maybe during the noon whistle they could pop over—"

"Oh, Lordy, Franklin, for a moment there, when you were saying 'outdoorsy' and 'active,' I thought you were suggesting Terry and Tomata."

"No, no. I was talking about . . . well, wait. That's kind of a brilliant idea, too," I say.

"It wasn't an idea," she says. "That was me misunderstanding, not spitballing. I'm heading back upstairs."

"No, but, Wendy, think about it for a minute. I can't speak for Jimmy and crew; they may have a tight lunch break. But my guess is Terry and Tomata and some of their friends are available, which already places them ahead of the A-H-uh-E-T-C group. I think you're brilliant."

"The AMHCNJ. This makes no sense, Franklin."

"It makes perfect sense. You need outdoors people—check. You're looking for people who do a lot of walking, or, for the sake of today's activity, let's call it 'hiking'—check."

"Healthy lifestyle? Remember that aspect of the target demographic?"

"Okay, we're not going to check that box just yet, but let's not jump to assumptions."

"Today's focus group session is really more around aesthetics, anyway. We need to get their reactions to the look of the packaging more than anything else."

"Even better. They're artists!"

She pauses for a moment, drumming her fingers on my desktop. "Listen, don't worry about it. I really just came down to kvetch, grab a cup of coffee and say hi to you. Your presence was needed for all three. I've got to go make some calls," she says, heading back to the elevator.

"But, Wendy," I say, "if I am able to round up some folks, may I text you?"

"Listen, you can text me anytime you want," she says, getting onto the elevator. "I'd be stupid to say 'no.' At this point, a few hours out, all options need to be looked at."

Before entering the elevator, she tosses something, with a certain level of gusto, into the garbage can. After the doors shut, I walk to the receptacle to see what Wendy deposited. In the bottom of the can is a partially wrapped, half-eaten *On the Gaux* Bar.

◆   ◆   ◆

Recognizing that Wendy may not have fully appreciated my insouciant tone or was adequately grateful toward my unsolicited counsel, I leap into solution mode and attempt to replace her mislaid wanderers. Having discerned a measured degree of prioritization on her part, I head outside and walk down the block to see if Jimmy and his associates might not be able to lend a hand in this situation. After all, they had been quite helpful in untangling last week's traffic snarl and food delivery, albeit with the inducement of free lobster and beer. Let's see if they rise up to respond to bars of another type.

As I head toward our building's street construction entrance, I notice there is a certain aura, a certain essence that seems to be missing from the milieu this morning. Cabs are racing, cars are honking, planes are zooming, people are rushing. All seems to be in order with the city, but something . . . something is absent. And then it occurs to me.

No clanging, no hammering, no buzz-sawing, no . . . Jimmy and Co. in the Fitzger's space.

The sounds that I had grown accustomed to, to the point that it became only so much background noise, were missing.

The ways and schedules of the urban construction crew remain a mystery to me. For days on end, work will transpire at a dizzying, unabated, raucous pace, much to the annoyance of neighbors and pedestrians. And then, after days of nonstop noise, it mysteriously stops. The project is not completed; far from it—we are still clearly a work in progress. But the workers, as in this morning's instance, have disappeared. No clue as to where they have gone, nor when—or if— they will return. And so, what had been a chance of presenting itself as, yet again, a brilliant solution turned into only so much marsh gas. Gone, dissipated; much, perhaps, like my suit of white, shining armor.

And so I head back to our front doors, a little less jaunt in my step, a little less hitch in my ride, a measurable drop in my giddyap.

"What's got you down, man?"

"I'm sorry?" I say to a squirrel looking down upon me from a low-hanging branch on one of our street's lindens.

"No, not him Scrape," Tomata says, directly behind me. "But I understand your thinking it was him. I run into some talking squirrels on occasion in the park. The crows, though, they're the chattiest."

"Tomata!" I shout. "Just the person I wanted to see."

"I don't have that said to me too often in this neighborhood."

"Yes, well, there you go," I say. "By the way, first things first. I want to thank you for the tour the other day. Very edifying for both Wendy and me. Great fun, all around."

"No worries, happy to do it. Terry and I get a ton of inspiration every time we go in there. Our art's what keeps us going, keeps us moving forward."

Now to the matter at hand.

"Tomata, I'm wondering if you'd be willing to do a favor for me, uh, actually, for Wendy."

"What do you need, man?" he asks.

"And I insist on paying you for it. So let's get that out on the table right from the get-go."

He nods his head at this proclamation. Alright then, onward with our agenda.

"Would you and Terry be able to round up eight or so of your friends and join Wendy and me over on the other side of the park in a couple of hours? We'll need you to eat some protein bars."

"Some what now?" he asks.

"Protein bars?" I say, somewhat questioningly.

I interpreted his facial expression to be what could best be described as blank or, perhaps, empty. Vacuous also comes to mind.

"What the fu—oh, do you mean, like, space sticks?" A reference that is lost on me. I mirror the vacuous look.

"Um, maybe. I guess, in theory, they take up space, presumably within the stomach region. They're meant to take the edge off one's hunger. Popular in certain active circles, it seems. Anyway, Wendy's company is running some tests on the product this afternoon. You and your friends will have the opportunity to taste the article and then answer a few questions about the packaging, I think it is. Quite simple, really, as I understand it. And then, you're off. Shouldn't take more than an hour, probably less. Has the opportunity to be a very pleasant experience, for all involved. From the state of her demeanor this morning, I suspect Wendy'd be greatly relieved if you were able to do this."

"So, you're talking about a focus group? Okay, boss, my calendar's pretty flexible today. But I've got to round up a dozen friends, did you say?"

"Well, eight or nine, including you and Terry. Ten seems to be the prescribed number for these undertakings. Is that possible? Do you know where Terry is right now? He was here not long ago, dropping off a painting. Can you find him quickly and gather others? If so, I'll meet you at the same spot outside the Met that we met at on Saturday. We'll head from there to the marketing firm's offices, on West 72nd Street. We need to be there by twelve thirty, so let's plan on meeting at a quarter to noon. It's just after ten right now, which gives us less than a couple of hours. Will you have enough time?"

"Yeah, yeah. I'll have your guys for you. Can we look at this as freelance work? What did you say the gig pays?"

Ah, yes, the detailed portion of the pecuniary matter returns. Not being entirely sure what the going rate is for paying people to look at and eat crunchy granola molded into the shape of a petite brick, I offer up, "Well, let's say, thirty dollars an hour? Is that okay?"

"For the whole group? Thirty bucks?"

"No, each person. Would that cover your time sufficiently?"

The left half of Tomata's mouth curls into a smile, with the right half being slightly more coy and subtle. "Yeah, that should just about cover our time today, Scrape. I'm not sure any fellas I round up would believe that rate, though."

"Too high, then? Bring it down a bit, should I?"

"No, no, no," he's quick to say, "that's not what I was going after. Just a comment."

"Do you guys have an hourly minimum, or anything? Like, four hours?"

"Yeah, not really. I guess I wouldn't consider Wendy's space stick program to be union work or anything, but I'll check with the head of our operation."

Bit of a pause between us; a pregnant one, some might say. "Well, then, very good," I offer, hoping to reengage the momentum we had a moment ago, "perhaps you'll need to use your most persuasive skills upon your colleagues."

"Scrape," he says, "credibility ain't always on hand in my community. Money talks pretty convincingly, though."

"Aha. A 'sweetener in the pot,' is that what you're getting at?"

"Yeah, pretty much," he says. "It'd help."

"Yes, well, if you wave a bunch of twenties around, will that get their attention?" I ask, reaching into my pocket. The thought occurs to me, however, that if there is to be any exchange of money at this juncture, it would be best that it happen a few steps away from the front of our building, or, at the very least, away from Charlotte's oversight of the street.

"Yeah, Scrape, that'll get their attention," he says. "That should get their attention just fine."

"Very good then, Tomata," I say, handing him ten twenty-dollar bills. "Go get their attention."

"Jesus, you're like a fucking ATM. We'll see you at the Met, Scrape. I've got some guinea pigs to go round up for you." He turns, rushing toward the park.

"Oh, and Scrape," he adds, "our rate goes up a lot if they start pushing any tofu into our mugs. We go into double time for that gunk. Hah!" he laughs, walking off quickly.

# INTERREGNUM

> Good news! I've rounded up your focus group.
> J

Um, maybe yay.
Is it the construction crew?

> Terry, Tomata, etc.

Tell me you're kidding, Okay?
We were kinda kidding about
that earlier, weren't we?
Kidding, right? RIGHT?

> No, we've pretty much moved on to Plan B
> Or are we at Plan C? I've lost track.

No no no no no
That's me hyperventilating

> Do you have other options?

Still hyperventilating
Give me a sec

> It's 10:15, Wendy

You're under deadline.

Not helping

We can do this

Are you still there?

Yeah. I just came to.
What is the "etc." part of Terry and
Tomata? How many do you have?

I told him we needed 10

Who are the others?

Let's refer to them as associates

I might be hyperventilating again
PLEASE help them understand what the deal is
This is so important

All over it.

Okay . . . you get them here, I'll work on
the, um, proper positioning

Should be easy . . . I get people through
doors, you market.
Let's play to our strengths

Yes, let's play

# CHAPTER 23

Monday, 11:43 am

And so, upon informing Wendy that a focus group was, indeed, on its way and having negotiated with Charlotte to allow me to take an earlier and lengthier off-premises lunch, I head out for the Met to pick up the soon-to-be granola-eating focus groupers.

I recognize and acknowledge that this could end up being an irrefutable disaster, but I'll hold off on that line of thought for the time being. I also recognize that when I arrive at the Met, there may, in fact, be no one to meet me for the purposes of a marketing convening. It might only be Tomata and Terry waiting for me at the top of the stairs, Tomata having been unsuccessful in rounding up other compatriots. For that matter, it might be him, Terry, and twenty other park denizens who were attracted by the waving of the green. I'm just not sure what awaits me.

But then, as I wend my way past the 5th Avenue street vendors who are still in the midst of setting up their sidewalk stalls, I see them: Tomata, Terry, and their ensemble. I quickly eyeball the situation—one, two, three, etc. Ten. He's brought the exact number of people I had requested. Two emotions quickly wash over me; first, a wave of relief followed closely by an echo wave of guilt. Tomata had given me no reason to doubt him personally, but society had given me every reason to do so.

"Hey, Scraper, yo!" Terry shouts, waving. "We're up here, man. We're ready for our all-expense paid outing."

"Hello," I shout back. "Well done, Tomata and Terry, well done." At this, a portion of the gathering begins to laugh.

"He called him Tomata," says one of the men, chuckling. He is an older gentleman, with arched black eyebrows, a salt-and-pepper goatee, and an air of genteel theatricality radiating from him.

"Is that not correct?" I ask. "To call him Tomata?"

"Yes, sir, it is absolutely correct," he says. "Just sounds humorous coming from a man of your bearing. Akin to calling Clayton over there Squirrelbait, as certain members of our band are wont to do."

"Yeah, yeah," says Terry, taking charge. "Good enough, Cad-man. Happy to handle the introductions a little later. Let's move out, what d'ya say, Scrape?"

"Yes, kind sir, we are but travelers all. Deliver us, young ferryman," says the gentleman referred to as Cad-man.

"You know, Scrape, we're all God's creatures great and small, right? The colors of the rainbow so pretty in the sky, and all that shit?" Terry asks me, discreetly, as we start out. "Well, Cadillac over there is a little more colorful than the rest of us, okay? But he's totally harmless. In fact, he's probably harmless-er than the rest of us, too. Don't worry. He's a great artist. Used to design and paint theater sets. Worked on lots of Broadway shows. I think the pressure kinda got to him—thinks he's one of the actors, what with his cape and beret. Always reciting Shakespeare or some such shit. Least, we assume it's Shakespeare. If we don't understand what he's saying, we say, 'There goes Cadillac with his Shakespeare shit.'"

I lead our unit—eight men, two women—around the south end of the museum. I have exactly a half hour to deliver this lot. I recognize that if Charlotte were to catch wind of just how I'm spending this particular day's lunch hour, she would have a provocative point if she were to say I've gone so far outside of my written job purview that it was truly, once and for all, grounds for dismissal. But am I not, as the doorman, in a way, opening doors? Could it not be said that I am—quite effectively and expertly—seeing people from one realm to another, from one setting to the next? Am I not easing one's movement from the here-and-now to the there-and-after? And am

I not, appropriately, delivering upon a request that has been made by one of L'Hermitage's residents? Am I not solving three—no, no, *four*—distinct problems, thereby making this city and, by extension, L'Hermitage run just a little more efficiently? First, and perhaps most important in the eyes of Charlotte—helping resident Wendy solve a personal and professional problem; second, helping Wendy's small, boutique marketing firm maintain their slim footing among the giants of Madison Avenue; third, helping midwife into existence a fine— although, arguably, overpriced—snack product; and number four, feeding a segment of New York's population who would benefit from a pocket full of nutritional products.

Yes. But to that first point, helping Wendy, I suppose if I were to be honest with myself, that is ultimately what this exploit is all about. Wendy.

We come to a juncture in our odyssey. We, as a group and a single unit, must expeditiously circumnavigate The Lake without losing a single one of our cohort.

"Where the fuck are you guys going?" asks a woman amongst us with bushy red hair, a grey sweatshirt, and a seeming inclination to lead through volume and jackhammer-paced articulation. "If we're going to 72nd, the quickest route is to go this way."

"No, Suze, it's faster this way. Trust me." This from a dark-haired fellow. The posse seems to be dividing up—half of us appear to be following him, the other half clustering around Suze, with Terry and Tomata standing judiciously in between the two groups.

"You moron, what are you talking about?" Suze shouts, but with a laugh thrown in to soften the blow. "You haven't a clue about this park, Johnny. You're going to get lost going around that way. The trails are all messed up on that side. That's why it's called the Ramble, dumbshit." Again, a punctuating cackle.

"You go your way, Suze; we'll go my way."

"Okay, okay, wait a minute, folks," I say, sensing a bit of an unraveling occurring.

"What *won't* work well is if I lose half of you as we're trying to get to 72nd Street."

"Well, I ain't going that way," Suze says.

"I sure as shit ain't going her way, the long way," Johnny says. "This gig might be paying well, but it's paying me to look at wrappers and eat, not to take a hike."

"Yes, well, about that 'taking a hike' part, now might be a good time to—" I say.

Terry jumps in, "C'mon guys, pull it together, Jesus Christ! We spend our whole fucking day—sorry, Scrape—our whole fucking day walking around this city. At best, one of you is right by no more than five minutes. Come on, Johnny, let's just go Suze's way and get over there."

"Forget it, Terry. You're just siding with Suze 'cause she's your squeeze. I'm going this way."

"I'm not his fucking squeeze, Johnny, ya asshole. Christ, who talks like that? I told you before to knock that shit off," she says.

The dissention among the ranks is growing. My focus group is rapidly losing both focus and grouping, two key qualities of the forthcoming exercise. Suze's and Johnny's set-to has taken five minutes off the clock. Had we simply taken either of the routes, we'd be halfway to 72nd by now.

"I have a compromise," I say, eyeing the nearby idle row boats and their two lounging keepers, both of whom appear to be enjoying our sideshow. "Let's all stay together and take the boats across. That's probably the fastest way, anyway. And, that way, no one need be concerned about which way is the longer or shorter walk. We can all sit comfortably."

"Fine, but I'm not paying for that," Johnny says. "Especially since I know my route is the shortest." Disagreeable character, this Johnny. I must remember to warn Wendy that his On the Gaux Bar survey and accompanying critique may skew unnecessarily negative.

"Well, I know *something* of yours is the shortest, Johnny, but it ain't that route!"

Suze spits out a gravelly laugh directly behind.

"Who here is the chief gondolier?" I ask the man at the rental booth. "The gondoli-est, as it were, hmm?" With my repartee seemingly lost on both audiences—the Terry-Tomata Gang, as well as our seaman—I leap straightaway into the necessary act of negotiation.

"Well, to begin with, these aren't gondolas," one of the keepers informs me. "They're just row boats. You row 'em on your own. We're not gondolians, or whatever you just said."

Following our brief discussion, it is determined that three boats will be needed for our voyage across the waterway. An appropriate number of twenty-dollar bills pass between the captain and me.

"Damn, Scrape," Terry says under his breath to me. "I've never seen a dude spit out so many of those bills. You don't, like, deal on the side do you? 'Cause that would surprise me a little."

"That does appear to be a growing perception of my actions," I say. "Perhaps I should be more careful."

"Yeah, well, you got a damn fine expense account for a doorman. How do I get me one of those jobs?"

"Depending on how this all plays out, L'Hermitage may be hiring."

# CHAPTER 24

Monday, 12:09 pm

The assigning of boat buddies, the clambering into row boats, and the eventual sailaway eat up another sizable portion of our remaining time, to the point that I am becoming outwardly agitated. Being in the lead boat—the Santa Maria of our flotilla—I choose to seize the opportunity to exhort the rest of our naval force.

"Put your backs into it, men. Posthaste. This is no leisurely outing. The goal is within reach!" And other positive, inspirational messages and directives, to little effect.

"Oh, captain, my captain, shut the fuck up," Johnny says, in his own exhortative manner, from boat number three.

"Uh, Mister Terry," I say, taking my seat at the front of our boat, with Terry sitting directly behind me. "This Johnny fellow. Is he on board, so to speak, with the spirit of this adventure? I mean, he seems slightly rougher around the edges than our marketing friends may be comfortable with. Any way to ask him—in a manner that is persuasive, if you know what I mean—to tone it down a notch?"

"What . . . Johnny?" Terry asks. "Aw, he's harmless. Don't you worry about him. All bark, no bite. I don't even notice him anymore."

"Yes, well, I'm not entirely convinced he'll achieve the same level of invisibility with the marketers and the clients with whom we're about to engage. Anything you might say to him in the next five minutes—or even four—would be greatly appreciated by me."

"Yeah, yeah, got it man. No problem." And then a shout across the waters, "Hey, Johnny, shut your fucking trap. The only time we want you to open your maw is when you're shoving one of these damn cookies into it, okay? You got that?"

"Okay, fine. Yeah, don't get all hyped up," Johnny says, saluting Terry.

I look over at Terry, who is displaying just a slight indication of smugness. "Quite the alpha male, Mister Terry. That seemed to adequately rectify the situation. Most impressive."

"That's me. Your little alphabet man."

We land on the opposite shore with ten minutes to spare. The disembarking exercise isn't totally uneventful, what with three of our passengers stepping into the muddy waters up to their ankles prior to fully arriving upon dry land, Suze being one of them.

"Goddammit," she sputters. "This water's cold. Now what am I going to change into?"

"What, Suze, you didn't bring a change of wardrobe with you?" This from Tomata, who follows it up with his ashtray-laden laugh.

"Okay, folks, we're just a block or so away. Let's continue on, please," I say, attempting to keep a fragment of focus among the troops. "If anyone's hungry, just remember, buckets of Gaux Bars await us at our final destination."

"And fifty bucks, right?" Johnny asks, with a few others murmuring their support of this line of questioning.

I look over at Tomata. "Sorry, boss, the rate had to go up a bit," he says with a shrug. "I was getting some pushback, for some reason. You did give me the leeway to negotiate, right? Because I got to have leeway to negotiate."

"Yes, of course," I say to him. "And, yes, Johnny, you will certainly get fifty dollars for today's efforts. All the others will be paid in Gaux Bars." I allow a comedic pause, waiting for Vesuvius to erupt, but before it can, I say, "No, no. My idea of a joke. I trust you all found it amusing. Let's keep going, shall we?"

"May I ask you a question, young man?" Cadillac asks me as we emerge from the park. "Do the people at the end of our journey know our circumstances? I mean, *I* know we're heading to a marketing firm, but my question is this: does our audience know what's about to transpire? Has the stage been appropriately set?"

Cadillac's question makes me realize that prep work is required on both ends. I have assumed that Wendy is taking care of the necessary details at the 72nd Street headquarters, but it dawns on me that I have left much of the prefatory legwork to Tomata during his earlier rounding-up exercise. His emphasis may have been more on payment schedules rather than end goals, tasks to be accomplished, et cetera.

"Hmm, yes, you bring up a good point. Perhaps we've reached the moment in which I supply a few more details to our expedition. Everyone, can I have a moment of your attention?"

The troop gathers around me. I do a cursory accounting to make sure none have gotten lost between the lake and the street. All good. A pair of elderly strollers not associated with our outing join us as well, expecting, one presumes, an edifying dissertation on nearby birds and trees of Central Park.

"I'm sorry," I say to them, "but this is a closed-door meeting."

Apparently, my announcement was too subtle for my intended outcome, as they continue to stare at me, expectantly, in a gawping manner.

"Hey, Gramps, beat it," Suze slings out. "And take the old broad with you, too."

This one hit home and the two shuffle off. "Have a nice day," I offer up, hoping to soften their departure.

"Now then, may I go over a few ground rules? The thirty-dollar stipend covers the following—"

"Fifty dollars," Johnny reminds me.

"Yes, yes, of course. The *fifty*-dollar stipend covers the following: We will go into the marketing agency momentarily. As Tomata, I believe, has told you, you will be a focus group for an item called the *On the Gaux* Bar. It falls under the industry category of nutritious snack bars. As I understand the exercise, you will not be commenting so much on the taste of the item—although you are certainly welcome to knock back a few—as you will be on the look, the packaging of the item. The curb appeal, so to speak. Oh, and one more thing, you might be presented to those gathered as an outdoors club. A hiking club, if you will. I would ask that you simply play along with that part of the event."

"An acting role?" Cadillac verifies.

"Of sorts, yes. I suppose you might look at it in that light."

"Will this be an equity job, then? Will you require proof of my union card?" he asks, reaching into one of his pockets.

"Let's consider this a nonequity position. But if you'd like to list it on your CV, I would be happy to vouch for you."

"I see. And what is my motivation within this part?"

"The easiest fifty bucks you'll ever earn, asshole. Now shut up," Johnny says.

With Johnny bringing down the curtain on my scene-setting preamble, we continue our journey.

"It might merit mentioning, young man," Cadillac says, joining me at my side, "that Terry and Tomata have assembled an unusual group here. Although I tend to introduce myself as a thespian these days, I am also a trained artist, as are all the others, practicing within various mediums. It is through the art world that we know each other."

"I knew Terry and Tomata were artists, and I had heard you designed sets. But everyone here is an artist?"

"Verily. That's how we met; that's our connection. A shelter on 1st Avenue offers space for art classes. It's a hangout. We've all been professionally trained. Another point of connection, beyond the art, is that we've all had some muckish luck. Everyone's story is different; it's just that we've ended up in the same place. We don't see ourselves as scary homeless people. We *know* the scary ones; we stay away from them just like you do. But I'll tell you what—you put a three-piece suit on Johnny over there, give him a haircut and a shave, and everybody'd look at him as a leader. A man of action. But in that outfit, with that hair and beard, he's scary to you—"

"He's not scary to me. A little overly assertive, perhaps—"

"I don't mean scary to *you* you. I mean the collective you. You who have your own doors to lock at night, roofs over and pillows under your heads. Like so many others, Johnny has been dealt a rough hand and because of that, he has a chip on his shoulder. It's because of the judgments that people cast upon us. You know, I get it—people's prejudices against those of us who happen to be a little down on our luck at this very minute—or decade. They're probably thinking, *There they go—too much alcohol, too many drugs, too many demons*, when, in fact, they should actually be thinking, there but for the grace of god."

◆　◆　◆

At last, we arrive at Wendy's place of business. It's a narrow townhome that has been taken over by BergManPR, a firm established in the mid-'90s, a time in our nation's storied development in which spaces within company names were deemed outmoded and, potentially, wasteful, and letters in the middle of words became syllabically capitalized.

We enter the front doors and gather, haphazardly, around the reception desk.

"What is—? I'm sorry, what's going on here?" the receptionist asks, standing up from her desk, not quite as friendly—as *receptive*—as one may have hoped for, especially taking into account our grueling land and water travels during the past thirty minutes. The sign on her desk says, *Ashley Emerson, Director of First Impressions*. So far, both sides seem to be failing in that department.

"We've just taken our morning jog in Central Park, and we're famished for something in the form of an energy bar. We thought your establishment might be able to help us." Yet again, my elevated style of wry humor this morning has flown high above its intended mark.

"I'm sorry. Are you a part of the . . . are you here for the market testing?" A question asked of me, but with her eyes scouring the full team.

"Yes, we—" Before I can finish, Wendy is upon us, descending a nearby staircase.

"It's okay, Ashley, I've got it," she says. "Franklin, can I see you for a moment?"

We walk to a corner of the reception area while the others congregate around Ashley's desk, apparently to her consternation.

"Shit, shit, shit," Wendy says. "I haven't been able to clue Candice in as to what's going on. She's been in meetings all morning. She hates surprises. She knows the AMHCNJ is not—"

"So impressive with your command of acronyms. I have trouble after the A-M part. I suspect you'd be very good at crosswords were you to give it a—"

"Franklin! She knows the AMHCNJ is not coming in, but I've not yet told her the solution—if that's what we're calling it. Alright, let's go up, but just go with the flow."

"That pretty much sums up my life motto. Alright, troop, up we go. Company—move."

Wendy leads us up the carpeted stairs to a large conference room overlooking 72nd Street. There are seven people in the room: three standing at the far end of a cherry conference table; three seated in chairs along the windowed wall, intently staring at their cell phones; and one conducting a reconnaissance mission of the supplied refreshments.

"Ah, our hikers," says a man with a prominent chin thrust conspicuously in our direction. "Welcome, welcome. Make yourselves comfortable. Everyone, take a seat." Although Chin has an encouraging smile firmly affixed to his face, the woman he had been talking to upon our entrance has a slightly different expression upon her own, one indicating either displeasure or a disagreeable encounter with a midday lemon drop.

"Wendy, are these our focus group members?" Lemon Drop asks.

"Yes. These are our focus group members. Yes, they are," Wendy says, taking a hand, firm or otherwise, to the current situation. "You see, Candice, as I think I may have said earlier, the Appalachian Mountain Hiking Club of North Jersey is stuck out West due to flight delays, so they're unable to be with us today. We have, however, found a group who will be a very good fill-in until the time we're able to bring the Mountain Club to us. We'll shift things around and make the Mountain Club our final focus group at a later date. I didn't want to have to cancel this opportunity, since Harold and others had flown in from Milwaukee specifically for *this* focus group. So, on short notice, we've been able to round up the, uh, the—"

Gently shaken from my reverie upon the amount of focusing those associated with boutique marketing firms must do within the course of any given workday, I leap to Wendy's aid. "The Urban Hiking and Camping Club. And Painting," I offer, helpfully. "The U-H . . . C . . . C. And P. Club. No, wait, that makes too many Cs. The U-H- . . . let's see, the U-H—"

"The UHC-and-P Club," Wendy blurts out.

"What is she calling us?" Suze mutters. "You see and pee?"

"Very well branded," Candice says. "I can't help but wonder who their fortunate agency was—"

"I kinda like the Agency for Community Programs over on 40th," Johnny says.

"Oh, they're very good," Cadillac chimes in.

"Psss, shut your traps," Tomata says. "That's not what she's talking about."

"I'm sorry, but I think that under the circumstances . . ." Candice looks disapprovingly at our gathered troop, all the while letting her unstated conclusion waft about the room for a moment or two before seeing upon which perch it might land. Some members of our assembled band had begun taking their seats, while others simply stood to the side, waiting to see how the drama would play out.

"This isn't our hiking club? The one we were expecting?" Harold asks.

"Well, it isn't *our* hiking club, but it is *a* hiking club," Wendy says, rising more fittingly toward the spirit of the moment.

"No," Candice says, "This is *not* our hiking club. Harold, we'll need to reschedule. I'm sorry for this unfortunate calendar snafu with the Appalachian Hiking Club. Flight delays are unavoidable, however. I'm sure you understand."

"Well, I think I heard the words 'hiking' and 'camping' in this club's title, Candice," Harold says. "Why would we not use this group? They may not be the club we were expecting, but I certainly wasn't attached to the Appalachian group. I mean, my team and I have flown in for this session and, it would appear Wendy has pulled together a group of people. What's the Broadway phrase, 'On with the show'?"

"Yes, exactly. That's the spirit—on with the show!" says Cadillac.

"Harold," Candice says in a manner that some might interpret as dismissive, "I admire your chi, but—"

"Did you say my—"

"But I don't think this would be a good use of your time. We've helped you establish a very specific target market. Yes, we could pull in a dozen people anytime you want. We could pull in some copywriters and a couple of interns from our own office here. But the value of a focus group is to test a product with your key demographic. I . . . we don't have that right now. You don't just slap a bunch of people into chairs and say, 'What do you think?' and pretend that you'll come up with worthwhile results. I'm sorry, but it just doesn't work that way. Not here. Not in New York."

"Well, that sucks," Suze says. "Cuz I've lived in New York, like, all my life. I'm overflowing with opinions. I'm a virtual fountain of opinions for you, Hal. Hell, I've even worked up some fresh opinions about ole Candice here, newly formed."

"Suze," Terry says, attempting to still the storm.

"Well, she's right, Terry," Johnny says. "What's wrong with us, lady? You think we can't tell you whether your little bars taste good or look pretty?"

"It's not that. Please, don't get me wrong," Candice says. "We know the bars taste good. But we had very specifically planned on their packaging being tested on a narrow demographic and market segment. This is aimed explicitly at active outdoor lovers."

"Ain't nobody more outdoorsy and lovey-dovey than this group, lady," Johnny says. "That I can promise you. And by the way, since I have the floor, let me ask you something. Who do you think actually buys this crap?"

"It's not *crap*, and as I said earlier—"

"What you said is that active outdoors folks will buy them. And that's where you're wrong right off the bat. It's people who like to *see* themselves as being active outdoor folks. Here, hand me one of those things. Your actual market is folks who sit on their lard asses all day long in tombs like this one and think they're being active by moving their jaws around these five-hundred-calorie bars—"

"Johnny," Terry says.

"Thank you for that assessment. So very rich in detail," Candice says. "Everyone, please take a couple of bars with you. Enjoy them. They're wonderful. But we're not having a focus group today. Harold, our afternoon is better spent nailing down the timeline and reviewing the launch budget before you fly out."

"Yeah, well," Suze says, getting up to leave with the others who have started for the door, "I wish you had spent your time this morning going over the *lunch* budget a little more carefully, 'cause right now it's my lunch break, and these stupid little bars of yours ain't going to cut it. Plus, I fell out of a goddamn boat and got my shoes wet for this adventure."

"If I may intercede for a moment," I offer up, hoping to bring the level of discourse down just a notch among our gathered trekkers, "as you may be aware, the originally scheduled group has been delayed by travel problems. I have brought this group—"

"Wait, who . . . who are you?" Candice asks.

"I'm sorry, ma'am. My name is Franklin Hanratty and I'm—"

"Are you, like, what? A doorman?" Candice asks, eyeing my outfit.

"Yes, but only during the daytime. As I was saying, I'm the one responsible for delivering this group of outdoor enthusiasts and visual artists—"

"Oh, artists," Harold enthuses. "*Visual* artists. That's very good. That's very good, indeed."

"Yes," Wendy says, jumping in upon seeing that this particular categorization has brought a new light, at least, in Harold's mind, to our proceedings. "New York City plein-air artists, healthy-eaters"—a couple of snorts can be heard with this particular aggrandizement—"and lovers of the great outdoors."

"Well, then, Wendy," Harold says, "We're certainly interested in gaining the perspective of artists, especially if we're looking specifically at packaging in this session. Plus, you said they're members of the, uh, what was it? The Outdoor Hiking Club?"

"Yeah, I think we're calling ourselves the Urban Hiking and Painting Club or something," Suze says. "Whatever. It's very exclusive. Low entry fees, though. Careful, Candy. You might just become our next honorary member, if this meeting is any indication of what goes on here."

"Okay, then, we're good here," Candice says. "I think we've tapped out on this particular game. Wendy, please, show your guests to the front door."

"Yeah, good, we'll leave. Anyway, your bars aren't going to sell worth shit." This lob from Johnny, who makes a dismissive hand gesture over the array of bars.

"Thank you, all," Candice says. "Wendy? The door, please?"

"Wait, Candice," Harold says, "I would like to hear more. Why do you say that, that the bars won't sell?"

Johnny snorts. "I know these things are good for taking care of hunger. I know the different brands—Clif Bars, PowerBars, Balance, Tiger's Milk, even Luna, all that shit. And I'm here to tell you, your box of bars is going to remain untouched on the shelves while people buy the other ones."

"Wendy? Door?" Candice says, indicating that the meeting is over.

"No, wait, Candice," Harold says, "I want to hear why he says that."

"It's because your packaging is ugly as hell," Suze says. "I'm not sure what Johnny's thinking, but I'm thinking that's some god-awful packaging."

"That's exactly what I was thinking. Who's the color-blind graphics dude, Candice?" Johnny asks, pronouncing Candice's name dangerously close to candy-ass.

"That's ridiculous," Candice says. "Those colors are highly contemporary. They are the look of today. They will play perfectly to our target demographic. Harold, *please*, let's—"

"We're not saying they're not nice colors," Johnny says. "They might be fantastic colors for a clothes dryer or a box of Kleenex, but unless your target demographic is something other than a human, ain't nobody going to buy a food item wrapped like that."

With this proclamation, those gathered around the table lean in for a closer inspection of the displayed bars, including me. Even Candice feels it necessary to take a more detailed look at the Johnny-maligned *On the Gaux* Bar packaging.

"Go on with what you're saying," Harold says.

"Tomata, why don't you jump in here. You gotta have some thoughts on this," Johnny says.

"Oh, yeah, I got some thoughts," Tomata says. "Maybe I oughta introduce myself first. I'm a painter—of canvases, buildings, murals, that kind of stuff. Same with Johnny. And Terry over there, too. Anyway, we've painted a lot of restaurant interiors in our days, so we know our colors. Black and blue packaging for something to eat? Whee-ew. That's going to kill you folks in sales—"

"Of course it will *not* kill us in sales; that's exactly what it will NOT do," Candice says, a few of her well-sculpted hairs now falling slightly akimbo over her narrow-eyed countenance. Her face, over the last few moments, has approached the look of celebrities captured during unflattering moments and plastered on the covers of cash-register tabloids. "That Faded Denim Blue is wildly, enormously contemporary. It's one of the hottest colors on rising designers' palettes. We selected it for its freshness, and for the very fact that it would stand out from the competitors—"

"Please, Candice," Harold says. "I'm interested in what the artists are saying. You've brought me some artists; let's let them finish. Please, go on, Tom—uh, is it Tomato?"

Candice lets out what I would typify as an irritated growl as Tomata continues. "Yes, sir, thank you. It's a beautiful color, ma'am. No doubt about it. But it's just not a beautiful *food* color; that's a whole 'nother pot to boil in. You'd never see that color anywhere near a restaurant. That color's what we'd call an appetite killer. No one's going to buy that bar, and most people won't even know why they're avoiding it and picking up the bar next to it instead. You may have tested the color, and everybody liked it, but I'm guessing you didn't test it in connection with food."

"But it's got to stand out against the competition," Candice says, rising to the debate. "That's how you gain first-time sales. The bars have a very distinct taste and flavor, and the packaging appropriately calls attention to—why am I even having to justify this?" she says, looking at the staff members behind her, but not at Harold.

"You'd do better with a bunch of natural colors, that is, colors you actually find in nature," Terry jumps in. "It's the old saying, ma'am. There ain't no blue food. The competitors' bars use browns, greens, and a little bit of red for a reason. We react to those colors. They make us hungry. You go into any self-respecting restaurant, and those are the colors you'll see. That's for a reason. These are time-tested findings. Anyway, that's just what I'm thinking."

"Hmm, yes," Harold says, looking obliquely at Candice. "I see what you mean."

"Your images are wrong, too," says a young woman heretofore unheard from within our slate of speakers.

"Whoa, Emily, way to lay it out there, baby-cakes," Suze says, laughing. "She speaketh."

Emily has been with us since the beginning of our adventure, but one would barely know it. This is the first utterance that she has emitted, hiding, for the most part, behind her black bangs and beneath her red hoodie.

"Go on, honey. What are you thinking?" Suze says.

"It's just that the image of the athlete is backward," Emily says. "He should be facing to the right, not the left. Images facing to the right are positive. And the mountain that he's looking at. You might want to make it snow-capped, white. White means hope. Optimism. Anyway, that's what we were taught in design school."

"Well there you go," Suze says, slapping her hand on the table. "That's our graphic artist right there—you tell him, Emily. I knew she didn't drop out of SVA for nothing. Get yourself some damn snow in that picture, lady. Hah!"

"Yes, yes," Harold says. "That makes sense to me. You know, I always felt there was something missing with that mountain image. It was too plain."

"Oh, my god," Candice says, easing herself into one of the chairs at the table. "Harold, we've gone over these images dozens of times these last two months. We're set to launch this fall. If we open up our discussions on the packaging again, we're going to be totally off our timeline. We're tight as it is."

"Yes, but Candice, wasn't that exactly why we were gathered here today? I'm not going to market with, with . . . *unappetizing* colors and, and . . . *unhopeful* images. Besides, this was intended to be a focus group, not a rubber stamp group. Was there not a possibility that we might need to make some alterations coming out of our discussions? We're depending upon BergMan for proper guidance in these issues."

"And well you should," Candice says. "Our staff of graphic designers are the best in the market."—Snort. This, I believe, came from Johnny. Possibly Cadillac. I'm mildly confident it wasn't me—"I greatly appreciate the opinions we've just heard, but what you have here is cutting-edge. We're making this brand and product as distinctive within the marketplace as possible. I'm sorry, can we continue this discussion in my office, Harold? We needn't detain these folks any longer. Wendy, see them out, please. Thank you all for coming. Please take a couple of bars with you as you leave the premises. I mean, as you depart."

Being summarily dismissed for, at latest count, the eighth time, Wendy leads us out of the conference room. We go down the stairs quietly, with a few occasional grumbles and gripes to be heard among our number.

"Wendy, I'm sorry if this has caused you problems," I say.

"If it has, I'm sure I'll find out soon enough," she says. "This is her agency and Candice needs to be in control at all times. Clearly, for the last twenty minutes, she wasn't. Anyway, I appreciate your getting them over here; it was worth a shot."

My entourage and I head outside, a tad bit less ebullient than when we arrived on our mission.

"Well, that just kind of sucked," Suze says, summing up the situation in a tight and succinct manner. "I always knew I hated marketing. Turns out it was because of the marketers."

After I pay each of them the agreed-upon rate, they go off in their various directions. Most of the crew head back toward the park; a few move in the direction of Columbus Avenue. I throw a concoction of apologetic and appreciative comments their way, but they all fall somewhat flatly on the concrete between us. Terry and Tomata, however, do their best to bolster me up.

"Hey, man, forget about her," Terry says. "Every fruit bowl needs a prune."

"Yes, well, I feel bad for all of you. A bit awkward back there. And do all bowls of fruit really need prunes?"

"Nah. Just came up with it. Don't inspect it too closely. Anyway, we'll catch you in the 'hood, Scrape," Terry says. "We gotta go see if Zabar's is carrying this swell new product yet. What's it called again,

Tomata? Oh, oh, yeah . . . *Gaux Bars!*"

"On . . . the . . ." I begin but decide to let it drop.

Tomata lets out a large whoop. "Yeah, *Gaux Bars. Gaux Bars* at Zabar's. Them ain't the kind of bars I feel like visiting right now, though. Later, Scrape. As the man once said, it's been a little slice of heaven; thanks for another terriff outing!" The two head off toward Columbus Avenue, following the others who have headed in that direction. I hail a cab on Central Park West to take me back to L'Hermitage.

"Wait a minute, man. What are *you* doing getting in?" the cabbie asks me, as I open the door and settle myself into the back seat. "I'm used to doormen flagging me down, but they've never gotten into the cab themselves!"

"Yes, well," I say. "I'm just chock-full of surprises today. Take me to the other side of the park, please. And here, enjoy a Gaux Bar. Don't look at the wrapping, though."

# CHAPTER 25

Monday, 4:12 pm

The afternoon is full of typical odd jobs that don't require much heavy lifting on my part, and for this, I'm grateful. The drama and angst of the noon hour, the absolute *sturming und dranging* that accompanied my adventures beyond the outer reaches of L'Hermitage left me somewhat spent. And so it is with relief that Mrs. Hill requests a dinner be ordered up for her from Roxie's, that Mr. Cooper requests a plunger be brought up to his apartment, that Mrs. McAdoo pops down to go over next month's catering schedule, that Mr. Harrison visits the desk to show me his latest charcoal creation, and that Charlotte petulantly ignores me.

At around a quarter after four, Wendy enters from the street burdened with a large box, seemingly full of an assortment of knickknack items.

"Hello," I say sheepishly, but with an attempt at displaying a certain level of derring-do, hoping to place the earlier events of the afternoon sufficiently behind us. "I'm sorry about the meeting . . ."

"Yeah, well, I guess these things happen," she says. "Easy come, easy go, right? Or maybe I should say, easy come, easy gaux bars. Fuck it, I just got canned."

"Aw, Jesus," I belch out, loud enough to precipitate a quick gander from Charlotte as she clickety-clacks from the mailroom to her office.

"Did we cause that?" I ask, doing my best to avoid the first-person pronoun, opting for the safety and sanctuary of the first-person plural.

"No, not really," she says, setting her box on my counter. "Candice has had it in for me the last couple of months and for her, today was just a final straw. She said I jeopardized a very important account and that I would have to go."

"Jeopardize?" I say. "I thought you saved it. In fact, I thought Terry and his friends were a pretty good solution for the other focus group—"

"They were, Franklin. The problem wasn't so much them. Candice was embarrassed in front of Harold and the others. She felt I had deceived her all along, that I hadn't told her the full truth about who I was bringing in. That's something she can't tolerate. Fact is, Terry and Tomata and the others were actually making really good points. If Candice hadn't backed herself into a corner by immediately dismissing them, and had she allowed the session to take place, everything would've been fine. Harold thought it was a very productive session. Anyway, onward. I'll be okay."

Of course, she will be fine. The thing about Wendy's situation— being well-educated, wealthy and presumably well-connected—is that small setbacks like this don't cause the same ripples they do with others who live on more tentative ground, those who are one check away from a missed rent payment. Having a large checkbook allows for quick bounce-backs. It's the Terrys and Tomatas of the world who have trouble rebounding, not the Wendys.

"You know, I think I'm going to need a drink and if there's one thing I hate, it's drinking alone. Do you have any interest in joining me? I mean, after your shift ends?" she asks.

After a momentary hesitation, I say, "I'd love to. And given the fact that I may have aided, not to mention abetted, in your situation, I insist on picking up rounds one through, oh, let's say, three?"

"I'm not in the mood to go out. I've got a cabinet full of pretty bottles upstairs. Just come to 8D."

◆　◆　◆

"Why the hay-hoo you rushing off so fast tonight, son?" Jacob asks, fifteen seconds after he arrives at the front desk for his shift and five seconds after I've wished him a good night.

"I have plans, Jacob," I say, heading toward the elevator bank.

"Oh, you have *pla-anns*. Well, what kind of *pla-anns* do you have? Hey! Wait a minute! Get back here. I'm talking to you," Jacob shouts, leaning over the counter as I get on the elevator. "What the hell you doing getting on the 'vator? Do you got *pla-anns* upstairs? Damn, Franklin, you one helluva player, I always said that you—" Although the doors have shut, it's a good half-floor up before the elevator's creaking machinations have fully drowned out Jacob's warm-up act.

When the doors open up on eight, all is silent. I tread softly down the hall to 8D and, as I'm about to knock on the door, I hear a small, quiet—but loud enough that I can hardly ignore—voice say, "Oh, Franklin, you startled me. I'm not used to seeing you up here on our floor. Unless, of course, I've requested you."

"No, I suppose not, Mrs. Hill," I say. "Well, you have a nice evening, then."

"Yes, okay."

We're at a bit of a standoff at this point. I will knock, discreetly, upon Wendy's door once Mrs. Hill shuts her own door. But, of course, all actions depend upon Mrs. Hill actually shutting said door. Which she doesn't do.

"Were you coming to bring me something, Franklin?"

"No, ma'am."

"Hmm." Pause. "What, then?"

"Ma'am?"

"What are you doing up here, then?"

A hand prop would have been good—would have been *handy*—I now realize. Something which would have forced the action, as they're wont to say in the theater world, could have acted as the reason for my nocturnal visit to Floor Eight at the end of my shift. But I am caught not red-, but empty-handed, so to speak.

"I . . . have to relay a message to Wendy."

"Oh, how nice of you to do so in person," she says, "when a phone call would have done the same. Always going above and beyond, Franklin. That's what we like about you." At this, she shuts the door. Whether her last comment was sincere or sardonic is uncertain.

◆　◆　◆

Upon entering Wendy's domain, I describe to her my brief interaction with Mrs. Hill.

"Oh, yeah," Wendy says. "She's all over the comings and goings of this floor. Keeps close track of all of us. Very pleasant to me, but quick to tell me about the activities of our floormates. She says that she's been asked by the building's owner, Mr. Franken, to keep an eye on matters. Kind of a hall-monitor type of arrangement, she says."

"An arrangement between her and Mr. Franken, eh?" I say, more to myself than to Wendy, but she responds, "Yeah, so what's up with that guy? Never see him. People say he owns half of New York."

"No, no," I say, perhaps a bit too quickly. "He's not that wealthy. Nowhere near. That's ridiculous. Why would they think that?"

"Oh, do you know him well?" she asks.

"No, not well. But I can't possibly imagine him being that wealthy."

"Too bad," she says. "I'd love to meet him someday. Very mysterious, owning buildings and such things, but never seeing him. You work for him—tell me what he's like."

"Oh, he's . . . I don't know. Kind of tall, I suppose. Pretty quiet, I guess you could say. Well-intentioned, let's put it that way. He means . . . well. Big reader, too."

Wanting to move on from this particular topic, I move around the apartment, eyeing the surroundings. To a certain extent, I felt as if I had entered either a movie set or a designer showroom. The walls and shelving are a stark white, with a dark wood flooring. Area rugs are scattered about, along with low-slung, cushy furniture defining room sections. Low black tables contain designer books and magazines. Although all furniture and floor dressings are in shades of either black or white, there are splashes of color obtained through large pillows and throw blankets. A designer might describe it as ultrachic. Wendy has been doing well with her entry-level marketing position. Trust fund babies—as I say; I can spot them a mile away, or even close up in their apartments.

"I hope you didn't think it odd that I invited you up here this evening, Franklin. I just didn't want to be, you know, alone right now. I've enjoyed getting to know you better and, quite honestly, I don't know that many people outside of work yet. And I certainly wasn't in the mood to be with anyone from . . . from . . . Berg—"

At this, she ambushes me with a rock-solid, grade-A bear hug. Not being entirely certain what to say, I simply hug her back. Not so much in a doorman kind of way as in a good friend kind of way. The doorman arms would have embraced her, briefly, in the shoulder area; the good friend arms give her a lower back type of embrace. Quite charming and cozy, really. The right hand breaks rank first and begins exploring in an adventurous and independent manner, moving up and stroking her hair.

"I'm sorry, Franklin," she says, coming up for air but not exactly extricating herself from my friendly, nondoormanesque embrace. "I'm probably the last thing you need to deal with right now, a slightly on-edge resident who's just been canned. It's just that I wasn't seeing this day end the way it has."

Nor had I, for that matter. "Well, I do like to regard myself as a full-service type of doorman," I say, and at this, she lets out a generous laugh. The thus-far amicable comforting I'm giving her veers into more of a, well, what one can only describe as a canoodling type of activity, with lips pressing against flesh, hers in the general vicinity of my cheek, mine in the neighborhood of her soft eyes and battering eyelashes. All quite tender but, nonetheless, still harmless and fully innocent, if not mildly flirtatious.

Certainly, no inappropriate boundaries have been breached.

Until they are. Our lips, which had seemingly felt quite at home in the previously described outer regions of our respective faces, suddenly find themselves together and, to all appearances and experienced sensations, greatly enjoy the none-too-brief encounter.

Yes, enjoy it quite a bit. For several enjoyable minutes.

And so now, clearly, a line has indeed been crossed and one life—perhaps two—has become immeasurably more complicated. On this particular night, the complications rest only within the physical divide that has been crossed. But whether the intimacies continue or not, the nature of our front-desk encounters has changed dramatically. From here, we can either go back to the casual remarks tossed back and forth but in a far less casual, and more fraught manner, each comment examined and weighed for specific meaning, tone, and nuance; or we can enter our own world in which secrets are kept between just the two of us, leaving others within L'Hermitage to guess for themselves why it is we talk a little more quietly and look at one another in a slightly different manner than we did before.

# CHAPTER 26

Saturday, 8:40 am

"**Y**ou will be fired; you know that don't you?" Judith asks during our next Saturday morning chat. "You may not be willing to make a decision on your own, Henry, but your actions will force an end game in and of itself, okay? And then, once that happens, you'll no longer be able to make a decision. It will be made for you—totally out of your hands. Get it?" She's irrepressible, having entered my domain at 8:30 on this cheery, sunny morning, fully dressed in her lawyerly, adviserly, godmotherly outfit. Given the morning on hand, there was a side of me that hoped to have received a phone call from Judith explaining that she wouldn't be able to make it today, but no such luck.

She's nothing if not dependable.

"So, if it wasn't enough that you've expanded your realm of oversight from the front desk area to some marketing firm over on the West Side, you've added boinking one of the residents to your repertoire? At a certain point, Henry, you've gotta realize, you've outgrown this doorman shtick."

"Well, to begin with," I offer, "I'm not 'boinking'—as you colorfully describe it—one of the residents. I mention the incident only under the guise of full disclosure, per your and my relationship. I was only comforting Wendy, I wasn't—"

"Yeah, fine. One moment you're comforting, the next you're boinking. I understand the progression of these things. So, my timeline's off by a night or two. The fact of the matter is we both know the direction this one's going, right? I haven't memorized the building's bylaws, but I can assure you there's something in there about doormen not boinking residents. I *promise* you, okay? So I'll say it again—it's time for you to, very soon, rip off your cape and mask. You've got far bigger opportunities in front of you. Ducking and dodging Charlotte's anger is not a part of that plan. And now with this little dalliance with what's-her-name? That may just force your hand, okay?"

"It's Wendy. And no hands will be forced if we're discreet about it."

"Yeah, right," she says in more of an editorial grunt than an utterance. "Because as we both know, Upper East Side apartment buildings are always discreet in such matters. These types of details *never* leak out, right? As the doorman, Henry, you know better than that. You've heard more goddamn secrets since you took over the front desk than you have in your entire lifetime. Guess what—you and Wendy are about to become topic number one in the mail room, if you're not already."

"Well, anyway, Judith, I'm just a plaything to her. Trust me, she's not serious about this—it'll be over before it starts. I've been in her unit—she's rich. I'm just the doorman. There's no way Mummy and Daddy are going to allow her to step down to my level for an extended period of time."

She looks at me for a moment before theatrically swiveling her head to take in our surroundings. "Step down? To your level? You mean this level right here, in the penthouse? That level?"

"Oh, well, yes," I say. "I suspect that sounds slightly odd to you, perhaps."

"I think your charade is starting to muddle your mind, Henry. Let's just let her and the rest of the building in on your game and call it a day. Your life would be much easier and more even-keeled had you never set up this deception."

"We've been over this before, Judith. I was in a bit of a shock, all right? I didn't know what I was doing. When I got to the front of the building, I saw the 'Doorman Wanted' posting. I had just come from the conversation with you about my financial status. And, by the way, you may recall, you had given me a drink, so there was that factor—"

"Toughen up, sailor. Speaking of which, since you're offering—"

"It's nine o'clock in the morning, Judith."

"It's nine o'clock in the morning *on a Saturday,* Henry. We do have our standards."

"Well, anyway, I was in an emotional state. Maybe a little drunk. I took the posting as a sign from God—it was an opportunity for me to hide, to buy some time."

"A sign from God, Henry? A sign from God was the fact that you were born into a family worth hundreds of millions of dollars. There's your fucking sign from God. The Doorman Wanted sign? That was a sign from Charlotte. I had told her to put it up that morning—God ain't got nothing to do with that one. Had I any inkling that you would think that sign was meant for you, I would have had her hold off a day, okay?"

She sits down at my kitchen table and drinks from her coffee mug. I do respect Judith's inclination toward ritual. I suspect she, at first, regarded these get-togethers as a slow-motion intervention that, by a defined point on the calendar—long before now—would no longer be necessary. Her initial visits, I suspect, were done more out of obligation to the friendship she and Dad had with, perhaps, a nod toward her responsibility as godmother tossed in. I recognize that, at some point, we'll no longer need these meetings, and we'll probably both miss them.

"Getting back to our earlier discussion, Henry, you need to appreciate that Charlotte's your problem. She's not going to put up with any nonsense from you. As flighty or as spacey as you and I might think she is, she does—believe me—have an agenda, okay? That's clear to me. Your farce is increasingly causing problems all around. And, what's more to the point, it's causing problems for me. Do you know how many phone calls I've had to take on your behalf—on *Henry's* behalf, not Franklin's—during the past couple of days, with her wanting to get through to you—the *rich* you, not the doorman you—to discuss her concern over her head doorman's cavorting with the homeless people out on the street? She has her suspicions, Henry, and she's tossing about the idea of firing you. The *working stiff* you. You are aware that every single one of those calls from her, asking for Henry Franken's approval to can Franklin Hanratty, are costing both of you, oh, about two-hundred-fifty bucks, special rate? That is, unless she gets to yammering away, and we sneak over the quarter-hour billable. Then, it's costing you upwards of five hundred dollars. Again, I point out, special rate. She hasn't gone to three quarters of an hour yet, but we are developing quite the relationship, little Hot-cha-cha and me."

Judith's pep talk this morning is not effective. In fact, I find it altogether to be quite unpeppy.

"She called you, did she?" I ask.

"Oh, yeah. She's demanding to set up a meeting with Henry Franken in order to talk about personnel here at L'Hermitage. That's her code word for wanting to talk about *you.*"

"I find it odd, Judith, that she wants to fire me when I'm probably her best employee. I mean, I could understand if I were to have to protect Jacob from her, with his special brand of, let's see, what's the word I want . . . loquaciousness?"

"Yeah, she ain't wanting to talk to me about Jakey."

"Or, even Morgan or Lester—"

"Them, neither."

"—with their admirable ability to sleep through every one of their shifts. But, why me? I'm conscientious, I'm trustworthy, dependable, and, perhaps of greatest import, the residents like me."

"Thank you, Stuart Smalley. Let me ask you a question. How old are you?"

"You know I'm thirty-three."

"Yes. So young. Don't you see? You're only a few years younger than her. You're clearly educated. And, yes, you're all those other things you mentioned . . . trustworthy, dependable, whatever. But your biggest issue—and most threatening one to her—is the last one you mentioned. All the residents like you. They love you. Hell, why wouldn't they? You're easy on their glaucoma-filled eyes. But all those items you mentioned only make you a threat to her."

"Threat? How could I possibly be a threat?"

"She knows you could replace her in a heartbeat. And that fact makes you a threat. Jacob replace her? Yeah, right. Lester? Morgan? Hardly. They're both closer to the pearly gates than they are to the front doors. Altogether, their ineptness makes her indispensable. But you? She's looking for any reason to can you. She wants someone in that position who's more controllable, someone who's not going to see that she's messing up or dinking around on her computer, someone who doesn't shine quite as brightly with her residents. And here's some news for you pally-boy—you ain't it."

"I see. So, you think I'm upstaging her?"

"I don't, she does. It's an old story. The understudy takes over the star's role. She can't be comfortable until you're gone, so she's looking for any reason she can to get rid of you, or, at least, hold a power chip over you. If you insist on keeping up this pretense, you'd best keep that in mind. I think you're ready to, to—what's the word I want?"

"Move on?"

"Hmm, bigger than that."

"Evolve, perhaps?"

"Yeah, close."

"Metamorphose?"

"Yeah, that'll do. Metamorphose. It's time for little Franklin to *metamorphose* into Henry, y'know? You've been caterpillaring around long enough, as far as I'm concerned. Let's get you into that butterfly stage. At least one of the two of us is ready for that."

I sigh, sitting back against my chair. "Yeah, okay, Judith," I say. "I do hear you."

"C'mon, *liebling*. The quicker you move on and assume responsibility and ownership of this building, the quicker I can move on, okay? And, for that matter, the quicker everyone else can move on, too. Besides, I promise you, if you think your new girlfriend likes you in your doorman uniform, just wait till she finds out what's in your back pocket. That should be enough incentive right there, right? Okay, I'm out of here. You got a stack of papers to go through. If you haven't noticed, your retail space has become a sinkhole. Lots of expense, no revenue. I'm trying my damnedest to rent it out, but we might have to get creative with that square footage. Make yourself useful and talk it up while you're standing out there on the sidewalk, okay? Go get yourself a sandwich board, or something."

And with her usual flourish, Judith gets up from the table, puts her cup in the sink and leaves. Her words, though, continue to echo throughout my large, empty apartment.

# CHAPTER 27

Monday, 7:30 am

I come in early on Monday morning, if for no other reason, because I've done nothing but toss and turn all night. I'm normally a sound sleeper, but that gift has seemingly been returned, at least during the past two days.

Upon entering L'Hermitage, I am mildly surprised and inordinately pleased that not only is Morgan at the front desk where he should be, but he's wide awake, alert, and working on his shift report. My insomnia must be catching.

"Alright, then. Morning, boss," he mumbles, looking up at me from his report. "You're in early."

"Yes, well, I thought I'd get a jump on the week," I offer up. "Quiet night?"

"Yep," he says. "As usual. I have a pretty easy shift, this Sunday night business, I gotta admit. This may be the city that never sleeps, but L'Hermitage makes up for the rest of the town, know what I mean?"

"Speak for yourself," I mutter.

"Wuzzat? Hmm. Anyway, pretty quiet. Mrs. Hill called down a cupla times, asking me to go check on some sirens a few blocks over. The guy from 5A was down reading for a while, middle a' the night. But, that's it. Oh, and the girl up on eight. She was down for a while, too."

"Wendy?" I ask.

"Suppose so. Don't know her name. But since you're here, do you mind if I knock off a little early this morning? I'm beat."

"No, that's alright, Morgan," I say. And then, after a nonchalant pause, I pursue the subject a tad more while arranging the coffee cups on the cart. "So, what was she doing down here?"

"Who?" he asks. Good lord, the attention span of a gnat.

"The, uh, that girl from eight."

"Oh, you mean Wendy?"

Pause.

"Yes," I say, wishing dearly to push the conversation along. "Wendy."

"Oh. I dunno. Kinda walking around a bit. I think she sat in the living room for a while. Went into the mailroom at one point, or something."

"Was she reading? Sitting? Writing? Sobbing hopelessly?" This last suggested possibility was, perhaps, a bit over the top, even for the dense mass otherwise known as Morgan. He looks up at me from his crouched position beneath the desk as he searches for his lunch bag.

"Well, I wasn't giving her my full attention, I guess, but I don't remember there being any sobbing, hopeless or otherwise. I prolly would have remembered that," he says, before turning back to his lunch bag duties. "Interested in what the guy from 5A was reading, too? No, maybe not so much. Okay then, boss, I'm outta here." And he stands up, straight and tall, or, at least, as straight and tall as an eighty-three-year-old, hunched-over short man can do, and departs.

"See you next week," he says.

◆　◆　◆

As I putter around the lobby, making coffee, straightening chairs and magazines, greeting our early morning dog walkers, I continue—as I have all weekend—to think about what Judith told me on Saturday morning: that it's time to move on. I suppose, in taking over my father's wealth, it's a bit like a vice president being thrust into power after the president dies. Is anyone truly ready for that level of responsibility that quickly?

"Good morning, Mr. Hanratty."

Mr. Harrison has entered the lobby—earlier than usual—newspaper in hand, and heads immediately to the coffee urn, as is his routine.

"Monday morning, sir," I say. "Given your mastery over the crosswords in the early part of the week, our visit, I suspect, will be short this morning."

"Ah, yes, no doubt," he says, waving his paper and approaching the desk. "Bat it out in seven or eight minutes, eh? Really more of a speed-writing exercise on Monday mornings than coming up with solutions. I should shoot off a letter to Mr. Shorts over there at the *Times*, asking him to kick it up a notch for us veterans. Not so much that the rookies are put off, mind you. But keep us seasoned solvers interested."

"Yes, well, sir, were everyone as brilliant as the two of us, we'd lose our chronic joy of gloating, now, wouldn't we?"

"Hah! Yes, you're absolutely right about that, Mr. Hanratty. Damn good thing they're not, eh?" He laughs, then takes a sip from his coffee.

"Damn good thing they're not," he repeats, turning slowly toward the living room. "Oh, Mr. Hanratty," he says, turning back. "By the way, I wanted to apologize for my behavior on a couple of recent occasions."

"Sir?"

"The other morning," he repeats. "Regarding Mr. Stewart when you were heading out to fetch a painting for him. I threw some unsolicited advice your way regarding how best to deal with him. Do you remember? And then, also, I'm a little embarrassed about the way I, well, I guess you could call it 'heckled' Mr. Stewart the other afternoon. Very uncharitable of me. Beneath me, I'd like to think."

I do recall a certain amount of disquiet on Mr. Harrison's part—perhaps a level of unhinging that occurred in his otherwise calm demeanor. But we all have our moments now, don't we? Certainly, can be overlooked; after all, I am in no position to cast judgment on those of us who have multiple sides to their personality.

"Well, it was wrong of me," he says again. It would appear he wants to air the matter out. At this time of day, I'm happy to be an audience for him.

"We have a complicated relationship, you might say. He and I were once good friends; actually, both my wife and I were—with him, and his wife. And that's, perhaps, where we should have left it, as just a friendly relationship. The problem, you see, is that we entered into a dangerous territory as friends. My wife and I became clients of his. And as will often happen, the relationship changed significantly."

He pauses and takes another sip of coffee, perhaps wondering whether he has said enough or if he should continue. I say nothing, offering no encouragement one way or another. A proper doorman does not pry, but certainly enjoys listening to a good yarn when one is offered up.

"It turns out that Mr. Stewart has a touch of the flim-flam in him," Mr. Harrison continues. "Although, given his proclivity for not following through on matters properly, let's give him credit for only having the flim in him, eh? Close enough. You see, he sold us a couple of works from an artist who, as it turned out, had an entirely different backstory from that which had been presented in all the advance and print materials. Margaret and I went to a showing of his a few years back. The artist had one style and, seemingly, one tube of paint—red. Every painting had variations of solid red splattered on the canvas and were called things like Blood I, Blood II, and, of course, lest the story not be amply or richly told with those first two editions, Bloods III and IV. There were other depictions, as well. He had a Cardinal series, a Brick series, all quite subtle reddish sorts of nonsense. Perfectly suitable, I suppose, if one's living room required a large splash of red on the walls.

"But the artist's story itself was extremely touching. There was a large amount of press before the opening, so, of course, the event was packed. The artist was from Sarajevo, had lived there during the war. These art pieces were intended to be a powerful visual depiction and encapsulation of that experience. Blood everywhere. This showing was the artist's life work. It was the way in which he processed what he and his family experienced during the siege. The paintings were, indeed, beautiful. I unjustly simplified their depth of expression. The artist was able to communicate nuance through various shadings, colorations, and textures. I have the pieces hanging in my living room to this day. The artist, however, was unable to join the opening. According to the legend, his trauma prevented him from traveling—actually, prevented him from even leaving his studio in Sarajevo. His absence at the opening only added to the aura and the mood of the evening."

"But I'm unclear on what the problem was," I say. "It sounds like you're happy with the pieces."

"I do like them," Mr. Harrison says. "The problem is with the backstory that Brendan put forward. The artist—I can't even remember his name right now—would probably struggle to find Sarajevo or Bosnia on a map. He had never been there. It was discovered that he grew up somewhere on Long Island, went to Pratt for a few years—didn't graduate—and started doing commission work. He and Brendan somehow, somewhere tripped across each other and cooked up this scheme."

"I'm assuming there's some sort of law against that, no?" I ask. "Racketeering? Wire fraud? Forgery? Something?"

"No. The police never got involved. Brendan contacted those of us who had bought pieces and offered a discount once the story began to leak out. In essence, hush money."

"But how did it ever come out? How did you figure it out?"

At this, Mr. Harrison snorts. "The dope," he said. "He's got to pick his partners a little bit better. The kid—the artist—is the one who contacted us. He, himself, didn't trust Brendan. He didn't feel he was getting his agreed-upon cut. After getting paid by Brendan, he contacted several of us and filled us in on the scheme, presumably hoping to get a tip or a cut, or maybe just revenge of some sort. I'm not sure what his aim was. I wanted nothing to do with either of them. False representations are not appreciated by anyone."

At this point, Mr. McAdoo, 11A, comes off of the elevator, smelling strongly of Royal Copenhagen with a whiff of wintergreen chewing gum thrown in for good measure.

"Gentlemen!" he roars before heading into the mail room.

"Mr. McAdoo, how are we this morning?" Mr. Harrison says.

"Ted, I've never been better," he says, reemerging from the mailroom. "Never been better. And you know what it is? I'll be delicate with you, Ted, because I know you're a man of fine taste and upbringing. But let me just say, the little lady keeps me a very young seventy-eight. How the hell else could I explain getting out the door with a spring in my step at eight-fuckin'-fifteen in the morning, huh? Look at me! I'm nearly eighty, y'know? That used to be old, remember? But look at me. Strong as a goddamn bull is what I am. Marrying that bird a few years back was the best thing I coulda done. Fountain of youth, boys, I have discovered the very fountain of youth. Why, I feel like you look, Franklin. And she's upstairs right now, catching up on her beauty sleep. Whoof! See you, gents. Someone around here needs to keep the world of business spinning."

He starts out, but then swings around. "Frankie, boy, you're getting' some, right? Don't waste these peak years, pal. I'nt that right, Teddy, huh? Peak years!" And with that, he heads out the doors. A slightly indelicate quip given Mr. Harrison's recent entry into widowhood status.

Mr. Harrison turns back to me after the dust devil that is Justin McAdoo leaves the lobby. We stand for a moment, collecting ourselves. It takes a tick or two for the peace and calm that had preceded Mr. McAdoo's arrival to descend upon us once again.

"Yes, well, maybe Mrs. McAdoo has a baby sister. I'll look into that immediately. Now, what was I saying?" Mr. Harrison offers. "Oh, yes. About Brendan. Well, probably enough said, at least for this morning. I brought it up only because I felt it important that you understand my reaction the other day. Sorry to drag you into it, Mr. Hanratty. I guess I just feel that art—good or bad—deserves better representation, that's all. Now, to the puzzle. These things don't solve themselves. They need to be prodded."

He heads to his corner in the lobby and sits down, turning on the nearby table light. Within moments, lobby traffic picks up and the week is underway.

# CHAPTER 28

"**I**s there a raven at our front door?" Mr. Harrison asks from his seat across the lobby.

"Sir?" I ask, calling out from the mailroom. Mrs. Cooper, 3C, had handed me her mailbox key while rushing out the front door moments ago. "Be a dear and pick up the weekend's mail for me, would you, Franklin? I'm in a rush and haven't been to the mailroom in days. Just put it all inside my front door. Thanks so much."

"The tap-tapping," Mr. Harrison says. "I believe there's a raven at the front door. Or maybe it's your coyote friend. Whatever it is, we seem to be getting more doorknockers these days."

I poke my head out and look toward the front vestibule. Through the warbled glass, I make out the silhouette of Terry, face pressed up against his cupped hands at the window. He taps again with a coin. After Saturday's discussion with Judith, I'm resolved to be firm with Terry. Polite, but firm. Her words sunk in—that I was developing a growing list of relationships that was beginning to tear—or, at least, threaten—the ephemeral scrim I have created around my identity, to the point that, perhaps, I was no longer in control of my own timeline for extricating myself from a self-created sham. I walk to the door in my most absolute resolute manner, possibly more an issue of toe-heel volume than anything visually distinctive.

"Terry," I say, upon cracking open the door, "I'm sorry, but you really must—"

"Scraper, I need your help bad," he says with a pained look on his face.

"What's the matter?" I ask.

"Scrape, they messed him up really evil. Oh, Jesus, they messed him up."

"Who, Terry? Who messed up who? Whom?"

"Cadillac, man. They beat the shit out of him, and he's just an old man. Goddamn. You gotta come, Scrape. We need your help."

I step through the door and let it shut partially behind me. I don't let it latch, though, keeping one hand on the frame.

"Terry, what happened? Who beat him up?"

"A pack of kids . . . some shitheads—I don't know. We're not sure. No one was with him at the time. It happened sometime late Saturday night. We found him this morning near where he normally sleeps. We need your help taking him to the hospital, Scrape."

I shake my head. "I can't leave here, Terry. I'm on duty. There's nobody here to cover for me right now. Take him to the emergency room at Lenox Hill. They can't refuse service—"

"Scrape, they'll make us sit there for hours. Cad is messed up bad, man. If you take us over there, I promise, they'll look at him immediately. Between the way you talk and the way you look, you're going to get their attention. They'll just blow us off. Trust me, man, I been there. It ain't going to happen if Tomata and I take him alone."

I look at him and begin to speak, "Terry, I'm sorry—"

And then, from somewhere in the very bowels of the building, or maybe just a few feet behind me, I hear, "Franklin? What are you doing?"

Charlotte. Again, Charlotte. Always Charlotte. All roads lead to the Charlotte, to the Charlotta, to the . . .

"Shut the door, Franklin. Shut the door now. Come into my office."

I turn to Terry. "Mister Terry, I'm sorry. I have to stay on duty here. I can't help you right now. The hospitals can't turn you away, though. Get Cadillac to Lenox Hill as soon as you can. They'll take care of him." I look over my shoulder to make sure Charlotte is no longer behind me before I pull my wallet out of my pocket. I pull two fifties and as many twenties as I have out of the fold and offer them to Terry.

"Take these," I say.

"I didn't come here for money," he says, looking at me with an expression that effectively mixes anger with disappointment and disgust. "Or your coffee, for that matter."

"Please, Terry."

"Keep your money; you keep throwing it at us like its air, anyway. It's your help I need right now." He turns and scuffs back toward the park, but not before spitting out one last comment, "Doorman. Shit. More like doorboy, if anyone were to ask me. Door *mat*."

"Wait a minute," I say, "That's not fair."

"There's a whole shitload in this life that ain't fair, Scraper," he says. "Cad-man lying under a tree in Central Park with blood coming out of his ears ain't fair, man. You got more important things to do, never mind. We'll take care of it, like we always do. You just stay here and keep opening your doors for the rich folk, though, okay?"

I go back into the lobby and let the front doors click shut quietly behind me. Mr. Harrison is standing at the elevator, newspaper in hand, as the doors part. "Mr. Hanratty," he says with a slight smirk. "Give my best to Ms. Marbury, would you? She seems in a particularly . . . hmm, Monday morning sort of mood. Best wishes." And then he enters the elevator and the doors shut. The lobby is empty.

"Franklin? Come in here please," Charlotte calls.

"Yes, Charlotte?" I say, entering her darkened office. Charlotte prefers muted lighting; I assume because of its flattering qualities. "How was your weekend?" I ask, somewhat flatly. "Did you get out in your new car?"

"I have more going on in my life, Franklin, than just a new car, okay? And, yes, I had a very nice weekend."

"Good. Then I suppose you called me in here to talk about my dismissal—per your earlier request—of those who have no business with L'Hermitage."

"Your what . . . my what? Wait, what are we talking about?" My initial thrust has, seemingly, effectively parried her anticipated opening offensive move.

"You had asked that I turn the street people away from our building. I was in the midst of doing so when you called out to me in the lobby. The guy was asking for assistance and, you'll be happy to know that I moved him along." And then, for further emphasis, I spit out, with an intended edge about it, "I have absolutely no doubt that you're *very* happy about that. Is that correct, Charlotte? Didn't I do the right thing?"

"Well, yeah. I guess I am happy with you doing your job. So, uh, good job." She squints at me, uncertain of the flow of our conversation, uncertain who is controlling our exchange.

"Is there anything else you need this morning?" I ask.

"Yes, actually there is," she says. "It's not just keeping him away from our front door. I don't want him or others anywhere near our building. Again—"

"It's New York City, Charlotte. When I last checked, the streets of the city are still public and there is no wall that has been built to prevent anyone from walking on those sidewalks," I point out to her.

"*Again* . . . I hold you responsible for the issue of undesirables approaching—"

"We don't call them undesirables anymore."

"I hold you responsible for the issue of people-*formerly-known-as*-undesirables hanging around our building," she continues. "They shouldn't feel any reason that they can be walking anywhere near L'Hermitage. Anywhere near it."

This time it's my turn to squint at her. I'm working from the angle that a heavy, editorial pause will allow the ridiculousness of this comment to achieve full effect.

"Well?" Charlotte asks. "That's it. You can head back to your desk now, Franklin."

"I will, Charlotte. But I need to point out that I am the doorman. That title limits my responsibilities. Although I do sweep and hose down the front sidewalk on a regular basis, this position does not allow me to restrict passage of any individuals from those sidewalks. But I'll do my best to ensure that any and all residents of this building, and cleared visitors, are allowed unhindered passage into L'Hermitage. And, perhaps important to note, the reason that person—*Mister Terry*—was here is he was seeking assistance. Not a handout, but assistance for a friend of his who was badly hurt—"

"We can't help him here, Franklin. We're an Upper East Side condominium building, not urgent care, okay?"

"Oh, I'm quite clear on that, which is why I sent him away. You'll have to excuse me, Charlotte. I hear folks in the lobby."

Charlotte is one who enjoys a good set-to. Her timing of this particular engagement happened to be poor, given the incident that had immediately preceded it. A man can only be pushed so far, after all. As a wise Greek poet once said, timing is in all things the most important factor.

# CHAPTER 29

Monday, 4:20 pm

"Hey, lady bird, wake up."

Jacob has entered the building, the front foyer to be more exact, and has caught me in what can best be categorized as a blank-stare fog, an unusual bit of inattentiveness on my part.

"Hello, Jacob," I say, returning to business.

"*Hello, Jacob. Ooh, hello Jacob,*" he says, in a miming fashion. "Busted. You were off in la-la land, boss-man. Ooh, wait, don't tell me you have another big date tonight? That's going to play havoc on your once-a-year average. You and one of your L'Hermitage ladies hitting the town, huh? Gonna paint it red? That what's going through your mind? Oh, wait a minute. If it's you leading the 'genda, maybe just paint the town pink. Not even a hot pink, just one of those little baby-girl soft pinks. That what you going to do?"

"Yes, yes, Jacob. Paint the town pink. Got it, very good."

His loud, cackling laugh is interrupted only by Wendy's approach, as she gets off the elevator and heads to where I'm sitting at our front desk.

"Uh-oh, here we go now," Jacob says, heading toward the mailroom. "Who's walking down the streets of the city, indeed?"

"Hello, Franklin. How are you?"

"I'm great, Wendy. How'd your day go?" I ask.

"You know, still adjusting. I was thinking of coming down earlier and visiting, but I didn't want to disturb you. The last thing an *employed* person needs is an unemployed person hanging around their desk, disturbing their work."

"No disturbance at all," I say. "Distraction, yes. Disturbance, no."

"By the way," she says, "you left this upstairs the other night. I've been meaning to get it back to you." And, at this, she hands over my pocket square which, quite honestly, I hadn't even noticed was missing.

"Oh," I blurt, looking down at my lonely, empty pocket, touching it. "Thank you."

When I look up, I lock eyes not with the lovely Wendy, but rather with Jacob, who has just returned, carrying packages from the mailroom. His eyes are open wide, and he mouths the words, "You *fuckin'* dog!"

"Whoo-hee!" he shouts out, clearly comfortable with communicating his excitement over this development with more than just me. "I'm gonna splode over here in my neutral corner. What am I, chopped hash? Coo-coo-cachoo. There's three of us here, kiddies. Towel it down, now."

"Oh, Jacob. I'm sorry. I didn't see—I thought you had gone into— sorry," Wendy says, looking awkward.

"Oh, don't you worry about it, baby. You probably didn't even notice me wandering about the premises, little ole wallflower, Jacob. Always being outshined by the overpowering presence of Franky-boy."

"Yeah, well, anyway, I'll see you guys later. I'm going for a run." At this, Wendy turns, goes out our doors, and heads toward the park.

"Goddamn—you quiet ones," Jacob says to me. "It's *always* the goddamn quiet ones. You're like fricking stealth submarines, just skimming below the surface. Most of us don't even know you're around—well, sure as shit, *I* don't know you're around. I barely know you're around when we're in the middle of a conversation. But here we gunboats are, up on the surface, shooting off our cannons, doing our thing, then all of a sudden, KA-BOOM! You got yourself a brick shit-boat. And all this time, Franky, I wasn't even sure you fell on that side of the fence, know what I mean? I mean, you got your Mr. Leatherdale up on four. Ain't no doubt which fields he's plowing—all musky bluster and coming back late at night with the young ladies—I'll tell you that story someday. And then you got your Mr. Gabamonte from six who's always heading down to the Village to check things out. But you—couldn't ever quite tell which way you were bending—to the Village or the fields, know what I mean? And here, all along, you've been heading upstairs to pay a call on our own little Miss Wendy. Whoo-ee and a ram-alama-goddamn!"

"Okay, shhh, stop it. Shut up," I say. I can't help but smile, however, but doing so in a manner which, I hope, communicates that he tone it down. I hand him the evening's log book with L'Hermitage's coming and goings and wish him a good night.

"Whoa, whoa, whoa, don't be giving me that crap. Get over here and spill me some details. That little art outing that you went on the other day—that must have gone somewhere, huh? Did you show her all the sexy paintings like I said? Did that work?"

"Jacob, you know there's an explicit order that building personnel are not to get involved beyond a professional level with residents of the building."

"Oh, yeah. Fascinating, Franky. To begin with, you ain't said shit in that statement. I watch my share of cop shows. That's what they call a nondenial denial, 'kay? So, secondly, that little clause about not fraterizing with homeless folk out front ain't holding you back too much from what I'm hearing, now is it? So, we know what you think about company laws, right? Whoo-wee! You quiet ones. Goddamn!"

"Yes, Jacob, we quiet ones have all sorts of secrets up our sleeves—"

"Yeah, those sleeves are full, but your front vest pockets are running a little light these days, ain't they? Huh? Huh?" he says, sticking his index finger in the chest pocket normally reserved for my pocket square.

"Yes, very good, Jacob. Your sartorial sense is top-notch, as always. Now, I can't help but wonder if you're up to the task of manning the desk, or do you need a little more time to collect yourself from your perceived revelations?"

"Oh, no, boss, I'm good to go. Fact, I'm thoroughly energized for the evening. I can feel the secks-u-all tension all over this place. Good goddamn! This is one crazy-assed building."

◆   ◆   ◆

There is a side of me that understands Jacob's incredulity. I'm certainly no virgin; I've had a statistically appropriate number of one-night stands for a single man of my age. It's the second-night stands that have always been problematic for me.

My hesitation in establishing anything that resembles a relationship comes back to money, always money. At an early age, I was told by my father to make sure I was clear on the difference between people who wanted to be with me because of my personality and those because of my wallet. That simple advice created a confusion within me that remains entrenched to this day. How does anyone know why someone wants to spend time with them? Everybody's motivations became immediately suspect if they knew the least bit about my family's background or my father's wealth. Were they laughing at my uproarious humor because it was truly funny or because the world I inhabited was intoxicating? Did they want to spend time with me because they found me interesting or because they found the *thought* of me interesting? The thought of my world?

Wendy's motivations seem clean, unadulterated. Going out with the type I represent may be a safe and impermanent form of rebellion. I know there are wealthy young women of her stature who consider my type to be playthings, trophies to be collected during their early professional lives and certainly before their years of marriage to Ivy League-educated Wall Street managers. They brag to their girlfriends about the auto mechanics, utility men, manual laborers, and, yes, doormen they have been with. She may simply regard me as one of those collectibles, though, were I to be wholly honest—and may it be noted, I'm working on this facet of my personality—I would display a marked hesitancy toward technique were I to ever be handed a deburring tool or a wheel-kit abrasive. My looks are merely an added bonus; and the fact that I have an interest in literature, art, and non-sports-related conversation is doubly alluring, thereby extending the timeframe of the superficial relationship.

But for me, within my disguise, I feel no need to maintain my well-honed antennae. I can relax, knowing that the interest in me has nothing to do with my family's financial situation.

"What's the difference?" Judith invariably asks me on those occasions when we get deep into this topic.

"What do you mean, 'what's the difference'?" I ask.

"Just what I said. What's the difference if they're after you for your money or after you for your blue-collar status? Everybody's after someone for something, Henry. All I'm saying is that we're drawn to one another for lots of different reasons and we choose to stay together for fewer reasons. Sylvia was drawn to me because of my loud mouth and unending charm, okay? And, yeah, my partner status at the firm sweetens the pot. But she stays with me 'cause I'm such a sentimental pussycat. You're wasting your time by posing as something you're not. You're not a doorman; you're rich, okay? Get out there and have some fun. And, yeah, you know what? There're folks who may be attracted to you because of your money. And guess what, pal—a whole lot of others may hate you and go running the other way for the same reason—because you're rich. Bizarro world versions of you, ya know? Deal with it."

# CHAPTER 30

Pushing her loaded walker off of the elevator, Mrs. Hill turns to look at me.

"Hello, Franklin. I'm glad to see you down here."

"Mrs. Hill, how are you this morning?"

"Fine, thank you," she says, moving slowly toward the coffee urn, inch by inch. Her walker, as usual, is covered with the jetsam and flotsam of her life—two half-empty pint-sized water bottles with napkins rubber-banded around them, half-folded and half-read newspapers, Q-tips, a washcloth, a partially-eaten candy bar, and two wristwatches. I observe for a moment to see if there is a game plan behind her acquisition of coffee and subsequent movement into the reception area.

"Mrs. Hill," I say. "May I get you a cup of coffee? Perhaps you would like to be seated and I'll bring it to you."

"Oh, would you? That would be so nice of you."

"It would be my distinct pleasure, ma'am."

At this, she emits a giggle as she moves off into the living room. "You're so charming, Franklin. 'Distinct pleasure'—people don't talk like that anymore."

*Did they ever?* I think. I bring her coffee. Today, three trips between the sofa and coffee station are required to adjust the cream and temperature to her desired levels. The coffee, of course, will sit on the table next to her for the rest of the morning, largely untouched. It is not the coffee she desires so much as my focused attention on her caprices.

"You know, Franklin," she says as I begin to return to my desk, "I heard about you turning away your friend at the front door the other day."

I stop and pause, and then turn slowly back to her.

"I'm sorry," I say. "To what are you referring?"

"Your friend. That fellow who comes around. I heard he asked a favor of you, and you turned him down."

I blink and attempt to form a sentence, but the tongue is not quite as silky as I prefer.

"How did you . . . what did . . . how could . . ."

"How did I know?" she asks. "Oh, Franklin, we women have our ways, hmm? Our feminine intuitions."

Oh, dear lord, the woman's flirting with me. "I'm sorry, Mrs. Hill. I'm just very curious as to how this bit of news traveled up to 8B. It was such a small event that happened so early in the morning. Rather insignificant, I would hope, in the grand scope of things."

"Hmm. Yes. Maybe insignificant, maybe not. Tough to say. This building is a small village. There are no secrets. You'd best know that."

Perhaps a few are safely kicking about, I think to myself. But the speed with which this one particular story made its rounds is rather astounding.

"People talk. Especially that one," she says, nodding in the direction of Charlotte's office. "I don't think she has enough to do in there. I really don't. But may I tell you a story?"

"Uh, well, yes. Certainly, ma'am. Although, by sitting down and listening to your story, am I, perhaps, risking imparting the impression that *I* don't have enough to do?"

"Well, right now, you have your hands full listening to me. Right now, I'm your job. Sit down, sit down."

As she utters these words, Mrs. McAdoo gets off the elevator, quickly observes the scene, and heads directly into the mailroom without her usual greeting, highly resembling what, in some circles, would be classified as avoidance behavior.

"Were you aware that I knew Emily Bedohr?" Mrs. Hill asks me, in a stage voice for the benefit of the mailroomed Mrs. McAdoo.

"I had no idea," I say. "And remind me, who is Emily Bedohr?"

"Who is Emily Bedohr?" she asks. The astonished question allows her to amp it up a tad in the decibel department, again, presumably, for the sake of Mrs. McAdoo, as well as Mrs. Stewart, who has just entered the lobby. "Beverly, Janey, can you believe Franklin doesn't know who Emily Bedohr is?" Ah, well, there you go. Just in case her previous unnaturally loud reactions were missed. I have become a mere prop on Mrs. Hill's stage.

"Hmm, they mustn't have heard me," Mrs. Hill says as Mrs. Stewart rushes out the front door and Mrs. McAdoo, seemingly, exits through the mailroom's back door.

"Anyway, Emily Bedohr was married to Herb Bedohr, Mayor Lindsay's righthand adviser," she informs me. "Probably the most important behind-the-scenes man in all of New York City politics during the sixties. Herb guided Lindsay beautifully through those difficult years. Anyway, I got to know Emily very well at that time. Herb and Emily and Joe and I all ran in the same political circles. Emily and I would have lunch together regularly. When Joe and I divorced in the eighties, I got the condo, he got the Bedohrs. Emily and I stayed in touch on occasion after the divorce, but certainly not as often as we had before.

"In what ended up being our last lunch together in, oh, this was years ago now, we met at a restaurant near here, on Madison Avenue. I forget what it's called, but *very* hard to get a noontime reservation. It may not even still be there. It was the first time we had seen each other in months, maybe even a year. We got a table in the window, overlooking the street. The other tables around us were crowded. It was a popular lunch restaurant—the kind that we liked to meet at.

"After our wines were brought to us, I was in the middle of telling Emily a delicious story. I noticed that she looked out the window for just a moment, had a strange reaction, and then turned back to me.

When I finished my story, I, too, looked out the window and saw a man lying half on and half off the curb of the street, with his shopping cart overturned and blocking one of the lanes of traffic. Cars were going around him and no one was stopping. I didn't quite know what to do. I realized that he was what Emily had reacted to when I was telling my story, what she had gazed out upon. At that moment, the waiter came up and described the lunch specials. We gave him our orders. When he left our table, we turned back to one another and, at that very moment, the woman at the table next to ours screamed out, 'Oh, my god, there's a man lying in the the street.' Emily then said, 'I know. He's been there for about ten minutes.'

"The woman said, 'Has anyone called for help? Did you call 9-1-1?'

"Well, neither of us had. Pocket phones were relatively new at that time and neither of us, certainly, carried one. The woman at the next table pulled a phone out of her purse and called for help, quite loudly I might add. A few men from tables around us jumped up and ran outside to try and help him. By this time, a city truck had pulled up and parked near the man, blocking him from oncoming traffic. The woman who shouted out gave us both a nasty look and said, 'Why didn't you say anything? I can't believe it.'

"And you know, Franklin, I don't know why we didn't say anything. It was one of those moments that required immediate action and neither of us did anything. I think back on that incident quite a bit. I believe I didn't do anything simply because I was following Emily's lead. I guess somewhere in the back of my mind, in those few minutes in which I should—or could—have done something, I was simply figuring that, well, Emily didn't do anything. I guess I won't either. I didn't consciously think that, but I guess I use it as rationale. To this day."

I am not quite used to this level of conversation with Mrs. Hill. These are the first introspective comments I have heard from her.

"The man," I say. "And what happened to the man?"

"The man on the street? I'm not sure. An ambulance came quite quickly. They took him away. We watched it during the course of our conversation and lunch, but we never addressed it directly. I don't know if he fainted, had a heart attack, or died. We just, we just carried on with our lunch."

"Well, it's always tough to know what to do under difficult circumstances," I offer.

"Yes, I suppose you're right," she says. "But these would hardly qualify as difficult circumstances. We didn't even tell the waiter to go call an ambulance—it could have been part of our order, I suppose. We sat there and listened to him recite the day's specials and then we ordered our food. It's one of the greatest regrets of my life. And I have a few of them, Franklin."

"Oh, Mrs. Hill," I say. "I would never have guessed that you have regrets in your life."

"How could you ever know?" she asks, quite rightly. "My guess is that many of us are weighted down with regrets of some sort or another, don't you think?"

"Well, possibly," I say. "Did you and Emily Bedohr ever talk about that incident afterward?"

"No," she says. "In fact, we never saw each other again. I never called her, and she never called me after that day."

"Really?" I ask. "Did that lunch break up the friendship? I thought you said you were close."

"Yes, we were close," she says. "But, you see, we had exposed to each other what you could call our ugliest and most fearful sides. I didn't wish to see her again, and, I assume, she felt the same. Who wants to be reminded of the person we don't want to be? I've never gone back to that restaurant, either—it had wonderful calamari, by the way—and I've even avoided that section of Madison Avenue. Easier to do these days, I guess," she says, kicking at her walker. "I wish it hadn't cost us our friendship, though. I do miss her. We always did have such interesting political discussions, trying to save the world and all. But, I suspect, it was inevitable. It wasn't that I was judging her—I could certainly put up with *her* weakness, her flaw, her inability to act. But I couldn't put up with her seeing the same in me. It's like the embarrassing thing you do as a child and hope that everyone who might have witnessed it has forgotten it—that the memory is gone. Only, in this case, far, far worse." She stops talking and looks down at her hands.

"Well, that's quite a story for a Thursday morning," I say. "Thank you for sharing it with me."

"I share it for a reason, Franklin," she says.

"I understand, ma'am," I say.

"So now that I've given you a level of entertainment, if that's, indeed, what we can call it, I can't help but wonder if my coffee has gotten cold?"

"It very well may have. May I top it off for you, Mrs. Hill?"

"Oh, would you? That would be very nice."

"Happy to. It would be my distinct pleasure."

# CHAPTER 31

Thursday, 5:39 pm

Long after my shift was to have ended, Jacob enters from the back hall, singing about him and Julia down in the pool hall.

"I think you mean *Julio*, Jacob," I say. "You and Julio."

"Nope. No Julio with me," he says. "This here was Julia. Believe me, I know Julia and *that* was Julia. Don't know no Julio, didn't see him mucking about."

"And I'm quite sure Paul Simon had you in the schoolyard. Not in the pool hall."

"Hell, no!" he says. "We sure as *he-ll* warn't in no schoolyard, I can tell you that, my man. It was me and *Julia* down in the *pool hall*. Had it all to ourselves. Don't know who your Paul or Simon are, but, 'less they was peeking around some corners or some shit, doing some creepy stalker-like stuff, they don't know shit about what me and Julia were doing, 'kay? It was beautiful, man—shoulda been there. You coulda been watching with your pals, Simon and Paul. Did you know you can get carpet burns from the tops of pool tables?"

"Okay, very good. I believe we have plumbed the depths of that topic to its fullest extent," I say, attempting to bring a certain level of decorum to the evening proceedings within L'Hermitage. After all, there is sufficient traffic in the lobby that would dictate a more professional demeanor among staff. "Are you ready to assume your duties, Jacob?"

"Hell, yeah. Besides, Julia ain't coming around until your skinny ass is tucked into bed, most likely around nine fifteen or so. What you don't know won't hurt you. Hah!" he roars. "I'm just messing with you. Don't go getting all serious on ole Jakey, 'kay?"

"Very good," I respond. Though Jacob is late tonight, I would happily have continued overseeing the front desk, feeling slightly at sixes and sevens. I'm not quite ready to head upstairs and so, after giving him the evening report about expected visitors, deliveries, and ordered cabs, I stroll down the hallway to inspect the progress of L'Hermitage's retail space, rather than heading out to the street via the front doors.

Although the workers have nearly finished renovating the interior, the space has still received only limited interest among potential renters, making Judith nervous. She deals regularly with our hired real estate broker, badgering her to get more showings and, if necessary, lower the required rent.

I unlock the door and enter the dim space, lit only by the diminishing light coming from the bank of windows. Street sounds bleed into the space: passing cars, taxi horns, pedestrian conversations, and . . . a saxophone? I look and see my squonky friend—or a very good impersonation thereof—from the other day outside of Mr. Stewart's gallery. He is playing an insouciant version of "Every Time We Say Goodbye." Either that or a very slow version of the theme to *The Umbrellas of Cherbourg*. Uncertain.

I survey the space. The workers have been making progress in their restoring and updating efforts, bringing it back from the sixty years it spent as a jewelry shop. As with any decades-old space, the "bringing it back" consists primarily of gutting it, stripping it, taking everything back to the original walls, and starting over. For the past month, workers have been covering the original brick walls with drywall, and painters have been coating all surfaces, including ceilings, with white paint. Judith, in her ever-efficient manner, felt that this space needed to be as neutral as possible in order to attract the largest number of potential renters.

"If we keep it looking like that jewelry dump, then the only folks who will even consider renting it are old jewelers, and that's too small a market segment. I want dressmakers, flower peddlers, gallery owners, glass blowers, doggie-salon owners, chefs with the latest restaurant ideas, insurance sales twits—I don't give a shit—I want them all looking at this place. Got it, Henry? Right now, it's dead space, a huge cash cow, and I want it doing nothing but giving you sweet milk. Okay, kid?"

"Looks kind of like a museum, doesn't it?" a voice behind me says.

I spin around and see the back-lit silhouette of Wendy standing at the door.

"Uh, Wendy, hi—I was just, uh, check—checking into the progress of the workers."

"Really?" she asks. "A doorman's work is never done, is it? It even stretches into areas which I wouldn't think had anything to do with a doorman."

"Yes, well, curiosity and whatnot. The entire building is my realm, so to speak."

She enters the space, walking slowly, gently touching the recently painted wall to her right with her fingertips.

"What's it going to become, Franklin? Was I right? A museum? It has that sense about it."

"I don't know," I say. "Nobody has rented it yet—I believe. I hadn't heard any interest from museum directors, however."

"All this white—it's so sterile. It's like a big canvas."

"I have been told that real estate agents like it like this. Helps prevent future renters from being distracted. They can see its potential, rather than its history."

"Well, looks like a big canvas to me. Why don't we suggest to Charlotte that she recruit our friends Terry and Tomata to see what they can do on these walls? Keep them off the streets; keep them warm. Would also be far more artistic than just this . . . white blankness, don't you think?" She suggests this while continuing her slow walk along the perimeter of the space, right hand still gently touching the wall, rising, falling, rising, falling. And as I watch her from the middle of the room, as the sax player segues into the highly unusual sax-solo song, "Isn't It a Pity," one of the best—well, if we were to be quite honest, *brilliant*—ideas I've ever had begins to form in my mind. It's so brilliant and so obvious, in fact, that it almost seems as if it's been sitting there, all along, just waiting to be invited to—

"Dance?" Wendy asks. She had slowly approached me during my musings and now stood fetchingly close.

"Right here? Right now?" I ask. "Wouldn't that feel slightly awkward to—"

"Yes, it would. And, no, I'm not talking about right now, but I am talking about right here. The space has a high ceiling height, there'd be good acoustics. Wouldn't it be fantastic if the building were to convert this space into an intimate music club? With a small dance floor. Where couples could dance? It would be a tight space, so couples would need to dance closely. And, no doubt, quite intimately. Don't you think that would be, um, fun?"

My brief visit to the building's retail space has taken a turn that I had not predicted or, certainly, foreseen. What had simply begun as a quick once-over pop-in to check on the progress of the work crew has progressed into a brainstorming sesh with distractingly suggestive undertones—or is it overtones?

After a moment, I say, "Good thought—let's table that conga line of thinking for just a moment and hear me out. What if I—what if L'Hermitage were to turn this space into an exhibition gallery? A place where Terry and Tomata and other artists who might be homeless could show their artwork? I have no clue where they store their canvases now—if they store them at all. But has there ever been anything like it in the city? Certainly not on the Upper East Side. It could be so very cool—"

At this juncture, a throat-clearing interjection occurs behind us. Has this space always had this level of foot traffic in the evenings?

"Franklin? I've been looking for you. Jacob told me I might be able to find you here. Good lord, it's like you're in the belly of the whale. What a dank space."

Although my only view is of a back-lit silhouette in the door, I recognize the voice to be that of Mr. Stewart's.

"Franklin, tomorrow I have an important meeting in my apartment and I'm afraid that it may not have been mentioned to you. Wait, what was it you were just saying? What is this space becoming?"

"Well, *I* was saying it should be a small dance club," Wendy chimes in helpfully, "but *Franklin* had an even better idea—a gallery for homeless art. Isn't it a wonderful idea?"

"Excuse me, Wendy," I say, recognizing the problem of exposing brilliant ideas to the light of day before their time, especially to gallery owners like Mr. Stewart. "We were simply playing a little game, sir. Kicking about ideas for this space—no wrong answers, you understand. I think our most intriguing idea, actually, was the one you came up with, Wendy, about a . . . about a, uh, small, intimate nightclub. With a dance floor. And a . . . a sax player. Who plays . . . out on the street. Really quite clever, don't you think, sir? Something . . . quite similar to, well . . . this."

"Yeah, yeah, okay. Sounds great. Anyway, Franklin, I just need you to make sure the caterers get in without any problems at nine thirty. They need to set up for an eleven thirty event with some clients of mine. I need you to personally greet them, indicate your awareness of this event, and point them in the right direction. This is an important meeting for Mrs. Stewart and myself, alright?"

"Of course, sir. Quite clear."

The mood on the dance floor has been irretrievably snapped, at least for one half of our dance team. Not so much by Mr. Stewart's interruption as by my realization that the homeless art gallery idea is a topper and that it will be extremely complicated to bring about, particularly because of the likes of Mr. Stewart, Charlotte, and, possibly, others. But it occurs to me that, for the first time in months—years, really—I feel as if I have a game plan. Wendy and I walk from the darkened space, heading toward the lobby.

Doors need to be opened.

# CHAPTER 32

Friday, 6:41 am

I come down early the next morning from Wendy's apartment, fully dressed in my doorman outfit. A threshold has been crossed, so to speak, within our relationship and although I would prefer to go up to the penthouse for my morning ablutions, that, clearly, is out of the question. As far as Wendy knows, my apartment is located in Queens, not four floors above her.

After a bit of straightening up in the lobby and the making of fresh coffee for the soon-to-descend denizens, I head outside for my front stoop duty, sweeping and hosing down the sidewalks. When I am nearly finished, in the shaded light of early morning, I see a familiar figure approaching slowly from the park.

I haven't seen Terry since I turned him away—him and his request to help Cadillac. I feared that he would no longer come around to L'Hermitage following that encounter.

"Hey, Scrape," he says, somewhat mutedly, with a gesture resembling something between a half wave and a swat at a fly, "you got any extra coffee for me this morning? Today I'll take one of your handouts."

"Yes, of course I do," I say. "Wait here for—" And then, I pause. "Come on in, Terry. Why don't you wait inside while I pour it for you?"

"Nah," he grunts. "Too claustrophobic in there for me. Too *santa*-claustrophobic in there. You know what that is, man? The fear of getting gifts in small places—and your lobby is way too small for me," he says. "Why'n't you go tend to the coffee and bring it to me al Fresca. Gimme that hose—I'll finish taking care of the sidewalk for you. We can call it earning my keep, okay?"

I head inside and go to the coffee station. Mr. Harrison has taken his seat in the lobby, already working on his crossword. Mrs. McAdoo and Mrs. Cooper are talking quietly in the mailroom, their two dogs leashed and ready for their morning promenade. I greet them all, pour Terry's coffee, and head back outside. Terry is halfway down the block toward Madison, spraying the sidewalk, the trees, the parked cars, and even the second-floor windows.

"Very good, Terry," I say. "I think you've adequately doused the neighborhood. Here, I'll swap you the coffee for the hose."

"How do you hit those flowers up there?" he asks, referring to the second-floor window boxes. "That takes some pretty good aim to squirt them. I gave them a shot, but I noticed that a couple of the windows were open. That ain't good. I might have gotten some of the indoor plants, too."

"We have a service that tends to those, normally from the second floor. Thank you, though, for giving it a go."

"Damn, this tastes good," he says, taking a loud slurp of his coffee. "Bit of a nip in the air this morning, have you noticed?"

"I did notice, yes," I say. "I'm glad you're enjoying the coffee."

After a moment, I begin. "Terry," I say, "there's something I wanted to talk to you about." I pause a moment before taking the plunge. "Is Cadillac doing alright?"

"He's doing a little better, I guess," Terry says. "They messed him up bad this time, though. Real bad. Bunch of fucking animals went after him that night. College kids on a drunken spree. What the hell do they teach these kids in their fancy schools, huh?"

"Is he in the hospital?" I ask.

Terry snorts, almost spilling his coffee. "Naw, Scrape. No. Old Caddy ain't in no hospital. Caddy ain't exactly a hospital kind of guy. I know I came here asking you to help us get him in one and all, but that was probably pretty stupid on my part. I kind of panicked after finding him. Didn't know what else to do or who else to go to. There's no way—even with you—that he would have gone to the hospital.

Naw, that ain't Cadillac. We were able to hunt down his daughter the next day—which he was none too happy about either. He hadn't seen her in months. She came into the city and picked him up. She's from somewhere out in Jersey—Baskin Robbins or some such shitsville or something."

"How did you ever find her?" I ask.

"He had a little book on him. Was always pulling it out and writing notes and stuff. I knew he kept some phone numbers in there and I knew her name, too, from his having mentioned her over the years. Anyway, he's gone now. I don't expect to see him again. His daughter will put him away somewhere in Jersey—sure as hell not Central Park."

He pauses and takes another sip from his coffee. "Yeah, old Caddy's gone, mm-hmm," he says.

"I want to ask you something else, Terry. Actually—a few things, if you wouldn't mind. Wendy and I were talking the other night. What do you do with your artwork?"

"We sell it, as best we can. Set it out on sidewalks and stuff."

"And do people buy it?" I ask.

"Hell, yeah, they do," he says, adding a proud wiggle of his shoulders to support his statement. "Course they do. How do you think I live the high life like I do? Beg? Shaww—I'm an artist, man."

"Yes, I know you are. You and Tomata, right? And the others?"

"Yeah, yeah, of course," he says. "Tomata's terrific. Great landscapes, a little more abstract than I sometimes like, but he's good. Johnny's the best, though, of all of us. His stuff'll blow you away, Scrape. And Suze, well, she builds these incredible—I don't know what you'd call them even, little sculptures or something, from the shit, uh, from the crap . . . from the stuff she finds out on her rounds. Turning other people's garbage into things of beauty. She's incredible. Little crazy at times, but what artist worth their salt isn't, huh?"

Yes, a triumph over chaos. I look at him as he displays a broken-toothed smile, not directly at me, but in my general direction.

"And, may I ask, Mister Terry, where do you store the art that you don't sell? Or the art that is in progress? Do you keep it all in the park?"

"Yeah, kind of," he says. "Some of it we keep in grocery carts and boxes and tuck it in under bushes in the park. A lot of times it gets destroyed—like the other night—or picked up by the park cops and tossed. Used to be easier to hide it away than it is now. Some of the shelters let us keep it in their lockers and stuff. You know, Scrape, it ain't like we each got tons of canvases or sculptures that needs a big warehouse. We each get a few things together and then hold our little art bazaar wherever the spirits move us. Or where we think the cops ain't going to hassle us."

"What if you were to have an indoor display space?" I ask. "What if you were to have an actual gallery to display your works and a studio to create them in?"

He looks at me for a moment with a sideways smile and one squinty eye, as if trying to comprehend what it is I've just asked him—or offered him. As if trying to read my face to determine if I'm pulling his leg, something I've never done with him before.

"Yeah, well, that'd be a pretty cool thing," he snorts before taking another sip of his coffee. "But what are you asking me for? Are you joking? If you are, I guess I don't get it."

"No, I'm very serious, Terry. What if you and your colleagues were to have a studio space, here on the Upper East Side? Is that something that would be of interest to you?"

Again, he stares at me, trying to read the meaning in my face. In a world in which people pass him every day without acknowledgment, connection, or even eye contact, being presented with the offer of a space—an indoor space, at that—in a prime storefront in New York City for the display of one's artwork is highly unusual. A smile begins to form on his face, but then, just as quickly, a dark expression takes over.

"Wait a minute," he says. "What's the hitch, Scrape? What would I have to do—for you, I mean?"

Oh, yes. I see. The trade of the streets.

"Paint, Terry. That's what you'd have to do—just paint. Nothing more than that. Create product. You and your artist friends would keep a majority of the proceeds."

We go back and forth—somewhat tediously, I might add—in this vein for several minutes. Neither of us is particularly good at it, this back-and-forth questioning and answering, if that's how it can even be characterized. He is not in the habit of knowing how to acknowledge offers; and I am not in the habit of personally extending them. At last, he admits being open to the concept of this proposition.

"I've got to go talk to my partners about this," he says. "You know, we get a little set in our ways, Scrape. May not want all the pressure that comes with your idea. We kind of like it just the way we got it. You may be trying to solve something that ain't looking for a solution."

"Terry," I say, "this is an unusual opportunity. I am merely saying that, if you're interested, I would explore the possibility of converting this building's retail space into a display room—a gallery—for your and Tomata's, and Suze's, and anyone else's artwork. I admit that it would be a very unusual gallery in New York. It would own a niche, shall we say? But there are many hurdles to be leapt on my end before anything is a done deal. And before I can begin leaping those hurdles, I need to gauge your interest."

"No shit, man," he laughs. "You got tons of hurdles. I don't doubt you're a great doorman. And I have no doubt that people inside the building like you and give you their five-hundred-dollar tips come Christmas. But what the hell, Scrape? How much clout you think you got? They ain't going to give you the fucking store in their building," he laughs.

"You may be right," I say. "But I'll tend to my own hurdles. In the meantime, here's what I suggest—get to painting. Do nothing but paint over the next couple of weeks—you and Tomata and the rest of them. Come back tomorrow and I'll have some paint supply money for you. Come early. I'll need your best examples as I float the idea by the residents."

"Shit, and people think *we're* the crazy ones," he says, turning back toward the park. "Damn, Scrape," he shouts, "you are on-ne un-use-u-*al* doorman. Ain't no other doorman like you in this city. No where, no how!"

He lets out his high-pitched cackle as he walks, limping, down the street. As I reenter the building, Mr. Harrison shouts from across the lobby.

"Ah, there you are Mr. Hanratty! Where on earth have you been? I'm horribly stuck," he says while holding up his folded *New York Times*. "What are they going after with this clue: 'Easy peasy'? Ten letters, starting with N-O-P, ending with E-M-O, and several blanks in between. That E-M-O looks wrong, wouldn't you say?"

"'No problemo,' sir."

He looks at me, not too dissimilarly from the look Terry just gave me when I offered him retail space, but perhaps a wee bit more subtly.

"Your answer, sir. 'No problemo.'"

"Ahh. 'No problemo,' indeed. A most extraordinary young man," he says, shaking his head, filling in the blanks.

# CHAPTER 33

Saturday, 6:28 a.m.

I leave Wendy's apartment at 6:30 Saturday morning. Our sleepovers—or, I should say, more pointedly, *my* sleepovers at *her* place—have become common and the risk of detection of our nocturnal activities by other building residents increases dramatically. We've already had the brief, but awkward, run-in with Mr. Stewart in the retail space, as well as Mrs. Hill's occasional monitorings of eighth-floor arrivals and departures. Charlotte encourages the doormen to go above and beyond, not below and within. Grounds for dismissal and whatnot.

Wendy's unit is a pleasant space to spend an evening, as far as overnights go. Long hallways, white carpeting throughout; floor-to-ceiling shelves filled with books and items from her travels; a large kitchen with recessed lighting, marble countertops, white cabinets, and expensive-looking appliances of various sizes and purposes—some even appear to have been used; three bedrooms, one being employed as a well-equipped home office; and a den with a home entertainment center, a gas fireplace, and more book-lined shelves. It's as light and sophisticated as my penthouse is dark and cavelike.

"When do I get to see your place?" she asks sleepily as I put on my uniform.

I am still in a bit of a groggy state of mind, shower notwithstanding, and am tempted to blurt out, "Let's pop up there now, hmm?" before catching myself. Instead, I simply say, "Oh, it's nowhere near as nice as your place. I'm a bit embarrassed by it, really, if you must know. Pretty small and insubstantial."

Not much one can argue against when presented with a statement like that, seemingly, but she presses on, ineffectively squelching another gaping yawn, "Oh, I don't care about that. I like small places. I'm actually more comfortable in them. It's not like I'm expecting you to be living in a penthouse or anything, you know. I'm sure you've made it nice."

At the mention of *penthouse*, I look up quickly from my busy buttoning endeavors at her reflection in the mirror to gauge her intent with this comment. Is she testing the waters? If so, she's playing it coyly as she stretches, arches her back, and scratches her arm. All's well. I go back to my buttoning activity. Double-breasted doorman uniforms are relentless in that way.

"So why are you rushing off?" she asks. "Who are you meeting with so early on a Saturday morning?"

Not many doormen have standing meetings with lawyers-slash-financial advisors on a weekend morning, so I simply say, "My godmother."

"Your godmother?" she asks. "What, are you from a fairy tale? What do you mean your godmother? Is that still a thing?"

"She's an old family friend. Kinda plays the role of a mentor, you could say."

"Well, off the top of my head, I can think of far more interesting things for you to be doing this morning than meeting with an old family friend. What about your *new* family friend, lover boy?"

Saturdays present difficulties in my highly choreographed migration from Wendy's apartment to my own. There is no way to get from point A to point B—either via elevator or stairs—without traversing through the lobby. That's all well and good with the exception that my presence on the premises on a weekend day would invariably raise eyebrows. From Monday through Friday, nobody would think twice about my being anywhere in the building—in fact, seemingly, the residents would prefer that I be *everywhere* in the building. But on weekends, my appearance would border on trespassing. I would just as soon avoid the inevitable questions.

I crack Wendy's door open and peer out in the hallway. With the exception of a vacuuming hubbub coming from the far end of the hallway—the instrument seemingly being employed more as a front door battering ram than a cleaning device—and some boisterous shouts emitting from the Williams's unit—visiting grandchildren—the hallway appears quiet and, more importantly, empty. Quiet to the point that my journey to the stairwell would, seemingly, be undetected.

Except for Mrs. Hill.

"Oh, good morning, Franklin," she says from behind her cracked door, just as I am quietly shutting Wendy's door. "I'm surprised to see you here on a Saturday morning."

"Yes, quite surprising, isn't it?" I say, feeling my cheeks flushing. "Uh, but you see, I thought that, since I had popped into work this morning to pick up my paycheck, I would, I would, uh––" sweet inspiration! "—take an extra minute to deliver some newspapers to this floor. A bit of added value and what have you. Here's yours, ma'am."

I happened to have picked up the Quinson's, 7C, unclaimed *Times* from the mailroom the evening before, knowing that they were gone for the weekend, with the intention of perusing it at some point Friday evening while in Wendy's apartment. That moment of newspaper-reading had never quite manifested itself, so I, once again, grabbed it with the best of intentions as I was exiting. It happens to be of great use at this particular moment, as I extend it—perhaps a bit too demonstrably and with an effusive amount of fanfare—to Mrs. Hill.

"Ooh, my," she coos, "such terrific service. You *do* go above and beyond. Wonderful."

"Enjoy, Mrs. Hill. Enjoy!" I splurt, rushing toward the exit sign above the stairway door.

"Oh, Franklin!" she blurts. "This is yesterday's paper, not today's."

"Very slow news day yesterday, ma'am," I say over my shoulder.

"I thought that strange, too, but they seem to have repurposed the previous day's offerings. We are in the rerun season, would seem. Unusual—not sure that they've ever done that before, hmm?"

Before the stairwell door shuts, I hear a slightly dispirited sound emit from Mrs. Hill, something smacking of a combination of disappointment and disbelief.

◆　◆　◆

"Huh," Judith harrumphs after listening to my plan. "So now you're an art dealer? Where'd this come from?"

I had spent the better part of the last hour explaining my idea of converting the retail space into a gallery for artwork created by homeless artists.

"Well, no. I mean, not exactly. I wouldn't be an *art dealer* art dealer. And it wouldn't really be a *gallery* gallery."

"Have you developed a stutter this week? Carpal tongue syndrome?"

"No. So it wouldn't be a gallery like Mr. Stewart's."

"Good. But, why not?"

"For openers, he represents artists from throughout the world. The art in this gallery would be from, uh, the park."

"Yeah, there's that point of distinct differentiation. Weren't you telling me that Stewart represents artists that paint in—what was it, again—soot?"

"Yeah."

"Okay. Based on that alone, I would put your artists up against sootian artists any day. You're going to need to work on your marketing message a bit though, Henry. But, what the hell, you have something that sounds like a plan or, at the very least, let's refer to it as a talking point. And quite honestly, I've heard far worse schemes than this one, even from your own dad. It actually sounds kind of interesting to me, but it's going to take a shitload of work to pull off."

"Isn't that what I overpay you for?" I say, before immediately adding, "That was a joke. Totally a joke. Have some more coffee."

"Yeah, good one. But I will say, looking at it financially, the tax implications are actually pretty good, assuming you turn your idea into a nonprofit, which it would have to be. I don't see this being a money-making endeavor. Its only success comes in its feelgood effect, nothing more. You've got the capital, Henry. So, pick up the ball and run with it."

Mangled metaphors notwithstanding, Judith helps me think through the next steps, including the fact that the approval of any entity moving into the retail space would require majority consent by the owners of the condos within L'Hermitage. If a condo is under one person's ownership, that person has a vote. If, however, a condo is under joint ownership—a married couple, for instance—then both owners have individual votes, potentially canceling each other out or doubling down on one outcome or the other.

"I *do* own the building. Is that correct?" I ask.

"You own the shell, the ground, the air rights, and the penthouse unit, thanks to your dad's negotiating around the debt issue during the purchase. But the building comes with bylaws, as you're well aware," Judith says. "Think of yourself more as a benign—but *absent*—monarch, one whose power is dependent upon staying within the good graces of a parliament—the board of directors. This is a very democratic condo organization. I should know—I reviewed the existing bylaws before your dad agreed to the purchase. But doing it in this manner falls within the best practices of Upper East Side condos—it happens to be excellent for resale value. People will only pay top dollar if they feel they can have a firm say in the governance of the building they are buying into."

"Is there any reason to believe that this might be controversial, that folks wouldn't agree to use the space in this way?"

At this, Judith lets out a loud stage laugh, throwing her head back in a broad and theatric manner. "Oh, you are a babe in the woods, aren't you, love?" she asks, in a perhaps slightly more condescending tone than is appreciated by all those gathered. "It's a vote, Henry. And whenever you vote on something, you have the potential for some to vote *one* way and for others to vote *another* way, right? The reason this bylaw is in the building's charter is to ensure that something doesn't move in there that might be upsetting to the residents or problematic for future sales. It was a bylaw established to ensure that something loud didn't move in—"

"A gallery's not loud," I say.

"Or something stinky—"

"Well, it's certainly not stinky either."

"Or something which might be perceived as bringing down the value of someone's individual property by having a bunch of homeless folks trompsing around the outside—and potentially *inside*—the building."

"Well, yes, I see there is that aspect about the undertaking."

"Scary as hell, Henry. To lots of folks. There's no such thing as a slam-dunk vote—in the building or in the nation. And an issue such as this requires leadership, a certain level of politicking, making the case for why this is a good idea, why it works well for L'Hermitage. If this comes up at the next board meeting without someone pushing for it strongly, there's a better-than-even chance it goes down in flames. We're a conservative lot, we humans. We're wired to avoid change. Change is scary. So, here's the million-dollar question: are you ready to assume the mantle? To lead the charge? To act as the sponsor of this action? 'Cause there ain't no one else who's going to push for your vision."

"Well, uh, back to your role. Can't I pay you to push for it?"

"Hah! To perpetually act as your surrogate? To live your life for you? Naw. You're rich, but you're not that rich and, at this age, I'm not that hungry. Think about it, Henry. Your identity will have to be revealed at some point. Do you do it when you can do the most good, or after the fact, when it's too goddamn late? You've got an interesting cause here; I'll give you that. Run with it—and do it right or don't bother doing it. Ain't no way your dad would have done something by just sticking his toe in the water. But you may have to kill Franklin, okay? I'm not convinced your doorman is the one who's going to get this one across the goal line. No offense, *Franklin*."

"None taken," I say. I get up from the kitchen table where we're sitting and head over to the windows overlooking the street. I pull the drapes and look out.

"Don't jump," Judith says. "It's not all that bad."

"That's the thing with high units," I say. "They give you the opportunity to enjoy great views while at the same time wondering what it would feel like to take the leap. Both at the same time."

"Yeah, well," she says, "one needn't preclude the other. It's just that if you do jump, your nice view becomes increasingly—and rapidly—diminished. It's not a perfect long-term strategy. See you next week, hon."

# CHAPTER 34

Thursday, 10:15 am

"**O**ff to today's art lesson, then?" I say, greeting Mr. Harrison as he pauses at the front desk to put on his jacket.

"No, not today, Mr. Hanratty," he answers. "In fact, I've skipped the last couple of lessons."

"Why is that, if I may ask?"

"To put it quite bluntly, I've been creating nothing but absolute shit," he says, spitting out the last word.

"Given what I am led to believe from Mr. Stewart, there appears to be a ready market for that. Shit art, that is," I say, taking a faint stab at humor.

"Hmm, yes, no doubt," he says, smiling. "Mr. Stewart should know all about shit art. But even my brand of shit art wouldn't sell. It's really quite bad, as it turns out." He walks to the reception area's coffee urn, where Mrs. McAdoo, 11A, and Mrs. Tang, 9A, have been engaged in a lengthy discussion on some bit of low-volume gossip. He interrupts them with a flirtatious comment or two, pours himself a cup of coffee, and returns to my counter.

"What happened?" I ask.

"You mean with the art lessons? Gone. Dried up. Kaput."

"But your talent is in there, is it not? I understand being a bit rusty—you didn't think you'd be creating masterpieces by week five, did you?"

He smiles, takes a sip of coffee and looks out the front door. "Time passed, that's what happened. I can't tell you how many dreadful meetings I sat through in my career, how many briefs I filed, how many clients I put up with, all with the firmly established thought in my head that someday, *someday*, I wouldn't have to endure this nonsense any longer, that I could get back to what I thought was truly important to me, not to anyone else, but to *me*. Creating art. It's what I had loved to do throughout my childhood. I would daydream, saying to myself that I will retire from the law once Father died, that I needn't continue living out his dreams for me. There's no way I could have done so prior to his death. I was a pleaser, not one of those kids who tried to punish his parents by making poor choices. But once Father died, our kids were in high school—private schools—and it didn't seem like a fitting time to put on the beret and pull out the oils. So, again, I held off. I became a partner and had a full pension dangling in front of me. It would *not* have been a responsible decision to leave so soon after achieving that status. And then, what I was most afraid of, what played at the back of my mind for years, turned out to be true. The talent—if it was ever there—was gone. As it turns out, there was an expiration date on that particular talent."

"But, sir, isn't it the act itself—the act of creation—that attracted you to the activity? Does it truly matter if it's good or not? If you enjoy it, why not do it?"

"To me it matters," he says. "If I'm just spinning my wheels, not producing anything of value, then the activity itself is meaningless, eh?"

"Well, maybe," I say, "but it seems—"

"Why spin our wheels, Mr. Hanratty? We're not caged gerbils. Our talents should be put to better use, don't you think?"

I look at him for a moment, and then look down at the pile of papers in front of me. A day's worth of delivery notifications, maintenance calls, and prearranged visitor listings. Mrs. McAdoo and Mrs. Tang loudly part one another's company and others spill from the elevator, heading toward the mailroom or outdoors. A series of morning greetings and shouted instructions are tossed in my direction. Within minutes, the lobby is quiet once again.

"Yes, well," I begin, "I suppose you may be right."

"I'm afraid I missed it—my window," he says. "Thought it would always be open for me. As I get older, I realize these opportunities might not always be there for us. And there's something a little sad in that, I think. Wish I'd have considered that when I was younger. I let a job get in the way of the things that I really cared for."

I've not seen Mr. Harrison in this type of mood before, somewhat maudlin and mawkish. But I recognize that there is far more to Mr. Harrison than his crossword puzzles and less-than-museum-quality etchings. A touch of the philosopher in him, really. He buttons his sport coat and heads toward the door. But before he exits, he turns and holds up his coffee cup, as if in a toast, "And so, young Hanratty, here's to the lawyer I never wanted to be, and to the artist who never was."

Once he steps outside, I push the papers on my counter off to the side. I open the drawer on my left, pull out a sheet of paper, and begin making a to-do list. The day's priorities have changed.

# CHAPTER 35

Thursday, 4:16 pm

There is a heightened level of excitement in the lobby this afternoon, a different energy from most Thursday afternoons. It is as if the wind has shifted direction a tad, or perhaps a rare and portentous bird has alighted on a nearby branch, or perhaps tea leaves at the bottom of a demitasse have arranged themselves in a meaningful and significant manner, or, perhaps better yet, a—

"What the hell is this?" Mr. Stewart bellows, to really no one in particular, as he explodes out of the mailroom holding a leaflet of paper. "Janet, do you know anything about this?"

Mrs. Catledge, 2E, who happened to be discussing the very topic with Mrs. Turnblad, 9C, in the living room, replies, "It's talking about a gallery moving into Fitzger's Jewelers."

"Isn't it great, Brendan?" Mrs. Turnblad asks.

"Great? No, I don't think it's so great. In fact, I think it's terrible. I think it's the most ridiculous thing I've ever heard."

"Oh, no, truly, Brendan, it's great," Mrs. Turnblad says. "You needn't be afraid of artists—they're really not so bad. I think it will be a wonderful addition to the building and the neighborhood." I surreptitiously jot down on a notepad in front of me—Mrs. Turnblad, yes; Mrs. Catledge, maybe?

The flyer Mr. Stewart is waving about in what I would typify as a slightly hysterical manner is the agenda for the building's next board meeting. Included within the agenda is Agenda item #1a: "Action Item: Discussion and vote on proposal to allow retail space to be leased as gallery space to Homeless Art Project (working title), 501(c)

(3), Mr. Henry Franken." I assume this is the item that has caught his attention, since the other listings are simply run-of-the-mill items: review of last month's minutes, approval of the semiannual hallway art rotation, review of maintenance expenditures, discussion of proposed themes for quarterly building mixer, and so forth.

At this precise moment, Charlotte comes out of her office, seemingly heading out for the evening, sunglasses on, purse on arm, perfume freshly spritzed, lipstick applied, and diet soda in hand. From her point of view, a more ill-timed exit would be difficult to imagine. Charlotte catches a whiff of the energy that is ricocheting about the lobby, stops dead in her tracks, and—none too inconspicuously—attempts to slowly back into her office once again, but too late.

"Charlotte!" Mr. Stewart roars. "What is this about an art gallery moving into Fitzger's? Do you know anything about it?"

"Well, uh," she opens, none too strongly as she pushes the sunglasses further up her nose, "I, I don't know too much about it. Something that Mr. Franken requested be put on the agenda."

"Oh, Mr. Franken did, did he? Give me his number, please. Right now. I am *really* frustrated by the fact that in the months since he's taken over the penthouse—since he's taken over this *building*—he hasn't once seen the need to introduce himself to any of us, but yet he puts a bombshell like this on the agenda for a vote, with no explanation?" He continues on in this manner, quite effectively filling what I believe those involved in the radio or television broadcast industry might refer to as dead air, as Charlotte, within her office, rummages about for my penthouse phone number or, perhaps, Judith Guncheon's number. Mr. Stewart's attempt to fill this lull continues, quite loudly, from outside her office while her muffled responses can be heard intermittently emanating from within her office, along with the sounds of drawers slamming, piles of paper and folders being shifted about, and cabinets being rapidly opened and closed.

I pick up a pen and Post-it note and begin to write down two numbers.

"Charlotte," I say.

Charlotte sticks her head—hair now disheveled and white-rimmed sunglasses placed at an odd angle amongst the mass of black curls—out of her office to shout instructions to me to look through the contact database on my computer for both Mr. Franken's and Judith Guncheon's phone numbers.

"Wait," says Mr. Stewart, "you don't even know Franken's phone number?"

"Charlotte—" I attempt again.

"I'll have it for you in a moment, Brendan. Franklin, would you *please* hurry? Brendan needs those numbers. I totally agree with you, Brendan. It is so weird that Franken would put a bombshell on the agenda like this and who knows if he'll show up for the meeting? I would, of course, have confirmed with him, but I haven't even met the guy yet. How am I supposed to do my job, huh? How am I?"

"Charlotte—"

"Franklin, would you *please* hurry up and look for the numbers? I don't want to keep Mr. Stewart here waiting." And then, in a confidential stage whisper, "You know, Mr. Stewart, I think it's really weird how we never see Franken, don't you? I mean, don't you think that's creepy? After all, I'm the *manager* of this building and I've never even met him face-to-face? And now he's moving ahead with a vote on something as important as this and he's never met with the residents? I mean, I just find that peculiar. Maybe that's just me, but what am I supposed to do? Franklin!"

"Char—" I say.

"He just keeps sending that lawyer chick, Gucci, or whatever her name is."

"Judith Guncheon. And Charlotte I have the numbers you're looking for right here." I hand her the Post-it with two numbers, the penthouse unit's and Judith's.

"Where did you get this?" she asks. "You didn't even go to your computer."

"I've got a mind for numbers," I say.

She looks at me with a questioning expression over her sunglasses, which have fallen to the end of her nose, before turning to Mr. Stewart to hand him the Post-it.

"Brendan, if you're successful in getting through to Henry Franken, you tell him he owes me a call—or, like, fifty. Tell him I wouldn't mind the opportunity to meet him—my *boss*, I might add—someday."

Mr. Stewart, with Post-it in hand, is already at the elevators. "Yeah, okay, Charlotte, got it. Although only one battle is going to be fought at a time and, right now, yours ain't it. A deep second." The elevator doors shush open, and he is gone. Charlotte turns back to me from the elevators.

"Say, Franklin? You never even got near your computer to write those numbers down—Franken and Guncheon's numbers."

"Oh, I did, though, Charlotte. While you were looking in your office, I took a moment to open the database and pull up the numbers. Nothing more than that."

"Let me see," she says. "Turn the screen around."

Confounded woman, this one. Really quite tenacious when she sets her mind to something. I start to turn the databaseless screen toward her, when all of a sudden, coming out of the mailroom, we hear——

"Hey, Franklin-wiener, how's the schtuppin'—Ho! Charlotte! Hey-hey-ho! Did *not* see you there. So DID not see you there. No way, no how. Say! Am I early today? Or are you working late? Wha-hat is going on in this here lobby, huh?"

"Oh, Jacob, shush," she says. "Help us pretend you're a doorman, just this once, would you? Knock off the fucking street talk when you're on the premises, okay?"

"Yes, you are absolutely right, Charlotte. Consider said street talk—fucking or otherwise—to be off-knocked. That goes for you too, Franky. Wa-ay too loud in here—bring it down, now. You heard what the lady said. I'm on it, Charlotte. I've got your, uh, back. Hmm-hm."

The lobby is filling up with the evening rush. People are greeting one another, asking how each others' days were. Clusters of short conversations begin and end. A deliveryman from Hour Drop approaches the front counter and signs in. There are sufficient distractions at this point that Charlotte loses interest in the mysteries surrounding jotted-down phone numbers.

"Franklin, can you and Jacob handle all this? If so, I'm going to take off," she says, halfway out the door.

"No problem, Charlotte," I say. "Many thanks."

"Goddamn, I'm losing my timing in my advancing years," Jacob says. "Time was, I wouldn't see her for weeks—like the saying, two shits passing out of sight."

"Yeah, that's not, uh, really the—"

"But now, hell, I might just as well move in with her. You have GOT to scoot her out earlier, Frank-man. You springing your little surprises of having her hang around here until I show up is just about giving me a major heart attack-ack-ack. Ain't no damn way I can be my charming self to the fine residents of L'Hermitage with little Miss Dark Cloud floating about here. I gotta smile, man. I gotta make people feel good, know what I mean? I gotta be up. I swear, when I'm working and she's around, she throws me off my game, you with me on this?"

I certainly want everyone to be at the top of their game, so, suspecting that I might be putting a slight crimp in Jacob's style, I beg his leave.

"Yeah, yeah, yeah," he says, with a dismissive shooing gesture. "Go, go. But I'd ask you to give thought around some sort of signal system that you can rig up letting me know when Charlotte is and isn't here, got it? Maybe just a warning text, or, no, no, no, better yet, just shoot me one of those 'moji things, maybe the one that looks like the devil, that'll be our code. That wouldn't be so difficult, right? You don't want your number-one man croaking from another, what do you call it, corollary. Isn't that right, Mrs. Richards? Howdy-do to you. And to you, too, Mrs. Berger. Don't think for a minute I didn't see you ladies over there looking all lovely and hotsy too."

As I head for the door, I hear the ding of the elevators and out walk Mrs. Turnblad and Mrs. Tang.

"Oh my god, will you look at these two CATS heading out for a prowl? Me-OWW!" Jacob says.

I turn back, aghast, expecting the two to be furious. But, instead, they break out into shrieks of laughter.

"Meow yourself, Jacob," says Mrs. Tang. "By the way, sweetheart, the Bonairs are coming over at eight tonight for a little canasta."

"Got it down right here in the schedule, ma'am. Here's what it says: 'The boners are gonna erupt tonight like Mount Shasta.' It's all down here in black and white; I'm on top of it. I don't care what you say about him, Mrs. T., my boy, Franky, keeps excellent notes. I've trained him well."

Again, screeches of laughter from the two ladies. Although my shift and Jacob's have certainly overlapped—it's part of my job to see that they do with the passing on of notes and updates—I realize that in the half year that I've been here, I've rarely seen him in action with the residents. And while his style might be radically different from my own, what with his insouciance and, shall we say, irreverence, he does, indeed, seem to know how to play to an audience.

# CHAPTER 36

Thursday, 4:53 pm

I walk down the alley toward the penthouse vestibule of L'Hermitage, giving thought to both Mr. Stewart's reaction to the distributed agenda, as well as Jacob's interaction with Mrs. Turnblad and Mrs. Tang. Though he had often been impertinent with me, I thought that was simply our shtick—his routine with his direct supervisor, his indifferent shrug at authority, laughable of a representation of authority as I may be. I had not realized that it actually stretched into a floor show with the residents. And, quite frankly, if Mmes. Harrison and Tang can be considered a dependable focus group, his performances are not only put up with, but seemingly appreciated, enjoyed, and perhaps even anticipated, at least on this particular evening.

As I put my key into the vestibule's lock, a noise behind me brings me out of my deliberations.

"Franklin? What are you doing?"

I turn quickly to see Mr. Stewart standing near the utility dumpsters.

"Mr. Stewart, uh, hello," I say. "What are you doing back here? Can I . . . can I help you?"

"No," he says, shaking his head and slowly approaching. "*I* don't need any help, but I can't help but wonder, Franklin, why it is you're going into the penthouse entrance. Aren't you off duty right now?"

"I am, sir. Yes, indeed I am." I pause, hoping he'll jump in at this point and swerve this particular conversation in another direction. Nothing. More dead air. "I would think this probably looks a little, well, uh, suspicious," I say.

"Yeah, as a matter of fact it does," he says. "So, what's going on?"

"Well, part of my job—at the end of my shift, well, actually, at various times throughout my shift, as well—is to check and make sure the penthouse owner's door, uh, Mr. Franken's door is properly locked and hasn't been tampered with."

"Uh-huh, check the door," he says, tilting his head back and looking down his nose at me. "And you need to actually unlock the door with the key you have there to determine that the door is locked and . . . hasn't been tampered with?"

Jesus, this inquisition. Although I had certainly known there always existed the possibility that someone would see me entering the building by way of the penthouse's private entrance, I had assumed, incorrectly, that it might happen by someone looking out of their small utility room windows on the upper floors. It hadn't occurred to me that I would carelessly overlook someone standing by the dumpsters. I had always played it out in my mind that if I were to chance upon someone in the alley, I could explain it away by yammering on about perimeter reconnaissance or some such nonsense. People, for the most part, observe actions and personal presentations within a given context. But, presently, Mr. Stewart is working against that particular assumption.

"Well, yes. It simply is part of my job description," I say, opening the door, sticking my neck in for a nanosec, and then shutting and locking the door.

"All clear, Franklin?" he asks.

"Seems to be," I say. "All seems to be in order. As usual. Well, good night, then."

"Take me up to his apartment, Franklin."

"Sir?"

"I said, take me up there. I've been waiting back here for a fucking half hour to meet this Mr. Franken and talk to him about his stupid plan for Fitzger's. Homeless art gallery. Goddamn. He doesn't return calls. He doesn't introduce himself to anyone in the building, but he sure as hell is comfortable imposing his cute little idea on the rest of us. Well, it isn't going to happen—I'll make damn sure of that. But I want to talk to him. So . . . take me up there."

"But, sir, I can't do that. Besides, I don't think he's up there at present."

"Well, who would know? No one has seen him enter or leave the building. He doesn't return calls—"

"But doesn't his lawyer, Ms. Guncheon, return calls?"

"Oh, yes, I've talked with her, but it's *him* I want to talk to now," he says, nodding his head skyward. "So, let's go. Open the door, Franklin."

"No, sir. I'm afraid I can't do that."

"You know, Franklin, it looked a lot like you were trying to illegally enter this unit. Do you do that with the other units, too? Have you tried to enter my unit, Franklin? Convenient that you always know when people are home or away, isn't it? And that you have keys that would allow entrance to any unit within the building. All very convenient for a doorman, isn't it?"

Oh. I see. We're going down that path, are we? Now it's my turn to stand up a little taller, a little straighter, and look down my nose.

"Sir, are you aware of items missing from your apartment or from others? To my knowledge, there hasn't been a rash of break-ins or burglaries within our building. In fact, I'm unaware of any one unit being illegally or improperly entered since I've been here. So, I'm afraid, I'm not quite sure of the direction of this conversation."

"Oh, Franklin, you clearly are not schooled in the myriad forms of theft—"

"You are correct about that, sir. I am not. Although it has been brought to my attention recently that theft does, indeed, take many forms. Now if you'll excuse me, I'll be on my way. Best wishes in your attempts to get ahold of Mr. Franken. I know, for a fact, that he oftentimes comes home not at—" I look down at my watch——"ten after five, but, rather, more often after midnight. Bit of a night owl, as it turns out. And, yes, he does, most often, enter through the front doors, not through this alleyway."

I turn and head back to the alley's entrance. What I assumed was a conversation heading down a path in which Mr. Stewart had made the realization that Henry Franken and Franklin Hanratty are, in fact, one in the same had veered off in a far more nefarious direction.

It's becoming clearer that a reveal might be necessary. It's no longer easy hiding behind a doorman's cape.

After killing three hours of time by walking in the park, eating at Baluchi's, and browsing at Westsider Books, I work my nerve up to return to L'Hermitage. This time, unlike my nonchalant stroll through the alley earlier, I am vigilant and cautious. I proceed slowly, staying along the sides of the buildings, rather than walking obliviously and incautiously down the middle, as I had done earlier in the evening prior to my run-in with Mr. Stewart. I return to my previously established procedures, when my charade was brand new, looking for movement or any signs of human presence.

Prior to crossing the alley to approach the vestibule, I carefully examine the back windows of L'Hermitage. Satisfied that no one is watching, I cross, unlock the door, and enter the elevator.

Although I had initially felt like a stranger in a very strange land when entering my father's condo months ago, my feelings toward the penthouse have changed in the last few weeks. As I enter my space, lights from the city flood the living room and entryway, so much so that I needn't initially turn on any interior lighting. I walk to the windows and look out. I see people in their apartments across the way, eating, watching television, talking on their phones, pulling blinds, walking between rooms. In the top unit in the building directly across the street, I see a man looking out from his windows, arms behind his back. At first glance, I mistakenly think he, in his window, is simply a mirror image of me in mine, somehow a trick of light, reflection, and space. But then a woman walks up behind him—his wife? His lover?—and hugs him, looking out on the street scene with him. She says something that makes both of them laugh. They turn away from the window and walk out of the room together.

I turn and face the emptiness of my apartment. My cell phone flashlight is blinking, which means only one thing—Judith has left a message. I listen to it—Judith at her shortest and most succinct. "Call me, kid," it says. The timestamp indicates that the call came in while I was wandering the West Side—after my conversation with Mr. Stewart. Since Judith rarely calls in the middle of the week, saving up any news items for our Saturday morning visits, I assume there is a certain sense of urgency behind her call and that the urgency might just be related to Mr. Stewart.

"Oh, yeah, kid, I got some news for you," Judith says upon picking up my call, eschewing any howdy-do pleasantries and jumping right into the matter at hand.

"Let's see," she says, "where should I begin? Here's a good spot; maybe you can help me out. I got a problem because I have two screaming headlines for you, and I just don't know which one to lead with. Kind of like when the news producers had to decide between opening with Reagan's inauguration or Iran's release of the American prisoners—kind of like that, you know what I mean? Maybe I'll save the historical references for later. Tonight, let's stick to the hysterical ones, shall we? 'Cause I got a ton of those."

She is clearly enjoying this, savoring the moment, working at stretching it out for as long as possible without breaking it, which is never a good sign with Judith. Given the slight slur of her speech, I suspect she might also be savoring and stretching out her second—possibly third—cocktail.

"Is this windup an attempt to run up my bill?" I ask.

"Yeah, okay, on with the show. Here, let's try this on," she says. "I'll approach it from this angle and see what you think. I'll combine the two and we'll just see how it plays. Brendan Stewart thinks you're a cat burglar—his term, not mine. Kind of cute, though, don't you think? And he now wants to rent out the jewelry space. So, there you go. Which one you wanna discuss first?"

The cat burglar issue is news to Judith only, so I set this one aside for the time being. The rental of the jewelry space, however, is a genuine, bona fide headliner.

"What are you talking about? He wants to rent Fitzger's?" I ask. "It's been available for months. Why hasn't he stepped forward earlier?"

"Well, if you were a poker player—which, sadly, I suspect you most definitely are not—you would understand that you have, in effect, forced his hand. Stewart wouldn't have given a shit if a shoe store or a candy shop was moving in there. But an art gallery, no way. He can't stomach that. He feels threatened by this move, the fact that a competitor is moving into his very own building, right under his nose. And a big part of this, I suspect, is that Brendan Stewart—or 'B. S.,' as I will now affectionately refer to him—feels dissed. A little of his reaction is concern about one more art gallery competing in the neighborhood against his own. But, quite frankly, it may be more about his own goddamn pride."

"But he can't take this personally. We're talking about an organization aimed purely at helping homeless artists. We're just giving them studio and display space. How can that possibly be threatening to him? To him and his, his . . . soot artists?"

"Oh, snap, as my neighbor's kid would say," Judith says. "The boy has some fight in him after all. Yeah, well, you know, competition is in the eye of the beholder. Or, at least, in the eye of the gallery owner who is fighting for his life to stay solvent. It's a tough market out there, Henry, especially for the Brendan Stewarts of the world who, as I understand it, happens to be teetering on the edge of bankruptcy. If he doesn't feel painted in a corner, he may feel like he's been, at least, pointed to the corner. And he doesn't like it. So, here's the deal: he's planning on growing his way out of his debt. And he wants our retail display space for his inventory that's been doing nothing but sitting in storage. Maybe he was wavering before over that space and the agenda item forced him to commit and, quite honestly, I think he increasingly talked himself into the wisdom of his move while he and I were talking. In any event, we now have a new action item on the agenda. The board will now be asked to vote on which occupant they want in Fitzger's—Brendan Stewart's upper-end chi-chi gallery—again, his words, not mine—or a nonprofit homeless artist gallery. So now, my young friend, you have a bit of a fight on your hands. Because I'm Henry Franken's representative, I can make as strong a case as possible within the context of the meeting, but I'm simply an intermediary. Your neighbors are getting restless that the real Henry Franken never shows up. And, you know what? Stewart is going to be in the meeting, twisting arms, looking people directly in the eye, and saying he needs this space. A building owner who can't even make the time to be at a meeting and make a case for this nonprofit organization won't get a great deal of consideration. I'm just sayin'."

I let out a heavy sigh and fiddle with a pencil and paper that are sitting next to the phone.

"Is there anything else, Judith?" I ask.

"Well, yeah, just this thing about you being a cat burglar and breaking into every unit in L'Hermitage, and some poop about you possibly being a drug dealer, but, I suppose, we can table all that until our next meeting."

"Yeah, I'd prefer that," I say. "I need to do some thinking."

"Yes, I suppose you do. But your window, Henry? Not the one you're probably staring out right now, but the window that is allowing you the luxury of noodling about and playing the Hamlet shtick? It's closing rapidly, know what I mean? It's unhealthy for cat burglars to get locked in on the wrong side of a closed window. Yeah, okay, that metaphor might be a bit of a stretch, but you get the general drift. Anyhoo, this conversation has just gone long enough that I can justifiably and with all clear conscience charge you another quarter hour. And, more important to one of us, I gotta go freshen up my G and T. See you, sugar plum . . . Sylvie! Make me another—"

Judith clicks off and I go to change out of my doorman's uniform.

I put on blue jeans and a summer-weight sweater, slide on my two-tone sneakers, and take the elevator down. The main elevator, not the service elevator.

# CHAPTER 38

Thursday, 9:03 pm

One can overthink these things, I suppose. Judith asked that I drop the Hamlet act, but her comparison is not quite right. I suspect she imagines me to be mucking about castle parapets and whatnot—or, at least, the roof of L'Hermitage—with overwrought expressions of agony and despair on my face, wondering if I should dash myself onto the building's canopy below as a means of escaping my frozen indecision.

But, I'm not. There is no such thing as a great epiphany, at least within my experience. I know exactly what needs to be done and have known—in one form or another—for a long time. The issue, as with so many matters, comes down to one of timing. Timing and, now with Mr. Stewart's annoying entrance onto stage, odds.

I exit L'Hermitage from the front doors. Both the lobby and the reception rooms are empty—no idea where Jacob has headed off to. I walk towards 5th Avenue. It's evenings like this that I seek the solitude that only the park can give me, whether there are hundreds of walkers like me or not.

I think back to a conversation my father and I had when I was thirteen or fourteen.

He had told me to watch for the sparks of life and when they appear, grab them.

"I don't get it," I'd said in my sullen, early teenage posturing way. There's no stupider creature to walk the planet than a fourteen-year-old boy's father.

"Too often, we miss the clues and magic that surround us," he said. "But there are sparks, Henry. And we need to see them and harness them. That's where the magic of life comes in."

My grunt of semiacknowledgment must have sufficiently encouraged him to continue along this line.

"When those sparks come along, grab them. Follow them. Use them to create something wonderful, Henry."

"Like what, a bunch of bland buildings?" I asked.

As soon as I said it, I regretted it. The phrase "bland buildings" was not my own. It was a phrase used within a *Post* editorial column about the problematic growth of corporate landlords within the New York metropolitan area. Dad's company was mentioned as one of the key offenders of the growing trend, how these practices take advantage of low-income residents and destroy a community's fabric. It was a column that made an impression on me, not only because it provided a greater sense of how Dad spent his days and made his money, but, more importantly, informed me of a sensitive weak spot within his makeup. The columnist had ended with the throwaway line, "and, furthermore, Franken's new construction simultaneously insults and assaults the cityscape with its patently bland buildings." Dad was seemingly willing to accept the charges pertaining to moral turpitude; it was the imputation of a pedestrian aesthetic that most offended him. Of this, I was keenly aware.

"Yeah," he said, after a painful pause. "Build yourself a bunch of bland buildings." I would rather he had slapped me at that moment rather than giving the defeated response he did. He was simply trying to pass on a lesson to his son—"Build something"—and my retort was both painful and superfluous. I didn't have the ability to apologize. The moment stuck with me, if not him, for years.

◆　◆　◆

I enter the park at 69th and begin meandering in the direction of the bandshell. In what remains of the dim summer light, I can see that there is some sort of show taking place on the stage. A small but appreciative crowd is listening to a trio of young men, two on violins, one on bass, perform an eclectic combination of classical and rock music. It is the type of music that allows me to sit on the periphery, enjoy, soak up, but yet continue to fashion a game plan of sorts without an inordinate amount of distraction or unfocused concentration.

If nothing else, my conversation with Judith clarified for me that I have turned a corner in my thinking about the next steps. Up until that call, I had been mildly ambivalent about the use of the retail space, the creation of an organization focused on helping homeless artists, and in revealing my very identity. A fun idea, an *interesting* idea, but is it a solution, either for me or for those it might serve? But with the slightest whiff of having it removed as a possibility at this point in time, I feel both protective and defensive. And that whiff, that flutter of a response within me, would be what my father, were he here, might label as a spark.

The on-stage trio shifts effortlessly from "Hallelujah" to "Shenandoah" following polite applause from the audience. That all transitions could be so elegant and uncomplicated, I think. I prioritize my to-do list as follows: Number 1—form an organization that provides a safe space for homeless artists to create and display their art. Number 2—build that space within a well-trafficked area, thereby helping the artists more quickly get back on their feet. L'Hermitage certainly fits this criterion and, well, since it's my own building, that's exactly where I would like the gallery to reside, Mr. Stewart be hanged. And, Number 3—if it turns out that it advances the cause, step forward as the building's owner to properly make the case.

But this leads to another important realization. These three to-do items, which I thought might be separate and unconnected, now seem not only connected, but perhaps, as one. And although I have ranked it as the third priority of to-dos, my disclosure might actually prove to be the critical step that allows the two other pieces to fall into place.

Best, however, to ease into the revelation. Perhaps best to test the waters, in a manner of speaking. To float a trial balloon by a sympathetic and fully understanding audience might help me hone my message once I take the main stage, should it come to that. And so, I get up from my park bench and head back to L'Hermitage, despite the fact that it is 9:30 and past the hour that most genteel people would consider the cut-off time for the unannounced pop-in. After all, sparks do fly.

# CHAPTER 39

Thursday, 9:53 pm

From the elevator bank, I walk down the long hallway to Wendy's apartment. The corridor is empty, which suits my present mood, although in this instance, unlike within the alley earlier this evening, I am better prepared to run into a resident.

I knock on Wendy's door and, a moment later, I hear a voice behind me.

"Oh, Franklin, I didn't recognize you, at first. More messages? At this hour?"

"Good evening, Mrs. Hill," I say. "Feeling well, I trust?"

"Oh, yes, yes. Not bad this evening, although I certainly wouldn't mind feeling better, of course. If I felt better, I could go out of an evening, you know. Perhaps to the theater with friends, but probably not tonight."

"Yes, well, anyway, I hope you feel better soon, ma'am. Have a nice evening."

"Hmm," she murmurs, continuing to look at me.

"Yes, well, you have a good evening then . . ." I say.

"These messages, Franklin, who sends them? Are they telegrams, or cables, or some such thing?" she asks, while looking down at my empty hands.

"This is, uh, actually a verbal message that I'm delivering tonight," I say with a slight smile and wink. Most mysterious, I am, but I allow the proverbial door to open just a crack for our bit of collusion.

"Hmm, so unusual in this day of pocket phones. Oh, and computers . . . and the like."

Finally—finally!—Wendy's door opens. She is dressed in a bathrobe with a towel wrapped in her hair.

"Oh! Franklin," she says, "and Mrs. Hill, too. Huh—hi. How nice to see . . . both . . . of you."

"Hello, Wendy. I am here in my official duty. That being of bringing a message. Uh, to you," I say. Mrs. Hill continues to stand in her doorway. "Well," I begin again, "it is of a somewhat personal and confidential nature, so—" looking at Mrs. Hill and then back at Wendy—"perhaps I should enter your apartment—this one I've never, or, not never but *rarely*, been in before—to deliver . . . said personal . . . and confidential message . . . that has been given to me . . . to deliver to you. And just you."

"Yes, yes, of course, come in," she says, "to deliver your confidential message. To me."

"Very good. Well, goodnight then, Mrs. Hill," I say quickly before jumping across the threshold.

"Goodnight, Franklin," Mrs. Hill says. "Oh, and Franklin—did you bring any messages for me? Did any come in?"

"I'm afraid not, Mrs. Hill," I say. "But as soon as I get downstairs, I'll check once again for you, if you would like."

"Good night, Mrs. Hill," Wendy says while shutting the door. Before the door clicks shut, however, we hear one more utterance from Mrs. Hill, "Most myster—"

"Hmm, such a deep, deep mystery," Wendy says, putting her arms around my neck. "Can't wait to find out what your personal and confidential message is."

"The message is, 'Get dressed.' We're going out tonight."

"The two of us are going out? Together? Wow . . . brave young boy. This is a first."

"It's time to celebrate my birthday," I say.

"Well then, I'm dressed appropriately," she says, letting her robe drop and kissing me, pulling me close to her still-damp body.

◆   ◆   ◆

An hour later, we jump in a cab on Madison.

"Carlyle Hotel," I instruct the cabbie.

"Carlyle?" Wendy asks. "As in John Pizzarelli, Woody Allen Carlyle?"

"Yes, but I'm not taking you to the Cafe Carlyle tonight—and, by the way, before we go any further, this entire evening—what's left of it—is on me. I'm taking you to another bar within the Carlyle, Bemelmans. Have you been there? It was Dad's favorite in all the years he lived here. He always said there was no finer bar in the entire city."

"That sounds like high praise," she says. "I've never been there. But if it's your birthday, shouldn't I be the one paying?"

I turn from the window and say to her, "Yeah, probably, but it's not really my birthday. I lied. My birthday is months off. I just feel like celebrating."

"Well, anything within the Carlyle sounds expensive. Truly, I'd be just as happy celebrating with you at Taco Bell."

"I wouldn't," I say. "Tonight, this doorman doesn't worry about costs. Besides, I do very well with my tip money and my coupon clipping."

We ride the next several blocks in silence, Wendy sidled next to me and my arm around her. Our cabbie, who I suspect was an ambulance driver in a previous career, deftly weaves his way in and out of Madison Avenue traffic, gunning through yellow lights, passing other cabs, and putting his horn to good use—depending upon one's viewpoint. For the first time in months, I feel comfortable contemplating my future and allowing myself a sprinkle of optimism and excitement. Hence, the spontaneous celebration.

The cab pulls up in front of the Carlyle and a doorman opens my door.

"Good evening, sir. Ma'am," he says. I pay the cab driver and hand the doorman a ten-dollar tip.

We enter the Carlyle, go up the stairs and to the left to enter Bemelmans. This was the venue Dad always wanted to go whenever a celebration was in order, and if there was no reason to celebrate, he would make up one ("Another day of life? Close enough.")

Wendy lets out a small gasp upon our entrance. "Franklin, it's beautiful," she says.

The bar area is fully occupied, but a few tables remain available near the midroom stage. My preference, however, is the same as my father's the first time he took me to Bemelmans. I hand the maître d' two twenty-dollar bills and ask for a table in the back corner.

"Yes," he says, "I believe that can be arranged."

After a few moments, he leads us to a table with a perfect view of the piano and musicians, who are just coming back from their break for the final set of the evening. The bar's decor is an intersection of childhood and adulthood—from one angle, it could be a kid's bedroom; from another, a speakeasy. The bar is lit softly by table candle lamps, each with small Bemelmans-painted shades. While the Café Carlyle, just across the hall, receives most of the attention due to the standing or renown of the musicians who perform there, the distinct artwork of Bemelmans is what always attracted Dad. "The martinis are cold and deep and who wouldn't mind sitting inside a children's book for a few hours, Henry? Just keep the little kiddies on the outside of the book; that's all I ask," he would say, unsentimentally, whenever he took me here on my visits to the city.

"Please don't do that on my account, Franklin," Wendy says, seemingly out of the blue since I haven't done a thing for her as of yet.

"Do what?"

"Ten dollars for a doorman to open a cab door? Forty dollars for the maître d' to walk us to this table, which, if you hadn't noticed, was open anyway? It's all very impressive, but I truly don't want you throwing money away like that for my sake. Don't worry—you impress me already. You don't need to do that."

I'm not sure what to say at this moment. To begin with, I had attempted to be subtle with my tips. Secondly, I thought I had handed over the currency in such a way that, were she to have noticed, she could not see the denominations.

"I tend to be generous with those in the service industry," I confess. A true statement, but my intimation is misleading. "We're a subset of the population that tends to take good care of each other, that's all."

"Franklin," she says, in a tone that is slightly less endearing than the last time she uttered my name, "please. I know about these things—how people can sometimes throw money around in a way that's meant to impress those around them. Trust me, I know all about those motivations. All I'm saying is that it's not necessary to do so with me. I would like for us to be able to be ourselves around each other. No pretend games, no posing. I just find it takes so much energy."

At this point in our conversation, the three musicians, led by the piano player Loston Harris, take their spots and begin tuning up. Judging by the badinage that takes place between the piano player and a few chaps at nearby tables and at the bar, there appear to be several regulars in attendance tonight. And then, as if a switch has been flipped, the three go from chatting, tuning up, and taking swigs from their drinks, to launching into a finger-snapping version of "From This Moment On."

The waiter quickly comes to our table—no doubt made aware by the maître d' that a generous tipper has entered the premises—and takes our orders. In tribute to Dad and the history of this place, I order his favorite drink, a Bombay Sapphire martini with a thimble of Lillet Blanc wine and a lemon twist.

"Well, if it's a cocktail evening, I'll have a Cosmopolitan, made with Absolut Citron," Wendy says.

"Very good, then," he says. I order the croque monsieur, the cheese plate, and eight fresh oysters on the half shell for appetizers.

Once the waiter has left our table, Wendy turns to me and says, "Franklin, this place is incredibly expensive. What are you doing?

And, by the way, what was it you just ordered?"

"The croque monsieur. It's just a ham and cheese sandwich on soft bread. The French name allows them to jack up the price by fifteen bucks."

"But, about the expense—please, let's just split the bill. Look at the people around here. I love this place, but aren't we a little out of our league?"

Her question surprises me, coming from a person who is accustomed to playing amongst this league, but I say to her, "We're celebrating my coming out."

She has a blanched look on her face, and I realize my statement might lead to a misinterpretation that doesn't necessarily work toward the betterment of our relationship. "Oh, sorry," I say. "I was speaking broadly. Here's what I mean: ever since my dad died, I've been in somewhat of a fog. I've put my life on hold, hidden within the comforts of a doorman position. But, recently, I've been feeling I'm ready for new challenges, to maybe move on from this position. And so, I'm . . . excited to be celebrating this decision with you."

"Ah, now I get it. You scared me for a moment. Well, not scared me, that's not the right word. More like . . . concerned me. But, you can afford this splurge tonight?"

"I told you—I do very well with my tips, all in all." For a moment, I'm tempted to go the full distance with Wendy, telling her the whole story of Franklin Hanratty and Henry Franken, but right then, our drinks arrive. I pick up my martini, take a long pull on it and, as Dad always did after that first sip, say, "Doesn't that take the edge off the day?"

"You're a very unusual man, Franklin," Wendy says, after taking a sip from her drink. "So unlike most of the guys I've dated —oh, wait. We are dating, right?"

I take another sip before heaving a bon mot in her direction. "Well, you're in very sophisticated company right now." The trio begins a mid-tempo version of "The Lady is a Tramp" at just the moment that

Wendy slides over to me and puts her arm through mine.

"Franklin, there's something I've been wanting to tell you for a while," she begins. "My . . . the condo I live in? I just, well, really, have a problem with money."

"*You* have a problem with money? *I've* got a problem with money," I say. "I've been wrestling with it for years. I've wanted to talk to you about it, but I was too ashamed. But I feel I'm ready to come out from under it, you know? You and I just need to . . . you know, the thing is, I'm coming to believe it's all right. Accepting our financial situation is a necessary part of maturing, don't you think? It's taken me years to come to that realization, but I truly think—for the first time in my life—that I'm coming to grips with it. And it feels great, I have to say. In fact, it feels so damn good, let's have another round. I got a plan for the first time in my life. And it feels so good."

"Jesus, give the man two sips of a martini and he turns into a regular jukebox Saturday night. Anyway, I was afraid you wouldn't understand. I was afraid you would think poorly of me. So to speak."

I look at her askance. "Well, it's not exactly like your situation was a secret. You are, after all, living in Unit 8D. It's one of the building's most beautiful units."

"Thank you, Ella Fitzgerald," Wendy says, in a slightly tipsy, nonsequitorish sort of way, hoisting her glass up in a mock toast to the trio. I realize that the musicians have just segued into "They Can't Take That Away From Me" and her gesture becomes clear.

"You're good with music," I say.

"They can't take that away from me," she says, smiling. "But I'm afraid they can. And will."

She puts her head down on my shoulder. The waiter walks over with another round for us. "Sir, this is on the house. It sounded like the two of you were celebrating something, so Bemelmans would like to be a part of that celebration. Compliments of Anders, our maître d."

Anders gives a nod from his post at the door. "Ah, terrific," I say, thanking the waiter and holding my hand up in Anders' direction.

"Very nice touch," I add. A second waiter comes up behind the first waiter and delivers our ordered hors d'oeuvres.

"You see?" I say to Wendy. "That's what a generous tip just bought us. I assure you, they are not sending free rounds to everyone in this place who exudes a hint of celebration. A generous tip always puts everyone in a good frame of mind—both the giver and the recipient. And that's the point, Wendy. It's okay to have and to give. It took me a while to get there, but I believe I've finally arrived. And that, my friend, calls for celebration."

She looks up at me slightly glazed—the cosmo has gotten to her—gives me a kiss and sits up to take in the food that has just been brought to us. "All I know, Mr. Doorman, is we're both very good at the giving out—*that* I've seen tonight. What we need to improve on—fast—you and I, with our money problems, is this part about bringing it in, that you've touched upon so elegantly."

A bit of a lull descends upon our table as we begin the eating portion of the evening, a welcome relief to the heady—and slightly woozy—drinking segment of the festivities. Wendy appears to be drawn more to the croque monsieur than she is to the half-shell oysters. I slurp two down, take another sip of my martini and broach another topic with her. Since we're on such an agreeable course, it only seems right to take the opportunity to do a little backroom politicking, so to speak.

"Wendy, you're aware that we're having a condo board meeting, right? And you're aware that there's an important vote coming up regarding the Fitzger's retail space, yes?"

"Yes, but I don't go to those meetings. Too busy."

"It'll be very important that you attend this meeting, however," I say, in my best lobbying mode. "To begin with, we'll need a quorum, but we'll also need as much support around the art gallery proposal as possible. I know Stewart is pushing hard for his agenda item, which has done nothing but muddy the water. Anyway, I know we haven't discussed this directly, but may I assume you're in support of that space being used as a homeless artist gallery and studio space, like what we talked about the other night?"

"Yeah, but I'm not entirely sure I can be there," she says. "I'll do my best, okay?"

Odd, this. I would've thought she'd jump at the chance to assist me in this endeavor. But, of course, though she may regard it as my idea, she doesn't recognize it as my endeavor. For all she knows, I'm simply wrangling a crowd on behalf of Mr. Franken.

"Well, in a large way this would certainly benefit Terry and Tomata and others. But beyond that, there's something else you need to understand about me."

"And now, a little something for our two lovebirds in the corner," says the piano player. I look up and see both him and Anders, the maître d', smiling in our direction.

Good heavens, a big tip certainly goes far these days—some might say, too far. I hold off on saying what I was about to say to Wendy for the time being, but I realize that the moment may have passed. I settle back in my seat, put my arm around her, and hold up my martini glass in a toast back to our hosts.

"Ladies and gentlemen, this is a little song we like to play when we see two lovers snuggled up in one of our corner tables," Harris says. "Whenever folks are as cuddled up as those two are in a dark corner, *and* when they order eight—not two, not four, but *eight*—oysters on a half shell, then we know there's some secrets floating about back there, isn't that right, Anders? When they order eight, someone's gonna 'preciate, hey?"

At this, both Anders and Harris let out an all-knowing stage guffaw, which the audience joins in with a smidge of laughter and a few catcalls.

"Anyway, young lovers, this is a song some in this audience will recognize from their old Frank Sinatra or Doris Day albums. It's a beauty called 'Secret Love.'"

# CHAPTER 40

Friday, 3:42 pm

That there is an energy in the lobby this afternoon—the afternoon of our vote—is palpable. People have been gathering in clusters throughout the day, primarily during the morning's rush hour, and even more so now, as increased traffic moves and dawdles through the lobby in the late-afternoon hours. There is an anticipatory party atmosphere as residents, rather than rushing through the doors to head to the mailroom or directly to the elevators, linger, looking for the latest news or gossip about the evening's proceedings.

I, too, have been doing a bit of politicking or, at least, canvassing and surveying, in my own subtle, doormanish way. In my arguably unscientific method of research, I am sensing that the vote will be a close one, but that the tide, in recent days, has been moving in the direction of the homeless art gallery and away from the rather off-putting horse trading Mr. Stewart has recently resorted to.

"I discern the slightest aroma of panic," Mrs. Rubin, 6D, said to me under her breath yesterday morning after passing one of Mr. Stewart's strong-handed jawboning sessions, this time with Mrs. Pelletier, 5D, at the coffee cart. "A most repugnant smell, wouldn't you agree, Franklin?"

I only smile. Any further reply or encouragement of such remarks would be highly impolitic on my side.

"Franklin, come over here please."

Mrs. Hill has entered the eye of the storm this afternoon. She has not been feeling well lately and has been absent from the lobby space for the past week. This afternoon, however, she has managed, albeit slowly, to make her way with her walker into the living room to assume her favorite seat near the fireplace. Her progress from the elevator to said seat, while residents flow quickly around her, would not inaccurately be likened to a human version of Frogger.

"Franklin? Please come over here," she says again quietly, once seated.

I approach her quickly, for I cannot be away from the front desk at this time of day for too long a period before Charlotte begins to bellow my name.

"Any messages for me, Franklin?"

"Ma'am?"

"Any messages? I'm just wondering if any have been delivered for me that you may not have been able to bring me yet. Like the ones you've been bringing with a noted frequency to Wendy?" She asks this with the greatest of sincerity and not a hint of irony.

I cough into my hand, the better to stifle a guffaw. "No, Mrs. Hill. I'm sorry. No messages for you this afternoon . . . like . . . the ones I've been . . . delivering to Wendy. None. Sorry. Were you expecting any communications?"

"No, no, just wondering."

"Oh, wait a minute, that's not entirely true," I say. "There was something that came for you. Wait here, please."

I head back to the front desk, pull six yellow roses out of the overly large desk bouquet, and bring them to her.

"How silly of me," I say, before presenting the bouquet to her. "These came for you, just within the last hour. From your secret admirer."

Could it possibly be that a blush has come across her face?

"Oh, Franklin," she says, "What a wonderful surprise. They're beautiful. Who's my admirer?"

"Well, if I were to tell you, he could hardly continue being your *secret* admirer, now could he, ma'am? The gentleman swore me to secrecy, but I have no doubt he'll reveal himself soon," I say. "Speaking of surprises, I'm glad to see you up and about this afternoon. May we assume you will be in attendance at this evening's board meeting? There's an important vote, you know."

"Yes, I believe I will attend. It's an important issue tonight, isn't it, Franklin?" Although Mrs. Hill is, clearly—as I like to phrase it—in the sunset years of her life, and, seemingly, almost at the green flash portion of said sunset, I am aware that, not so very long ago, she was deeply connected and heavily involved in the politics of this city. She has indicated as much within stories she has told me but, beyond that, Mr. Harrison gave me greater context around the topic within various morning discussions. He informed me that she would hold well-attended gatherings on the Monday nights before national elections, in which invitees would make their predictions for the next day's results. In the '90s, it became a fairly coveted invitation to receive. Due to intermittent health issues, however, Mrs. Hill has been unable to hold the party for both of the past two election cycles but vows to renew the tradition once again. To look at her today, slumped over in the leather chair in the building's living room, one would never know or fully appreciate the political circles she once ran in. According to Mr. Harrison, no one loved a political discussion more than Mrs. Hill. And no one was more informed.

"It is, indeed, an important vote, Mrs. Hill," I reply. "If I may be so bold to ask, I can't help but wonder what your opinion is on the matter of the Fitzger's space and Mr. Franken's proposal of a gallery for homeless artists?"

"Hmm, yes, well I do love art," she says, her voice quavering. "And you do know that I sat on several museum boards, don't you?"

"And, so . . .?" I prod after a moment.

"Yes, I love art," she repeats.

After another pregnant moment, I realize Mrs. Hill is either unwilling to commit or hasn't yet fully made up her mind.

"Well, from where I sit, this seems like a wonderful opportunity," I say. "A wonderful and interesting way to help a segment of our society.

Is there anything I can get to make you comfortable, Mrs. Hill?"

"Sandra, there you are," Mr. Stewart says, addressing Mrs. Hill. He comes blowing in and I back up, returning to my desk. As I do so, I hear him continue, "I've been trying to reach you. I'm glad you're here."

At this point, Charlotte comes out of her office and approaches my desk. I lose the thread of the conversation between Mr. Stewart and Mrs. Hill.

"Franklin, what time are you off tonight?" she asks.

"My usual departure time, Charlotte."

"Impossible. Forget it. I need your help at tonight's meeting."

"Are you asking if it's possible for me to work overtime tonight?" I ask.

"Yeah, yeah, yeah, okay fine. Might it be possible for you to work overtime tonight? Just say yes."

A most persuasive argument, and quite well approached. There is a side of me—a slightly sadistic side, I do admit, but I do have one—that would like to watch this sheet twist in the wind, in a manner of speaking. It would be akin to dangling a piece of yarn in front of a kitten, just out of reach, watching it stretch for something it so desperately wants but can't quite have. Just one dangle.

"Hmm, I'm not sure if I can juggle my schedule this evening to accommodate this last-second request—"

"Please, PLEASE," she says, timber rising. "These people drive me crazy when they're all hopped up about something. It's like the whole fucking building is going to be in the common room tonight. I'm supposed to take the minutes, and for a normal meeting, that's fine. But this happened one time before when everyone got into this Excited States of America bullshit about the roof's HVAC system, and they all showed up for the meeting. I was trying to take minutes, but then they all kept asking me to get them sodas and stuff and THEN they would ask me to read back the minutes from a half hour ago. Come on, Franklin, I need your help. I just need another pair of fucking hands in the room with me. *Your* hands. To get them sodas and stuff."

"Well, when you put it so nicely, as you just did, and impress upon me how important my role will be, I can't possibly turn you down."

"Oh, thank god," she says. "Go ahead and get some dinner, expense it, and then be back here a quarter to seven."

Charlotte's request, little does she know, actually helps a conundrum I had been in. Although I had told Judith that I was not going to be in attendance—despite her strong recommendation that I be there, as Henry Franken, in order to make as strong a case as possible—I did, indeed, want to witness the discussion and the vote. Being the soda server allows me to be the necessary fly on the wall.

"Franklin! What the hell?" roars Mr. Stewart from the corner of the living room. The corner in which he has been conferring with Mrs. Hill. This shout by him, following my recent conversation with *her*, would seem to indicate something unpleasant this way comes.

"Franklin, what the fuck?" he says again, approaching the desk in as quick a manner as possible, nearly upsetting a table lamp and floor planter on the way. Charging bulls are not widely known for their grace or light-footedness.

"Sir?"

"I just told Sandra to vote yes for my gallery, but she just told me that you had convinced her to vote for the homeless shelter."

"Uh, Mr. Stewart, I'm assuming you're referring to the homeless artist gallery. I can assure you, I didn't instruct her to vote one way or the other," I say.

"Like hell," he says. "What was it you said, Sandra? 'Franklin was most convincing?' Was that it?"

"'Persuasive,'" Mrs. Hill says. "I said Franklin was most persuasive. And he truly was, Brendan. You should listen to him."

"Yeah, persuasive," he says, turning back to me. "What the fuck, kid? Why would you be lobbying for one of the agenda items? You're the guy who's supposed to open doors half the time and distribute Amazon packages the other half." And then, under his breath, "Don't go confusing the old ladies, got it?"

"Sir, she may have misconstrued a comment I made. I was only making idle conversation as I was helping her settle into her place by the fireplace. Nothing more than that—"

"Most persuasive, Franklin was," Mrs. Hill says from the living room. "And charming. He was also very charming, Brendan, as always," Mrs. Hill adds, bringing the recently delivered roses up to her nose, in no way helping my interaction with Mr. Stewart.

"Has the meeting begun, Brendan?" Mr. Harrison asks, having just entered and noticing the flow and energy of the conversation. "Because if it has, I want to make sure my vote is cast."

"No, Ted, it hasn't be*gun*."

"Good, because I had set aside some time to do some arm-twisting, make sure the right votes are cast."

"Oh, Ted, please. Can we move beyond all that shit? You've been trying your damnedest for years to make something very grey into something black and white. We both know that putting a homeless shelter—"

"Homeless artist gallery," I helpfully toss in.

"Semantics! A homeless *make-and-play center* in that space is ridiculous—"

"What part of it is ridiculous, Brendan? If you're concerned about a nonprofit organization being a part of a residential building, that model plays out throughout the city. Go on down to Battery Park and visit the Poet's House. It works, Brendan. Is it the gallery space you don't think can work in this neighborhood? Please. You can't swing a cat on the Upper East Side without banging into an art gallery. They seem to work. So, is it the homeless angle that makes you uncomfortable?"

At this, I feel it is time that I intercede, to tamp the tempers, so to speak. There is, after all, work to be done. "Gentlemen," I say. "I'm sorry, but I'm wondering if this might not be tabled until this evening's meeting. There's a bit of paperwork I must deal with here and it needs to be done before I turn the reins over to Jacob."

"Fine," Mr. Stewart says, turning to head to the elevators. "I'm wasting my breath here, anyway."

"Brendan," Mrs. Hill calls out, as best she can. "You really should listen to Franklin. He's most persuasive on this matter. And charming, too. It strikes me that a little more charm would go a long way in this building, you know."

"Ah, god!" Mr. Stewart shouts before entering the elevator. "Loonies! I'm living in a damn loony bin!" And, with this rather inelegant exit line, the elevator doors close.

"A born politician," Mr. Harrison adds, before heading to the elevators. "A born *New York* politician."

# CHAPTER 41

Friday, 6:42 pm

The common space, or The Commons, as the room has been dubbed and labeled, is one floor above the front entryway. It is a converted space, formerly two smaller private units that were combined into one large community room in the early '90s, when such amenities became a requisite of upper-end condominium buildings, just as a shared workout and exercise room became in the early '80s. The room is used for monthly board meetings, occasional all-resident mixers—primarily around the holidays—as well as for private parties. For this particular meeting, the room has been redecorated. In place of the original oil paintings and signed lithographs that normally hang upon the walls are numerous offerings from the relatively unknown artists by the names of Terry, Tomata, Johnny, Suze, and Emily. Judith had called Charlotte earlier today, purportedly passing on a request from Mr. Franken, asking that the new artwork be put in place for this evening's meeting. Charlotte delegated the task to me ("Can you believe this bullshit?"), as I knew she would.

Charlotte and I are the first to arrive, in order to make sure the chairs and tables are arranged properly. Judith comes in at 6:45, casts me a slightly quizzical look, throws in a smirk for effect and greets Charlotte.

"Charlene, how ya doing?"

"Charlotte, Judith," she says, barely containing her irritation.

"Aw, dammit," she says. "Why can't I ever get that straight? I'm sorry, hon. Problem is, I used to know someone who looked exactly like you. Gorgeous, lots of hair, lots of strong personality, big teeth, know what I mean?"

"Yes, I understand," Charlotte says. "Her name was Charlene?"

"Nah," Judith says. "Cindy or Jackie or something. I can't remember. You just look like a Charlene to me. Anyway, we all set for tonight? I see you brought the doorman with you."

Charlotte looks over at me quickly. I know her well enough at this point to know her thought process, how this innocent observation of Judith's plays out within the Charlotte brain. It will have occurred to her that what may have been intended initially as a proactive gesture may now appear, to some, as a possible sign of weakness. As a sign that she is unable to handle her duties appropriately or, worse, singly.

"Well, I . . . we can send the doorm—Franklin—away if you feel it's not good for him to be here. Will Mr. Franken be here tonight? Would he rather the doorman—Franklin, sorry—*not* be here?"

"I don't care. Franken's not going to care if the doorman's here, this much I know. I was just surprised, that's all. Hey, the more the merrier, right . . . *Franklin*?"

"Ma'am," I nod.

At this point, people begin entering The Commons, largely in pairs and clusters. The Longworths and the Wallins, two sets of spouses I know to be casting opposing votes, enter together, wife paired with wife—two "yes" votes for the homeless gallery—and husband paired with husband—two "no" votes.

"Ah, Jesus, it's going to be a mob scene tonight," Charlotte says to me. "Nobody ever comes early to these meetings. In fact, they don't normally start until a quarter after. I swear, if people start shouting and I'm supposed to be taking minutes, I'm just going to toss my pen across the room. Truly."

"I'll do what I can to help you, Charlotte. I know you're doing the best job you can under the circumstances," I say to her, attempting to put on my most comforting smile.

"Yeah, well, thanks," she says, softening somewhat. "Tell that to Franken."

Mrs. Rubin of 6D enters, sees me, and says, "Why, Franklin, I didn't realize *everyone* from the building was coming to this meeting. Such a surprise to see you."

"Well, ma'am, in a way, I'm with her," I say, with a touch of humor, pointing toward Charlotte. "I'm her plus one. Actually, I'm here just to lend a hand, where needed."

"Yes, well, you're certainly very good at that. We appreciate everything you do."

At 7:06, Judith, from the head of the table, begins to make peremptory-type noises and grunts, in the hopes of ending the table chatter and calling the meeting to order. I look around and am disappointed—and mildly surprised—that Wendy has not yet arrived. I have brought the topic up to her twice since broaching it at Bemelmans, and both times, she seemed eager to change the topic.

As Judith is about to bang the gavel, or what she employs as a gavel—a can of diet soda—a further noise comes from the entryway. Mrs. Hill, with Jacob just behind her, slowly enters with her walker.

"Please wait until I'm seated, everyone," she says. "It took Jacob more time than I expected to come get me from my apartment."

"Oh, ma'am, that's cold," Jacob says, holding Mrs. Hill's purse, newspapers, and other sundry items that are typically on her walker's tray. "You can't go blaming your man Jacob for your being late. Un-uh. No way. That move's going to cost you extra in your tip. I ain't taking the fall for your tardiness. No way! I swear, Jacob's the fastest dude around these parts. In fact, Sandy, let's you and I have a race down the block tomorrow, we'll settle this once and for all. You and me—let's do it!"

Mrs. Hill giggles in a coquettish way as she makes her way across the room to an empty seat at the table. Step by minuscule step she walks, with Jacob's attendant patter continuing behind her. This routine works for both of them—achieving a level of attention, drama, and notice.

Finally, Mrs. Hill is seated, Jacob moves to the door, and the meeting begins. In the opening minutes, Judith makes note of the fact, while glancing in my direction, that Mr. Franken has asked her to speak for him and that she, Judith, has been fully briefed on his intentions and can speak firmly thereon as well as knowingly cast votes in an appropriate matter.

"As has happened in the past, and as is written in the corporate bylaws, I will cast Henry Franken's vote only if need be, that is, in the case of a tie, much like the Senate president," she explains.

She also points out that the first two action items—the proposed uses for the Fitzger's space—do, in fact, compete against each other. A yes vote on one precludes the possibility that the other can be voted on in the affirmative. A discussion takes place in which it is decided that the two action items be combined into one item: a vote for the homeless art gallery, or a vote for Mr. Stewart's private gallery.

"Okay, at this point, with the changes made to action items 1a and 1b, we can proceed with discussion around the use of the space, known as Fitzger's, prior to taking our vote. I open it up for discussion."

A slight disturbance occurs at the entryway. Jacob, who is still watching the proceedings, moves aside as Wendy sidles in. From my post at the sink at the opposite side of the room, I attempt to make eye contact. Wendy, however, is focused on finding a seat. None are available at the table, so she sits at one of the folding chairs lined up against the wall. Mr. Harrison scoots his chair closer to Mrs. Delacroix, and motions for Wendy to pull her chair up to the table.

"Discussion, folks? If not, do we have a motion?"

Several arms shoot in the air and Judith does her best to preside over the spirited discussion that follows. Mr. Stewart angles to play off the fears that the homeless can so often elicit. He does all but give assurance that, if the homeless are allowed to enter any portion of the building on one day, they're bound to appear in your living room with their feet propped up on your coffee table the next.

"Oh, god, Brendan, let it rest," Mrs. Pelletier jumps in. "That's just fearmongering garbage to—"

"Excuse me, excuse me, one at a time, please," Judith says. "Bob was next, I believe."

And so it goes. Comments, counter-comments, questions, assumed answers. From the gist of the discussion, the vote will be as I suspected—close. Based on recent conversations, both direct and overheard, I know how many people fell on the subject. A few comments and clarifying questions surprise me, however. I assumed Mr. McAdoo was in the Stewart camp, but his reactions to Judith's answers around lease length, assumed hours of operation, the number of homeless served, etc., makes me think that he has moved into the homeless gallery camp.

"Think of the cachet this would bring," Mrs. Pelletier opines. "Whether you like the art or not, or whether you like the artists or not, we're the ones living in the building that became a home to homeless artists. It's a true point of diff-er-en-ch-ee-ha-shun, don't you think? We become a—whadya call it?—a landmark building. And my friend, Natalie, she's a real estate agent. Natalie says that kinda cachet brings all kinda ka-ching. That's a saying of hers. She's very clever with wordsy things—"

The to-ing and fro-ing goes on for more than thirty minutes until finally it begins to peter out. Folks are repeating themselves, repeating what others have said and, at 8:05, Judith closes the discussion.

"Ladies and gentlemen," she says. "It is time to vote."

"Wait a minute, Judith," Mr. Stewart says, "I just want to make sure everyone is clear on my point about unit *de*valuation. I also want it understood that Stewart Galleries is ready to move in immediately, while the homeless people still need to establish a 501(c)(3) organization, which could take months—"

"Sorry, Bren," Judith says, cutting him off. "You've made both points very well throughout this young—but aging quickly—evening. You're bordering on filibuster. Unless you have a new point to make, I'm going to ask for a motion."

Mr. Harrison moves that the Fitzger's space be allowed to be used as a homeless art studio and gallery, seconded by Mr. Cohen—another surprise from my tabulations. Mr. Cohen, I'm quite sure, had entered the Stewart camp but, perhaps, has been persuaded through the course of the conversation.

"Alright, we have a motion on the table," Judith says. "All those in favor, please raise your hand. Charlene, count up the votes."

Twenty-two hands are raised, some immediately, some more slowly. One hand that is conspicuously missing from the group is the one that is attached to Wendy, who is slowly pushing her chair back from the table.

"Twenty-two yes votes, Judith," Charlotte says. I quickly do the math. I had counted the people at the table at the beginning of the discussion, noticing there was an odd number of people—forty-five, not including Judith, which means we would not be in a tie-breaker situation. Twenty-two yes votes means . . .

"All those opposed?" Judith asks.

Again, some hands go up immediately, others more slowly. Perhaps the tentative hands are an attempt to show that, while, yes, they are voting in favor of Stewart's gallery, they are doing so reluctantly. Again, Wendy fails to cast a vote.

"Charlene—"

"Charlotte!"

"Dammit! Sorry. *Charlotte*, gimme a count."

"Twenty-two, Judith."

"Goddamn it," Mr. Stewart mutters, knowing a tie vote goes to Judith.

"Wait a minute," Judith says. "Is someone abstaining? I'd counted forty-five available votes around the table. Did somebody leave?"

"No, there's forty-five, Judith," Mrs. McAdoo, 11A, says. "But you might be counting Wendy in your total."

"Yeah, so?"

"Well, she can't vote," Mrs. Hill says, quite matter-of-factly. "She's not a unit owner."

I look from Judith's quizzical look to Wendy's blushing face.

"She's just house-sitting, Judith. She's in Wendith's condo. Wendith is in China," Mrs. McAdoo explains.

"Who the hell's Wendith? Isn't that you, Wendy?" Judith grunts.

"Wendith is my aunt," Wendy finally says. "I'm named after her. I've been house-sitting."

"For, like, *years*?" Judith asks.

"Yes. Well, during college. And work. I'm sorry if I've caused any confusion by being here. Am I allowed to vote for my aunt? If I can, I would like to vote for the homeless art gallery." At this, Wendy shoots a quick glance at me.

"You can't vote by proxy if you haven't signed the affidavit ahead of time saying that you've discussed the matter with the owner and know exactly how they want to vote," Judith explains. "That's why I mentioned up front that I had spoken with Henry. It's, essentially, absentee voting. Have you spoken with your aunt about this?"

"No," Wendy says. "I haven't talked to her in months. She's in Shouzhu, China. Working." She, again, looks to me and quickly looks down.

"Uh-huh," Judith grunts. "So, it would appear that Mr. Franken and, yeah, me, have had a bit of confusion between Wendy and Wendith in the building's ownership files. That differentiation may not have been abundantly clear when he bought the building last year. We'll sort that out tomorrow. But for tonight, not knowing Wendith's—the unit owner's—intentions around Fitzger's and with no allowable absentee vote, it would seem we have a tie. In that case, I will cast the tie-breaking vote—"

"Wait a minute," Mr. Stewart interrupts. "This voting-by-proxy bullshit is unfair."

"Brendan, it's in the bylaws," Mr. Harrison says. "Maybe, at some point in your life, you'll appreciate established rules and laws."

"I don't care if it's in the bylaws or etched in the cornerstone of the building. There are certain votes—this being one of them—that are more important than others. We're not allowing Wendy's aunt to vote on a technicality. I know Wendith. I have no doubt she would have sided with my gallery, had someone taken the time to contact her. In a vote that's this important, I demand that either Henry Franken—who started this entire shitshow—take it seriously enough to be here and vote, or we end deadlocked and bring it up again at next month's meeting. And, by the way, there're lots of people missing. This should be the type of issue where everyone—every owner—votes, not just those who happen to show up on any particular evening. Hell, I'll even trust mail-in votes if people don't want to spend time in a meeting."

There are so many things of import that have just happened that my head is slightly swimming. I am attempting, as quickly as possible, to process the revelation that Wendy, in fact, does not own the unit which she had always positioned to me as her own, as well as this offensive thrust by Mr. Stewart, which could quickly gain traction and, quite honestly, makes a degree of sense. I realize that, as Judith might put it, my hand has been forced.

"I'm sorry, Brendan, but it's in the bylaws," Judith says. "My casting Franken's vote is not out of order."

"Judith, please," I say, stepping forward. I hesitate for a moment before saying, as simply and elegantly as possible under the given situation, "Allow me."

The entire room has turned to me, their doorman. Charlotte is somewhat slackjawed as her charge—her water boy—has stepped forward; she no doubt assumes my actions will reflect poorly on her decision-making capabilities. As our eyes meet, she inaudibly mouths the words, "What the fuck?" Others merely turn with varying amounts of bemusement and curiosity. What is this new entity that has entered the stage?

"The final vote is mine," I say. "And I would like to break the tie. As owner of the penthouse in L'Hermitage, I vote yes for the homeless art gallery. And, Mr. Stewart—uh, Brendan—Henry Franken is, indeed, in attendance. 'Tis I."

"What'd he just say?" Mrs. Pelletier whispers. "Tizzeye? What's a tizzeye?"

"Sorry, too theatrical?" I ask. "It's me. The doorman. I'm Henry Franken."

"Franklin, what the fuck?" Charlotte blurts out, this time around, audibly, in a manner less professional than I, as the owner of the building, would have preferred. "Go stand back by the sink and be quiet. What, are you delusional? Mr. McAdoo needs another soda, and you can't vote."

I look at her for a moment, waiting for the reality of the situation to sift down through her layers of grey matter and realize that others, as well, are a tad slow on the uptake of what has just transpired. Judith sits back in her chair, with a slight smile on her face, and tosses her pencil onto her pad of paper. Mr. Harrison looks at me with a smile and says, "Henry Franken, Franklin Hanratty. Damn it, Franklin, I knew you were better at word games than I was. I should have seen this from a mile away, eh? Hah!" At this, he claps loudly, tilting his head back, and the rest of the room fills, for the most part, with soft murmurs and laughter. Brendan appears more pained, however.

Jacob, from the door, shouts out, "Good goddamn! This is one upside-down, topsy-turvy world we're all living in. The doormen are taking over. Look out, people! Rise up! The revolution has begun, y'all!"

At this, Wendy jumps up from her seat and runs from the room, a reaction I hadn't totally anticipated in the seconds before my declaration.

"See there, what'd I just tell you?" Jacob continues. "The hermit of L'Hermitage has done risen up; people are heading for the hills! Grab the children and all the old ladies. And Mrs. Hill, I'm looking right at you. Get out while you can!"

To fill this somewhat awkward void, Mr. Longworth, 7E, says in a loud stage whisper to Mrs. Wallin, "Had I known these meetings were so entertaining and richly produced, I wouldn't have missed the last six years' worth."

Brendan, sitting with both hands flat on the table, looks up over his glasses and simply says, "What . . . the . . . hell, Franklin?"

"I'm sorry, folks," I begin. "I probably owe you all an explanation—"

"Yes, and Henry will be more than happy to give you one," Judith jumps in. "But before we get to that, I'm going to suggest we take a five-minute break. Anyone need to take a wee tinkle?"

# CHAPTER 42

Friday, 8:51 pm

The evening show's intermission commences, and Judith approaches me, briskly, and spins me around by the elbow, while others talk animatedly amongst themselves, both at the table and as they head to the outer hallway. I have, after all, tossed a bombshell in their midst. I recognize the fact that their world order has been upset. Seemingly, half the room understands what has just transpired. They explain, while filing out of the room, to the other half who thinks that I have lost my mind, or they theirs.

"Are you ready for this?" she asks.

"Well, it would seem a bit too late to ask that question, no disrespect intended, Judith," I say. "You have, after all, been exhorting me to come out of my shell, or, out of my penthouse, as it were. I would say that we can now, most assuredly, check that to-do off the list, hmm?"

"Yeah, well, you certainly came roaring out, pally-boy. As a lawyer, I have to say, I'm not real comfortable with courtroom bombshells, know what I mean? I wouldn't have minded being told in advance what the game plan was. I think you've been watching too many Perry Mason reruns."

"Uh, a reference I'm not entirely clear on, but I think I understand the general drift. So, duly noted. But then I guess neither of us foresaw a twenty-two to twenty-two tie with one abstention, now did we? I felt the need for a little impromptu tap dancing right at that moment."

"Yeah, speaking of which, what the hell? I thought your chicky-poo owned her fucking condo. This little topic never came up during your pillow talk? Seems you're not the only one throwing out surprises in this meeting. Nothing like a little mystery in a relationship to keep it fresh and alive, huh, kid?"

Judith is admirably able to keep a sense of humor in moments like this, but I'm currently neither so inclined nor disposed. I'm not sure which of the news events has me more rankled—my unmasking, Wendy's revelation, or the long-term implications of both.

"So, what do I do now?" I ask. "What do you recommend? I mean, when everyone comes back?"

"Hah!" Judith snorts. "There's nothing for me to recommend. Not like you got a lot of options here, eh? No, no, wait. Here's a recommendation. Go pour yourself a big glass of scotch from your bar over there, take a long slow drag from it, and tell us a story. Trust me, everyone loves a story, Scheherazade."

The residents begin reentering the room and taking their seats at the table. Many had not left, perhaps refusing to give up their ringside seats to what, no doubt, is one of the greatest dramas to unfold at L'Hermitage in years. All have returned, with the exception of Wendy and Jacob, who, presumably, was instructed by Charlotte to resume the reception desk. Either that or he's securing the battlements.

Judith opens Act II of our meeting by saying, "Let's see, where were we? Oh, yes, now I remember. We were about to begin the financial report. Just kidding, ladies and gentlemen, settle down. Unless there are objections, we're going to go off agenda for a few moments. Henry—*Franklin*—well, to me, Henry, to the *rest* of you, Franklin, would like to address you. Henry, you now have the floor."

I move from my post near the sink to the head of the table, opposite Judith's position. "Ladies and gentlemen," I begin. "I would first off like to apologize to each of you. I am sorry if any of you feel deceived. That was never my intention. I am, indeed, Henry Franken, owner of the penthouse unit and, for that matter, of the entire building in which you reside."

At this proclamation, there is a round of eye darting, nudged elbows, some head shaking and grimaces, and smiles and laughter.

"Good, god," Mrs. Pelletier interjects. "Our doorman's richer than the Donald."

"Yes, well, so's everyone in this room, as fate would have it," says Mr. Harrison.

Only Mr. Stewart remains firmly focused on me, perhaps trying to make sense of not only this evening, but the past six months, as well.

"So, wait a minute," he says. "Let me see if I got this straight, Franklin. When I saw you in the alley, you weren't testing the lock—you were just going home."

"That's correct. Nor was I cat burgling. As you say, I was simply heading to my home after a long day at the office. And on this one particular evening, unlike most others, I just got careless."

"Jesus," he says, shaking his head and looking down at the table.

I explain to them how shocked I was when my father passed away; shocked not only over the premature loss of my father, but also by my financial gain, and the accompanying responsibility—a responsibility I was, in no way, prepared for—that was attached to that gain.

"Hey, kid, what's the problem?" Mr. McAdoo shouts out. "When ya got it, flaunt it, baby. That's what MY daddy taught me—har!"

"Yeah," Mr. Pelletier chimes in. "We'll give you lessons on how you can spend that fortune. No problem. Our hourly rates are cheap, too!"

"Yes, were it that simple," I say. "I fully understand how odd this affliction, if I may call it that, must sound to you."

I explain how, starting as a teenager, I often attempted to hide my father's wealth, or, at the very least, avoid conversations in which the source of that wealth was touched upon, to the point that, during and after my college years, I purposely entered social service work, followed by my current position.

"When I came to L'Hermitage after Dad died, it wasn't my intention to become the doorman. I was headed here to sign some papers." I look to Charlotte for a sign of recognition or acknowledgment of the events of that day. "Remember, Charlotte?

You had an appointment with me—with Henry Franken—that morning, but Henry never showed up. Instead, an applicant for the doorman position, Franklin Hanratty, came into the building. When I came that day and saw the 'Doorman Wanted' sign out front, something, quite candidly, snapped. Instead of appearing as Henry Franken, I entered as Franklin Hanratty—a name transposition that I simply pulled out on the spot—and applied for the job. It was stupid, I admit that. But it allowed me to hold off the reality of my new situation a bit longer. And then, I was trapped. But, I must say, I was kind of partial to the cap and cape that came with the job."

My attempt at levity is met by blank stares, so I soldier on.

"You can probably keep those, Franklin," Mrs. Hill says, helpfully.

"Yes, well. As most of you know, Judith became my surrogate. Until finally, this evening arrived. Again, I humbly apologize to any of you who feel deceived by my actions. Charlotte, to you, especially, I apologize. This deception put you in an awkward—and perhaps, at times, frustrating—position."

"Yeah, well, shit—stuff—happens," she says. "By the way, am I supposed to be taking all this down in the minutes?"

Judith snorts at this. "No, honey. Sit back and enjoy the show. I've been recording the whole thing, anyway," she says, waving her cell phone.

"If it's any consolation, I do want to say that I was consumed with pulling myself out of this situation, more or less the moment I got into it," I continue. "Very much to her credit, Judith pushed me constantly"—I look at Judith, who looks around the room with a subtle smile of satisfaction on her face—"to shed my doorman uniform. Figuratively."

"Yeah, well, what else are you going to do for a thousand clams an hour, eh? Push your client to move on, right? Huh? Hey, am I right? That's a family-friends-only rate, by the way."

"In this position," I continue, "I learned a lot. I learned that many of you were willing to share things with me—your doorman—that you probably would not have chosen to share with me if you knew me as the owner of the building. Your perception of who I was and what my background was affected our interactions. And that, in a certain way, was what I dislike the most about my financial situation. I'm treated so differently than if you were to simply see me as the doorman.

"I also learned a lot about the people who walk by the doors of this building, those with whom I interacted in my position—the creators of the artwork on these walls, Terry, his friend Toma—Tom, and several others. In my uniform, they were comfortable in approaching me and talking with me, in a way that, I'm confident in saying, they probably would not have done were they to have taken me for just another resident in an Upper East Side condominium building. Through those conversations and interactions, I realize that the line between their existence and ours is a far thinner space than any of you might like to think. In many cases, certainly in my own, where we all land is just the luck of the draw. But what I would like to do, once I shed this uniform, is help reverse some of the misfortune that has fallen upon these artists.

"Look at their art on the walls around you. These are examples of the work they can do. Terry and his friends are good—really, *really* good. Their voices and their take on the world are substantially different from those you represent, Mr. Stewart. They're not your competition. Their art, their message, their perspective is radically different from artists such as de Smet—"

"Well, that makes you a lucky bastard, then," Mr. Stewart says.

"—and they're passionate about the healing qualities of art, both in creating it and owning it," I continue. "I've seen that passion. Go on a tour of the Met with them if you're in doubt. They're characters, yes, but, my god, so was Pollack. So was Kahlo. So was Warhol. And, so, all I ask, is that you, the residents of this building, come along on this journey with me. Be supportive of this endeavor, no matter what your motive may be, whether it simply is out of the goodness of your heart, or if you love the creation of interesting impassioned art, or, as Mrs. Pelletier said, because it will bring some cachet—"

"I emphasized the ka-ching part!"

"—*cachet* to this address. But whatever your rationale, please help give this a chance of success."

"Where will they live, Franklin?" Mrs. McAdoo asks.

"They won't live here, Mrs. McAdoo, if that's your concern. I know that's been on some of your minds. Clearly, we're not set up for that. This studio is simply meant to be their workplace. It's where they will have the opportunity to earn their living and display their creations, their works of art."

"But, Franklin, are they truly what you could call artists?" This, from Mr. Prasad.

"Yes, look at these examples. When you walked in and saw the art, I have no doubt that it was the emotional impact that struck you, not what the background of the artist was. They have a firm grasp on not only art history, but design, the creative process, the direction and the importance of art. I've witnessed their artistic passion up close. I want to provide them with an outlet, a conduit, to express themselves. These are voices that have something important to say."

Mr. Prasad turns to Charlotte and asks her to reread the results of the vote, taken twenty minutes earlier.

"Twenty-three to twenty-two, in favor of allowing the homeless art gallery to take over the Fitzger's space," Charlotte says.

"Yeah, well, I know it's a moot point, but I'm wondering if I can change my vote," Mr. Choates says. "I voted against Franklin's gallery, but I'd be more comfortable if my vote was reflected in the minutes as being in favor of it, rather than being against. Now that I understand it better—you should have come out before the meeting, Franklin, and explained what you wanted—but, now that I understand it better, I'm all for it. Sounds pretty great. That okay, Judith?"

"Well, Roberts Rules would probably object," Judith says. "But, we'll let it slide."

"That makes the final vote twenty-four to twenty-one," Charlotte says.

"Make it twenty-five to twenty," Mr. Pelletier says.

"Twenty-six to nineteen," Mr. McAdoo says.

At this, much noise and confusion erupt around the table, with everyone chiming in. There seems to be a land rush, of sorts, for those who had voted against the measure to shift their vote into the pro column. When the dust settles, the vote, which had moments earlier been a squeaker, can now be considered a landslide, forty-four to one.

"Brendan, care to make it a clean sweep?" Judith asks, looking at him with a slight smile.

"I get the merits," Mr. Stewart says, "and I understand what Franklin—or Henry, or whatever the hell we're going to call him now—is attempting to accomplish, so I get all that. But I still don't buy it. This has nothing to do with my line of work, or a competing gallery, or anything like that. It doesn't make sense for this building to add a nonprofit organization into its mix. For years, Fitzger's rent underwrote a ton of the maintenance costs in this building, and a nonprofit is not going to have the wherewithal for that kind of cash flow; that's all I'm saying."

"Oh, admit it, Stewart, you've been beaten fair and square," Mr. Prasad says.

"Well, perhaps, if I may be so bold," I interject, "I would suggest we not position those of us within this building as falling into winner or loser categories over this particular matter. We're doing an important thing here and there are many who will benefit from our efforts, both artists and customers. And, although it's irrelevant to this discussion, *I* will benefit greatly from this endeavor. For me, it's time to move on."

At this, Judith suggests our meeting get back on agenda. I excuse myself, asking that Judith continue to represent me within the meeting, and leave The Commons.

"Franklin," Mr. Harrison says, as I arrive at the threshold, "well done."

# CHAPTER 43

One month later . . .

The weeks that follow the board meeting were a whirl of activities. I tendered my resignation as head doorman at L'Hermitage; promoted Jacob to that position which he, reluctantly, accepted ("Shit, man, there goes my freedom of the night shift—keep Queen Char-lotta butt out of my face, got it? Lonely at the top, my ass. I *like* lonely. We comedians are always inter-verted, you know"); filed the necessary paperwork—along with Judith's help—for the establishment of the nonprofit organization, entitled *Opening Doors Art Gallery and Studio*; began soliciting community members for board positions, starting with Mr. Harrison as chair, Judith as vice chair ("Clever, Henry—you're just looking for a way to get my services for free"), and Mrs. Hill as head of our development committee. Her knowledge of the giving community will be priceless.

Over the course of the past three weeks, I have, on numerous occasions, attempted to reach Wendy, whom I haven't seen since her quick departure from The Commons on the night of the vote. Repeated visits to her unit—her *aunt's* unit—have been unsuccessful. I have called her cell phone, with the call on each occasion going directly to voicemail. Emails and texts have gone unanswered. I have even knocked on Mrs. Hill's door to see if, by chance, she has caught a glimpse of Wendy since the board meeting.

"I've heard the door open and close on a few occasions, Franklin," she said. "But I haven't actually seen her. When I have heard the door shutting, it's been either early morning or late at night. I'm not such a good sleeper, you know, so I'm aware of people's odd hours."

And then, tonight, as I'm working on the paperwork and financial statements necessary for an upcoming *Opening Doors* meeting, my cellphone rings.

"Are you in your unit? Can I come up?" Wendy asks, without any preamble, small talk, or hint of an explanation as to why she disappeared.

"Yes, of course," I say, "please do." I tell her the elevator keypad code and then, she asks, "By the way, what am I supposed to call you? Franklin? Henry? Something else?"

I sigh quietly. The anger and disconnection are audible in her voice. "Call me Henry," I say.

"Yes, of course—Henry. Henry Franken. I'll be up in a moment."

I set the phone down and arrange my papers back in their folder. I move from the kitchen, where I had been working, to the living room, turning on lights throughout in order to make the space more welcoming for this visit. I suspect Wendy may appreciate a tour, current state of the relationship notwithstanding—it is a Manhattan penthouse, after all—so I turn lights on in the library, the living room, the back hallway, the bedrooms, the family room, the dining room, the recreational room, the media center, the office, the walk-in closets, and the bathrooms, including mine. Although it's a summer evening, there is an early indication of autumn in the air; the seasons will soon change. I turn on the fireplace in the library, but leave those in the master bedroom, living room, and recreation room off. I open the sliding doors between the living room and the deck and, for good measure, turn on the deck fireplace.

At which point, the elevator doors open. Wendy enters the marbled foyer, the one area in which I had failed to turn on lights. She pauses in the middle of the space, backlit, until the doors close.

"Well, if I do say so, you've been a difficult one to reach," I say. "But I'm glad you've come."

"I needed to be by myself for a while, Franklin," she says. "Sorry—Henry. God, that sounds strange to say. I never realized how important a person's name is to a sense of identity until the name—*your* name—was changed on me."

"You can certainly continue calling me Franklin, if you'd like."

"No, I'll call you by your name. It's so disorienting, that's all. By the way, nice place you have here. Must be a step up from your modest Queens apartment."

I smile at this jab. "Yes, well, certainly makes for a more convenient commute. Or, *did*, considering I technically no longer have a job here."

I show her around the condo, a tour that takes almost twenty minutes, allowing us to avoid the topic before us. When all that can be said is said about the art on the walls, the lighting throughout, the fireplaces, the walk-in closets, the walk-out patios, and the rooftop views, we arrive at the point of the evening's visit. We stand on the outside deck, leaning against the balustrade, with the firepit behind me and the city lights serving as an appropriate distraction, if needed.

"I came by to say goodbye to you. Properly, this time. This one won't end with me running out of the room. I guess we've both said goodbye to Franklin, in our own ways, and for me that was hard. That goodbye is what I've been trying to get my arms around since I last saw you—him. As far as saying goodbye to Henry? That won't be so difficult. He," she says, looking at her surroundings, "I don't know so well. That'll just be like saying goodbye to an acquaintance. Like saying goodbye to Ted or Lorraine or Sandra—just some people who lived in the same building as me. I'm leaving tomorrow morning to go back to Wisconsin. That's actually where I've been the past few weeks. I went home to sort things out."

"And, in sorting things out, you've decided that you're done with New York? That you're done with me?"

"Yes. I should also probably mention that I've had several conversations with the OTGB team to—"

"The OTGB team? The overtime . . . Green Bay team? The Occidental . . . transportational . . ."

"Sorry, the On the Gaux Bar team—"

"Yes, of course."

"They're based in downtown Milwaukee. Anyway, I've been talking to them about a position, a senior-level position, in their marketing department. I'm thinking seriously of accepting it. Kind of funny how these things work out—I'd be a part of the team overseeing BergMan's work."

"Yeah," I say. "Funny."

I shake my head slightly at this. In the weeks since I last saw Wendy, I realized and appreciated how important a part of my life she had become. In the days immediately following my coming out, I was looking forward to tearing down the walls of deceit that I had built up prior to and during the course of our relationship. I was looking forward to acknowledging that we lived in the same building. I was looking forward to having another presence within this condo, sharing it at times with someone else, beyond the weekly visits from Judith.

"I feel you're running away from me, more than running away from New York," I say. "And, if that's true, I'm, quite honestly, surprised by it. I would have thought that my revelation—my disclosure—would have pleased you. After all, weren't you the one who was posing to be rich? I was only posing to be . . . not rich."

"But that's just it. You deceived me. How could we ever have any form of a relationship—be it a friendship or something more serious—when I can't even trust you? When you don't even present yourself in an honest way? Turns out I didn't even know your name— your *name*, for god's sake. I don't even know who you are or what to call you."

"But, Wendy," I stammer, "I'm sorry about the name issue. That and my entire facade had been fabricated well before you and I ever became friends. I was simply maintaining it with you—it wasn't developed because of you. But, please, keep in mind, I'm not the only one in this relationship who was misrepresenting themself. You regularly presented yourself to me as the owner of your condo. An Upper East Side condo."

"I never said that to you. You, as the doorman, assumed that. I never once actually told you that I owned that condo."

"Yes, I guess I failed to ask for your title of ownership, but your reference to the condo—on numerous occasions—was misleading. You consistently referred to it as 'mine' whenever—"

"But, what did you want me to say each time, 'my aunt's'?"

"Well, it wouldn't have been entirely inaccurate had you done that perhaps once or twice, or consistently. The thing is, the irony of all this is that I had assumed that you were the rich girl slumming it with me, the doorman. And, in fact, I found that terribly comforting. I went through high school and college, Wendy, never entirely sure if girls were interested in *me*—as in myself—or in *me* as in my wallet. Dad always told me to be careful in that differentiation. In fact, he said it so many times while I was growing up that I came to believe that any girl who was interested in me was *only* interested in my money. I came to distrust anyone who expressed the slightest bit of interest. Dad was only trying to protect me, but it got to the point where I couldn't possibly conceive of anyone being interested in me for myself. So, in a way, my relationship with you felt so gratifying. There was none of the doubt or suspicion that came with earlier relationships. It just felt so comfortable. Of course, I would have eventually told you—had it not been for the vote the other night—but I enjoyed knowing you were interested in just me, not my money. Not my penthouse. Me. But let me ask you this—why did you continue the charade around your status when you knew that I was assuming you were wealthy?"

She looks down at the street below, bites her lip, and says, "I guess I just liked being who you thought I was. Most everyone else in this building knew I was just housesitting—they knew my aunt. But you saw me differently, and I liked that. I liked being able to slip into that persona. Everyone wants to be rich, Franklin. You may not be aware of that or appreciate it because of your situation, but that's the way it is. This is America, right? You've got to be rich in America—certainly in New York—or you're nothing. But then, at a certain point with you, I didn't know how to get out of it. I was feeling trapped in my mask, too, because I knew what you were assuming about me. It's kind of like when someone calls you by the wrong name and you don't correct them that first time. Then they do it again and again. And, at a certain point, it becomes too embarrassing to correct them. Well, that's kind of what happened here. I didn't know how to correct you and I'm not even sure I wanted to. I liked seeing myself through your eyes."

"So, you're not averse to wealth, is that correct?"

"Well, sure. I guess."

"Which would seem to imply that you're not entirely averse to wealthy people. Am I correct again?"

She smiles. "There are some who are better than others," she says.

"Then it would seem to me that we have solved our problem. Gotten past our impasse, as it were. Wouldn't you agree?"

And at this, her face clouds over and she turns from me, looking at the buildings beyond us.

"No, Franklin, my leaving was not about money or wealth. It was about trust and honesty. I don't know that I can truly trust you not knowing what other secrets are hiding just beneath the surface. I need someone who's *transparent* with me."

"So, speaking allegorically, maybe you were looking for a window washer and not a doorman?"

"Stop it."

"But didn't we just have a little laugh over the fact that *neither* of us was upfront—or *transparent*—about our backgrounds or our piggy banks?"

"You don't understand," she says. "Everybody in America poses to be richer than they are. We all buy big houses because we want to be seen as people who live in big houses, whether we can afford them beyond one paycheck or not. People buy big, expensive cars because we want to be regarded as the kind of people who can drive around in big, expensive cars. That's just who we are; we can't control it. But what you did, I . . . it just felt like . . . lying straight to my face. We're breaking up, Henry, because we—"

"Is that what we're doing right now?" I interrupt. "Breaking up?"

"Yes. I just need to get out of this city for a while. I need to collect myself back home. I'm not saying it's forever. I do love New York. But I need to leave for a while. Please tell me you understand that."

And like that, it's over. We stand for another moment before undertaking the obligatory awkward, parting hug. She walks off the deck, passes through the living room and turns left toward the kitchen.

"Uh, Wendy," I say. "Unless you're wanting me to serve you a quick bite before you leave—which, believe me, I'm happy to do— you'll want to turn the other direction. Maybe I should lead you out."

"Dammit," she mutters. "No, you stay there. Don't move. I can't leave you dramatically if you have to lead me to your elevator. I'll find the damn thing myself."

And at that, she disappears, this time in the correct direction.

# CHAPTER 44

Nine months later . . .

As I enter the gallery, the band that has been hired for our opening night event begins playing, "Didn't Leave Me No Ladder," which, given my arrival at that very moment, strikes me as a tad bit theatrical, but I did, after all, leave the playlist up to the bandleader. I grab a glass of champagne from a wandering server, as well as a lobster canapé from another.

The walls are lined with scores of paintings from Terry, Tomata, Suze, Johnny, Emily, and others. They have been working for months on creating new paintings, gathering up old ones—many of which had been left in the storage closets of Manhattan shelters and community centers—and exploring new media.

The gallery, I'm pleased to say, is packed. Beyond most of the building's residents, along with numerous friends, there is also a strong contingent of neighbors, council members and representatives from the mayor's office, press members, and those who are simply curious. I see Terry addressing a cluster of a dozen or so attendees near his largest displayed painting, a depiction of the Majestic Apartments and the Dakota at night, as seen from the far side of Central Park Lake. It is a beautiful, moody painting and anchors the centerpiece wall of the gallery, the first thing a visitor sees upon entering from our street entrance. Within the foreground are the silhouettes of two people gazing upon the skyline. The multiple shades of blue within the painting are deep, dark, and prevalent.

"Yes, well, what you have here, of course, are two small figures, diminutive against their surroundings," Terry says, giving me a slight head nod in recognition of my approach. "What the artist—*I*—am attempting to say is that nature is a far more powerful force than man himself. Notice that I have incorporated a whitish hue, a slight tinge, within the western sky. That is intended to give a sense of hope and optimism. Also, the fact that the two figures' backs are to us immediately draws us in as viewers."

"Yes, I see that," says one of Terry's audience members. "It draws you in immediately. Do you see that, Frankie?"

And so on.

About half of the paintings have a red dot affixed to the wall next to them, indicating that they have been purchased. In the world of New York City art openings, these paintings are highly affordable, ranging in price from $500 to $5,000. I suspect that, given the energy in the room, all will have a red dot upon them before the night is over.

"I believe we may have a hit on our hands, Mr. Franken," Ted Harrison says to me. "Well done."

"Well, you, sir, are a big part of the reason for the success," I say. "Your guidance and expertise in the legal matters helped us get this up and running far more quickly than I could have."

"Ms. Guncheon took the lead on that matter," he says. "I simply filled in a few empty squares, so to speak. Speaking of which—"

"Kid, I gotta hand it to you," Judith says, before clinking my glass with her own, "You done well."

"The artists did well," I say. "They just needed someone to believe in them."

"Spoken like a true director," Ted says. "By the way, speaking of needing someone to believe in them, did I tell you that Terry has offered to give me painting lessons starting next week? He said he saw a spark of talent within some of my recent doodles. He's willing to take me under his wing. All is not lost yet, Mr. Franken. All is not lost."

At which point, Charlotte approaches and asks, "Are you ready for your comments? You guys need to get going. Let's go, let's go." Charlotte takes her new role as gallery manager seriously, moving tonight's speakers, me included, into position. I offered Charlotte the post contingent upon her taking provided courses on diversity and inclusivity training; she accepted with the stipulation that she have regular access to her immediate supervisor. She pointed out that her last position was less than satisfactory in that regard.

As board chair, Mr. Harrison makes the introductory comments, acknowledgments, and thank yous before introducing me. I move to the microphone stand, look at those gathered around me, at the artists standing near their work, and begin.

"Let me paint you a picture," I say. "One nowhere near as provocative, engaging, or captivating as what you are surrounded by, but I'll do my best. My name is Henry Franken."

I continue, explaining the genesis of the gallery, brief synopses of each of the displayed artists along with their individual backstories, and the vision and mission of the *Opening Doors* organization.

I conclude by asking that all in attendance consider supporting our mission by becoming members of the gallery, by contributing, and, most importantly, by purchasing the art. As I make my final appeal, I notice a recognizable figure at the back of the crowd. I step down from the platform to welcome Wendy but am immediately surrounded by folks wanting to shake my hand or ask further questions.

"How did you conceive of the—"

"I'm Laurie and I represent the mayor's office of cultural—"

"Henry, will you be expanding the gallery space or moving into—"

Peter Pelletier, 5D, wants to introduce me to a friend from Connecticut who has collected twentieth-century folk art for decades. Lois Wallin, 2B, wants to make an introduction to her younger sister who runs a gallery in Tribeca. Brendan Stewart— even Brendan—approaches me and asks me to introduce him to the artist behind the blue series on the eastern wall ("He captures the depressive spirit perfectly, Henry. I could really do something with that artist."). After weeks of threats of legal action from Brendan following the board vote, he eventually came around to seeing that the *Opening Doors Gallery* did not actually put either his own gallery or his reputation in danger. It may have had something to do with my purchase of eight of his larger de Smet canvases for hanging within the public spaces of L'Hermitage. The words *quid pro quo* were never spoken, but they seemingly were understood.

Finally, I break free and find her holding a glass of champagne while speaking with Ted.

"A board chair's work is never done," Ted says upon my approach. "How did I ever let you talk me into this role, Henry? Excuse me, both of you, while I go mingle and twist arms for some contributions."

"Discreet," I say to Wendy upon his departure.

"Some would say transparent," she replies.

"It's an important quality, I hear."

"Meh," she says. "Occasionally overrated."

We joust like this for the next couple of minutes, with me asking about her current professional status ("I turned down the Gaux Bars position. Who wants to market overpriced snack bars for the rest of their life, or even for the rest of the year?"); her residential status ("Moving back to New York temporarily. Neither Aunt Wendith nor her orchid collection seemed pleased with my rash decision to leave"); her months in Wisconsin ("You can't find good cheese *anywhere* back there. I *so* missed Zabar's").

"Well, should you know of anyone, I'm aware of a fledging organization that is seeking marketing expertise. I could put in a good word for you. I think it pays fairly well and, if I'm not mistaken, they toss in a cheese platter for all new hires."

"Pfhh, not a chance," she says. "I've heard the boss can be detached and, worse, duplicitous."

"But my sources inform me that he's been working on that issue."

"Well, we Wisconsinites have a saying around such matters."

"Go, Packers?"

"No. Never say never."

And then a cheer arises.

"Ah, my thoughts, exactly," I say, responding to the outburst. Or possibly Wendy's comment.

"Ladies and gentlemen," Ted shouts out. "May I have your attention, please? Hello! Attention please. I would like to make a very important announcement to the full room. Our designated centerpiece work of art—Mister Terry Matthews's painting, *Two Men Contemplating the Skyline*—has just been purchased for five thousand dollars by an anonymous art collector with the stipulation that the entire amount goes toward the artist—"

Cheers and hand clapping momentarily drown out Ted.

"Beyond that," he says, once the applause has died down, "Beyond that, the collector has contributed an additional five thousand dollars to *Opening Doors*."

More cheers and huzzahs.

"This might just be the start of something good," Wendy says to me, and, if I'm not mistaken, her eyes appear a bit more moist than normal. "But you know," she adds, "I always felt a more appropriate name for the organization would have been Starting Over. You may want to get your marketing director thinking about that."

I open my mouth to respond—something glib, something clever, something, perhaps, transparent—but the band's renewed startup drowns me out.

# ACKNOWLEDGMENTS

How many people does it take to write a book? A family, a village, a city, a metropolitan community. I would like to first thank Minneapolis's Loft Literary Center. Without the guidance of the many wonderful teachers I studied under and the talented classmates who sat beside me, this book would not have been completed. In particular, I would like to thank instructors Lori Lake, who sounded the starting gun, and Peter Geye, who was there at the finish line.

Thank you to the fine folks at Koehler Books: to acquisitions editor Greg Fields, who read the manuscript and said the most thrilling words a writer can hope for, "Do you have time to talk?" To editor Becky Hilliker, who provided kind, experienced guidance throughout the editing process; to Lauren Sheldon, Danielle Koehler, and Christine Kettner, for their wonderful design sense; and to publisher John Koehler, who provided generous hours of help, insight, and guidance from beginning to end. Thank you, also, to Andrea Kiliany Thatcher and Kellie Rendina at Smith Publicity for their tireless work and enthusiasm around *Doorman*-related efforts.

Thank you to my beta readers, who read not just sections of the book, but the whole damn thing. It takes a lot of fortitude and generosity of spirit to read a 340-page Kinko's copy, and so, dear friends, I thank you. Dylan Hicks, one of my earliest readers who provided insightful feedback and careful editing; Colin Hamilton, who, after many thwarted requests to read the manuscript, said, "Attach the damn thing to an email and hit *Send*. Now!"; Judge T. J. Conley who, at perhaps my lowest moment in the process said to me, "I think this is really good;" and Caroline Hale-Coldwell, who provided a critical editing eye and some greatly appreciated positive feedback. Many thanks, also, to readers Chuck Coldwell, Joanna Glover, Lisa Lange, Liz McGillivary, and Jim Peterson.

Thanks to those individuals and organizations who helped me gain a deeper understanding of certain elements within this book, including Minneapolis's Plymouth Congregational Church and their focus and dedication to homeless populations within the community; and to Dan Peterson, a former doorman who allowed me to quietly sit in the corner of his lobby to observe interactions between him and his building residents.

Thank you, also, to the supportive friends and family who asked often about the progress of this book and, in so doing, encouraged me to continue on: Philip Bither and Kathleen Gavin, Angie Conley, Laura Davis and Eric Roberts, Missy Staples Thompson and Gar Hargens, Beth Schoeppler and Todd Pearson, Roger Hale and Nor Hall, Nina Hale, Leslie Hale and Tom Camp, Tom and Marcia Wood, Iris and Jay Kiedrowski, and Dawn and Brian Hoy. Thanks to Liz Petrangelo and Mike Lundeby, both of whom spent hours helping me wrestle with website-related matters; Rachel Fulkerson, who generously answered many questions about marketing issues; and Marly Russoff, who shared numerous insights into the mechanics of the publishing industry. And thank you to the He-Man Book Lovers Club—a group of fellers I've been getting together with once a month for the last twenty years ostensibly to discuss books and literature, but with numerous segues into family, careers, and life: Joe Bollettieri, Canadian Neil Crocker, Finlay Donesky, Folk Singer Neal Hagberg, John Reimringer, Daniel Slager, Rob Vischer, and Andy Wahl.

Oh, how I wish Mom and Dad were still amongst us to see their son's name on the spine of a book. It was from both of them that I developed my deep love of reading, varied though it may be. Mom encouraged me to read any and all novels, comic books, *Mad* magazines, and the backs of cereal boxes. Dad did the same, although with a stronger bent toward history and biographies. To this day,

I always have two books going at the same time—one novel, one history book. My Goodreads thread looks wildly disparate. Book recommendation algorithms aren't sure what to make of me.

And, of course, my alpha and omega—my "Dedicated to . . ." and my "In acknowledgment . . ." Jocey Hale. You, dear reader, are holding this book in your hands only because of her belief and insistence in this project. She read every page several times, as well as every version. And when, after numerous agent rejections, I said, "I'm done!" she only replied, "Fine. Sleep well, get back to it tomorrow." We should all have a Jocey Hale in our lives. I'm fortunate enough to have *the* Jocey Hale.

And speaking of alphas, a heap of love and thanks to the two sons we begat—Roger and Teddy. They put up with numerous dinner-table conversations and musings around plot points, character development, theme reinforcements, and the importance of resiliency. I can't think of two finer sequels.